C000193316

Hiraeth

a mark – marc

≈

Liz Riley Jones

Copyright © 2015 Liz Riley-Jones

www.hiraeth.me

The moral right of the author has been asserted.

Apart from any fair dealing for the purposes of research or private study,
or criticism or review, as permitted under the Copyright, Designs and Patents
Act 1988, this publication may only be reproduced, stored or transmitted, in
any form or by any means, with the prior permission in writing of the
publishers, or in the case of reprographic reproduction in accordance with
the terms of licences issued by the Copyright Licensing Agency. Enquiries
concerning reproduction outside those terms should be sent to the publishers.

Matador
9 Priory Business Park
Kibworth Beauchamp
Leicestershire LE8 0RX, UK
Tel: (+44) 116 279 2299
Fax: (+44) 116 279 2277
Email: books@troubador.co.uk
Web: www.troubador.co.uk/matador

ISBN 978-1784621-315

British Library Cataloguing in Publication Data.
A catalogue record for this book is available from the British Library.

Printed and bound by CPI Group (UK) Ltd, Croydon, CR0 4YY
Typeset in 11pt Minion Pro by Troubador Publishing Ltd, Leicester, UK

Matador is an imprint of Troubador Publishing Ltd

I holl Bobl
Teyrnasoedd y Môr

For all the People
of the
Sea Kingdoms

Hiraeth

Dwedwch, fawrion o wybodaeth
O ba beth y gwnaethpwyd hiraeth;
A pha ddefnydd a roed ynddo
Na ddarfyddo wrth ei wisgo.

Derfydd aur a derfydd arian
Derfydd melfed, derfydd sidan;
Derfydd pob dilledyn helaeth
Eto er hyn ni dderfydd hiraeth.

Hiraeth mawr a hiraeth creulon
Hiraeth sydd yn torri 'nghalon,
Pan wyf dryma'r nos yn cysgu
Fe ddaw hiraeth ac a'm deffry.

Hiraeth, Hiraeth, cilia, cilia
Paid â phwyso mor drwm arna,
Nesa tipyn at yr erchwyn
Gad i mi gael cysgu ronyn.

Hiraeth

Tell me, masters of wisdom, from what thing is
longing made;
And what is put in it that it never fades through
wearing it.

Gold fades, silver fades, velvet fades. Silk fades,
Everything fades – but longing never fades.

Great and cruel longing breaks my heart,
When I am sleeping in the deep of the night
Longing comes and wakes me.

Go away longing and don't weigh so heavily upon me,
Let me have a moment of sleep.

Anglesey
Ynys Môn

Irish Sea

Amlwch

Cemaes

Dulas Bay

Din
Lligwy

Moelfre

Holyhead

Isle of
Anglesey

Rhosneigr

Llanfairpwll

Bangor

HMS Conway

Newborough

Menai Strait

Gwynedd

Sea Kingdoms

Alba

Eire

Ellan Vannin

Cymru

Kernow

Breizh

Galicia

Celtic Britain

Pagan Year

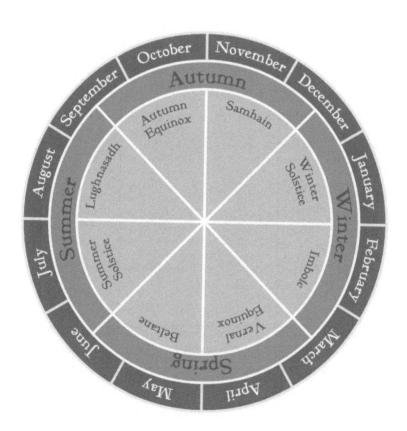

List of Places and Pronunciations

Cymru (Cum-ree)	Wales
Gwynedd (Gwin-eth)	North Wales
Ynys Môn (Unis Maughn)	Anglesey
Moelfre (Moil-vra)	Village on Anglesey
Swnt (Sunt)	Area of Moelfre, on the sea
Traeth Lligwy (Traith Ligwi)	Lligwy beach, Moelfre

List of Characters and Pronunciations

Mona Jones (Moh-nah)	
Idwal Jones (Eed-wal)	Mona's brother
Tom Jones	Mona's father
Molly Kelly	Mona's mother
Brendan Kelly	Mona's uncle

Principal Welsh Druids

Cai Owens (Kai)	
Sioned Owens (Shon-ed)	Cai's sister
Rhiannon Owens (Rhi-an-on)	Cai's mother
Gwilym Owens (Gwil-im)	Cai's father

Ifan (Eev-ahn)	Archdruid
Hywel (Huh-wel)	Cai's grandfather
Emlyn (Em-lin)	Ifan's eldest son
Arwel (Arr-wel)	Emlyn's son
Dafydd (Dah-vith)	Ifan's younger son
Nansi (Nan-si)	Dafydd's wife
Siân (Sharn)	Ifan's daughter
Nia (Nee-A)	Siân's daughter

Nesta	
Rhona (Rho-na)	Nesta's granddaughter
Ieuan (Yey-an)	
Geraint (Ger-eyent)	
Dai (Die)	
Cerys (Keris)	
Bryn (Brin)	

Irish Druids (Wicklow)

Seamus (Shay-mus)	Archdruid
Diarmuid (Derm-ot)	Seamus's eldest son
Cian (Key-an)	Son of Seamus
Colm (Col-um)	Seamus's brother

Irish Druids (Newgrange)

Niall (Ni -al)	Archdruid
Aislinn (Ash-lean)	Niall's eldest daughter
Kathleen	Niall's youngest daughter

Others

Rob	A Cumbrian Druid
Cadan	A Cornish Druid
Peder	A Cornish Druid
Carmen	A Galician Druid
Maria	A Galician Druid
John and Liz	An English couple on Eigg

Language

Language, not race, has always been the unifying component of the Celts: Welsh, Irish Gaelic, Scots Gaelic, Breton, Manx and Cornish. Though all derived from the ancient Brythonic language of Celtic Britain, they are now so distinct from each other as to be mutually exclusive. Yet they are still here.

In Hiraeth, Druids from the different Celtic regions use English to communicate with each other, though they all have a smattering of each other's mother tongue.

The Welsh used in some of the dialogue in this book isn't textbook Welsh. A word or two in the local Moelfre, Anglesey dialect has been used to indicate when Welsh is being spoken between characters.

Contents

Rhan Gyntaf – Part One

Rhan Gyntaf

Part One

Blean Woods, Kent, England 2007

Twenty years of hiding, of running, and it had come to this.

Tom pulled her along behind him, willing her to keep up, but she staggered again. She'd run too far, for too long, and Molly knew she would die tonight.

They called these ancient woods by their first name, *Blaen* – their Welsh name. Molly had brought Tom here this morning to celebrate Beltane and to consecrate their love, but she should have been more careful. Never the same place twice was the rule, but she'd broken it. It was too late now, and Molly could hear the men gaining on them; crashing through the undergrowth in the wet dawn.

Tom could feel her waning, and slowed to a jog. "We'll make our stand here – after all there's only five of them left now." He reached for a smile but the expression on his wife's face extinguished the attempt. "Where's Brendan?" It was almost a curse beneath his breath. Tom scanned the blanket of moist green, short sword in hand. They were back to back when the first Irishman broke cover.

"Not bad for a couple of oldies," the youngster taunted, trying to control his breathing. "He told us you might be a handful." The tone changed as he gazed at Molly. "He wants you to pay for your mistake." Molly gagged at a memory and Tom tightened his body around her, as two more men entered the clearing. This Irishman was extremely young, not much more than a teenager, and his strong Wicklow accent jolted Tom back in time. "Nothing you can do now." The lad grinned, holding up a blackened blade. "The swords are tainted. It'll only take a nick."

Tom threw his own sword in a vicious deadly arc, the momentum of the steel sending the boy flying backwards and clutching at his ruined throat. "Now there's only four. Do you want to talk?" he spoke evenly, to one of the stunned accomplices.

"You fucking Welsh bastard," another lad screeched, the youngest by far, and Tom felt that malice again. "There's nothing to talk about. You'll die and he'll have her, at last."

Molly passed Tom her sword, eased a knife from her belt, and threw it into the nearest man's thigh; she knew it would have bounced from the combat leather on his chest. The boy swore in pain as he dug out the dagger, then advanced on her, tainted blade in hand – all piggy pink eyes and ginger hair.

Tom pushed Molly behind him, then regained his combat stance. The younger man wasn't well trained but he didn't need to be with that blade. He wielded it like a taunt, slashing up and down flashily but leaving his kidneys exposed. Tom feinted to the side leaving his opponent overextended and off balance; a brutal kick to the ribs knocked the runt flat.

Too late. Tom whirled to Molly, held in the arms of the third man, and all the air emptied from his lungs.

"*No!* Molly."

But the cut had been made; a large black swathe against her neck. The Irish pig laughed, and pushed her forward into Tom's arms; he knew ginger was limping towards him from behind with his black blade but that didn't matter now. Her eyes were flat with pain but there was love and life there too, and when he felt the blade sink into his back, it wasn't too deep or painful.

"You'll live to watch her die," the runt spat. There was a commotion behind him, and Tom knew that Brendan had arrived. He heard Irish bodies fall thick and fast. The grunting and squealing of combat was played out beyond his vision, but Tom had the satisfaction of knowing that none of the enemy would survive an encounter with Brendan, no matter how many black blades they owned. Each kick and punch meted out by his brother in law, delivered pain and death to the enemy.

Molly's breath was slowing; blood loss and poison made it a struggle to speak. "Mona, Idwal, they must live."

Cocooning her in his arms, Tom lay them both against the sodden ground, already feeling the heaviness of the poison in his own lungs and heart. "They will live."

He kissed her mouth for as long as it would stay warm, and when he pulled away Molly, was wearing the smallest of smiles on her beloved face. "*Ein bywydau sydd i ddod.* All our future lives, Tom."

"Wait for me," he sobbed into her strawberry hair, but she had gone.

Tom was taking too long to die, and his vision was still clear enough to focus on Brendan when he staggered over; breathing heavily and decorated with blood that was not his own. He fell to his knees at the sight of his sister. "Molly..." he uttered as he swallowed back grief.

"She's gone Bren... they took her from me."

Brendan's heart clenched in grief, as he watched the big man smooth back his sister's golden-red hair. "I couldn't get past them in time... too many at the southern gate... I failed her."

A seizure shook Tom but he smiled sadly, shaking his head. "It was always going to end like this, Bren. We've lasted so much longer than we thought possible." Brendan lowered his head and nodded; he knew Tom spoke the truth. "Look after them. He mustn't have them. Not Mona, not Idwal – please." The words were a struggle for Tom now, and Brendan gripped his friend's shoulder.

"*Nes i ni gyfarfod eto.* Until we meet again, Tom."

Tom's last words were a whisper in the rain. "Burn us, Brendan, ease our passing."

The rain pattered through the trees as Brendan stared down at his dead sister and her love. He wasn't alarmed by the voice of the dying Irishman – Brendan had nicked the boy with that dirty blade.

5

"I did her a favour. Better to die here than face what he had planned for her," the young man croaked.

Brendan was too numb to feel anger; his loss was beyond grief. "Why did they have to die? There are so few of us left," Brendan choked out.

"Seamus wanted her back."

"But why still, after all these years?"

"The *mark*... it was the *mark* – always the *mark*."

"I don't understand. What is this *mark*? Why does he need it?"

"Druids will return to their former power under it; it's the only way left now."

Brendan was well aware of the catechism. The mindless obsession with inherited magic, but he didn't understand the new fixation with this *mark*; the psychosis in Seamus must have hollowed him out over the years. Brendan needed one more answer before the man died.

"How did you find us?"

"Cameras, surveillance," the lad winced as the poison began to overwhelm him. "The new world order is technology, old man. He's been hunting you down with it for years."

A week later, on the Kentish coast

The pub was the only building for miles around and it teetered at the edge of the salt marsh. Brendan watched the arrival of the flashy black Mercedes, confident that it hadn't been followed. He and the lawyer knew each other by sight, and Brendan waited for the man in the suit to come to his table.

"Drink?" Brendan asked, knowing the answer.

"No. Thank you."

Brendan knew the lawyer was irritated by the remoteness of the location, but he was either too polite or too scared to complain. It must have taken a great deal of effort to find this place and Brendan might have been impressed – if he could get past his revulsion. It wasn't just the man in front of him to be fair; the warrior had a real loathing for the entire breed. The Ovate solicitors didn't take sides, only money, and from all of them – and yet these Druids still had the nerve to laud their academic superiority over any of the warrior class. They liked to move around in the soft, safe circles of mainstream society and claim they were 'doing their bit' for the greater good of the Druid community. It was just a load of arse licking and bending over in Brendan's eyes.

Brendan didn't feel safe anywhere anymore, but he'd taken as many precautions as he could; there were no cameras here at least – and he needed to sort out their future.

"Interesting spot," the lawyer noted drily.

"We're being watched."

Brendan was taciturn at best, but the lawyer knew enough to

leave well alone, and settled down to business, pulling the papers from his briefcase. "You're familiar with the will?"

"Some."

"Here we go then." The man passed the file across the table. "You have custody of the girl and her brother is in the army. The estate is to be shared equally between them, held in trust by you until Mona is eighteen. It's all quite straightforward."

"Not really. I have to make some changes to *my* will now. Are you sure you don't want a drink, we'll be here a while."

≈

Business was completed three hours later.

"Tell me again, just so I know you've got it," Brendan demanded and the lawyer sighed, rubbing his gritty eyes.

"If anything happens to you, Mona will know. She will contact us, and we will then drive her from the appointed location to the address in Anglesey…"

"Immediately, the same day, without stopping," Brendan interrupted, hoarse with repetition.

"*Yes*, how many more times?"

"I've paid you a lot of money for this," Brendan growled, and the lawyer continued, jolted back into compliance by the threat in the Druid's eyes. The man was deadly, warrior class, not a Bard or an Ovate.

"When she arrives there, we leave her with the papers." The lawyer fluttered a long-fingered hand over the table. "And the details of her contact."

"Yes," he sighed. "I'll be in touch."

The contact. Could Brendan stretch back into a bloody past and trust her life to him? Possibly not, but there had never been anyone else. If Brendan died, Ifan was the last and only hope for Mona, and he felt empty as he watched the red rear lights disappear. One last job, one huge deceit and he would have fulfilled his promise to keep them safe.

Brendan stood by the red post box, his gaze alternating between its slim metal maw and the letter in his hand. He felt the name beneath his fingers, one last time: '*Sapper Idwal Jones,*' printed neatly, above the boy's BFPO number. There was enough money in here for the lad to survive for a few years. The news would devastate him – but this would keep him safe. With a lump in his throat, Brendan slipped the letter in. He let it fall and turned away.

Immediately, he began to jog, already running from his decision and knowing that Idwal would never forgive him. It took Brendan over an hour to get back to the small caravan in the wood, and he made his plans on the way. Now that the cash was accessible, he'd buy a bigger caravan; they could keep it camouflaged and hidden in woods – moving on was easy with a caravan.

Slowing to a walk just outside the trees, he caught his breath and calmed himself, preparing to deal with Mona. At five metres from the door, Brendan knew something was wrong; the angle of the main plastic window had altered, there was movement behind the caravan and a strange snipping noise.

"Mona?" Brendan called out warily.

There was a brief pause in the odd noise, and he rounded the caravan poised to strike. His niece was sitting on a plastic chair, savaging her long, thick hair with kitchen scissors. Brendan blanched at the mutilation and the violence of her cutting action.

The girl glared up at him after a minute or so – she had obviously decided the haircut was over. "You locked me in." It was an accusation.

"I had to, Mo." Relief flooded his brain – these were the first words she had uttered in a week. The first words she'd spoken since her parents had died.

9

Brendan had tried to comfort her that night, to hug her against him, still covered with the stink of her parents' ashes. Mona hadn't cried, but she had slept – slept for almost the entirety of the week. He'd had to lock her in to keep her safe.

"I broke the window." Her stiff body language told him to keep his distance.

"It doesn't matter; we're getting another caravan, a bigger one." They were three feet apart but it felt like thirty.

"Will there be a funeral?"

"No, Mona."

"What about…?" her voice broke a little. "What about Id?"

Brendan took a breath; he'd prepared this speech, this little scenario, over and over again in his head. They were only words, so why were they so hard to say? "Sit down, Mona."

Grey eyes burnt him where he stood. "Tell me," she commanded, but somehow he couldn't do it; the words wouldn't come.

The teenager stood and strode at him in one smooth movement. At seventeen, Mona was big: tall, powerful and strong. She already owned the muscled body of a warrior and Brendan was struck again by her resemblance to Tom – his square jaw and sharp bones, emphasised now by the crude haircut.

"Tell me, Brendan." Her hands had already turned into fists at her side, and Brendan noticed the pink music machine was still clenched tightly in her grasp – it had been last year's birthday present from her brother, and the only possession Mona genuinely cherished.

"Idwal has deserted," he blurted too quickly. "He's on the run from the army. He went AWOL in Afghanistan – after they told him about the accident."

An invisible force struck Mona across the belly and she bent forward; there was nothing in her body to vomit up, but retching nevertheless wracked her. "He'll come back, though?" It was a whisper

10

from a sad, lonely girl. A girl he had loved and treasured as his own since her birth.

Mona's vulnerability broke Brendan's heart but speaking past his emotion, he fumbled as close to the truth as he dared. "No he won't. He can't come back here, it's far too dangerous."

She was sick then, heaving over and over again, but producing only bile.

≈

Things were better in the morning; Mona was awake and had finally eaten. Today he would tell her some facts. Not very much maybe, but just enough to keep her safe.

Talking about her parents' death was hard and Brendan wasn't a gentle man, but he explained with as little brutality as he could manage. "Your mum and dad didn't die in a car crash. They were murdered." Brendan was constantly surprised by Mona's lack of fear; whatever emotion he saw in her eyes, it was never fear. "I can't tell you much more than that."

"Why not?"

"It's too dangerous. The less you know, the better." Brendan knew his niece wouldn't be fobbed off; there was too much of her father in her for that. "Your life is in danger; that's all you need to know." He didn't want to sound hard but he couldn't help it, he just needed to keep her alive.

"What did they do wrong?" she asked, showing another rare glimpse of that vulnerability, and Brendan was torn.

"Nothing, Mo. Please don't ever think that. They were in the wrong place at the wrong time. That was all. It was fate."

Mona was silent for a long time after Brendan had talked, after he'd explained how they would survive and how their life would be. His hand crept to hers over the small Formica table, touching her fingers and pulling her out of her reverie.

11

"What is it, Mo?" He could see a question forming in her eyes.

"I want to learn to fight. Really fight. Can you teach me?" she asked fiercely.

Brendan smiled; his first in a week, and he squeezed her hand tightly in reply.

1

Moelfre

Four years later

Watching the English countryside whizz past, through the tinted windows of the car, lulled Mona into a trance. Her eyes flicked backwards, over and over again, picking out random details: the pink blur of a cyclist and the shape of a lake.

It had finally happened.

Brendan had not been there at the appointed time – after four years of unfailing consistency. Mona had made the call immediately, hoping that it might be a test, a dry run, to check if she could follow orders. So, she had packed, and the car had come – but Brendan hadn't leapt from the bushes with a big grin and a carrier bag full of shopping. Her uncle was dead then.

The lawyer all but confirmed it with his tone, and then he handed her the paperwork. Mona wasn't feeling shock, or even surprise. After all, Brendan had reminded her of his imminent death almost every morning since she was seventeen. What she felt was crushing loss and complete loneliness.

As the sumptuous, chauffeur driven car slid through the English countryside, Mona tried to seal her memories of the man away; it was the only way to deal with crippling grief and survive. They had endured four years of running – avoiding all cameras and most people. Mona had hated her uncle some of that time, and loved him

13

at others, but she had respected him through all of it. Now he was gone, and she was totally alone.

For the first miles of the journey, Mona read and reread the will. It was baffling. The lawyer was taking her to a remote village in Anglesey, a place called Moelfre, which she had never heard of. On arrival, she was meant to find a man named Ifan – there was no mention of a surname. Once she had made contact, Mona was supposed to search for some relatives. If none were found by the end of the month, she was free to leave.

There was no get-out clause. It was a particular requirement of the will – like a punishment, she thought; Mona wouldn't inherit her parents' estate without enduring it.

The slick lawyer assured her that he knew nothing else, and was singularly mute for the duration of the journey. Until Mona noticed the sign for 'The North'. She didn't pretend to be a geographer, but Mona was pretty sure that Wales was south and west. Sitting up suddenly, she confronted the man opposite.

"That sign said 'North.'" Mona made it sound like a threat, which the lawyer seemed to take seriously for a few seconds, before lapsing into laconic law mode.

"Anglesey, Ynys Môn, is an island off Gwynedd. This is the quickest way." His tone told Mona he was used to explaining to idiots, and she had an urge to lift her leg and give him a sharp kick to the throat.

"I've never heard of *Gwinith*." She copied his pronunciation in a growl, but there was a slight nagging in her mind; Brendan would have hated this smarmy bastard.

"You don't trust me." It was a lazy statement.

"I don't trust anyone."

"Maybe that's just as well, Ms Jones." His smile showed teeth but no warmth at all and Mona had the feeling he was nurturing a big, fat secret. "How's your Welsh by the way?"

"*Welsh?*"

For the first time, the man opposite her showed some real emotion – and it was shock. He shook his head, regained the well-worn composure and returned to his own paperwork.

Mona had heard that it always rained in Wales, and that at least was proving true. The weather in Kent had been a flaming June, but the further north-west they travelled, the wetter and colder it became.

The car left the motorway and glided through grey, wet towns and tunnels that ran through mountains. After a long time of fighting sleep, Mona looked down at a swirling expanse of water from the height of an ornate bridge.

"The Menai Strait," the lawyer noted – his first words in four hours. "Not far to Moelfre now."

"That's a funny name, *Moelfre*." The word didn't sound the same coming out of Mona's mouth. "Does it mean something?"

"Yes," he replied quietly, "it means 'barren hill.'"

The driving rain worsened the further onto the island they travelled, and as Mona finally stepped from the car at a bus stop on the side of the road, it could have been February.

"Four weeks today, then, we'll be waiting here at nine a.m." He didn't pause for an answer; the electric window slid shut, and the lawyer's car receded into the rain.

Mona began her search. There was a shop, just across from the bus stop. It was a general store, selling everything from beach balls to home-cooked ham. The sign was in Welsh, '*Rhen Fecws*' and Mona tried to say the words in her head, but her brain couldn't turn the letters into sounds.

The writing may have been Welsh, but all the voices Mona heard were English – northern English. There seemed to be an entire extended family of them stuffed into the small shop and they were loud, wealthy and dripping in technology.

A sullen-looking teenager was propped against the doorjamb, just shy of the busy drainpipe. The youth was plugged into several machines at once, and was sporting a comedy-sized pair of earphones. Mona and Brendan had read newspapers and she knew all about the swift development of the smartphone – though she hadn't expected to see so much evidence of it here.

As Mona waited in line behind the wet tourists, she wondered how the slimy lawyer had got it so wrong. People didn't speak Welsh in this village. But then the small, older woman in front of her began a conversation with the shopkeeper. By their tone, the women seemed to be chatting about the foulness of the weather, but their language triggered a short circuit back to Mona's childhood.

Her parents had sometimes spoken that language to one another. They'd never explained its use, but then again, she'd never asked. Mona had always thought of it as a language of secrets – a code for keeping the kids in the dark or for when they got soppy with each other. Mona sighed. Perhaps she should have paid more attention, though to be fair she had always been crap at languages, and maths, and science, and geography... "Can I help you love?" The shopkeeper broke her reverie.

"I'm looking for Ifan," she asked simply.

The woman paused and glanced quickly at someone behind Mona in the queue. "*Ydi o'n gwybod pwy wyt ti?*"

Mona frowned. "I'm sorry, I can't speak Welsh."

The woman looked surprised and then wary. "Can you be more specific?"

"No," Mona shrugged, "I don't think I can."

"Best try down at Ann's Pantri. Sorry, love."

Mona turned to the door and the rain.

≈

The woman in *Ann's Pantri*, carrying plates of tasty-looking pasta, appeared too young to be Ann. The restaurant was filled with the smell of good food and the sound of English voices.

"Do you know Ifan?" Mona asked her.

"*Eevan? Cymraeg?*" the woman asked, seemingly confused.

"No, sorry," Mona muttered.

16

The woman moved nearer and Mona caught a waft of spice and two muttered words: "Lifeboat station."

At the tiny, pebbled beach Mona followed a sign to the RNLI station, along the coastal path. Even through the veneer of grim weather, she could see beauty; the ferocity of sea against granite and the smudge of distant mountains. The only face she saw on her journey was that of Dic Evans, a big bronze lifeboat coxswain, who surveyed the Irish Sea with a look of grim capability.

The sign said that the Moelfre Lifeboat Station was open to the public, but the door was locked. Mona swore and thumped it in frustration. She was deciding how feasible it would be to wee in the long grass at the edge of the coast path, when the door swung open. A big man stood there with a scowl on his face even before she'd opened her mouth.

"*Ar gau,*" he growled. "We're closed," he added, almost immediately, and began to turn away.

"I'm looking for *Eevan.*" Mona tried out the new pronunciation and the man stiffened. He turned back to her slowly – he certainly knew an Ifan, even if it wasn't him. "I've got papers," she added, hoping it would help her cause.

"Show me," he grunted rudely, and the hairs on the back of her neck rose in response – she didn't like this bloke one bit.

"Are you Ifan?" she demanded, matching his aggressive tone.

"No."

"Then you can't see them, they're for Ifan only." Mona thought that the man was contemplating violence. Not that it mattered; her bladder was too full for her to care.

"Come in," he growled eventually.

"I need to use your toilet." Mona didn't hide the edge in her voice and he pointed at another dark blue door, his glower deepening.

After leaving the loo, Mona edged her way around the lifeboat, which loomed and gleamed above her in all its glory. The boathouse smelt enticing – a mixture of seaweed, diesel and hot machinery.

There were voices above her, raised voices, so she found the almost vertical staircase, and climbed towards them.

The big man was the coxswain – it said so on his jumper – and he was growling into a VHF radio. He stabbed a finger at her, and then at a plastic seat. Mona obeyed but didn't rush to sit down as ordered. At least this was progress.

On another phone, there was a younger, slighter man, also sporting an RNLI uniform. The men looked related, brothers maybe, and they were having a heated debate with each other while simultaneously holding two phone conversations.

The big man added to the mayhem by stomping around and occasionally rolling his eyes in her direction. In some strange way he reminded Mona of Brendan; it might have been the way he moved – perhaps he was a fighter too. The younger of the brothers seemed calmer and placated the other from time to time. Mona felt she might have intruded on a family row, though she was almost beyond caring.

The rain was beating and sliding against the panoramic window, forced by the wind into its corners. Watching the weather was making Mona sleepy, and she reached for her mp3 player as a distraction. The machine was a touchstone for her, a talisman, a reminder of happy times. It came from a time before fear and running. Mona's life used to be normal; there had been telly, phone calls, music and freedom. She used to have a family, but now Mona had only herself and her memories. And those were all stuffed into the tiny, tatty machine in her hand.

Both men appeared happy to ignore her, so she stuck an earphone in each ear and put the player on shuffle. The familiarity of the music soothed her, but Mona hadn't heard any new music for far too long.

She was well into the playlist when Mr Grumpy came to stand in front of her. "Follow me."

Mona was wary; she hadn't expected him to help her. "Where are we going? Do you know Ifan?"

"I *said* follow me." He turned away abruptly, without looking to see if she was affronted by his ever-increasing hostility.

While following the coxswain down the stairs and out onto the coastal path, Mona secured her rucksack over both shoulders. If it came to a fight she'd need both hands free. The path wiggled down and round until it reached sea level. Grumpy was leading her to a row of ancient whitewashed cottages, only a hundred metres or so away from the foaming waves.

The tiny white houses were so low that Grumpy had to bend down to knock. Time yawned on and he chose not to make eye contact with her during the wait, but closed them, as if preparing himself for some great test. The door eventually opened to reveal a small, wiry old man, with a mass of white hair and eyebrows. Mona immediately claimed the old man's attention – he looked mortally panicked.

The big man eyed the old man warily before starting up a loud discourse in their native tongue. After some energetic exchanges between the two, both sets of eyes rested on Mona. "Are *you* Ifan?" she asked.

"I am," he managed. "Who are you?"

The old man's reaction convinced Mona that she must have found family – it was equally evident that she wasn't welcome. "I'm Mona Jones, and I'm here because Brendan Kelly sent me. He's dead." She'd finally said the words out loud, and they sliced at her chest as she offered up the paperwork.

If anything, the atmosphere deteriorated at the mention of Brendan's name. Ifan leant against the angry coxswain, who didn't seem to relish the close contact.

Mona was trying to work out what Ifan knew. He was mightily shocked, maybe even frightened. As he stood and gawked, the big man asked him some garbled questions, which Ifan didn't answer immediately. When at last he did, an awful silence descended between the two, and it was obvious that Mona had sunk even further in

Grumpy's regard. The big man stomped into the cottage, relaying the bad news to whoever else sat behind the door.

Ifan took advantage of their privacy and grabbed her arm, shock, dread and fear etched into every wrinkle. "Who are your parents?"

"Molly and Tom Jones," she replied swiftly, and braced herself before continuing, "but they're dead too."

"You should never have come here," he stuttered with uncomfortable finality.

≈

The inside of the cottage smelt old and damp. The windowsills were crumbling and there was a whiff of neglect in the air. The men left her in a room on her own, save for an assortment of frayed and bulging suitcases. Some were split and held together with string, but they were all still shiny and wet, as if their owners had also just arrived at the cottages through the rain.

When Ifan came back into the room, he appeared a little more at ease and Mona almost expected him to offer her a cup of tea – but he didn't. "So, I've read through your papers but I don't understand why your uncle sent you here – we weren't friends," he added with a dark edge, as he passed back her documents.

"The will says I'm here to find relatives." Mona reiterated what she thought he would already have learned from the paperwork. "Do you think we're related?"

"Almost certainly not," the old man replied quickly, and with some distaste, Mona thought.

"Then what the *fuck* am I doing here?" she exploded, launching herself out of the musty armchair towards him.

Ifan flinched at her sudden, foul language, and the little man backed away towards the door. There was an immediate reaction from the other side of the wall – someone was shouting and rattling the door handle. Ifan seemed to reassure the rattler but his eyes never left Mona's.

"So what now?" she asked, collecting her rucksack from the floor and slinging it over one shoulder. It looked like she'd reached a dead end.

"I could make some inquiries about your family, if you like?"

Mona shrugged; the man didn't seem sure about the offer, and it was probably a waste of time. "Don't worry," she said, moving towards the door.

The man backed off; it was almost as if he was scared of her. "Where are you going?"

"Back to the village." She shook the will in her hand. "I've got to stay here a month."

"Where will you stay?" Mona shrugged again; she hadn't thought that far ahead. "You could stay here?"

"I don't think I'll be that welcome, do you?"

Ifan grimaced awkwardly. "Sorry about your parents."

"Thanks." She didn't know how else to respond, and made to get out again but Ifan didn't move.

"Don't go just yet," he said, pushing his palm out to her. "I'll be back in a minute."

The old bloke was gone for much more than a minute; there were twenty minutes or so of muffled talking and shouting from the adjacent room. When he did re-emerge, Ifan drew someone in behind him – a small young woman.

She was essentially caramel; with long, dark, curly hair. Golden brown, fully lashed eyes peered soberly at Mona from a perfectly oval face. Dressed in semi-medieval fashion, she looked flustered. "*Bore da.*" The young woman muttered the phrase into her shoes but raised her eyes to Ifan in shock when he replied to her in English.

"This is Mona, she doesn't speak Welsh." Mona couldn't help but feel shamed by the accusation in the woman's eyes. Ifan saw and ignored the glance, then spoke to Mona. "This is Nia, my granddaughter. She'll be keeping an eye on you while you stay here…"

"I'm not staying here," Mona broke in.

21

"I think you should. It's what Brendan thought best, and after all, he's managed to keep you alive so far."

Mona tried to think of another option but she was all out of alternatives. "What do you want me to do here for a month?"

Ifan just shrugged. "We'll think of something."

≈

Mona had only unpacked her travel alarm clock and wash bag – not convinced she'd be here long enough to put anything into a draw. She supposed she'd come to some sort of agreement with the old boy, but the prospect of staying a month here was looking grimmer by the minute. All conversation stopped when she entered a room, and her mere presence could clear the place in seconds.

Mr Grumpy had turned out to be Emlyn, the coxswain and Ifan's eldest son. He lived next door or maybe even here – the row of cottages appeared to be interconnecting and was populated with all manner of RNLI crew. Dafydd, the younger brother, was also a resident, along with a constantly changing cast of others.

Everyone treated Mona with a sense of suspicion that she really couldn't remember earning, but Emlyn and Nia's mother, Siân, were the most hostile. Mona avoided them both whenever she could.

Since the moment of her arrival, there had been hushed and not so hushed conferences about her – it was all in Welsh but she wasn't an idiot. In some ways it was a relief to be surrounded by people again, but the language barrier isolated her and Mona began to long for the solitude of the trees and a lonely caravan.

≈

Next morning, Mona grabbed a slice of bread and slid from the kitchen to the conservatory with it; there was too much of a queue for the toaster. Picking up the *Daily Post*, she started to scan the jobs section. There was bound to be some local temporary work, and the will only seemed to stipulate that she stay in the village, not these cottages specifically.

Mona was formulating a plan involving bar work and buying a tent, when a delicate cough pulled her from the black and white pages. "What sort of job are you looking for?" Nia had a soft, lyrical voice and Mona was surprised by her interest.

"Well, I was looking for bar work but I'll have a go at anything." She sighed and flapped the paper. "Not much locally."

"No," Nia agreed and there was silence again while she churned her hands in her lap. "I was wondering if you'd be interested in spending the month studying? My grandfather has good links with the university, I'm sure he could..."

"No." Mona stopped her adamantly, cringing about having to reveal her lack of academic nous quite so quickly. She'd had an education, and was fairly pleased with her paltry clutch of GCSEs – she'd worked hard enough for them – but learning had never come easily to Mona. "I'm more of a practical person than anything else," she hedged.

Nia didn't seem to be able to come to terms with that very easily, but ploughed on valiantly. "When you say practical, do you mean chemistry..."

Mona laughed and shook her head at the incongruous image. "No, I mean woodwork, mechanics, plumbing – that sort of thing."

Nia's eyes had grown larger at the mention of each additional trade but she remained undaunted. "Perhaps we can enroll you on some sort of short-term course for a month. I'll see what I can do." Mona shrugged vague thanks at the offer and went back to the ads.

2

Sea

The Irish Sea really did want to come in through the little window tonight, and Mona watched its spuming progress from the bedroom. It was a small, bent little room but luxurious compared to her berth in the caravan. She was counting the waves, waiting for the next big one to make it to the top of the pebbled shore. Mona recalled a dim childhood memory of the *Mermaid Shepherdess,* with all the waves her sheep and every ninth her ram – or maybe it was every seventh.

There wasn't any fear that the water could breach the cottage; the walls were five feet thick, and appeared well used to the constant abuse. Her nagging preoccupation was why she was here at all. Most of the people who lived here weren't friendly or even polite. They were dour, and closed, and spoke in a language made entirely of consonants. Mona had been lured here with the hope of finding lost relatives, and now, at the beginning of her second week, she fervently hoped that she wasn't related to anyone – except maybe Nia.

To Mona's astonishment, Nia and the old man had somehow negotiated a month's worth of tuition up at the university for her. Mona had spent the last two weeks travelling back and forth to college on the bus with Nia each day, and the more time she spent with the quiet academic, the more she found to like.

They had enrolled her on a metal fabrication course and Mona had jumped at the chance, though she still suspected it was just a ploy to keep her occupied while the others argued over what to do with her.

≈

There was a mumbling kerfuffle of activity in the rooms below. From the odd snatched words, it was evident that an RNLI shout was underway. It seemed that June was a busy time for the rescue service, as all sorts of idiots pitted themselves against Mother Nature, by sailing and motoring into disaster around the cruel Anglesey coastline.

The excitement of rescues had already worn off for Mona, but tonight's shout did mean that she was free to venture downstairs to the kitchen, and make herself a cup of tea without the fear of bumping in to anyone.

Creeping down the steep stairs was an effort in the dark and Mona still had to feel out with her foot to gauge if she'd reached the bottom. In a well-practiced grope to the front door, she switched on the kitchen lights, and it shorted with a bang.

Mona rudely questioned the sanity of the electrician who had rewired the cottages as she shuffled back to a kitchen cabinet for the torch. She knew the routine now, and reset the ancient circuit breaker with ease. The place was a death-trap, and Mona muttered something to that effect, as she stuffed a single earphone into one ear, filled the kettle and waited for it to boil.

It was a Saturday night, and Mona was indoors with tea and pyjamas again, while most women her age were awash with men, music and mayhem. Mona felt she was watching from the side-lines while other people played.

Sipping the hot drink, Mona glanced over at the old Sunbeam motorbike in the lean-to. All the men in the cottages were obsessed by it. This week alone they'd taken off the carburettor four times, and it was still running lean. Mona had politely proffered the idea of a damaged gasket, but apart from looking at her with incredulity, she had been ignored.

However, she was alone now, and the lads would be gone for a good while, dealing with the drama. There would be no harm in unbolting it to check. If she was correct about the gasket, it might improve her relationship with the intractable Emlyn.

Mona turned off the light in the kitchen and made for the fluorescence of the tacked-on shed. The socket set was handy, and the carburettor came off in no time. It was soon obvious that they hadn't had a really good look at the gasket, because there, at the very edge, was a hairline crack. Mona only discovered it herself by holding it up against the light, but it was there all right.

Finding replacement gaskets for antiques like this could be hard, but it wouldn't be difficult to make one, or barter from an enthusiast on the Internet. Instinctively though, she doubted anything even close to a computer existed in this place – no one even had a phone.

Mona had resolved to speak about it to someone in the engineering department at the uni on Monday, when she heard the unmistakable sound of the lock being moved in the door. "*Shit, shit, shitty, shit,*" she hissed to herself, glancing over to the door. The kitchen light was off, but the carburettor was suddenly heavy in her hands. Maybe she could get it back on before he made it to the lean-to? *No... Shit.*

She saw him fill the doorway, throw down his rucksack and fumble for the light switch. *Bang.* Of course, the trip. Mona moved to reset the breaker again, but was slightly side-tracked by the strong, intoxicating waft of seaside that the coxswain had brought in with him. "It's OK, Emlyn, I've got the torch, I'll go and reset it," she called out as amiably as she knew how.

By the time she got back to the front door, Mona had decided to come clean. After all, what would he do in reality? Sulk a bit more, and eye her a bit more warily, she supposed. It was nothing she couldn't handle.

Emlyn was fiddling with the lock and trying to make a hasty exit for some reason. "I've done it, don't worry." Mona leaned past him, and switched the light back on, pausing in that split second for the blackout that didn't come. "There's something making it trip. It's intermittent, but probably needs looking at – it's been happening all day."

Mona knew Emlyn could speak English perfectly well; they all could. Yet he responded with nothing, and turned away from her. Emlyn didn't even know about the bike yet and Mona was already in for the silent treatment.

Deciding to cut her losses, Mona replaced the torch in the kitchen, and walked back to the bike, where she drained the mug of tea, and began to wipe the oil from her hands. It was inevitable that he would follow her in there.

"Look, Emlyn," she began, defying him under the full glare of the fluorescent tube. However, she wasn't squaring up to the coxswain. Mona was almost sure she had never met this man before, yet a sudden spark of recognition flared in her mind. Could he be one of the long-lost relatives she'd been searching for?

"Sorry, I thought you were Emlyn. I'm Mona." She put out a hand, which he didn't take. The man didn't say anything either but stared past her at the carburettor. A cap obscured his features, but Mona caught a glimpse of blue eyes and a scarred face. Well, another chatty Welshman – at least Brendan had talked.

The crewman picked up the carb and examined it in quite a disconcertingly stern fashion. Mona reached for the gasket and held it to the light, pointing to the damage. "There's a hairline crack, won't run right unless they change it." Still he remained mute, so she handed him the gasket and returned upstairs to bed. Let him explain it to Emlyn then.

≈

Despite everything she couldn't comprehend about the place, Mona found the mornings were almost always glorious here. Living a hundred metres from the energy of the Irish Sea had inspired her to train outside before breakfast – even on a Sunday.

It wasn't something she wanted to do anymore, it had become something she *had* to do, in order to stay sane. Brendan had euphemistically called them 'patterns' but there was nothing pretty about the vigorous routine. He had drummed into her the necessity of daily, hard practice, and in the end it had become habit for both of them, a physical shorthand to control.

There had been a week of readjusting to exercise on her own after he'd died, but Mona could still feel Brendan's scowl on her, each time she over-extended, or lost sight of her rhythm. This was probably a form of OCD for her now but habits are a lifeline when you don't have much else, and it almost worked for her, more or less.

There was a back door into the house, and Mona always re-entered that way; it often saved the trauma of breakfast. However, there was no avoiding it today, and the kitchen groaned with neighbours and crew, getting stuck in to tea and gossip. The morning after a late night shout had a timbre all of its own.

Mona couldn't help but smile as Nia waved her in to the kitchen, managing to somehow disguise the rolling of her eyes to everyone else. As different as they were, and with evident opposition, Mona and Nia seemed to have struck up an easy friendship. "Saved you some *bara brith*," she muttered, revealing the booty on the plate on her lap.

"She puts some sort of additive in this you know?" Mona whispered, savouring the rich fruity bread.

"Do you think?" Nia asked naively.

"Crack cocaine I wouldn't wonder."

Nia nudged her hard with an elbow, cautioning her even through the squeak of laughter. If Siân was in striking distance, the humour had to be of a strictly innocent nature, and Mona wondered again about Nia's attitude to her mother. Surely they were about the same age, and yet there was almost an immaturity to Nia, an artlessness that belied her years. It was more than that though; a Victorian air of subservience permeated the small community. Siân, Emlyn and Ifan, the patriarch, appeared to wield something other than age as a weapon.

"Was it a bad one, the shout?" Mona asked, as she pushed the crumbs from her lap.

Nia shook her head in exasperated reply. "No, they all seem to be congratulating my cousin Cai on his discovery with that bike. Apparently he's fixed it. *Bloody thing*," she added quietly.

"Oh really?" Mona seethed, trying to bore a hole in the back of his head, having recognised the RNLI cap. *Bastard*. "So he's your cousin?"

"Yes," she lowered her voice. "Doesn't speak any English." Mona raised her eyebrows in surprise. "He is *Welsh*, we are in *Wales*," Nia explained waspishly.

"But…"

"But what? Would you think it so strange if he were a Frenchman living in France?"

"No, but…" Mona had hit a nerve, and in all honesty couldn't think of a sensible reply, so she asked a safer question. "What's he doing here then?"

"Oh, he's doing some stuff up at the university, starting on Monday."

"What, our university?"

"Bangor's the only one around here, Mo."

"What does he do?" Mona wished he would turn around, so she could give him a dirty look for stealing her glory, but he didn't.

"He's an engineer of some description." Nia waved a hand at him in an uncharacteristically vague gesture.

Mona fancied a run to *Traeth Lligwy*. The beach was a glorious expanse of sand and freedom, and the weather would just about hold if she went now – but then Emlyn's pager went, and all hell broke loose. Suddenly Siân and Emlyn were involved in a domestic dispute, which only their father managed to calm.

"What's that all about?" Mona asked Nia over the chaos.

"Uncle Em said he was going to repair the electrics today – apparently they shorted out yesterday. Only now there's a shout, and he's got to go. Mam wanted to bake today, and well, you know..."

Mona had already started to slink from the room, when Ifan turned to her. "Cai said you would be able to help him rewire the damaged section," he said, halting her departure with his garbled phrase.

Mona glanced across at the newcomer, pretty certain that he hadn't opened his mouth at all. "Well, I'm not a proper electrician you know, I've picked a few things up, but…"

"Still, he needs a hand, so if you're not too busy maybe you and Nia could help."

In the end, Nia sat at the kitchen table studying, while Cai and Mona started to rewire the kitchen circuit. Initially, Mona tried some friendly banter, with Nia's help as translator, but it fell rather bad-temperedly at the first hurdle, so she resigned herself to her mp3 player.

It was abundantly clear that Cai was one of those fastidious, tidy, methodical men with all the right tools for every job. He knew electricity, and found the fault by careful and considered deduction. Quite unlike Brendan, who had always guessed and experimented in any given situation, whether it be electricity, plumbing or engineering. She missed her bizarre uncle at the most unexpected moments.

Mona watched Cai work for about half an hour, learning the pattern of the work: cable, wire strippers, crimp, crimp tool, socket and screwdriver. Soon enough, she was able to pass him exactly what he needed, at the right moment, for every application.

They fell into a rhythm of working together that Mona found strangely satisfying, and after a few hours, the job was nearly over. Mona noticed that Cai edged his tongue out between his teeth whenever extra concentration was called for, and while waiting for another glimpse of it she lost her place and rhythm. Their hands fumbled together to catch the falling crimp. His touch electrocuted her, there was a tightening in her head and Mona was left with a residual image behind her eyes.

Cruel blue eyes smile at her across the stink of battle. He lets fly the whistling stone from its sling, straight, true, and her head slams back as the rock shatters her golden diadem.

The static shock of the vision burned into Mona's mind, and she closed her eyes to clean it away. When next she looked, Cai had packed away his neat little tool-bags and was already leaving the kitchen. By the time she had joined Nia at the table, Mona dismissed the incident as a returning still from a long-lost film.

"That's funny-looking Welsh." Mona squinted at the open book nearest her.

"That's because it's Gaelic. Welsh and Irish myths are interchangeable; we're all part of the same stories." Nia didn't look up and Mona didn't take the hint.

"So how many languages do you speak?"

"Only the important ones." Nia's head remained bent over the book she studied.

"Which are?"

"I can read Latin and Ancient Greek as well as a few others." It didn't seem to be a boast.

"Why?"

Nia finally raised her head, shocked at the Englishwoman's ignorance. "Source material, Mo!"

"Of course." Mona smiled, wishing she'd never asked.

≈

Mona was awoken by the shouting from downstairs – it was a fairly regular part of her morning routine now. Emlyn was the deep intermittent rumble that punctuated Siân's incessant shriek, and Mona couldn't quite place the third calm voice but suspected it was

Dafydd. Even spoken in anger, Welsh had a sort of harsh poetry in it, and Mona lay patiently waiting for it to make some sort of sense.

When it didn't, she let her mind wander to the day ahead and the lovely Jack. The man in question was also a student on the fabrication course; he was a bit brash and coarse, but what he had in his favour were a pair of muscular forearms, and an acceptable sense of humour.

Mona had forgotten about Cai joining them this morning, and somehow resented him talking to Nia at the bus stop. He wasn't wearing his cap today, and she noticed just how extensive the burn scarring was down the right side of his face. She didn't want to look too closely but thought that it might have been wiser for him to wear the cap, as some of the local undesirables were moving in to openly stare.

There was the normal scrum as the bus arrived and the passengers boarded. Cai sat in a single seat at the front, and the yobs managed to get a grandstand view of him, by parking themselves on a bench that ran perpendicular to his. Nia was completely immersed in her texts and Mona watched as the talking and gesticulating from the kids got louder and more obscene.

The kids abused Cai in English but Mona was sure he'd be left in no doubt about the subject matter. English was the language of the bus – and the playground it seemed. "Why doesn't he tell them to shut up?"

"Oh, Cai's not like that. Anyway, they'll get bored of it soon enough." Nia had obviously kept half an ear on proceedings, but Mona was bored of it already.

"Can I borrow your book bag a minute?" Heaving the monstrous weight over her shoulder, Mona rose from her seat to speak to the bus driver. Being overly careful not to lose her balance as he careered around the country lanes, she edged forward. As she drew alongside the young lads, Mona finally lost her balance, and the bag swung with an indecent force into one of the young men's groin. "Oh, I'm *so* sorry," she apologised exaggeratedly. There was another lurch and her hand accidentally caught his friend in the kidneys, as she flailed around for the handhold above her. Mona had an extremely quick conversation with the perplexed driver, before making her overly precarious way back to the seat beside Nia.

"That was a bit clumsy," Nia noted, not looking up from her work.

"I know!" Mona smirked. "The driver's getting faster and faster around these lanes. I decided someone should say something."

Nia still didn't meet her eye, but Mona detected the slightest of smiles around Nia's lips. "Nicely done."

As the university stop loomed, the young men were the first to disembark. Good bloody riddance, Mona thought.

Nia didn't take much notice of the other students, seeming to reside in her own private, academic domain most of the time. She had both a BA and an MA from the university but was trying very hard to be accepted on to a fiercely competitive PhD course. The interview was today. "We're here." Mona nudged her. They were always the last off, as there was always one last paragraph to finish.

Nia was now looking a bit flustered.

"Good luck." Mona crossed both sets of fingers and grinned, not knowing how else to behave. Having any type of friend was novel for her, and she was amazed at how fond of Nia she had become; it made her feel normal, and somehow female for the first time in years – though it was taking a bit of getting used to.

It was odd that Cai accompanied Mona to the faculty and if he thought her circuitous but camera-less route there was strange, he didn't say. Mona took a couple of sideways glances at his face; his right eye had been pulled down a bit, and part of his mouth had been mangled. The pain of a burn like that must have been excruciating, but it didn't seem to affect him now.

Feeling a bit of a fraud, Mona walked into Engineering as if she was a legitimate student, rather than just a bluffer doing a short-term welding course. However, it looked like Cai really belonged here, as he slipped into conversation with one of the more senior professors – Welsh, she realised – and their paths parted.

≈

It would be fair to say that all Mona's strengths lay in the practical, rather than the academic subjects. Brendan had allowed her to study – not in colleges, but in industry. He had bribed small companies to teach her the fundamentals of plumbing, electrics, carpentry and mechanics.

She supposed now that it had all been in preparation for surviving alone, and Mona no longer wondered why he hadn't suggested hairdressing or accountancy. Mona had also helped him fix their endless troop of old bangers and she had been competent at all of it, but nothing had excited her until she'd started to work in metal. Metal felt right in her hands, and she could make it do things that wood couldn't even contemplate. Her welding was poor, but that wasn't going to be a problem; that was just practice.

Mona's tutor was a reasonable teacher; at least, he explained things well enough for her to understand. It was the old technician who was a bit odd. Colm used to be head of the faculty, a long time ago, and he was still there, making it his business to keep his finger on the pulse, and in as many pies as possible. He was quite old and fairly befuddled, had a poor grasp of English and a real interest in Mona. The lads on her course joked about it endlessly, with an ever increasing serving of innuendo. Though neither they, nor the tutor, seemed too concerned about it, as long as it kept him out of their way.

It was coming up to the last week of term, and the class had been assigned a project piece to be finished by Thursday. It dominated the conversation on the way to lunch, as the students compared notes and ideas. "What are you going to make Mo?" Jack asked, and her heart lifted an inch. "Have to be something clever to hide that chicken shit welding of yours."

34

It slammed back down in place as Jack's entourage exploded with adolescent exuberance. Jack was a big, strong, blonde Geordie; he was popular and confident. What on earth had ever made Mona assume there could be anything but friendly banter between them? "Very good Jack, dream on. We all know you can't take the competition."

"Bring it on Jonesey," he laughed, as he led the gang to a table of Media babes. She watched them go, and sighed. Jack really did have lovely arms. Mona chose a table on her own and pulled out the limp sandwich from its bag. They were all given the same packed lunch at the cottages each morning, and it was always a disappointment.

An idea for the project had been flickering around in the back of her mind all morning, and as she reached for her workbook, a cup of weak tea arrived on the table in front of her. Cai peered down from above, somehow asking permission to join her. Mona didn't particularly want his company, but she smiled back thinly, and he scraped back the chair to sit opposite. "Thanks, Cai."

Predictably, there was a long, awkward silence, and Mona began to pray for the swift reappearance of Nia. When Cai finally spoke to her, it was in Welsh, and she had no idea what he had said, but his voice was quiet and gruff, and somehow pleasant. Mona raised her eyebrows, and he pointed at her book. "My book?"

Cai shook his head and took one of her hands in his own before she had the chance to pull it away. She breathed out in relief when nothing but a nagging déjà vu filled her mind – perhaps they *were* related. "*Llaw.*" He said simply.

Mona smiled at him until she realised what he meant – and then she tugged her hand away brusquely. Working in metal was a dirty job, and though she had worn gloves and washed them before lunch, her hands and nails were tattooed with the black, invasive oil. "I've washed them, it's just really hard to get out." Why was she apologizing? This bloke had taken credit for the bike.

Cai shook his head again, and retook her hand in his, turning it over gently to reveal a metal cut on the inside of her palm. "*Torri.*"

Nia appeared over his shoulder, looking unhappy. "It's gone from six to three. They can't decide, so we've got a viva on Thursday."

Mona exhaled a relieved breath. "Well, that's great; you're still in with a chance."

"No time to revise!" Nia squawked, lifting both hands into the air with abject futility. "I've got to rehearse for the 'Lifeboat Day' concert on Thursday, Mam's asked me to help with the dinner afterwards and I've got to sort out the horses and chickens for the neighbour – she's away and I promised." Nia was panicking now, her pitch getting higher with each word.

"Calm down, Nia. Show me what to do with the animals, I'm not exactly busy." Mona didn't savour the prospect of spending any more time than strictly necessary with Nia's difficult mother, but she would, if it helped Nia.

Nia and Cai had a conversation that sounded more intense and important than animals and dinner, but Nia seemed relieved with the outcome, and it was settled.

Rather than being pleased with her daughter's success, Siân was apoplectic with rage at their agreement, and Mona made herself scarce as the shit hit the fan. She chose to walk the cliff path to the bronze coxswain, rather than watch the family meltdown. A walk turned to a jog, then a run, and finally she found herself pounding along the hard, packed sand of Lligwy Beach, chasing out the aggression from the collecting points in her body.

There was obviously some unresolved angst about Nia's dad, and though she hadn't asked, Mona wouldn't be surprised if he had left Siân. It wasn't any of her business, and she tried to avoid thinking too hard about anyone else's family – it reminded her too sharply of the lack of her own.

≈

There was still some evening light by the time Mona eased through the back door. There was no sign of the witch, but Ifan was lying in wait, and he beckoned her over. Mona capitulated with a sigh, acknowledging that she was in for more questioning. "Tea?" Ifan asked, with no intention of making a cup.

"Yes, do you want one?" she asked. He smiled; of course he did. "Ifan, is there any chance that I could be related to Cai?"

Mona slid the mug to him, and was surprised that Ifan looked so shocked. "Why would you think that?"

She didn't actually have an answer that satisfied. "I don't know, he's just... only that I feel I've met him before. Not even that really, but he's familiar somehow." Ifan said nothing for a minute, so she continued. "I mean, that's why I'm up here, isn't it? That's what the letter said. I thought it was a lead, that's all." He peered over at her pityingly. She could cope with anything but pity and her tone became abrupt. "So, it's been two weeks, have you found anything – from the archives or wherever?"

"The archives in both Wales and Ireland are notoriously incomplete – one of the inevitable drawbacks of English invasion and rule," he grimaced. "I've researched your names; your father Tom, your brother Idwal, and you of course, have local names. We know your mother was Irish but I'm afraid Jones isn't much to go on."

No, it seemed to Mona that half the island and a good proportion of the Welsh nation shared her surname. Mona hadn't ever considered herself Welsh at all, growing up in Kent and speaking with a normal English accent, but there must be some connection for her here. "Does Cai remind you of anyone then?" Ifan appeared uncomfortable asking.

"Not really. My dad was dark with blue eyes but not the same, not as blue, if you know what I mean. Mum had green eyes and strawberry blonde hair." If she concentrated hard enough, Mona could remember its softness and comforting smell. "My brother looks like her, but big, very big."

There was the same pregnant silence for a while then, "So, were you never curious when your parents spoke Welsh?"

"They only spoke it to each other, and not very often. Id and I thought it was a joke."

Ifan looked truly offended by the comment but continued with the interrogation, though a little more stiffly. "And they never told you anything? Anything that sounded like a faerie story?"

Mona shook her head; he knew this already, he'd asked before. Perhaps he was losing his marbles. Ifan stared through her, his worn profile looking even older and more sinister in this light. What was he hiding about her past? What wasn't he saying?

It suddenly infuriated Mona that everyone was pussy-footing around this issue. She'd never had the gall to ask Brendan directly, but she'd been sure, almost since the day her parents had died. "It was some sort of sectarian killing, wasn't it?" Ifan was startled. "Come on, you knew my mum and Brendan were Irish, it doesn't take a genius."

Ifan shook his head but still appeared to Mona as if he was harbouring some mysterious secret. Their conversation came to an end when Nia joined them in the kitchen. It was clear she had been crying.

"Coming up to do the animals then?" she asked Mona in a quavering voice.

Looking after the animals was a little more involved than Mona had imagined, but it was a strenuous, outdoors job that she was looking forward to. "I've written it down for tomorrow, but you'll soon get the hang of it," Nia assured her.

Mona scanned the page; it all looked fairly straightforward. "You can tell your mum I'll help on Thursday as well."

"No." Nia responded a little too quickly. "No, it'll be over for me by then; I'll do it. I wouldn't want to inflict her on you."

"Is she going through a tough time?"

"All time is bad for her since Dad."

"He left?"

"He died."

3

Mark

Mona's new job allowed her to practice the patterns up in the horse field. The grass was different up here on the island; it was springier somehow, and it cushioned her slow, deliberate moves. Brendan had said that the constant practice kept open the neural pathways from brain to muscle. Mona didn't know too much about that, but the vigorous morning routine kept her strange little life in some sort of order. She missed Brendan, she missed the release of fighting with him, but at least she had her patterns.

The horses didn't seem to mind what she did around them, as long as they were eating. Horses smelled lovely; if Mother Nature had a smell, Mona thought on the way back to the cottage, it would be horse, strong and earthy – it was almost the smell of life.

The kitchen was uncomfortably full and tense, so she gulped down her tea and started for the back door. It was preferable to hang around with the strangers at the bus stop than to endure the horrible atmosphere in the kitchen for one more minute.

She'd noticed that the huge, dusty ledger was open on the table, and that was always a cautionary sight. Mona suspected that the small community had money problems and it hadn't surprised her that Ifan immediately accepted her offer of cash for food and board.

Mona closed the door quietly behind her, glad to be out of the way. She scuttled past the conservatory, where Cai was leaning elegantly against the ancient dry-stone wall. Mona wasn't entirely sure whether or not he was waiting for her, until he stopped her with a gesture to halt.

Cai picked up her injured hand, administering a TCP-doused cotton ball to the wound and covering it with a substantial plaster. Mona was stunned into a stupor by his unexpected kindness; it had been a long time since anyone had stuck her back together again. He held her hand for a little longer than necessary before letting it drop, then stooped to pick up the litter that his first aid had created.

Mona took great pains not to look at Cai on the way to the bus stop, and though they chose to sit together on the bus, there was an invisible demarcation line between them that left her muscles weary from the effort of not crossing it. "Thanks," Mona mumbled as they parted in Engineering, not hanging around to see if he'd heard.

≈

Colm was prowling again but Mona tried to ignore him. She'd been sketching a symbol that kept coming to her, over and over again. Soft triangles, shapes within shapes – endless and eternal, never ending and never beginning. The design was Celtic in style but it wasn't right yet – nearly, but not quite, even after twenty pages of scribble.

Old Colm shuffled right up to her workbench, peering myopically over her shoulder – then appeared to have a bit of a choking fit. The old boy was all bulging eyes and red face, but after a glass of water and a sit down, he made it over to her again. "If that's what you want to make, you should do it in iron, soft, pure. I can get hold of some if you'd like." His accent wasn't the same as the others when he spoke English, but as he said the words, Mona realised that *yes*, that was exactly what she wanted to do. "I'll have it by Friday," he murmured with a strange, soft excitement. The piece had to be in by Thursday, but that seemed less important now than the actual making of the work. "I can help you with it." He licked his lips. "It will be a magnificent thing." Colm was whispering, and it made Mona wonder if there was a black market in soft, pure iron.

≈

As the return bus neared the village, the rainclouds, which Mona had hoped would stay whole, burst. It hadn't rained for three days now, so they couldn't really complain, but she felt like doing so. "I'm going straight up to do the horses, see you back at the cottage." Nia was distracted, but heard Mona over the din, as their fellow passengers fled from the bus to find quick shelter from the driving downpour.

Mona jogged up to the field, reasoning that speed would get her less wet. The padlock was stiff and slippery in her hands but she eventually managed to wrench it apart. Mona's hood was up so she hadn't heard Cai over the sudden squall but saw him now as he closed the gate behind him, heedless of the two hungry horses galloping in their direction.

Mona wasn't at all experienced with horses but Nia had told her to expect this occasionally, and she stood stock-still, reaching to grab Cai back before he thought of running. As she did so, her fingers scraped against the exposed flesh of his neck, and the slight contact scorched another bizarre image onto her mind's eye, leaving her breathless.

A clash of swords and the tingle of reverberation shot up her arm, but she'd got the upper hand, and the sword was shunted from his grasp. A look of shock and then she was on him – climbing all over him, lips, mouth, breasts and hips.

As the two horses came to a skidding halt, six inches in front of them, Mona felt Cai dragging himself free and backing away from her to the gate. Her body was shaking with adrenaline as she patted the wet nose of the nearest animal. It was clear that Cai had fled from her through the rain.

Once inside the stables and cropping on their hay, the horses were much less formidable and Mona used her chores to steady the panic in her mind. Had Cai shared that eerily vivid image with her? His reaction certainly suggested that was likely. She glanced down at her hands – it had happened twice now through an accidental touch. As the adrenaline receded, Mona was left shocked but fully awakened by the snapshot sexual encounter.

She turned her attention to the horse at her side, leaning against its massive body for warmth, and breathed in the calming aroma as she scratched its ears. Perhaps it was just grief, perhaps she'd lost one too many of the people she loved. Yet, while mental illness might be a possibility, Mona was pretty sure it wasn't contagious.

Mona received another soaking before she made it from the paddock to the house. She dribbled into the kitchen where Sian's sharp eyes were immediately drawn to the t-shirt, made translucent by the rain. Apart from Siân, the kitchen was empty and for a split second Mona feared that the woman would attack her, such was the rancour in her eyes. Mona moved rapidly around her and up the stairs, attempting to cover her ample breasts by tucking her arms around them – they were a bloody nuisance.

≈

Both Siân and Nia were missing at supper and the evening meal was excruciatingly silent. Mona wondered if Cai had tried to explain their bizarre encounter to his family – she couldn't work out what else might have sparked the increased resentment in the air.

Mona cursed her long-dead parents throughout the tortuous meal. She'd only just about forgiven them for dying and now it seemed they were still punishing her from the grave. A bunching urgency surged in Mona's forearms and it begged her to sweep the table clear of clinking crockery.

It would be delicious to watch their faces, as the bowls of thin stew crashed to the ground around them. Mona resisted the violent urge and took her bowl to the sink. She stuck to the rigid chore rota by starting to wash the dishes and was stunned when Cai joined her at the sink with a tea towel.

Not so much as a glance was exchanged between them, and Cai kept a meticulously accurate distance from her. Mona was more disappointed than she ought to be; she remembered the TCP and plaster, then realised that the delicate fragrance of their fledgling friendship had been snuffed right out.

When Cai was back within the bosom of the Conservatory Motorbike Club, Mona took her textbook to the armchair nearest the fire and tried to study. She had shrugged on a jumper, still vaguely conscious of the t-shirt moment before dinner, and was becoming comfortably soporific, the soft nonsense from the men following her into sleep.

≈

Ifan sat in the darkest corner of the room. He had watched the woman read, and then fall asleep by the fire. He could feel the pulsing of Mona's power from here, and his scalp tightened anew at the memory of first seeing her at the cottage door.

The throb of Mona's potent energy frightened him and her presence here struck him daily with a sense of foreboding. If Brendan Kelly had sent her here for her safety, he must have been a truly desperate man at the end, and her potential very great indeed.

Ifan's mind travelled back twenty years to the image of the drowning Irishman. Saving Brendan's life had been the single most foolish act in his life. It would not have been something he would do again, given the choice. That moment of weakness had heralded a bitter chapter of personal and tribal tragedy.

Mona was either a really competent liar or completely ignorant of her heritage. However, the fact that she'd come from Brendan was the real problem and he sighed wearily at the thought. Ifan was old now and this was a young man's job – not that he'd ever shone as Archdruid, he reflected bitterly. Ifan yawned, preparing to grip the arms of the chair and haul himself upright, but froze as someone approached.

Cai was so intent on Mona that he didn't see the old man, and he was getting close to her now – too close. Ifan almost winced audibly, as the auras of power around each of the young people touched and roiled.

The Archdruid could see power in others as a haze and feel it in his scalp; it was never a comfortable feeling, but it wasn't something he felt very often now. Ifan had watched and waited for power to emerge, as every generation was born. Sometimes he was sure there must still be power in these youngsters, but that was probably just wishful thinking. The magic had been dying out gradually over the centuries; Cai was rare but Mona was rarer.

"Cai." The young man jolted, and peered into the gloom at Ifan, not uttering a response. "I hope you know what you're doing boy. She's mighty powerful."

Cai bridled visibly, before ignoring the old man and backing off. Ifan breathed again as the lad left. If he was honest, Ifan wasn't sure he liked his young nephew all that much. There was a cruel arrogance to the man that seemed to fit the face he now wore. He had learned to live with Cai's aura over the years, but had never been able to understand it.

Ignorance was a disease that Ifan would take to his grave, though he knew enough to fear the way the boy's power had shifted and flared as he had neared the sleeping woman.

≈

It was a beautiful morning and Mona was properly warmed up by the time she closed the gate on the grazing horses. She looked up to see Cai hovering nearby. He appeared to brace himself at her approach, before reaching out for her injured hand. He was too swift for her to avoid and her mind screamed a warning, even as a frisson of expectation fluttered in her body.

But there was no strangeness at their touch this time and Mona was loath to pull her hand away as he inspected the extremely grubby plaster. A new hint of sexual tension haunted them now and even this minimal physical connection was affecting her – a change in breathing pattern, a slight shiver.

Cai took an age to decide what to do about the plaster, before gripping her hand much tighter, and slowly unpeeling the dressing from one end. It was a disconcertingly sensual experience, and Mona had to add a drying mouth and raised blood pressure to the list of her symptoms. When Cai lifted her cut hand to his lips and blew, her stomach clenched and she knew immediately what to do. Snatching her hand back, she fell into a sprint start. "Race?"

Cai may not have spoken English but it was a pretty good mime. Mona made a cracking start, but could hear him gaining on her as she relaxed into a steady run. Mona was an accomplished runner but she didn't have great style. Cai, on the other hand, moved with an elegant minimalism; he had a longer stride, and Mona knew immediately that he would beat her.

That fact didn't prevent her from competing though, as she spied the finish line of the front door. They both sped up as they moved into the back straight, and it may have been gallantry, but for whatever reason, they arrived at the front door together, out of breath and laughing. Mona was amazed at the transformation and hoped that the laughter didn't hurt his scarred face, so that he would do it more often.

≈

There were too many people living in the little group of cottages, and nowhere near enough bathrooms. Having to queue for the shower made Mona late, forcing her to catch the later bus full of raucous youths. She braced herself for battle as the bus performed its large preloading arc. Nia must have taken an earlier bus in preparation for her test, but she could sense Cai standing exceptionally close behind her and was vaguely irritated with him when he gripped her arm tightly and held her back.

As the melee swarmed around them, anxious for a precious seat, Mona's face expressed her confusion, but Cai simply lifted his shoulders in a dismissive shrug and maintained a steadfastly deadpan expression. His idiosyncratic behaviour forced them to stand together in the aisle, crushed up against each other for the duration of the journey. Mona found that she had to brace constantly to stop herself leaning against him, though it would have been easier and more satisfying to let gravity have its way.

It was almost a disappointment to arrive at the campus and Mona thought how strange it was that the most erotic element in their closeness was his smell. In the cottages, they all used the same cheap shower gel, but that wasn't what Cai smelled of at all.

≈

Mona spent all day drawing the convoluted knot and trying to distance her mind from her libido. There was little doubt that she was becoming infatuated with Cai. She found him extremely attractive, despite his scarring – or maybe because of his scarring. But what was the point? She'd be gone in just over a week, and suddenly she couldn't wait to move on.

Mona snuck out of the workshop early. She was prepared and eager for tomorrow's metalwork and Colm said they'd even have the place to themselves. The bus was fairly empty and Mona snagged a seat at the back, switched on her music and closed her eyes.

Without needing to open them, Mona knew immediately that it was Cai who sat down beside her – sea air and diesel. Nia sat behind him, panting as if she had run for the bus. Her eyes were a little red. "Didn't you get it?" Mona asked, remembering Nia's viva.

"I did actually," she answered, though her lips wobbled. At Mona's confused look, Nia smiled. "I'm just not feeling all that well."

Mona grinned back and punched Nia lightly on the arm. "Well done clever clogs." The contact seemed to upset Nia further and

Mona wondered if she'd been a bit too heavy-handed. "Go back and rest, I was off up to the paddock anyway."

Mona's offer didn't improve Nia's mood, so she gave up and sank back into the music, half listening to Cai's hard Welsh consonants as he spoke in soft earnest tones to his cousin. The last of the shower gel on his body had evaporated with the warmth of the day and Mona was able to down lungfuls of Cai thanks to his closeness. It did remarkable things to her body.

Instead of leaving her to it, both Nia and Cai followed Mona up to the paddock. She was bemused, but Nia seemed too withdrawn to ask and Cai was typically inscrutable, so she carried out her jobs, relishing the sunshine on her face and arms.

Both cousins were still tense and morose when she joined them under the tree, hot and sweaty from her exertions. Nia didn't seem that happy with her success and Cai was sitting with his back bolt upright against the bark. He moved to pull something from his back pocket as Mona approached.

It was a small flat bottle of Navy Rum. "*Iechyd da*." He held it up towards her, unscrewed the lid, took a swig and passed the bottle to Nia – his eyes not leaving Mona's all the while.

Mona was too engrossed in watching Cai's tongue lick away a drop of rum from his lips to notice if Nia had taken a drink. But Mona accepted the bottle when it was her turn and took a large swallow herself. When she offered the bottle back to Cai, he made sure to touch Mona's hand, as if testing for their intermittent electrical connection.

As the cool liquid burned her lips and throat, Mona smiled back at the scarred man, who was unable to hide his interest in her chest. If Nia were not sitting beside them, Mona may well have made an advance. However, she was – and she had started talking. "So, you haven't told us anything about your childhood."

"Not much to say really," Mona shrugged, pulling her eyes from Cai.

Nia spoke again, with her eyes closed now – she'd clearly had a sip at least. "Your names are very Anglesey – I mean, *Mona*," she emphasised, making it sound like an attractive name. "You literally are the woman of Môn, Ynys Môn. And Idwal…" Nia's voice was taking on a fey quality. "That's an old, old name. It means ruler you know. I think you are related to us in some way, you *must* be." Cai coughed but his cousin continued to chat. "You should stay; I could help you do some more detailed research. I'll have more access now."

Mona was grateful to be asked but she couldn't see herself staying much longer than the month required, so the offer was left hovering between them. Cai passed back the bottle, she took another long drink, and lay back on the close-cropped grass next to Nia, whose train of thought had become random. "What's Idwal like?"

"He's a huge great lump of a man, with girly hair and stinking feet." Mona tried to joke his loss away.

"Have you got any idea where he is now?"

"No, but I was thinking about trying to find him, when it's all settled here."

"What sort of man is he?"

"The biggest party animal around; drinks too much, loves too much – you know the sort."

"You sound like you don't approve Mona," Nia noted, seeming a little more at ease.

Mona laughed. The sun was delicious on her skin and the alcohol-induced warmth in her brain made her talkative. "I do sound like that don't I?" She laughed. It wasn't true, Mona loved her brother too much to judge him. "It's not that; I'm sure we've all done our fair share of oat-scattering." Mona tried to energise the atmosphere by changing the subject and sitting up. "So what about music? Is it all Celtic and classical, or do you listen to other stuff?"

"Cai does, I'm a bit more old-fashioned."

"Really?" Mona grabbed the mp3 player from her jeans and rolled in Cai's direction. He remained propped against the tree, watching the women through half-closed eyes. Cai was very well put together, she thought, wiry but strong, and Mona had another powerful impulse to feel the muscles of his thighs. A full back, she supposed vaguely, he was too tall to be a scrum half. Fighting her rampant urges, Mona offered him one of her earphone buds.

Mona enjoyed almost all genres of music and though she had only a tiny amount on this player, she could use it to judge his taste. Cai liked some of the heavier stuff, but looked a little holier than thou about Imelda May. "Come on Cai, how can you not dance to this?" Mona demonstrated her lack of self-control, by wiggling to the thumps of double bass and drum. Cai made a noise which Mona hoped was a laugh.

"Did you live on your own?" Nia was still asking questions.

Mona sagged. The loss of Brendan was too recent, too painful, and she bypassed the question rather than attempting to answer it. "I've done quite a few courses, practical stuff. And I do a lot of sport, so I'm always busy."

"*Sport?*" Nia made it sound like torture, but after a bit of Welsh back and forth, it seemed that Cai wanted to know more about her sport.

"Netball, hockey, football, rugby, rowing, running, swimming."

Nia felt obliged to sit up. At the length of the list, and at Cai's request she asked, "What are you best at? I think he means what do you *enjoy* the most."

Mona didn't think that was what he meant at all. "I'm best at fighting," she qualified. "I practise a sort of mixed martial art, based on taekwondo."

"Fighting!" If anything Nia's disgust level had elevated.

"I'll show you. Come on Nia, get up."

"No, I can't move, it's too lovely in the sun. Do you know how rare it is here? Anyway, the only sport I'm even slightly interested in is horse riding."

Mona was about to question Nia about horse riding but Cai had teased his cousin. Mona guessed it was innuendo and there followed a little flurry of angry Welsh dialogue.

Mona felt a real need to move, and a bit of horseplay with Cai would suit her just fine. She stood and encouraged him with a draw of the head. When he didn't budge, she grabbed him by the arm and pulled him to his feet, forgetting momentarily to hide her strength.

Mona cocked her head to look at him but he seemed tense and rigid now – gone was the delicious sparkle in his eye. So giving up all verbal communication, Mona reverted to body language and moved his shoulders to face her square on. As she lifted her arms into the opening phase of Brendan's simplest pattern, she was surprised to find Cai pose an immediate counter.

Mona had wanted to block a few moves with Cai, just to give her an excuse to touch him, but his reaction changed everything, and within the blink of an eye they were fighting in earnest.

Some of Cai's moves were eerily similar to her own, but he lacked any decent technique. The punches and kicks were sloppy, his mind unfocused, and he wasn't using his core at all. He was fast and strong though, and Mona concluded that it wouldn't take much training to make him into a genuinely good fighter.

All musings were cut dead when Cai evaded a punch to the kidneys. He used the momentum of Mona's kick against her, forcing a one-legged hop. She'd been in this situation many times before though, and it was a great opportunity to use the flying scissor, striking his hands up and away from her with the other leg. Cai grunted with surprise and pain as he was felled by the ferocity of the kick.

Suddenly extremely sober and breathing hard, Mona rushed forward. *Please don't say I've broken his arm,* she prayed silently to herself. "I'm sorry. Are you OK? Look, that didn't go according to plan." Cai glared up at her from the ground, with a mixture of respect, fear and something on the edge of feral. "Let me look at your arms," she insisted, leaning over him and running her hands over his lower arms: they were muscular and veined with exercise. "You're OK, good, great," she breathed out and ran her fingers through her hair, chuckling in relief.

Despite the change in atmosphere, Cai took her offered hand, and she pulled him up to standing. He didn't move away or let go of her hand and she breathed in that strangely alluring smell. "Who taught you to fight like that, Mona?" Nia asked in a quiet, tense tone. Something about the fighting had upset her too.

"I've always studied a type of taekwondo. I've practiced a lot." It was almost the truth, but Mona didn't miss the silent communication between Cai and Nia and it brought the party to an abrupt end. Conscious that she had forced the awkwardness, Mona rather clumsily changed the subject. "What time have you got to do your singing thing?"

The diversion was immediately effective on the ever-conscientious Nia, who checked her watch. "I've got to be there in an hour. And just look at me." Mona looked, but saw only perfection.

Nia dragged Cai away and flew home to prepare herself for the performance. It was part of the village 'Lifeboat Day' celebrations, some sort of concert in the chapel. Mona was more than reluctant to go; expecting a school or village hall affair of wobbly notes and awkward, tentative applause. She was already predicting a cup of milky tea at the interval, or maybe an orange squash.

Still smelling of rum and sweat, she followed the family into the small, neat chapel and settled into the corner of a wooden pew, gradually getting more squashed against the cool stone of the wall, as the village arrived. Mona lost herself in the melodic and alien rustle of the Welsh, as people chatted and laughed quietly.

There was an understated usefulness to the chapel. Cleverly made and finished from quality materials, it lacked the extravagant embellishments of the Catholic or High Anglican churches that she'd seen in Kent. Mona was detailing the differences in window styles, when Nia walked on to the stage. The murmuring had wound down to an anticipatory silence as Nia inhaled and opened her mouth to sing.

Her voice was clear and pure but honeyed with delicious vibration. Mona was drawn in, pulled forward into the song. Nia sung in Welsh, and though Mona couldn't understand the language, she somehow understood the song. There was death and loss, love, betrayal and, at the end – joy.

As simply as it was cast, the spell was broken. Someone was nudging her arm and talking to her in the familiar, accented English. "Do you feel OK?" It was Ifan, a look of concern showing through his wiry, white brows.

"What? What, no, I'm fine, I just…" Mona couldn't find anything adequate to say. She rubbed her eyes to find them damp and her t-shirt soaked. Ifan discreetly palmed her a hanky and she mopped up. Mona couldn't remember crying, or even how long she'd been sitting there, but she was stiff. "I can't believe it, she's so good – her voice is so beautiful." Mona had never heard such an enchanting voice outside of the world within her earphones.

Ifan sighed wistfully. "Come on, we've been sitting here long enough, I need to stretch my old legs."

"What time is it? I've still got to put the chickens to bed."

"I make it seven-thirty," he replied.

What! Seven-thirty? But surely the concert had started at five? Time had been lost – *no*, she hadn't been aware of the time at all. It was as if only the music and the lyrics had mattered. Mona was the woman in that song; she had loved that man, she had killed that child. It was as if the music of the language had seared through her understanding, and imprinted the story on her heart. Mona thought that maybe she had come to terms with the language and tried to recall some of the Welsh words – woman, or child. But she couldn't – not now that Nia had stopped singing. Mona didn't know those words; she had never known them.

Suddenly aware that she was not alright at all, Mona mumbled something to Ifan and pushed past him and then through the other guests milling around the chapel entrance. The intensity of the episode and the lack of control it engendered in her was making Mona panic.

Outside was better, sitting on the low stone wall and taking down lungfuls of salty air. Nia arrived, beaming from within the bosom of her proud family; even Siân looked happy. Somehow this attractive, clever, bashful woman was at odds with the sound that had come out of her lungs a few moments before.

Still wrung out with emotion, Mona decided that physical activity would help steady her and she strode purposefully toward the field to put the chickens to bed. When she reached the stony paddock, Mona saw that Cai had beaten her to it, and he stood shaking the box of corn, enticing them in. She nodded to him, slightly awkward now about the sparring incident earlier. Mona had become quite good at hiding her strength, and she made a mental note never to let her guard down like that again. It was much better to slide under the radar here.

Cai wasn't doing a great job at shaking the hens in and he began to cluck at and cajole them. Mona immediately felt the promise of corn and clean dry sawdust, of shelter from rain and hungry foxes. She drifted towards him – stopping suddenly as he ceased calling.

Something peculiar was happening when Mona heard Welsh – but the compelling responses the language invoked in her seemed random. There was no way she could avoid it or defend herself from it, and Mona clutched at her head to rein in the jangling thoughts, before Cai noticed her confusion.

≈

There were still the evening festivities of 'Lifeboat Day' left to enjoy. Apparently, this culminated in a party, with Dewi from the post office doing the disco. Mona was seriously considering feigning illness when Nia came charging up the coastal path. She was wearing an expression that, for the first time, reminded Mona of Siân. Mona and Cai shared a glance of uneasy solidarity in the face of her anger. "Where have you two been?" she challenged.

"Putting away the chickens."

Cai nodded strenuously in agreement.

"Well, the party starts in half an hour. Aren't you getting changed?" The last comment was aimed at Mona.

"I wasn't planning on it; these aren't too bad," she said, resisting the urge to sniff her armpit.

"You're going to have to do better than that," Nia explained, as if to an infant, while catching her arm in Mona's and leading her upstairs.

Brief Welsh words were spoken to Cai, and Mona gathered they were along the lines of '*you too, Cai*', because he promptly sloped off to his own room. Mona wondered again why she was so slow at learning the language. She'd been here over two weeks now, and not one word had stuck. Apart from the strange incident in the chapel, Welsh made as little sense to her as Urdu. It was as if her brain had a Teflon coating when it came to any foreign language, and she sighed in frustration. Mona might be wise not to dive into bed with Cai, but it would be nice if she could talk to him at least.

"It's not going to be that grim, Mona. Get a grip will you," Nia snapped, while giving her the once over. "Don't you have anything better to wear than those old jeans?"

"Not really," Mona admitted. Brendan had never let her wander down a high street looking for clothes, and so an appreciation of fashion had passed her by.

≈

Dressing with Nia was a strange experience, as it brought the physical differences between the women into sharp focus. At 5'10", Mona was Amazonian and extremely muscular. She had a symmetrical face with non-descript grey eyes and a boy's haircut, whereas Nia embodied some sort of feminine ideal.

As it turned out, Mona did have better jeans, and Nia sourced a prettyish sort of white shirt from somewhere to replace her grubby t-shirt. Thanks to a liberal dousing of Nia's perfume, she didn't smell too bad either. Mona wasn't overly keen on the amount of cleavage that was now showing, and the blouse emphasised the t-shirt mark on her neck, so she wrapped a thin scarf around the distinct tan line and turned to Nia for approval. "Ta da!"

With her shiny hair and glowing eyes, Nia looked radiant in a simple dress, but she was nevertheless determined that they both add something extra in the form of mascara and lipstick. With a subtle veneer of Boots No7 and slightly higher heels, the women eventually wafted down the stairs on a breeze of jasmine perfume.

It was all bustle and locking up, amid warnings and instructions in two languages. Ifan rolled over to them, offering them an arm each, and they all made their way up the hill and into the village, leaving the moaning of the Irish Sea behind them.

"Where's Cai?" Mona asked

"Gone on ahead with the lads."

"Is he OK?"

"Aah," breathed Ifan, already a hint of rum on his breath. "He's young, so young."

≈

Once in the hall, Mona was back on familiar territory. Men, young and old, sporting RNLI emblazoned jackets filled up the bar while their wives, children and grandchildren chatted and played in the main part of the room. Families were filling paper plates with curling sandwiches and saving seats for each other.

There was a lot more Welsh in the air tonight and Mona suppressed a sharp longing for her parents as Nia arrived at her shoulder, with what looked depressingly like lemonade. "No rum?"

She was swiftly silenced by the clear menace in Nia's silent refusal. "Why did you rush off after the concert Mona?" Nia asked as she sipped her lemonade thoughtfully. "I know it went on a bit, but I didn't think it was that bad."

Mona was suddenly concerned that she'd offended her new friend, but she merely shrugged rather than explain. "Sorry." Nia accepted the apology with a smile. "What was the story about anyway?" Mona asked out of something more than courtesy.

"Rhiannon, the wife of Pwyll. I particularly love the story of her on the white horse, and I set a poem to music."

"Yes, no one could keep up with her, even when they galloped." Mona frowned at her own words, wondering how come she suddenly knew the Welsh folk tale. "But it was sad as well, wasn't it?" she asked.

"Yes," Nia nodded, "when her son is taken, and she is blamed for his death. But you don't understand Welsh?" She blinked slowly.

"I don't, but I understood what you were singing. I felt it… somehow." Mona trailed off, realising that she wasn't making any sense.

Nia frowned and then changed the subject. "Cai's trapped in the bar being bored to death about squalls and north-easterlies. Apparently there's a big storm coming." She tapped her hand against the side of her leg in time to the music.

"What's Cai really like?" Mona pondered out loud. "It's so hard to communicate with him when you're not there. You'd have thought he'd have picked up English from the telly or something – it's not as if there isn't enough of it around."

"What's so great about English?" Nia scowled.

"Nothing, I only thought…" Mona kicked herself mentally and groped for a less controversial topic. "How did he get all that scarring?" Mona felt Nia blanche; it must have been horrific at the time, and she apologised for the intrusion. "Sorry, that was rude."

"No, not rude." Nia muttered to her feet. "It's just a long story."

Mona abandoned that subject behind too and they both scanned the room, spotting him with some of the crew at the bar, looking belligerent and awkward. No change there then.

Dewi was desperately trying to get the dancing underway. His choice of music was an undeniable plea, even if Mona didn't understand his Welsh banter. He began with the Jackson 5 and all the mums and kids crowded on to the small square of dance floor. "I love this cheesy stuff, let's dance." Mona grinned. "I haven't danced in ages."

Mona loved to dance, in the same way she loved to fight – release through movement. She suspected that Nia might be a more decorous dancer than herself but she seemed game at the moment, and they stuck their lemonades on a nearby table and joined the throng.

Soon they were sidestepping hot and sweaty kids, who were running in between their families and seeing how far they could skid on their knees before being told to pack it in. Mona noted that all mums must be the same, whatever language they speak. The dance floor was becoming more and more packed, and Nia steered Mona to the periphery to accommodate some of her more exuberant dance moves. The music was addictive, full of oldies that the entire room knew.

Inevitably though, a song came on that even Mona wasn't that fond of, and Nia took the opportunity to drag them off to rehydrate. Their lemonade had gone. "I'm going to get some more." Mona mouthed over the music and waggled the glasses. Nia nodded and smiled pinkly, blowing her hair out of her eyes, while Mona made her way to the bar.

The queue was three deep when she arrived, and Mona was stuck behind a broad-shouldered old bloke with a liberal sprinkling of dandruff on the shoulders of his navy blazer. She saw Cai squashed between the bar and the queue, and he happened to be looking in her direction, while holding his pint. Mona smiled at him – but he broke eye contact. Cai glimpsed up again, taking a large swig of beer, and at that exact moment Mona treated him to her very best cross-eyed gurn. The effect was immediate, and beer squirted from both his mouth and nose in unison, spraying the nearby crew.

With a path effectively cleared through disgust, Mona easily found her way to him, as he continued to laugh and choke, while bending over and holding his stomach. Cai's laughter made Mona chuckle, and she grabbed him by the hand, leading him back towards Nia. "It's not *that* funny," she muttered.

Though apparently it was, and each time Cai tried to control himself it would take only a glimpse of Mona to tip him back over the edge into full hysteria. By the time they'd reached Nia, the hysterics had spread to Mona, and both of them were helpless as chicks and leaning against each other for support. Eventually, they subsided into silence as the laughter stuttered to a stop, while Nia stared open-mouthed at Cai.

The quiet was broken by the scream of a banshee, and Mona was transported back to her old living room in Kent. She was twelve years old and pressing the play button on the ancient CD player – track eighteen of Supafunky - Volume Two. Mona wondered how on earth this song was playing here – now. She was also vaguely aware of Nia sighing and drifting away, but her real attention was concentrated on the relentless, primal, rhythmic shriek of the woman still wailing in the background.

'Jump Around' by House of Pain was the most *'gangsta'* song that she and Idwal had danced to, and it wasn't music to dance *to* with someone. This music lent itself better to dancing *at* someone. Cai never really stood a chance to escape, and his eyes seemed to acknowledge this as Mona advanced on him, rolling her shoulders and hips in time to the thumping beat.

Reaching within inches of him, she began utilising the rhythmic, pointy, finger jab – a move designed to intimidate rather than debilitate. So it surprised her when Cai blocked the jabs. Mona briefly considered trying to twist her fingers out of the block to make full contact, when Cai firmly closed his hand around hers, and began to move with her and the rhythm of the pounding beat.

An electrical circuit began to form through and between them as the pulsing beat lit up their bloodstreams. Mona marvelled at the sensation, laughing as they were drawn together like magnets, so close now that she could feel his breath in her face. Cai smiled back, and moved his lips to her ear, speaking into it in an unintelligible whisper of soft, sensual sentences.

Cyffwrdd, cusan, teimlad, blas, gafael.
Mona's body knew their names.

Touch, kiss, feel, taste, hold.

By the time his alien murmurings had ceased, Mona found herself outside the hall and lost in the taste of his lips. Their kissing was slow and gentle at first, as if they were remembering an old familiar cadence between them. Mona's hands travelled along the hardness of Cai's back and it sparked an increasing urgency from his mouth.

The suddenness of Siân's appearance in the gloom shocked them apart but Mona was totally unprepared for her venom. "Get away from him, you whore," she spat in English, dragging at Cai's arm as if to protect him from a threat.

Mona quickly recovered from her embarrassment and shock. A powerful sense of frustration and fury pushed her to attack. "Siân," she enunciated with exaggerated precision. "For fuck's sake, I'm a woman not a child." That was enough, and Mona knew it, but the words kept on coming. "You're just a bloody bully, and you'll end up pushing Nia away." She registered Cai's shock from the corner of her eye but it didn't prevent her from saying her piece. "Why don't you try showing her a bit of love, instead of behaving like a queen bitch from hell? At least you've still got each other."

The strange calm that had enabled Mona to speak coherently, fled with the realisation of what she had just said. There was a distinct possibility that the situation could escalate into physical combat, or reduce to tears, and Cai stepped between them, steering his shell-shocked aunt back to the party.

Mona kicked the wall. "Nicely done as usual Mo," she muttered to herself as she turned down the hill to Swnt. There was just enough of a moon for Mona to see her way back, and it laced the sea with lines of erratic silver. On reaching the cottage, she breathed in the healing smell of sea.

'Hendre', the name of the cottage was carved into a small oblong of slate, and Mona touched it, wondering what it meant. All words seemed to mean something else in Welsh.

She was too pumped to sleep, her head whirled with recrimination already, so Mona turned to look out at the tiny beach.

The little island opposite appeared *so* close tonight – as if all she needed was a fairly big run-up to jump and land on the rock. Mona gazed at the odd-shaped hole in its centre, and could almost believe Nia's faerie story about the little elf man '*Robin Rogo*', who she said lived there.

Nobody else had come back from the party yet, so Mona turned back to the cottage, found the hidden key and went inside alone.

≈

It was during her allotted time in the shower that Mona formulated her apology to Siân. It was proving a difficult job though, because she wasn't sorry for what she had said; only that she had uttered it out loud. Mona's main concern was jeopardising her friendship with Nia, which was, she had worked out at three in the morning, the only real relationship she had left in the world.

But in the end Mona bottled out of the apology and went up to deal with the horses instead of taking her medicine at breakfast. Mucking out gave Mona another opportunity to berate herself. Siân had been cruel and vicious but Mona shouldn't have retaliated. Brendan had cautioned her often enough about her aggression. Mona's instinctive response was always attack, and Brendan had forever been extolling the virtues of calm and cunning. Mona wished he were here now, to tell her off.

Mona had a good forty-five minutes before the bus, so she lay on her back under an oak tree, enjoying the morning sunlight as it dodged the leaves and intermittently warmed her face. When she allowed herself the memory, Mona's body fizzed at the feel of Cai's mouth against hers. She sat up on her elbows and squinted through the sunshine; it didn't feel like there was a big storm on the way.

≈

Predictably, Nia and Cai didn't turn up at the bus stop that morning. Mona wasn't relishing the evening's confrontation and she'd already packed her bag for a swift, precautionary exit.

When she reached the department, Colm was already there, lingering by her workbench and muttering to himself. Mona acknowledged him, and started pulling on the leather gear. "Get a grip, girl," she cautioned herself, knowing she'd need all her concentration in order to make the strange symbol that populated her dreams.

Though the iron wasn't completely pure, Mona knew it would be much softer to work than steel. It would be the difference between soft eating liquorice and the cardboard hard, twisted ropes she'd had as a child. The raw material felt cold and heavy in her hands, but seductive and pliant, eager to be used. An image flared again in her mind: it was a symbol, interwoven but simple and complete. She must have seen it somewhere but, try as she might, its origin kept evading her.

With the design fixed in mind, Mona began to work. Old Colm stood by, offering advice and commentary while helping to keep the metal hot. The physical work of crafting the metal came to Mona easily, as if she'd worked with this metal her whole life. Her hands intrinsically knew how much pressure to force into the heated steel, and her mind knew how to twist the design to create the desired curves.

It was a relief to have the workshop to themselves, and as the piece progressed, Mona began to feel a driving urgency about the work, a need to perfect and conclude. The work was hot, and they were both overheating in their leather work wear. Another part of Mona felt the need to stop and cool down, to reassess and contemplate, but Colm, who seemed even more insistent about the outcome than Mona, was urging her on.

With the piece still steaming from its last quenching, Mona leaned forward over the bench to study it. She was filled with a sense of wonder at what she had achieved. The small knot almost vibrated with life, it was exactly right, exactly what she had envisaged.

Colm was already reaching for it with his tongs, when the door inched open. Mona glanced up at Nia and beckoned her over with a gloved hand, still mesmerised by her accomplishment. She was pleased to see that Nia was here; there would be time for a chat before she had to face Siân again.

Mona began unbuttoning the heavy leather coat, experimenting mentally with a few apologetic words as she did so. But as Mona started towards her, Nia's face slowly turned to alarm, and she shouted a warning in Colm's direction.

Mona was too late to prevent the old man from completing his trajectory, and as she spun around, he caught her full in the chest with the iron symbol. With an extra thrust of the tongs, he forced the hot metal shape into the exposed flesh of Mona's chest.

Nia screamed, a stink of sulphur and frying meat filled the air and Mona clutched at her chest where the pain of her seared skin began to throb. An explosive and exquisite energy pulsed its way through her body, intensifying into flesh and bone. Mona's spine arched back, bowing out her ribcage in a surge of elemental power that sucked greedily into all her extremities, changing from agony to ecstasy.

As the immense surge culminated and ebbed, Mona regained both sense and vision, whirling to see Cai skid to a halt, just inside the door. Nia was stumbling backwards away from the muttering old man and Mona lurched forward, trying to shoulder barge into Colm and knock him out of the way. In her panic, Mona forced the technician against Nia, and they both clattered down onto the workshop floor.

The old man had dropped the ironwork but inched himself up. He had some sort of blade in his hand now – and he stabbed Nia with it. "No!" Mona bellowed in rage, leaping over him, grabbing his skinny wrist and slamming it into the ground – away from Nia. She could feel the old man's bones through his thin skin, brittle and hollow, and now strangely hot. "Cai, help me," Mona pleaded, looking over at Nia, while trying to restrain the old bastard.

Cai was there instantly, checking Nia's pulse, and trying to bring her round. The smell of burning and sulphur increased, as did the heat in the old man's skin. Mona turned from Nia to look at him as the aged body began to scorch and blacken before her eyes. The old man's body was being burnt beneath her touch, and as she tried frantically to release her grip from his wrist, it exploded into grains of hot black ash that trickled through her fingers.

Chucking the grisly silt away, Mona threw herself in the other direction, raising trembling hands to her eyes, then peering back down at what little was left of the man. Her breath was out of control; it was as if she had forgotten the rhythm of breathing, and the oxygen kangarooed in her lungs. She was making strange noises that should have been speech but which had turned, by shock and fear into a keening babble.

Mona was shaking too much to stand, so she began crawling to where Cai had dragged Nia on to his lap. There was a small wound on Nia's arm, and he was rocking his cousin like an infant, and soothing her hair back from a pasty, waxen face. Cai couldn't tear his eyes from Mona and they were full of fear and loathing. She stopped crawling, curled herself into the foetal position and closed her eyes.

≈

A sharp kick in the small of her back was enough to rouse her and Mona scrambled away from its source. She'd managed to shift on to her knees now but the cold and trembling through her body was making it hard to get any further. Someone pulled her violently to her feet; it was Cai, but Mona was too stunned to question his roughness. All the while, he was spitting Welsh to someone beyond her. Police, she thought vaguely, people from university administration. I've just killed a man.

Nia.

Mona let go of Cai, and lurched around to where she had last seen her. "Nia, where's Nia?" Her friend was gone. So was everyone else but Cai and Emlyn. Mona's mind couldn't quite comprehend why the coxswain was here. "Where's Nia?" she whispered to him.

Emlyn screamed at her with sudden and savage intensity. "Don't you dare talk about Nia, you Irish witch."

Mona shuffled backwards away from the blow she knew was coming her way, and then Cai was between them shoving Emlyn back to and out of the door. When he had gone, Cai turned towards her and grabbed her firmly upright by the tops of her arms. His grip was harsh, it was hurting her, but Cai dragged Mona after him and out of the door. Dazed as she was, Mona allowed him to lead her away.

They ran down the service stairway to a fire door that exited on to an alley, where the Lifeboat Land Rover was idling. Cai bundled her through the rear door, and slammed it behind him as Emlyn lurched forward at breakneck speed towards the Menai Strait.

In the back seat Dafydd held his niece gently. "What's *wrong* with her?" Mona wailed, leaning forward to see for herself, only to find Dafydd snarling at her over Nia's prone body.

Cai snatched her backwards to face him, a finger on his lips, and a new hardness in his eyes. Mona turned from Cai and stared out of the window at the blurring hedgerow. The storm had come, rain was screaming past the windows and a strong north-easterly rolled the truck around the bends.

There must have been a plan, because suddenly they were all out of the vehicle, and running to the shore, then Emlyn was firing up the outboard on a rigid inflatable. Mona was finding it hard to even stand in the wind, and the sea that they were about to join was a roiling white mess. She tried to speak to Cai but the wind took away all breath and sound.

Even on the shore, the inflatable looked incapable of facing that sea, and Mona didn't want to get in it. Cai began dragging her to the boat as she backed away, but it was Emlyn who picked her up by the scruff and threw her in, before taking the helm and screeching into an Irish Sea battered by storm force winds.

Mona grabbed a handle and looked around for Cai, who was covering Nia and Dafydd with a waterproof. He answered her desperate look by pointing towards the Plas Newydd Estate in the distance. Somehow Emlyn and Dafydd had life jackets on and there was some sort of life preserver around Nia. Neither Mona nor Cai had a jacket but Mona had just enough sense to clip a line on to the belt of her jeans. She could see that Cai was scrabbling around to do the same.

But he was too slow.

As the boat abruptly changed course, it scuffed the top of a large wave and nosedived into the trench of another, firing Cai past her into the cavernous foam. He vanished beneath the waves and Mona knew there was no choice but to dive and pray that the line held – if she didn't get him first time, she knew there wouldn't be a second.

As Mona dived after Cai she told herself there must be a chance, there *had* to be. *Please, please…* she prayed, and then her flailing arms caught something – cloth, arm. She held, dragged and pulled, with slippery, weakening fingers.

Mona caught Cai's dead weight under his arms, knowing he couldn't make it back into the boat without help. She inched as much of his torso on to the sodden deck as she could, and then held him in place with an arm of iron, whacking him on the back arbitrarily with the other, until he choked up the seawater. After that, it was just a matter of not letting go.

The muscles in her arms and back were screaming agony when the boat finally slowed and stopped. Emlyn and Dafydd rushed Nia from the boat, bundling her into waiting arms. Mona couldn't tell how Cai was doing, his head and shoulders were planted in the bottom of the boat and she dare not let go to check.

Help must have come at some point, because Mona felt rough, gloved hands extricate him from her and drag them both from the boat to somewhere inside and warm. Clothes were thrown at her and the door was locked and bolted behind her. Mona fell to the ground, wrapping her drenched body in an old sleeping bag. Sometime later the convulsive shivering stopped and she fell into darkness on the wooden floor.

4

Lies

Mona was jostled awake by a completely unfamiliar woman, who was pulling at the sleeping bag and her still wet clothes. Her body was crusty and taut with salt and all her muscles had seized up. She knew the woman expected her to take off the wet clothes and shower, and Mona wanted to comply but her progress was so slow that the woman eventually intervened. Past embarrassment and care, Mona gave in to the rough assistance but was vaguely curious about the woman's gloves. She was allowed to shower on her own, and the hot water eased everything but her baffled brain.

Mona was given a well-worn tracksuit, socks and a pair of ugly rubber shoes, but no pants or bra. She dressed mechanically in front of the woman, awaiting the next command meekly, and wasn't totally surprised when she was handcuffed and led from the drying room across a dark corridor and into a cell. The woman lifted the corner of the duvet, and steered Mona into the narrow bed, relocking the cell door and walking away without a word.

Sleep was oblivion. Each time she threatened to resurface, Mona drove herself back under, until the ache in her bladder forced her to confront reality. There was a chemical loo and a screen. Handcuffs didn't make life easy but she managed eventually and then shuffled back to the bed. There was no natural light, so it was impossible to gauge the time, and though she wasn't actually ready for it, her brain had started trying to piece together the horrific events of the very recent past.

Despite the fact that she had killed a man – or at least somehow caused his death – her only cogent thoughts were of Nia and Cai. Not knowing if either of them had survived was a growing sickness in her mind.

She stood up when two men arrived at the cell door and, as they unlocked it, she asked, "Nia? Cai?" But, neither Dafydd nor Emlyn answered or glanced at her but they each took an arm and escorted Mona from the cell.

From the corridors and classrooms they passed, it was apparent, almost immediately, that they were in some sort of school. As they walked up through the building, there was a glimpse of light through metal-edged windows. Mona was swept past these and on to their destination: the school hall.

Even her rubber-softened footsteps clunked on the wooden flooring, reverberating in the acoustics. A meeting was in progress at the far end of the hall, among all the regulation gym equipment and rubber mats. The shouting stuttered and died as the party of three arrived, and Mona was pushed down on to the moulded plastic chair in the middle of the semi-circle. She knew some of the voices but recognising any of the committee was impossible, as they were all cloaked and hooded.

At any other point in her life, Mona would have laughed, joking about dodgy masonic handshakes and bearing your left breast. But it didn't seem that funny now, as Dafydd and Emlyn dragged her back up on to her feet and pushed her forward in front of one of the seated people.

As she approached, Ifan dragged the hood of his cloak back to look at her, an obviously unpopular move judging by the reaction from the rest of the group, but he snarled a retort and they settled again. "Mona, as you can probably appreciate, you're in a certain amount of trouble here."

She could only nod in response, as she had so many questions to ask, that nothing came out intelligibly. Ifan looked at her with sympathy and a fraught sort of sadness. "I promise to explain absolutely everything to you later, but at this meeting I need to ask you a few questions about what happened yesterday." He waited for her to acknowledge this, and motioned for her chair to be brought forward. "Please sit down Mona, you must be tired." The unexpected kindness unnerved her momentarily. "Now tell me, if you can, exactly what happened at college yesterday?"

Mona's voice was deep and croaky from salt water and lack of use. "I've been working on a project in iron, and I made it yesterday."

"Is this your project, Mona?" Ifan held up the woven symbol, swathed in leather, and offered it to her. Another wave of dissent swept over the meeting, one voice louder than the rest. Siân.

Unsure now whether or not to take the object, Mona looked to Ifan for help, and he nodded imperceptibly. As the iron passed into her hand, a shot of heated power stabbed her in the burn on her chest, a taste of the previous energy without the intensity. The metal itself remained cold to the touch, and Ifan's eyes widened as if he had shared the experience with Mona. "Yes, this is it," she replied.

The old man recovered well. "How did you come to make this design? Did anyone suggest it to you? Colm perhaps?"

"No, I must have seen it somewhere, I knew that's what I had to make. It appeared in my head somehow." More muttering told Mona that she wasn't doing herself any favours by telling them this, and Ifan continued again.

"And Colm? How long has he been helping you with your projects?"

"Only since the beginning of the week. We started chatting about materials, and he said he could get hold of some really pure old iron – if I wanted to make something special."

"Did he say where he'd got it from?"

"No, and I didn't ask, I thought he may have stolen it," Mona sighed. "He made it sound like something illegal."

"Was there anything unusual about Colm?"

"I found it a bit odd that he singled me out. I'm not a great welder but then I'm the only one in the class that enjoys experimenting. He said we were a dying breed," she added wryly, the irony not lost.

"*Siân!*" Ifan reprimanded, clearly frustrated at her continuous muttering, but Siân could hold back no longer, and leapt towards Mona, her hood whipping back in the effort.

"Stop lying you bitch. You tried to kill my Nia. She's... she's dying." The vitriol subsided into wailing and finally dry sobs as Emlyn clutched his sister to his chest.

Dying? The information triggered a kick-start in Mona's head, adrenaline pumped, and anger rose. "No, no, that's not what happened. I finished the piece, it was hot, and I was taking off my coat, while Colm did the last quench." Mona was wildly giving a shape to the events. "Nia shouted and when I looked up he was coming towards me with it. He burnt my chest with it." Mona's hands scrambled to the burn, which was sore and weeping. "Next thing I knew he was going after Nia with a knife. I got hold of him but not before he could stab her with it, and then..." She didn't want to say it out loud.

"What then, Mona?" Ifan prompted gently.

"Then, as I held him down, he burnt. His skin just turned black, and there was nothing left of his body... nothing but black sand."

In the silence that followed this revelation, Ifan continued his questioning. "Were there any flames?" Mona shook her head, and let it fall to her manacled hands. "Was there anyone else to witness this?"

"Yes, Cai was there," her voice muffled to a whisper.

"We're going to let you rest now, but before you go, I'd like you to show us your burn. Can you do that for me?"

Mona was strangely reluctant to reveal her wound, but it seemed pointless to resist at this stage. She unzipped the tracksuit with shackled hands, and revealed her burnt chest. There was a whisper of collective inhalation. Siân gagged visibly, and ran from the room.

Mona couldn't see what they saw, and realised now that she never wanted to; it made her feel dirty and abused – branded.

"Thank you, Mona."

"Is Cai…" she didn't need to finish her sentence.

"He's fine. Try to rest now."

Dafydd led her, not back to the cell but to a small simple bedroom, where she found a tray of food and a jug of water. He left without a word, locking the door behind him. After draining the water, Mona sunk onto the bed and slept, clutching her ironwork against her.

≈

Mona lay motionless on the bed long after she had wakened. There was a low-level thrumming of power throughout her body, and she felt alive, aroused even, and was immediately disgusted with herself. Her hand moved instinctively to the symbol branded on her chest. While the wound was still tender, it had healed well enough to touch and she marvelled at the speed of her recovery. Mona traced the raised scar tissue with her index finger; following the lines and getting lost in the curves.

She recalled the horror: Nia was dying. Concussion? A brain haemorrhage? It was beyond madness that Siân could blame Mona for intentionally hurting her daughter.

A scuffle in the corridor forced her to a seated position, and she held her breath. There were raised voices, perhaps even some punches being thrown. Mona was standing now but was still handcuffed. This could hamper her in a fight, though she would be able to use both arms as one weapon. The door bounced twice on its hinges, as if someone had been thrown against it from the other side, and Mona crouched in readiness. After half a minute of further shouting, the lock was worked in the door, and Mona prepared herself for the attack.

Cai barged through the door and into the room, slamming it behind him. Mona couldn't see his face as he marched towards her,

71

but she could sense that every fibre of his body writhed with fury. He held a set of keys, and she realised that they belonged to the handcuffs, so she held her manacled hands out in front of her.

Cai made no move to use the keys but grabbed her arms in a lightning-quick attack. His actions were rough to the point of brutality, and he held her far too tightly.

As they came together, her breath hiked with the force of her arousal and the smell of the sea filled her body and brain. There was a deep reciprocal groan from him, and then his lips were on hers, forcing his tongue into her mouth, hungry and hard. Devoid of affection and respect, his kiss spoke of punishment and greed but overriding it all was desire, and her body answered from its core.

Cai was crushing her against him, and pushing her back to the bed simultaneously. Her hips flexed forward, and he grabbed her backside, deepening the desperate kiss even further. Lust had seared almost all reason from her brain but she needed to take a breath, so Mona pushed him back, not very far, but far enough to see that he wasn't the Cai she knew.

Gone was the gentle, damaged engineer, and in his place stood a dark, savage god, full of lust and hatred. He was breath-taking.

Mona needed all her strength to push him away, but panic made her stronger, and he flew back. "Get off me. Who… who the fuck are you?" she roared. Her chest was heaving with action and fear; she had automatically resumed the combat stance. "Where's Cai?" she demanded, lifting her chin, though she knew it was the same man – from the tantalizing smell his body continued to throw at her. Her eyes scanned the room for an escape route.

"What have you done to me, you bitch," he barked, his breathing ragged from more than just passion now. This Cai was beautiful, unmarred – and speaking English. As the enormity of his deception dawned on Mona, her energy vanished, and she crumpled slowly to the floor.

"You can speak English?" Mona's voice caught in a painful cramp in her throat. He'd tricked her, they all had, even Nia. She felt sick.

For a long minute Mona sat dazed, collecting the memories of all the deceit and filing them chronologically. It armed her with rage and she stood again, wanting very badly to hurt him. "Tell me why?" she bawled.

Cai closed his eyes, and took a deep breath, trying to keep his voice steady. "I don't have to answer to you, *witch*. What have you done to me?" He sounded appalled, and Mona frowned; she had woken up in some sort of alternate universe. "In a community like ours, there are no unknowns," he spat. "Our family trees are traced and tracked; our lineage is written on our faces – the faces of our parents, our children. We know our own. You are *not* one of us. So who the fuck are you?"

Cai's anger made him frighteningly coherent, and Mona was struck dumb. He continued, but speaking English was an effort for him, and it took a while for him to collect his thoughts and translate them. "It was Nia's job to befriend and assess you, but she succumbed to your tricks and discovered absolutely nothing."

Cai paused for longer this time and Mona braced herself – she didn't want to hear any more. "Ever since you set foot in Ynys Môn, you have posed the greatest threat that our community has faced in years. It is only at the insistence of Nia and Ifan that you have not *yet* been destroyed." His tone was calmer and more measured now, but his accent was oddly alien, the grammar too good. "When Nia failed to discover your secrets, I was ordered to continue," his smile was cruel, "where she could not."

Mona's head dropped to her chest in a brief spasm of embarrassed realisation. She'd fallen for it all like a fool – he'd used her weakness as only a man could. "We have been watching you." He tipped his head at her in accusation. "We noticed the fighting moves in your daily exercises and became aware of your unusual strength. I was partly chosen to replace Nia, in case it came to a fight."

Images of a sunny day, laughing and play fighting with her friends, twisted sharply and she cringed at her naivety. Mona remembered the plaster, some kindness and a tender kiss. "Why did you change your face?" she finally spat back.

"As I said, we had been studying you, you seem to dislike…" He made a dismissive gesture towards his handsome features. "Anyway, they changed it with glue, some sort of glue."

Mona was appalled, but she knew what he meant. After all, she would have been instantly suspicious if a good-looking man had been attracted to her. In Mona's experience, beautiful people just didn't measure up. It was as if their outward perfection stunted some basic moral growth. Handsome men and stunning women had always been safer to avoid – if you didn't want to be disappointed. She thought of Nia and Cai, their beauty and their treachery, and it confirmed everything she had ever believed.

Mona had assumed she'd found friends, people who cared about her. The truth cut deeply. "Who are these people that I'm such a threat to, that you spy for? What is this stuff?" Her tone was acidic with hurt.

Cai ran his fingers through his hair, and then back down his face, as if coming to a difficult decision. "Druids," he stated. "We are all that's left of the ancient Celts, and we survive in patches on the Celtic fringe. There was a split, a war of sorts. That thing…" he pointed savagely at her chest, raising his voice again, "that *mark*, is their *mark*. It means you're one of them."

Druids? The only image that entered her mind was ritual sacrifice, a wicker man full of burning bodies. Mona was stunned by a sudden and overwhelming sense of claustrophobia. "What is this crap? It's rubbish, make-believe." This was sheer lunacy, and her brain started ticking. She had to escape. "You're out of your fucking mind!"

Cai was pushing into her space again and she neither knew nor liked this man. "Is it? Is it really Mona? I was there, remember? I saw you writhing in the power of the *mark*. I saw you burn that man to ashes with your touch, with *just* your hands. No one has ever had that power."

That look had crept back into his eyes again; fear and loathing. She didn't know what to believe but one thing was certain: "I wanted to stop him hurting Nia, that was all," she repeated woodenly, her lips still bruised from his kiss.

Cai watched her struggle to prevent an errant tear from falling over the rim of her right eye. The tear didn't fall and she cracked the knuckles of her manacled hands. Mona shook out the tension in her limbs; she'd have to be ready when he attacked this time. "So you're here to kill me now?"

It was a question that seemed to further enrage him, and he exploded. "I've been desperate to kill you from the moment I learnt about you, and I'm disgusted with myself that I didn't have the balls to do it."

The room was pure, vibrating tension. "Well, I'm not dead yet," she goaded. Her body was screaming for a fight. Mona knew exactly how to take this man down.

"How dare you save my life – you filthy whore!" His entire being radiated loathing. "Withdraw your spell," he commanded, producing a short sword from his belt – it trembled in his hands. "Free me from those fucking illusions."

Mona blinked. *Spells? Illusions?* He'd distracted her with the question, and had taken the advantage. Cai was on her again, pinning her to the walls of the cell. He'd slipped the sword between the handcuffs, and used the leverage to force her hands up above her head. His right hand was now free to strangle her. She struggled, but he was too close to kick.

Mona was as near to panic as she'd ever been; his hand was only pinning her in place at the moment, but once he started to squeeze, it would be over quickly. Mona bucked her hips out violently in an effort to dislodge him. It failed; he was stronger than he looked. Cai twisted her head away, and squashed it into the wall. He was breathing words into her ear. "Withdraw the spell," he begged, kissing her ear.

Mona felt the heat of his erection through her tracksuit. "Untie my hands and I'll break the spell," she panted, grasping at the chance.

His tongue was back at her ear. "I'm horny, not stupid." Mona's attempt at negotiation had ramped up his aggression, and he pulled her mouth to his again, forcing in his tongue. But Mona bit down hard and Cai pulled out in shocked pain, as she used the space and the immense strength in her legs to rocket him away.

The sword had fallen between them, and they glanced at it simultaneously. Cai got there first and brought it level with her face. Mona was gratified to see blood trickling from the side of his mouth. "Who are you?" he mouthed, cradling his stomach with his free hand.

"Mona Jones." She raised her chin, breathing hard. "What do you want?"

Cai's gaze told her what he wanted, but he lisped a different reply. "Nia wants to see you."

Now the scuffle outside her door made sense. Nia might want to see Mona, but no one else wanted her to. "How is she?"

"She's dying, it won't be long." He spat out each word, speckling the floor with blood.

"Take me to her?" Mona uttered blankly.

Cai knocked twice, as arranged, for the door to be unlocked. Mona noticed the gloves on the guards posted outside her room, and began to comprehend the level of fear surrounding her. They were startled at the sight of her leaving the room, and both moved in to challenge Cai, barking words at him. His reply was savage and curt.

Catching Mona's still-tied hands in his own, he pulled her roughly behind him. She snatched them back viciously. "Don't touch me," she enunciated with glacial restraint.

"Keep close behind me then." He granted her a chilling smile. "There are orders to kill you on sight, if you get out of line."

Mona soon found it easier to fix her eyes on the back of Cai's head, rather than confront the stares. To either side of them, the onlookers flinched or muttered as they swept through the labyrinth, but Cai brooked no opposition to their progress.

Nia was lying in a carbon copy of Mona's own room at the other end of the institution. She was conscious, and their eyes met briefly before two old men staggered arthritically in front of their charge.

Cai didn't shout this time, but appeared to be politely negotiating with them to let Mona see Nia. They didn't budge until Nia herself made the request; a weak rasp from the bed.

She didn't move to sit up as Mona approached, but was able to swivel her head slightly towards her, her gaze clouded with pain. Mona's movement towards the bed seemed to send Nia's carers into a state of extreme agitation, but Cai stayed them, and Mona gently picked up Nia's frozen hand, cupping it between her own bound ones. Nia grabbed a gasping breath, smiled at Mona, and closed her eyes.

Cai flicked her a nervous look but Mona was calm. "She's only sleeping; I'm staying for a while." She nodded to the old men. "They can check her over to make sure I haven't killed her, and then they must leave."

"That won't happen."

"Then we all stay. You'd better get some more chairs in here, or get the Chuckle Brothers to do it, just in case you need both hands free when I start my killing rampage."

Cai didn't react to Mona's spiteful words, and they sat for about half an hour in the room together. Mona and Cai were on one side of the sick bed and the old men on the other.

Mona didn't let go of Nia's hand; she was getting sleepy but noticed that Cai still hovered close by, his hand always on the hilt of the sword. Mona slumped forward to lay her head against Nia's leg, but it was thrown instantly back by Siân's shocked shriek from the door. Mona stood, her stomach churning queasily with the movement, and she struggled past Cai into the corridor.

Siân fought against Cai with a primal intensity, desperate to get at Mona, who was now walking away, looking straight ahead. Leaving an apoplectic Siân in the care of the ancient men, Cai raced to follow.

He found Mona leaning against the wall a few doors down, shaking, feverish and very pale. "Toilet. I need a loo. I'm going to be…" She heaved and vomited over herself and then him, eventually covering a large area of the corridor floor. Mona retched again, producing wave after wave of black, sulphurous vomit. The appalling stench made Cai gag, but he pinched the metal of her handcuffs and dragged Mona's convulsing body away from the worst of it.

As soon as she was lying on a clean stretch of floor, he reached for his sword again and held it out before him. Cai was surrounded now by physical proof of her dark magic, and his hand shook, as he pulled in a great lungful of the less tainted air.

Mona had finished throwing up and lay emptied against the floor. She didn't look dangerous now, and an errant part of Cai's brain had a desire to kneel down and help her. He shook the thought free, knowing it was her sorcery at work again.

From behind him, the Archdruid approached hurriedly, bending over the witch's body. "Don't touch her," Cai bawled, "she's poison." His advice came too late; Ifan had already stroked the woman's head.

"Get her up, Cai," the old man ordered. "Bring her to my rooms."

5

Truth

After snatching the keys from Cai and releasing her bonds, Ifan ushered Mona into his private bathroom. It seemed to be exactly the same as every other in the place, but was situated within a suite of rooms that appeared to be very much his own. Was this Ifan's second home? Mona couldn't fit all this absurd information together. *Druids?*

Mona felt better, now that she had washed the vomit from her body, face and hair, but fear was screaming at her through the water. Something profound had happened in Nia's room – Mona had felt a power leaching out of her and into the other woman. That power had a name. She was almost too frightened to consider it, but Cai's accusations of witchcraft still pinched at her thoughts.

Ifan had given her a bin liner into which she'd stuffed her clothes before showering, and she now toed it out of the door. "I haven't got any other clothes," she shouted.

An arm immediately shot through a crack in the door, depositing a pile of garments, and Mona was relieved at the inclusion of a sturdy-looking bra and good old pair of apple catcher knickers. The outer clothes resembled brown leather biker gear. She pulled on the trousers and found they were surprisingly lightweight and flexible, as was the sleeveless jacket that fitted over a black, dry-fit skin. Even the boots were light and comfortable, and everything fitted like a glove – though it was a little more closely cut than she would normally have chosen.

As soon as Mona had disappeared into the bathroom, and he was satisfied that she wouldn't hear the conversation, Cai confronted Ifan. "So it's some sort of virus then? Has she infected us all with it now?"

Ifan was busy incinerating Mona's clothes in the wood-burning stove, and puzzlement scrunched his elaborate white eyebrows when he glanced at Cai. "What are you talking about, boy?"

"That black stuff, the vomit. It's some sort of poison. She poisoned Nia?"

Ifan studied Cai slowly. "Mona has saved Nia's life. Just as she saved yours yesterday."

Cai worked a muscle in his jaw and shook his head. "It's a trap, trust me."

"Trust you? Like she did?"

"I had my orders."

"From whom? It sure as *hell* wasn't me."

Cai straightened but didn't answer. He stared at his leader, and realised the truth; the Archdruid had also been snared by the English woman's power. "She's bewitched us, Ifan," Cai whispered, even though he knew she couldn't hear above the noise of the shower. Ifan shook his head in doubt and it infuriated Cai, forcing him to invade the old man's personal space. "I'm speaking the truth," Cai urged through gritted teeth. "I've been affected since the first moment I met her. She draws me in – I can't keep away from her. I can't think straight around her, she's been controlling me with illusions." Ifan's eyebrows lifted but Cai continued urgently. "When she's near me I can't even control my body."

"In what way?" Ifan asked, finally curious.

"I want her Ifan," Cai said simply. "She's seduced me with her black magic."

Ifan chuckled without humour. "Forgive me my crudity, Cai, but isn't sex your primary pastime? Don't you feel that way about virtually all women, all of the time?"

Cai should have seen that one coming, but it wasn't only sex; he'd felt happy around her. Mona had made him laugh, despite himself. Cai was now certain that she was affecting the old boy, and he needed to be warned. "Ifan…" he began, "just look at her, she's not exactly the most…"

"Enough Cai," Ifan ordered. "You're making me sick, and it's not only the stench."

Mona walked out of the bathroom and straight past Cai; her leather clothes accentuating every muscle in her body. Mesmerised, he forced his eyes away from her and stepped into the bathroom.

While Cai showered, his foul-smelling clothes followed Mona's on to the fire. After completing this task, Ifan washed his hands thoroughly. "You look well, Mona. How are you feeling?"

"I want answers."

He frowned at her. "All in good time. You most probably need food now. Wait here."

"Who were those men with Nia?" Mona asked.

"We call them healers."

"Doctors, or *witch doctors*?" she scoffed.

Ifan grunted and set out to leave the room but turned back to her from the door. "How did you know what to do for Nia?"

"She seemed so weak and I thought I could pass her some… I don't know… energy." Mona couldn't deal with any other word. "It must have forced the other stuff out. I don't… understand."

Ifan left, muttering to himself, and Mona studied the room. It was a strange mix of scavenged seventies Formica and ancient library. The groaning bookshelves contained mostly volumes in Welsh, but there was quite a lot of Gaelic, and some French-looking stuff, along with the motorbike manuals of course.

Cai emerged awkwardly from the shower, dressed in similar leathers – they enhanced his physical appeal and she scowled again at her own foolishness. A lesson learnt. She could feel Brendan chiding her. *Nothing is ever as it seems, Mona. He's tricked you once already, you bloody fool.*

Cai retrieved his sword and laid it across his knees. They didn't talk.

Ifan finally reappeared with food and a large teapot. Over tea, he enlightened Mona. "We've known you're one of us," he glanced pointedly at Cai. "That is to say, a Druid, ever since you arrived."

"Look, Ifan, I've seen Druids on the telly." Mona was trying to recall the image and it didn't fit with what she was hearing now. "And I'm pretty sure it was mostly singing and poetry."

"I'm not talking about modern Druidism, Mona, I'm talking about a hidden Celtic community, unknown and unseen for millennia. Over the centuries, Celts have been pushed back from the whole of Europe and Britain into the far extremities of these western shores. The Celtic fringe."

Mona pulled a cynical face. "I've never heard of it," she sneered.

Ifan tried to hide his aggravation and continued with a forced patience. "Wales, Ireland, Scotland, Cornwall, Isle of Man, Brittany – these are our people, this is where we hide." Mona considered the distances and scepticism was written all over her face. "You can't think of them as countries, constrained by boundaries and roads. They are small strongholds connected by the sea – The Sea Kingdoms."

"The RNLI," Mona wondered out loud as the thought struck her, and Ifan nodded. "You mean…" Mona was shocked. "Do you mean that the RNLI are *Druids* then?"

"Don't be so stupid," Ifan tutted tetchily, "of course I don't mean that." Leaning back in his chair, he began to explain. "But we have good relationships with that operation. In many ways they are our link to and buffer against the outside world. Just think about where Lifeboat Stations are most prevalent." Ifan leaned forward again, pushing his battered old face in her direction. "We both cling like limpets to the savage rocks around this coast. We are the last people left who can read the music of the sea, and you'll find Druid fingerprints in the most remote and desolate stations. Boats are still our transport, and the water is still our path. If we have any friends in the world today – it's the RNLI."

Mona's mind was grappling with this new information but she couldn't link it to her own fate. "So how..."

"A long time ago, I saved Brendan's life; I found him half drowned while I was patrolling in the Swellies. I know he came here looking for your parents, but he told me nothing else." Ifan coughed and glanced quickly at Cai, who was studying the sword across his knees. "Shortly after that, we suffered the first of the attacks. No one is completely sure about the reason for that strike, but either way, Brendan was the catalyst, and many died. I would not have rescued him if I had known the consequences." Ifan was brutally straight talking. "Brendan was a dangerous man. Has he always been a part of your life?"

Mona nodded dumbly. "My uncle. My mother's twin." Mona was aggravated. "You know all this, I've told you who he was."

Ifan shook his head as if trying to negate something. "I'm not sure I've got this right, but I think your parents might have been on the run and in hiding ever since they met. Brendan may have been their protector, and then yours after their death."

At the mention of her parents, Mona stiffened and stood – *nothing is ever as it seems.* There were two of them now. She could probably take on both of them, but it would be messy; Cai had already proved he was physically stronger than her. A memory of his recent proximity sent a tingle through her body, pushing her off balance. She absolutely couldn't let him grapple with her.

"*Mona!*" Ifan hauled her back from the combat scene in her head. "Why did Brendan send you here?"

She looked back at him with confusion. "I don't know." Her voice was a rough croak. Cai got up and she whirled in his direction. "Keep away from me." The warning was low in her throat, and she glanced to the door, desperate for escape.

Cai didn't retreat but moved a step closer, and Ifan spoke for him. "You have to trust us."

Something broke in Mona's brain at that request. "Trust you?" she hollered. "My parents have been murdered, Brendan was killed three weeks ago... and my brother..." Her voice was thickening with emotion. "Everyone I love is dead or missing." She glared at Cai. "Laughing boy here wants me dead – by his own admission." She almost chuckled at the irony. "And you want me to *trust* you?"

Ifan changed tactics and his voice softened. "Please sit down, and I'll try to explain." She kicked the chair further away from both of them before she sat, and Ifan began again. "In essence, we're caught up in a type of religious persecution. That *mark* on your chest is the sign of our persecutors. We've seen it before – on their swords, their boats – it's their flag Mona."

"But I didn't burn it into myself. I was attacked."

"No, but you made the design – the design appeared in your head, if I remember correctly. I don't think that the iron mark has given you power – merely ignited it within you. I'm sure it would have emerged in due course anyway." Ifan didn't sound too sure of anything he was saying. "I believe your power will mature slowly from now on. It may have been the trauma of the attack that accelerated the process. I'm not sure – there's just so much I don't know."

"What do you mean you don't know? I thought you were in charge here. I thought you were some sort of Archdeacon."

"Archdruid," Cai corrected her evenly.

"Whatever," she replied without looking at him. "Surely you must have some idea about their reasons for attacking?" She changed tack, directing her questioning at Ifan, who merely shook his head slowly response. "What is my power then?" she demanded, irritated by his ignorance. "Burning people to death and puking up tar? Have you got any idea how fucking mad this sounds."

"I don't know, but whatever it is, you're full of it."

"How do you know that?"

"I'm not talented myself, but I can detect it in others."

"What do you mean, talented?"

"Magic, Mona. You're full of magic." Mona sucked in a jagged breath as Ifan used the word that she could not, but he drove on, almost apologetically. "I don't understand *how* or *why*. And because of this and despite my protection, you are in danger here." Ifan flicked a careless hand at Cai. "Though Cai will guard you – he'll protect you." Cai looked disgusted at the prospect of defending the woman he both loathed and feared.

"No. I don't need him." Mona didn't look over in his direction. "I can protect myself just fine." And then she asked Ifan a little more earnestly. "Couldn't it all be a coincidence, just a big misunderstanding?"

Cai barked sarcastically, but once again it was Ifan who spoke. "No, but things may have gone a little better for you here, if it weren't for your connection to Brendan."

"What about him?" This was the crux of the matter, she felt it.

"He was an Irishman."

The penny dropped. "Are you saying that Irish Druids are your enemies?"

A look of visceral pain shot across Ifan's brow. "The Irish are a fine people. We are kin and they have a birth right to the greatest of magic. My wife was a brave, strong Irishwoman, and I love her beyond time itself." He smiled   tenderly at the memory. "But something changed twenty-five years ago – it was like the flicking of a switch. The great friendship and loyalty between our lands dissolved – almost overnight." Ifan's voice faded, he took a steadying breath and focused on Mona. "You are branded now," he stabbed a finger at her healing wound, "marked for one of their own; your mother was Irish and you have been trained in combat by your uncle. Can you see how it might seem?"

"I'm not your enemy."

"Aren't you?" he asked softly. "No one knows that, Mona." Ifan smiled – it might have been benignly. "But you have saved two lives in our community over the last forty-eight hours." Cai shifted

uncomfortably. "And for that, if nothing else, I must show gratitude."
Ifan seemed to find it painful to stand up, but when he had, he threw
Cai a dirty look. "Others here will not be so lenient. Though for now,
you must stay, so I need to show you around the HMS *Conway*." The
old man took a minute to make sure that Mona was fully
concentrating on what he had to say next. "There is one rule that I
absolutely insist upon. I allow no technology here, nothing with a
microprocessor – it makes us vulnerable. No phones." Mona sighed;
he could have been Brendan.

6

Contest

The tour was extremely short. The site was an old naval school, previously used to train the sons of naval officers. Originally, the HMS *Conway* had been an actual ship, but she ran aground in the Swellies in 1953 and was eventually burnt out. The school moved on to dry land at *Plas Newydd*, retaining the former ship's name as a '*stone frigate*' until its closure in 1974.

Not long after that, the elusive Druid community had moved in together – when their numbers had exceeded the capacity of their various homes in Moelfre. There were a couple of large concrete blocks of classrooms and bedrooms with various shoddy outbuildings dotted between them. The Druids had their own beach and boathouse, from where they could launch their motley collection of vessels out onto the unpredictable currents of the Menai Strait.

"Why don't you drive in and out?" Mona asked, eyeing the closed, opulent gates.

Ifan's reply was to the point. "We're not actually supposed to be here. People take notice of cars, but very few people watch the water anymore."

"So what about the neighbours?" she asked, noticing the small town beyond the gates. "Doesn't anyone ask questions?"

"Sometimes they do, but we've got friends in high places." Ifan smiled vaguely. "And we keep ourselves to ourselves."

Within the squared off and austere group of buildings there was a canteen, kitchen, laundry and games room, but no television. It seemed a whole community existed in the institution. The place reminded Mona of a run-down *Butlins* holiday camp. No wonder they were odd, Mona thought, it was like a prison, and she deduced that the politics here must be excruciating.

Cai's attitude to her had changed; his aggression had morphed into sullenness and his continued presence aggravated her. "Why don't you just piss off?" she spat as they reached the hall.

Cai looked to Ifan for aid but the Archdruid didn't help him. "I'll be quite safe," he muttered. "I'm sure there's something else you'd prefer to be doing – there usually is."

While Mona's attention was drawn to the large hall, Cai scowled and moved to the rear of their group. The last time she was here, it had been for a trial, and Mona was still not sure whether she'd been acquitted or not. Ignoring her, Cai continued to screw his face at Ifan as they walked through the heavy, swinging double doors – and out on to a battlefield.

Men and women – but mainly men – fought together. Some held wooden practice swords but it was mostly hand-to-hand combat. Their fighting was disordered, and showed the same slovenly mistakes that she had seen in Cai's moves. Yet there was a clear similarity in style between this and what her uncle had taught her. As Mona continued to watch, she recognised quite a few of the crew from Moelfre. There were also some other lads from the stations in Holyhead, Trearddur Bay and Beaumaris as well – they'd visited the cottages from time to time.

At first, she didn't understand what was missing from their fighting, but as she scrutinised the brawling group, it dawned on Mona that they were lacking a vital element: taekwondo. Without the exacting precision of that martial art, the punches and kicks were reduced to ineffectual flailing.

As soon as Mona had walked into the hall behind Ifan, the room had stilled and silence had descended. Emlyn caught sight of them and barrelled over, eyes narrowed and locked on Mona. He argued heatedly with his father, clearly about her, though with regard to what specifically, she did not know. "Problem, Emlyn?" Mona's words were full of quiet menace, and they cut coolly across his furious tirade.

Emlyn launched himself at her but was prevented from reaching his goal as Dafydd pulled him back. Cai stepped in front of Mona and she balked at the gesture. "You're the fucking problem!" He was spitting fury but so was she, and there was nothing to lose.

"Oh, really? Go on then, tell me what I've done now." Mona was calm and resolute; something had given her the confidence to question this giant of a man – pillar of both mainstream and Druid communities. He had never seemed to like her, and at least now she knew why, but Mona couldn't see the need for tolerance anymore.

"Those clothes you're wearing – they have to be *earned*." He indicated to her leathers. "This is a mark of a warrior's ranking and it's governed by a strict protocol – trial by combat," he sneered, "or is that just another rule for you to break?"

Mona turned to Ifan. "You should have told me," she accused him. "How does it work?"

"It's a fairly straightforward system. A child starts off at the lowest grade and practices until they are deemed ready to fight someone in the grade above them. If they are successful, they can progress to the next grade."

"How many grades are there?"

"Seven. We start training at about twelve. Most people gain a grade a year."

"What grade is Cai?"

"Seven," Ifan replied without dropping a beat.

"So, if I fight Cai and win, I would become a seventh-grade *thingy*?" Ifan nodded. "And I could wear this gear?" She pulled at her leathers.

"Correct."

Mona turned back to Emlyn, unsure of what he was thinking,

because he didn't look annoyed anymore. "Do you think that would be a solution to the problem?"

"Yes, I agree you should fight a seventh-level warrior, but you won't face Cai. You'll face me. Cai has already proved he's too easy on you," he added acidly.

Mona moved to an area with a little more space, to stretch and limber up, but Cai stayed by Emlyn's side. For some reason, he didn't want Mona to fight Emlyn. Though when Cai thought about it logically, it was an elegant solution for him. Mona would die and be out of their lives, without him having to perform the actual deed. "You'll kill her," he said flatly to his uncle. Cai could see the fury behind Emlyn's eyes and the coxswain's constant battle to quell it.

"Someone has to, Cai." His eyes slid in Mona's direction and they were laced with disgust. "*Mi wyt ti wedi gweld y marc.* You've seen the *mark*."

Cai walked back over to Mona and addressed her quite rationally. "He will kill you."

"Really?" she answered, pulling one arm across her chest, to stretch her joints. "Saves you a job then."

Cai couldn't prevent himself from grabbing her shoulders. "I mean it."

"Take your hands off me," Mona warned. "I wouldn't want to put a *real* scar on such a pretty face." She wrenched herself away; appalled by his touch.

"He's right, Mona, Emlyn has killed many times. I think you need to pick your fights a little more carefully," Ifan said, as he watched Cai stalk out of the double doors.

Mona could hear them talking to her, but it meant nothing; this was where she had to make her stand. Blocking out the sound, she studied Emlyn as an opponent. He was huge; long in the leg and broad in the chest. He favoured his right knee, and was actively working the muscles over his left shoulder. Emlyn was older than her by maybe ten years, and some of his flexibility would be gone, though his power would exceed her own by quite some way. He would want to make it quick and final, and quite possibly spectacular.

Mona had a game plan by the time she had finished her stretching and she reassured Ifan. "Look, it's just a grading. I'll give up if he looks like killing me."

Cai's uneasiness was spreading from his stomach to his brain, and his hands were strangely cold and clammy. Staying here was turning into a monumental mistake. He should have gone straight from the hall to Gwen; she would have helped ease his straining groin. Instead, he was still loitering outside the doors, and peering in through the glass at the proceedings.

Dafydd beckoned Ifan over to him, a little shiftily. "You'll be seconding her I take it, Dad?"

"Yes, of course," Ifan agreed. He would now.

"Right, I have no doubt that Emlyn will beat her in a fair fight, but I'm worried that Mona won't play fair." Ifan stared at his son. Initially he didn't understand, but as the light dawned on him, Dafydd started nodding. "Yes, you see the problem? What's to prevent Mona from burning Em to death if she starts losing?" Seeing an opportunity for a climb down, Ifan admitted to the distinct possibility, and added that a postponement, or indeed a cancellation, was the best option all round. "That is *exactly* what I said," his younger son agreed. "But Em wants to fight her, no matter what. Though he has added a little caveat." Dafydd waited as the Archdruid raised his eyebrows with curiosity. "That we can shoot her, if she tries any of her burning tricks."

"*Guns?* You know I don't allow..." Ifan spat, horrified.

"I'm afraid so, Dad, she's just too dangerous."

Ifan relayed the proposal to Mona, and, after a short silence, Mona cocked her head to the side. "I agree."

"You're very confident."

"Indeed. Tell Dafydd I agree," she repeated, before continuing to loosen her neck muscles.

The entire room of warriors had turned into an audience, and with the hall filling up, Cai was finding it harder to see what was happening. "What's going on, Cai?" Ieuan asked noisily from behind him. "Is that Saxon bitch actually going to fight Emlyn? Who does she think she is?"

Cai's unease was disrupted by momentary rancour as his old rival's question stung his ear. He turned marginally to see Ieuan, freshly coiffured and surrounded by his ubiquitous posse of young idiots. Everything Ieuan ever uttered seemed to rattle Cai, though he wondered why these words rankled so much.

For a moment, Cai felt that he might not even be able to watch. The short and athletic Dai had been chosen to umpire and rang the bell to start. Mona and Emlyn joined the circle, both listening to the referee but assessing each other. Ifan took up his position as second, outside the circle, but close enough to offer advice. Advice that Cai doubted Mona would ever take.

Mona was listening intently to what Dai had to say. To Emlyn, these rules would be second nature, and she couldn't risk losing points on technicalities. As it turned out, there weren't many rules and the competition was based around a composite of martial arts. You had to fell your opponent, and they had to remain floored for three seconds to score a point. Other than that there didn't seem to be anything off limits.

Each round lasted for two minutes with a two-minute rest in between. There were five rounds, with two points for a win. The first to reach ten points was the winner, but a six-point lead stopped the game. If at the end of the eighth round, the fight was tied on points, there would be a decision from the referee.

Mona returned to Ifan, took off her boots, and to his amazement proceeded to remove her jacket as well. "That's all protection. See, here," he explained, holding up the jacket and pointing to the slightly raised and reinforced stitching around the kidneys, solar plexus and ribs. "It's well-designed."

Mona ignored him and looked right through Emlyn; her eyes

were granite. Cai tried extremely hard not to look at the fabric of the dry-fit skin as it stretched over her torso. There were just a few seconds left to warm up and then it would all be over. He tried again to look away but found he couldn't.

Then they were fighting. The bell had gone, and the room was hushed. Emlyn began the attack, a streak of raw power from a standing start, throwing an avalanche of whirling arms – which were blocked at every turn.

Mona absorbed ten different punches in as many seconds, waiting for the moment when frustration affected balance. When that time came, she raised her leg straight from the waist and extended her lower leg, snap kicking him in the solar plexus twice before watching him crumple.

Emlyn lay still for one, two, three seconds. Her point, two deep breaths and then he was up again and feinting to the right – which was a mistake. Emlyn was compromising balance again, and couldn't right himself in time to prevent a fast combination of open-hand slaps, culminating in an elbow strike to his kidneys. He fell to his knees and the bell rang. Mona straightened and returned to her second who mechanically passed her water and a towel.

Round two was chimed in, and there was cautiousness to Emlyn's approach this time. Mona could see that he wanted to grapple, to gain the upper hand through sheer strength.

Allowing him to reach her upper arm virtually unopposed, Mona swerved away before he fully clasped it, knocking his hand out of the way with a ferocious downward chopping action. Using all of his own momentum to throw him to the floor, she used a brief handstand on his chest to keep him pinned for the allotted time.

After that it was a blur to Cai, and he couldn't clearly see how she was destroying his uncle, as she appeared to have sped up as the bouts continued. It didn't go to a fifth round; Dai made the call, and Mona backed off. The only sound in the room came from the dragging breaths of the competitors. Emlyn lay on the ground, looking up at Mona with a mixture of awe and murderous intent. She walked away, back to her own corner.

The crowd was unnaturally quiet, and Mona began to question the wisdom of humiliating the big man. As people began to drift away, Mona drank the rest of the water and wiped her face on the towel.

"We're going to have to talk," Ifan warned her ominously. "Have some supper and come back to my rooms," he grumbled and shuffled off.

A few of the other men were hanging around, putting mats away, but she was essentially alone with Cai, who had returned for some reason and was staring at her as if she were an alien. Mona had no option but to talk to him. "I need a shower, where do I go?" She tried to make the question monotone.

"I'll show you to your room," he replied, his speech equally stilted.

7

Truce

Mona cooled off on the way back to the residential floors. They walked in silence and she noted that the animosity from the residents seemed to have increased since the fight. Cai stopped almost abruptly in front of a door with a tiny 172 in demo script in its centre. "This is your room," he said indicating with a wave. Mona grunted and pushed at the door, but Cai pulled her arm back and she flinched. "I've got direct orders from the Archdruid to protect you now. We should at least try to be civil."

Mona didn't turn back to face him. "What about my evil spells? Aren't you frightened?" she asked with quiet sarcasm.

"Those are my orders," he replied to her back.

Mona opened the door and let herself in but turned to him and nodded. "Where can I get more clothes? I'm dripping in sweat and all my stuff is back..."

"I'll see what I can do," Cai answered quickly, turning away down the corridor.

Cai had been just as surprised as Mona to find himself back in the hall, and he'd been trying his level best not to touch her since then. However, he had weakened and caught her corded forearm, and the memory of her muscle under his hand had done nothing to alleviate the overwhelming sense of arousal he'd felt while watching her fight.

As soon as she had closed her door on him, Cai ran to his own room at the end of an adjacent corridor and threw himself into the shower, and immediately began ridding himself of his untimely erection. He was completely bewildered why the recent fight had caused his body to react in such a dramatic way.

Once decent, he ran to the laundry and collected some clothes. Nesta assured him that they would fit her, and he sprinted back to Mona's door and knocked. "Cai?" Her tone was business-like.

"Clothes." He answered in kind. Mona's arm shot from a quickly opened gap, revealing the briefest glimpse of a bare arm and shoulder. *No, no, no. Not again.* It's not as if he was a teenage virgin, and he began breathing deeply, concentrating on some of the dryer facts from his engineering texts. Even to his own mind, the notion of Mona casting a spell over him was beginning to sound ridiculous – unless of course he was still being played. That might well account for the awful craving.

The truth was, she had affected him physically since their very first meeting in the kitchen, and the memory of her response to his advances this morning rolled deliciously in his groin. The compulsion to kiss her had been overwhelming; it had been wrong but unavoidable. Perhaps it was merely the novelty of forbidden fruit. The thought rallied him.

It was then that she opened the door: pink, clean and still tacky from the shower. Cai realised then that it wasn't just physical; he liked the way she was. Mona was wearing jeans, boots and a tight-fitting, low-cut t-shirt that struggled to contain her breasts. However, it failed entirely to cover the burn between them. Cai's eyes were drawn to the *mark* and Mona hastily covered it with her hand, embarrassed. "You can borrow a shirt of mine, if it would help." She nodded briskly and they both headed for his room.

Mona changed in Cai's shower room, putting on a baggier t-shirt that covered up the *mark*. "I need to eat." Her tone wasn't friendly but it was resigned, and Cai felt it was an improvement in relations.

The mess hall was almost deserted, and there wasn't much food left but she ate thankfully and quickly. "I'd really like to see Nia before I meet Ifan, just to check on her."

"Not a good idea. It's better to stay out of Siân's way. She could make life difficult for you, if you…" he searched for the word, "antagonise her."

Mostly because he was right, Cai's tone annoyed her. Mona was starting to miss her friendship with Nia, even though she had come to accept that it was essentially as false as her relationship with Cai. "It's such a shame they sent you to do their dirty work on me. I was actually beginning to like you." Mona found it awkward speaking to him now. "You've made me feel like a bloody idiot, but I'm going to try to be civil. OK?" She took her dirty plates to the sink, washed them and left.

Mona was glad she'd cleared the air with Cai. There was no point in perpetuating an anger that had started to fade, and she needed help in whatever form it came. Any trust between them had been obliterated though, and she certainly hadn't missed the shock on his face when she'd beaten Emlyn or when he'd seen the *mark* again in that stupid, bloody t-shirt.

≈

"Where's Cai?" Ifan asked, as soon as the old man had noticed his absence. Mona grunted. "Isn't he behaving?"

"You may have picked the wrong bloke to protect me. Cai thinks I'm some sort of evil witch."

"We'll see," Ifan smiled enigmatically.

She raised her eyebrows slightly. "So?" she started.

"So," Ifan replied, "You're a phenomenal fighter."

"And?"

"You're stupid and arrogant," he added more sharply. "Whatever possessed you to pull a stunt like that? You don't need enemies like Emlyn."

97

"Don't I?" Mona asked petulantly.

Ifan scrutinised her with real concern. "No, Mona, you don't." She knew Ifan was right: Emlyn was a bully and he deserved a beating but it had been a mistake to humiliate him. "Anyway, it's too late now. Just take my advice and keep out of his way."

Mona agreed with a quick nod. "Can you explain more about all this shit; I'm a bit of a slow learner. Are you saying my parents were Druids?"

"Almost certainly," he replied, and her face fell.

"But we had the most normal upbringing, boring even." She shook her head sceptically.

"Here's what I *think* I know." Ifan put down his tea and leaned forward over the desk. "Some of the strongest Druids were sent away from here, before the Roman invasion in about AD 61. Very gradually some of that bloodline came back, and some of it was scattered over the rest of the Celtic fringe. Not that we really know, nothing was written down until a long time after the events – by Christian monks." A look of strangled impotence twisted his mouth. "Our magic has been fading for centuries and I think there may have been some kind of master plan, to boost the strength and gene pool. Somehow, Mona, I believe you could be a part of the result."

"Are you talking about some sort of selective breeding?" Ifan didn't correct her, and Mona gasped at his cool objectivity, his complete disregard of any emotional response. "No, my parents adored each other, they loved us." Mona heard her own fear in the reaction. The thought of losing her own sacred memories of the best part of her life would be too much to bear.

"No. *Shh*, Mona, no, that's not what I'm saying." Her vehemence had startled him and he toned down the lecture. "I've been reading the manuscripts endlessly and I've come across a protocol where strong youngsters are introduced into a completely unfamiliar community and that is all. No coercion, no planning. After that, nature seems to take its own course." Ifan moved a couple of books around on his desk, as if looking for evidence to support his claim.

"Though there seems to be some evidence for the '*intended*', if you like, to be strongly attracted to each other, right from the start. I'm just saying that may have happened with your parents. I may be wrong of course."

They were interrupted by a soft knock as the door opened and Cai let himself in. "*Meddwl y dylswn fod yma.* – Thought I should be here," he mumbled sullenly.

Mona's eyes flicked to Ifan's as they passed between her and Cai. He seemed to find something about the two of them extremely entertaining. "So that means someone knows everything?" she asked, pointedly bringing him back to his theory.

"Not necessarily. The Ovate law firms have no affiliation to any particular community. The aim is anonymity. There isn't someone hanging around to see who falls in love with whom; they're not interested. They get the money when the job's done." Ifan didn't bother bringing Cai up to date, so Mona assumed he already knew the score. "Your father wasn't from this community; I would have known him. Though he may have come from somewhere on the island, your names suggest you have roots here, but he could be any one of twenty or more Joneses of the right age. Each community keeps a record of arrivals and departures, but not what happens to them afterwards. To go back is forbidden. It's like terrorist cells in a way; nobody has access to all the information."

Ifan stopped talking for a while, as if allowing her time to assimilate what he had said. Cai stretched out his legs, and Mona's thoughts were scattered by a sudden carnal appreciation of his quadriceps. Ifan resumed talking. "I have to admit that things may have been a little more complicated for your family. My guess is that both your parents were powerful, and the enemy started to hunt down these cells of potentially powerful Druids. Your parents were probably on the run as soon as they met." Ifan shook his head slowly. "But that need for secrecy must have become desperate for them by the time they had children... I'm sorry Mona; I've been going on, I didn't mean to upset you..."

"I'm not upset," she lied.

There was a firm knock at the door, and as they all turned to it Ifan caught their attention with a hiss. "All this is between us, not anyone else…" He waited for them to agree before calling out "Come in."

Dafydd and two other men entered the room. They were wearing combat gear and all three were armed. One of them was a man-mountain, bearded and hard-eyed. Cai slid to Mona's side and pressed his hand on to her shoulder, forcing her to remain seated.

Dafydd cast a critical eye over Cai and Mona, taking careful note of the contact. "Fraternising with the enemy, Cai?" His tone dripped acid.

"Easy, Dafydd," Ifan warned, provoking a violent reaction from his son.

"She should be locked up." He threw Cai a look of sharp contempt. "She's sent my brother to the infirmary, for fuck's sake. Look at her. She wears that fucking *mark* like a necklace."

Mona wondered why they weren't arguing in Welsh, then instinctively realised that he wanted her to understand, wanted to intimidate her. She responded in kind. "He'll be sore for a couple of days but I didn't damage him. *He* wanted the fight." Her tone was curt, business-like even, and it inflamed Dafydd still further, but she hadn't finished yet. "I held back; if I had wanted to hurt him, he would know about it."

The Welsh began then in earnest, a tirade of aggressive shouting from all sides. Mona could feel the breath and movement in Cai's body as he joined in. His arm had crept protectively around her shoulders during the confrontation and she thought better of shrugging him off; he was clearly on her side for the time being.

The controlled tension receded from Cai's arm as the posse left but both he and Ifan looked defeated. "What is it?" she asked tentatively, suspecting that her fate had been decided.

Cai let go and sank into the adjacent chair. "They've called for a meeting and a vote. They want you locked up in the meantime," he muttered sullenly.

"In my room or the cells?"

"Cells and an armed guard."

Mona wasn't surprised; fighting Emlyn had been a foolish move, and she was paying for her arrogance now. "Ok." She got up to face the music. "What will they vote on?"

"Expulsion or death. Bryn's coming back with the handcuffs."

"Who's Bryn?" she asked in shock. *Expulsion or Death?*

"The really big one," Cai explained dryly. "Please don't piss him off too."

"Cai will stay with you, Mona. Don't be afraid." Ifan's words were worryingly concise.

Only minutes later, the door opened again, and the man mountain, Bryn, approached with the handcuffs. Cai snatched them from him, muttering, but the ogre didn't react – Cai appeared to have some sort of power here. He fastened the handcuffs on Mona with a studied gentleness. "I'm sorry." She rustled up a brave grin.

≈

They wouldn't let Cai into the cell with her, so he leaned up outside the bars for the first few hours, cross-armed and sullen. "You should go," she tried again, knowing it was pointless.

"Would you like something to eat?" he asked, ignoring her suggestion.

"Are you thinking of smuggling a file in a cake?" It was a valiant attempt at humour and he smiled tightly. Mona sank to the floor with a frustrated huff, propping herself up against the steel. After a minute or so Cai mirrored her, on the other side of the bars. "So why did you want to kill me so badly?"

"Revenge," he answered immediately. He'd probably been expecting the question for a while. "They killed my parents, Nia's Dad…" A whirling hand movement indicated many more deaths.

"Who gave you that order?" she queried, "It clearly wasn't the Archdruid."

"My taid, Hywel. He's not your biggest fan."

"*Taid*?"

"Grandfather, he's my grandfather."

"Is it the *mark*?"

"Mostly," Cai nodded. "Though your English accent doesn't help."

Mona grimaced and frowned. "I thought you were fighting the Irish?"

Cai sighed. "Yes, we are." A brief flicker of sorrow clouded his eyes. "But it doesn't make any sense – this split weakens us both." Cai fiddled absently with the bunch of keys. "It's almost like," he peered at Mona dubiously, "we're playing at it. Characters from some Celtic myth, scrapping around on the floor while the ogre sneaks up on us both with a big hammer."

"The English?" Mona guessed wearily.

"Yes," Cai nodded back. "Saxon power and laws have devastated us for millennia. Though now the battle with them is more subtle than that – now we just run and hide."

"But surely that's ancient history?"

"Is it?" Cai asked, looking at her askance before tilting his head back against the bars and closing his eyes.

Mona noted his perfect profile and sighed. "Looks like I'm buggered either way," she mumbled and Cai merely grunted his agreement. "How will they try to… kill me?" she asked uneasily.

"That won't happen; they haven't passed a judgement like that in years."

"So?"

"You'll most likely be expelled." Cai's face darkened but Mona thought this was a really positive outcome, considering the alternative.

"That's not so bad, I'll go looking for Idwal."

"You won't make it far, Mona. The Irish know you're here now, and what you're capable of."

"How do they know?"

Cai shrugged. "Colm might have been a coincidence but I doubt it. He was more than likely lying in wait. I think you should stay here, until we've got some answers."

"Yes, you've all been incredibly kind so far." She rattled her cuffed hands, and Cai raked a hand through his hair.

"I was following orders," he groaned.

"And what about this morning? Who ordered you to kiss me? And if you say it was my evil sorcery, you'll get a punch in the nuts."

"I was improvising." Cai's mouth twitched and it made her smile.

"It was a great diversionary tactic."

"Really?" His smile widened but fell again as he saw Dafydd approach.

≈

The judgement was given in the hall and Mona was made to stand, still handcuffed, before the panel of nine cloaked men and women. They weren't wearing their hoods up this time and Mona recognised a few, Siân included. Cai hadn't answered her question about the method of capital punishment and her imagination dived into free fall for a second.

Ifan was refreshingly focused and brief. "The council have finally agreed on a verdict." He looked up to meet her eyes as he gave it. "Five of us voted that you should be free to stay or go as you wish, three voted for immediate expulsion and one voted for death." Many eyes moved to another white-haired old man, seated on Ifan's right. "You are free to go with immediate effect, Mona. However, you are welcome to stay until you have fulfilled the constraints of the will." Ifan motioned to Cai, pointing at her hands.

"Congratulations," Cai murmured.

"You like a bit of handcuff action, don't you?" she murmured, and he stopped mid-turn of the lock, staring at her.

"Why do you always joke?"

"Why do you never laugh?"

Emlyn strode up, too close for comfort, and Mona thought he was going to hit her. "Touch me and you'll get another pasting," she threatened through gritted teeth.

Mona saw Cai lift his eyes to heaven, and then squeeze them shut. Emlyn didn't touch her but he squared up. "I don't trust you, and I don't like you."

His brother and the giant Bryn had joined Emlyn. Their proximity forced her body into pre-combat preparations, and she checked her core. "Brought your friends to play?" she taunted.

Beside her, Mona felt Cai's need to restrain her, but Emlyn finally laughed. "Not frightened of very much, are you?" Mona raised an eyebrow, wondering how to respond. Was it merely a tactic to catch her off guard? "So you're here for another week, correct?" Emlyn continued in a surprisingly conversational tone.

Mona would have to stay if she wanted to claim the money, and her life would be a lot harder without cash. "Correct," she answered, rubbing her freed wrists.

"Then I'd like to make you an offer. Teach us to fight, and we'll allow Nia to research for you. Find out about..." He glanced at her hidden *mark*.

It was good news that Nia was well enough to work, and she *did* have seven days to kill, but Mona was curious. "Why do you want me to help you now? You wanted me dead this morning."

Emlyn leaned in closer at her question. "So we have more of a chance, if we meet any of your relatives." There was a residue of humour in the threat.

"Alright, Emlyn, but I'm not taking any shit from you." Mona scowled at all the men nearby, including Cai. "From any of you."

Emlyn snorted again; he seemed extremely amused by the idea. "See you in the training room at seven-thirty?" he asked, quite politely, considering.

Cai had already walked away, towards the other old man of the council, and they were disagreeing quietly but vehemently. "Who's that man?" Mona asked Emlyn.

"That's Hywel, Cai's taid – the one who voted to put you to death." He treated her to a not so polite leer.

Mona knew Emlyn wanted her to squirm, so with great difficulty she conjured a smile. "You know? You're such a delightful family."

Mona appeared to have found a way to keep Emlyn happy, and she left him laughing. She'd worked out the way back to her room now, and bed was calling her. Cai caught up with Mona as she turned into her corridor, and she thought he might try to talk her out of the job. "What will you need for the morning?" he enquired eagerly.

"Pads, mats, the usual."

"Pads?" he asked and Mona nodded. "It's just that we only use them with the kids," he muttered, slightly crestfallen.

"Interesting," she said nonchalantly. They had a huge shock coming in the morning, and Mona didn't feel like warning him. They had reached her door. "Night then, Cai." He didn't move away at the hint, so she opened it and headed in.

"Can I come in?"

"More improvisation?"

"I was thinking sex actually." He smiled at her expansively, and Mona laughed at his overconfidence.

"You seem to be over the evil witch thing."

"Maybe I just don't care." His eyes danced with lust, and Mona saw that he wasn't used to being denied.

"Oh, Cai. You romantic fool," she grinned back.

"Come on, Mona," he coaxed. "You can't deny there's something between us."

Mona moved slightly inside the door, using it as a barrier between them. "You're a difficult man to turn down," she chuckled, and then sighed. "But there's someone else actually."

"Who?" Cai was shocked, and more than a little annoyed at the thought.

"Someone at college, you wouldn't know him." Mona could see

his mind racing, and it probably ran to an image of Jack. "He's a bit of a geek really, an engineer; you know the sort. I liked him – he was kind." She closed the door, and Cai nodded to himself in rueful understanding.

≈

Mona was up in the hall setting out the mats early. She had slept well, tranquillised by the events of the previous day, but as dawn broke, she'd started to worry about the training session ahead. Mona wanted to do Brendan proud, but there were too many of them to emulate the way he'd trained her. Warming up and focusing on the patterns settled her nerves though, and she was soon floating in the calm that the movements always brought.

Cai watched her quietly from outside the door. He was lost with regards to Mona. He was supposed to hate her, had been asked to kill her, but had found himself entranced. He had hardly slept but had dozed between fitful fantasies of being tangled up in Mona's strong limbs, of pushing himself inside her. The visceral clarity of his imagination had sent him to her room at dawn, and then here, when she hadn't answered the door.

As soon as she had finished the intoxicating dance, he tapped and entered the hall. "How long have you been here?" Mona was direct, not hostile.

"A while. I didn't want to disturb you."

"Peeping Tom as well. You keep on showering yourself in glory, don't you, Cai?"

"I just want to learn." His face was deadpan sincere, until it wasn't. "I'm also extremely competitive."

Mona didn't trust Cai, but when his alter ego made an occasional appearance, he was lovely. She would have to keep her distance. "So what have you learnt from watching the patterns?"

Cai scrunched his face and angled his head in thought, answering with studied seriousness. "That your body is a lethal weapon." Mona nodded. He was right, but she was waiting for him to elucidate. "A man could easily suffocate between your breasts," he sighed, and smiled at the same time. "But what a way to go." Cai surprised himself with his bravery and the lightness of his mood.

Mona laughed loud and clear and he joined her. "OK, let's have a gentle warm-up bout." Cai straightened up and fell into an opening stance. "We'll start over here." She brought them both back to one corner of the room. "Do you mind answering a few questions as we go?" Mona asked.

Cai shook his head. "I'll do my best."

"You should stretch out," Mona told him and Cai began limbering up but took no real care over it. "Why do you all train so hard?"

"We were caught napping. The last time we were attacked it was here, on home soil. That just can't happen again. Ifan's petrified of history repeating itself, so we're always ready."

"Hardly," Mona muttered to herself. She didn't move particularly quickly and Cai blocked her punch. "How does this place fund itself?"

"Precious metals, but gold in particular. We've been around forever and hung on to the mines. Though it's coming to an end now." Mona blocked and parried, getting a little faster and harder but still within his tolerance. "The last funding crisis forced us to sell all the clan homes in Moelfre and move here."

"So you used to live in Moelfre?"

"We lived in all the old family houses; *Pen Y Bonc , Hen Gorlan, Bryn Llwyd, Dalar Gam, Bryn Wylfa, Llain Swch, Cocyn Uchaf.*" Mona's arms dropped and she stopped fighting as Cai listed the names of the ancient houses. He spoke them like poetry, and Mona was drawn in again by the Welsh, to the clan memories of a tight-knit community. "But that money's running out fast." Cai's change in language and tone snapped Mona out of her inertia, but she continued to listen. "We need to find alternative incomes. I've been trying to convince Ifan to branch out into renewables for years."

She started to use her legs now as well, and caught him with a light brush to the kidneys. "How do you prevent me from telling the world about all this, when I leave?" She brushed the other kidney and he felt a light slap make contact on his cheek.

Cai blinked and reformed, realising at that moment that he very much did not want her to go. "There's a leaving ceremony and you'll sign a legal document that the solicitors keep. The Ovate law firms have a lot of power, even in mainstream Britain, believe me, you won't want to tell." Cai made to extend his back leg for balance and it hit the back wall.

She smiled up at him, poised for a killer jab. "I've pushed you back the diagonal length of the room and you've only just realised." Their closeness fired up the now familiar electrical current between them and Mona stepped back to lessen the effect on her body. "Never let your opponent distract you Cai, every ounce of your brainpower needs to be focused on the fight." Cai nodded contritely but made a grab for her waist. Mona blocked and snatched up his leading hand before twisting it around his back and catapulting him forward on his knees. He was still there when her other students arrived.

Mona understood the difficulty would be to keep their interest in the patterns. She knew from her own experience that they could seem tedious and pointless at the beginning. "I want to show them the progression from patterns to fighting. Can I use you to demonstrate?" She smiled at Cai, and it seemed to ease the humiliation of his first lesson.

The room jumped with comments and sniggers, for which she didn't need a translation, as she led Cai into the roughly ringed area. "Don't be scared, I'm not going to hurt you," she whispered into his ear.

Mona didn't actually touch him at all, but used Cai to explain the transformation: from the simple repetitive move in the line work to the dance-like movement of the pattern, and from there to a deadly punch or kick. They worked well together physically, and before long he was able to pre-empt his positioning and stances, guessing with accuracy when they had finished with a sequence and were ready to move on.

Mona was entirely focused on the job, no banter and minimal explanation. All her moves against him, though fast, had fallen between ten and twenty millimetres short of contact, and Cai was in awe of her control, almost more than her skill or power. The simple demonstrations convinced the warriors of the effectiveness of line and pattern work, and before long they were ravenous for practice.

Mona was surprised how well the men received instruction from her, and now that she had been accepted by their leader, they were a fairly friendly bunch – all but Geraint.

Geraint embodied everything that Mona disliked in the male sex; he was a coarse, loud-mouthed misogynist, who did nothing but bully and complain a great deal. There was always one though, and Mona tried to rise above his constant digs and jibes.

At lunch, Mona tried to count how many Druids lived here at the *Conway*, and she got to over fifty before Cai began a catalogue of technical questions, in an effort to improve his own fighting techniques.

"I'm eating! Will you give it a rest with your constant chatter," she joked. Cai had a well-founded reputation for quiet moroseness, but was genuinely excited about this opportunity to learn what she knew.

"I wonder if you'd be that keen if I was teaching you the moves." Emlyn winked at Mona as he imitated Cai. "Oh, Mona, is this right? Or maybe I should stand a little closer? Perhaps I should put my hand here."

She laughed as Emlyn made a cupping motion with his hands. "Leave him alone, Emlyn. I'll see you back there – five minutes."

At least Druids didn't have unisex loos; she was sure Cai would follow her in if he could. As she sat down, Mona heard the familiar sound of gossipy women, congregating by the sinks. Usually they spoke in Welsh, so her access to any overheard information was negligible. Today, however, after the initial whispering, the conversation was held in English. "Why are we speaking in English, Cerys?" one of them hissed.

"Because the evil N woman from the laundry is in that loo, and she doesn't speak a word of it."

Nesta, Mona deduced – she'd heard the name bandied about. Cerys, Dwynwen and Gwen then proceeded to share their thoughts on various subjects; from hairstyles to jobs and the weather, and then inevitably to relationships.

"Well, I don't care what anyone says. I'm glad he's back," one of the women confessed.

Another of them groaned dramatically. "Bloody hell, Gwen, let it drop, why don't you. You knew what he was like, we all told you, even *he* told you."

"Don't upset her," one of them warned kindly.

"I just thought that once we…"

"Cai has sex with everyone. Always and only sex." The speaker seemed to labour each syllable: "At least he's clear about it from the start. It's more than I can say about Ieuan."

The women prattled on about Ieuan's proclivity for proclaiming undying love before moving on swiftly to the next love. Mona sat still, her legs numbing with inactivity.

"So what do you think is going on with the Saxon bitch? I think he likes her. I've watched him follow her around, he even talks to her." Gwen sounded upset, but one of the women laughed – she really hooted.

"Come on, how long does it ever last with him, a week? Two at the most. She's been here three days; I give her seven."

Someone else came in and the women left. Mona sat for a while, a little despondently. Cai had somehow made her feel special, but he'd merely tricked her again.

8

Brain Damage

It had been less than twenty-four hours since Mona had seen Nia, and she was a little apprehensive about how much improvement there would be. Her priority would be to avoid Siân – at all costs.

Mona knocked lightly on Nia's door and Siân opened it, freezing at the sight of the visitor. Over Siân's shoulder, Mona could see that Nia was fully clothed and sitting up in a chair, so she smiled into her eyes and turned away from the door. Mona heard the door close behind her but was dismayed to hear Siân running to catch up.

"Mona." She stopped, but didn't turn. "I owe you an apology," Siân mumbled awkwardly. "Actually, I owe you so much more than that." Siân's words began to sound more confident and genuine, but Mona continued to walk away. "Please stop, Mona. I know you saved Nia and Cai. There was no excuse for my behaviour." Mona slowed and then finally stopped to face Siân. "I was frightened of you – I still am; your *mark*, your power... but I want to trust you, and I need to thank you for saving my girl." It sounded like a rehearsed speech, but Mona heard the gratitude in the woman's voice. It obviously took a great deal of courage for Siân to take Mona's lethal hands in her own, but she did; and there she was, Siân, Nia's *real* mother.

"Would it be alright for me to talk to her?" Mona asked.

Siân's small smile said it all. "Please, go on in. I've got loads to do and she's desperate to see you." Siân gave Mona a final maternal squeeze of the hand, before continuing down the corridor and out of sight.

≈

"Alright, sicknote?" Mona joked tentatively as she pushed open the door. Nia was thin and pale. "How do you feel?" she asked a little more gravely.

"I just want to say I'm sorry, Mona. I never wanted to deceive you," Nia blurted out, eyes closed, so that she could manage her own rehearsed speech. "My friendship with you is not false, I want you to understand that."

Nia's hands were utterly frozen, and Mona tried to warm them with her own, shushing away the garbled declarations. "Yes, I don't think you're really cut out for espionage. That's probably why they had to send in the big guns, Cai did a much better job." She saw the pity in Nia's eyes and didn't want it. "Actually, I wondered if you could clear up a few things for me." Mona coughed, embarrassed, but she needed to know. "I heard some women talking about Cai…"

"And you want to know if it's true?" she sighed. "Well, yes, it probably is. He's a complicated man, but you must understand a vital difference in our cultures here, Mona."

Despite her frailty, Nia's energy level rose as she began to explain. She was once again in her element: knowledge and the imparting of it. "We are *not* Christian. We have our own beliefs, and though we have nominal gods and goddesses, our true belief system is pagan, built around nature and the turning of the seasons." Mona was getting used to being lectured by Nia and tried to concentrate. "Throughout childhood, we are taught that sex is an immensely powerful, natural and wonderful gift. To us, sex isn't something to be avoided at all costs until it's inevitable. Men and women are expected to have healthy sex drives, and there aren't the hang-ups about it that I've noticed in the Christian world."

112

After her synopsis, Nia wasn't going to pussyfoot around Mona's question. "Cai is a difficult man. His parents died when he was just thirteen, and though he wasn't alone in the job, he's been responsible for his sister, Sioned, since she was four. Cai's always got along fairly well with people, but has had no real friendships; he enjoys sex but seems incapable of intimacy. He holds a position of authority through his bloodline and that has made him arrogant – to say the least." Nia had a pained look on her face. "Cai can be quite cutting at times, cruel even."

"So he's broken a few hearts?"

Nia rolled her eyes and gave a short cynical laugh. "That scenario is becoming more infrequent. I think he's more careful about telling them what to expect now. Despite this, women still fall in love with him. I'm pretty sure it's only the desire of the unobtainable. Is that why you asked?" she queried directly.

"I find him extremely attractive," Mona confessed. "At least I know the score now." Nia had told her everything she hadn't wanted to hear.

"Just be careful."

"What, you mean condoms?"

Nia laughed. "No, he's always well prepared in that department. Never without one on his person, or so I've heard." Her smile was kind. "I meant that you shouldn't trust him with your heart, Mona." They shared a sad little laugh, and there was a knock on the door. "Come in, Mam," Nia called.

Cai pushed open the door. He'd been running and sank against the wall with exhausted relief when he saw Mona with his cousin. He started remonstrating with her in Welsh and Mona looked at Nia for an explanation. "He was worried about you – been looking everywhere, apparently." Cai seemed to be getting more, not less angry and decided to storm out.

"I suppose I'd better get back. See you after supper. Your mum and I have made a truce," Mona said lightly, and kissed the top of Nia's head.

113

"Only because I threatened her with Cardiff University," Nia smirked.

"You sly old thing," Mona grinned back.

Cai didn't give Mona a chance to apologise and the tirade began immediately and loudly. The thought that Nia was only the other side of the door and could hear each word he said, made Mona cringe with embarrassment.

"You said five minutes. You've been gone half an hour. How am I supposed to protect you if you don't take this seriously?"

"I was just…"

"It was dangerous and foolish. Don't do it again." Cai whirled away, obviously expecting Mona to follow. She didn't. "Come on, we've got work to do," he commanded when he realised she wasn't obeying orders.

Mona was appalled at his tone. "Don't fucking talk to me like that. What makes you think you're any real protection anyway?" His anger was infectious. "You've done nothing but deceive me since I met you. How can you possibly think I can trust you now?" Mona looked him up and down and found him wanting. "You're the very last person I need as a bodyguard."

"Where are you going?" he bellowed after her, as she marched off.

"None of your business."

Mona didn't have a clue where she was going, but it certainly wasn't going to be in the same direction as Cai. After twenty minutes of getting lost, she eventually found her way back to the hall.

Emlyn had asked about wrestling techniques rather than just the punching and kicking. Mona guessed that as a big man, these would be his weapons of choice.

It was hard to ignore Cai while they were working together. The key with close body contact work was to use your opponent's own momentum against them, and after two hours of throwing and being thrown by Cai, Mona was beginning to feel physically weak from something more than exhaustion. Their earlier confrontation had fanned the physical intensity between them.

Emlyn was good at wrestling but acknowledged that there was a wealth of technical help that Mona could provide. "Can we go over that tomorrow afternoon again? I've got a few favourite moves," he grinned, "but I'm wondering if you could improve them."

"No problem. It's just about getting in the right body position," she answered affably. Emlyn was talking to Mona now, maybe not as an equal but certainly not as a third-class citizen.

"How long have you been doing this?" he asked, intrigued.

"Since I was ten. Though I started seriously at seventeen."

"You love it, don't you?"

"It's my life, it's me," she replied truthfully, and he studied her as if she was some new fruit.

"I've never seen anyone fight like you."

"It's only practice. I've practiced a lot." She laughed and rolled her eyes at the understatement.

"We normally have a drink in the hall on a Friday. Be good to see you there."

The coxswain left Mona wondering if she'd just been accepted into the army, but the bastard hadn't offered to help tidy up. Cai seemed to have slunk off straight after training too, so she scanned around for help with the mats. There was a clutch of youngsters guffawing in the corner; being entertained by an attractive auburn-haired man. "Give me a hand with these," Mona called over to them as she wrestled with the corner of a dense training pad.

"Abandoned you already, has he?" the leader of the gang said as he sauntered over with a twinkle in his eye and a smile on his lips.

"Something like that," Mona grinned back, knowing he meant Cai.

"They're always much heavier after a session, don't you think?" he said, lifting the opposite corner.

"Ieuan, isn't it?" Mona guessed as they heaved the mat on top of the others.

115

Ieuan had a soft and attractive voice. His hair fell just shy of his shoulders and was glossy in a way that reminded Mona of a TV ad. The thought made her want to giggle, but she didn't. "That's right," he said, moving closer and ramping up the allure. "So, do you think you'll come to the hall on Friday then? We're an all right bunch, once you get to know us."

Ieuan gave her an enticing smile, which Mona returned. "That depends," she sighed. "I may not have the energy. There's a lot of work ahead with you lot."

"Are we that bad?" Ieuan asked in mock hurt.

"You're not too awful, though *you* could work on your reaction time."

Ieuan laughed and it was a lovely sound. "That sounds about right; I've always been a bit slow."

They stacked another mat and Mona took the opportunity to ask about something that had been nagging at her. "Why are there so few women who fight and train? I've only ever seen two or three and they seem to have disappeared completely now."

"Well, it is more of a man's job," Ieuan replied directly. Mona's face fell, and he realised his mistake immediately.

"No offence." He put up his hands in a defensive gesture. "It's only that most women like other stuff, don't they?"

Ieuan's allure was taking a rapid nosedive, but Mona was spared giving him an answer by the arrival of Cai, wet-haired from the shower. "I'm fine with these, Ieuan," he uttered quietly. It sounded more like an order to leave, which, after a curt nod, Ieuan obeyed.

They stacked the remaining mats in silence, Mona thankful that Cai had managed to partially mask his pheromones with soap. "I'm sorry I lost my temper with you today. I was worried." He spoke almost formally, but began edging towards her.

There was no way Mona could allow any more contact; not now that she was fully aware of his modus operandi. "I shouldn't have shouted back," she agreed, reversing towards the exit. "I've never been that good with authority."

Cai was still and serious. "I'd like it if you could try to trust me."

"Ok, I'll give it a go." Mona turned her back on him and was even tempted to break into a jog to extend the distance between them. "I'm having a shower. See you at supper."

"No, I'll be outside your room in thirty minutes."

"Forty," she called back.

9

Women

Now that she was aware of some of the politics, Mona risked looking around the canteen. It really was an *old school* dining hall, and she could imagine both the mayhem and formality that had existed here when the place was full of young sailors.

She was learning that breakfast and lunch tended to be staggered affairs, but supper was the time when people congregated. Mona upped her count of the Druids residing in the *Conway* to well over a hundred, and it seemed to be an aging population. After a while, she was conscious of the weight of many stares on her; women's mostly.

Cai remained fully deployed in bodyguard mode, and so close to her all the time that she was feeling a little claustrophobic. "Stand down, private; no one is going to attack me in here." Mona tried to make light of it, but he didn't seem to hear her and continued asking questions about the throwing techniques they had started today. Mona answered them fully, explaining that Emlyn wanted a bit more time on it. Then she asked her own question. "So when can I meet Sioned?" His eyes widened, and he suddenly found his dinner extremely interesting. "So?"

"She doesn't want to meet you – I've tried."

"Does she think I'm the enemy?"

Cai made a vacillating gesture with his head. "Sion can be a bit militant."

Mona was interested. "How militant?"

"Quite." He peeked up from his food with a smile of rueful affection, the sort reserved for siblings. "Extremely."

"Then why doesn't she fight? Ieuan said the women here aren't interested. Why is that?"

Cai baulked a little at the mention of Ieuan but answered her question. "I don't know, there have always been warrior women in our culture, it's well known – *Boudicca, Cartimandua, Gwenllian* and all those." Cai waved his hand as if he knew the women personally. "But despite the technology embargo here, there is more access to the outside world now. It seems that wearing a lot of make-up and talking like a Yank is the height of fashion." Cai thrummed his fork agitatedly. "It's probably her age."

Mona wanted Cai to take this seriously; the reticence of the women concerned her. "I think we should get all the women who want to fight involved in a bit of training; they shouldn't be unprotected." Mona let her idea sink in before continuing. "I know there's quite a lot of male chauvinism floating around here, even though you're not admitting to it," she whispered under her breath, and Cai moved nearer to whisper back.

He could sense the closeness of Mona's lips to his ear and he had to clench hard to stifle a gasp of pleasure at her nearness. She was talking about training the other women, and if it kept her close, he'd pretend to be interested. "What do you propose?" he murmured back.

"Women-only sessions, first thing in the morning, seven till nine."

"Do you seriously think that the men won't wonder where all the women have gone, at that time in the morning?" Cai asked, insinuating his body marginally nearer hers.

Mona scrunched her face, making her look quite child-like. "I'll leave that one to you," she was still near enough to whisper, "I heard you were quite bright." Mona elbowed him playfully in the ribs – it hurt. "I'll make some excuse to Emlyn about having to start the usual session at nine. If the men don't know about it they can't object, and the women will learn quicker without being judged or leered at." Their hair almost touched as they conspired, and Cai felt the old confidence returning. If all else failed, he could lure her in this way. "You'll need to get a feel for all the women who are interested." Mona continued with her plan, deadly serious for a moment, until she spotted the double entendre. Then she giggled extravagantly and winked. "It might take a while." Cai gave her an openly shocked look; someone had been talking. "Don't get cute with me, Cai Owens." She leaned in again to breathe in his ear, even closer this time, and it tickled in his groin. "I've been warned about you." Mona got up from the bench seat. "I'll speak to Emlyn. See you at Nia's in a quarter of an hour."

≈

Mona reminded Emlyn of their deal, and the coxswain thought it was entirely reasonable for Mona to want to work with Nia in finding answers to the *mark*. However, he wasn't at all happy that it left a two-hour gap in the daily training programme. If she only had a week to give, he wanted his pound of flesh, and he eventually convinced Mona to make up the time with some bouts after supper.

≈

The Archdruid was delighted enough with the plan to provide them with the key to the disused chapel across the quad.

Under cover of darkness, Mona and Cai lugged across some of the scruffier mats from the training room stores, and rearranged the pews. A couple of hours later, the dusty old church had been transformed into a perfectly serviceable workout room for the women's sessions.

They sat on a pew, exhausted. "How many for the morning?" Mona asked, massaging her neck.

"Eight, with Nia watching," Cai replied. "Do you want some help with that?" He wiggled his fingers playfully.

Mona just rolled her eyes at his clumsy tactics. "How did you entice that many? Or shouldn't I ask?" She nudged him and he did laugh but it was a little strained. "Come on, Casanova, I'm completely knackered."

"So, I like women, I like sex. Do you think there's something wrong with that?" Cai enquired archly. Mona was on the verge of an answer, when she realised she didn't know what to say.

Leaving Cai to lock up, Mona surveyed the grey walls of the shabby buildings surrounding her. "Thinking of escape?" he asked flippantly.

She was caught off guard, and it wasn't at his perception but at her realisation. Mona whirled around to face him. "You're not just my bodyguard, are you? That's why you were so worried this afternoon. You thought I'd legged it."

"No, it wasn't that. I care about… what happens to you. I thought we were friends?"

"We're not friends Cai, not even close. Did you think all you had to do was flutter your eyelashes?" Mona was pissed off now – her naivety knew no bounds. Of course he'd been upset and angry; he would have been in really deep shit if she'd escaped. "Fine, we're working together." Mona closed her eyes, furious at herself yet again. "I can deal with that, but you can drop the caring bodyguard act, it's getting boring."

To her surprise, Mona found she was hurt. Cai had drawn her in again, she felt ridiculous and had an urge to lash out in retaliation.

≈

It was easy to close the door on him when they reached her room, but Cai was there again like clockwork at a quarter to seven the next morning, handing her tea and toast. Mona was still fuming, and she stalked to the chapel ahead of him. Cai hung back, admiring how shapely she looked from behind, especially while furious. He parked himself at the back of the room, and waited for the fireworks to begin.

Ten women and girls turned up, in twos and threes. They varied in size and shape, and Mona couldn't help but wonder which one was Gwen. But when she strode in, it was immediately obvious which one was Sioned: a raven-haired, blue-eyed beauty who shared her brother's bone structure and surliness.

Mona introduced herself to the group, and not one of the class replied. They just started talking amongst themselves in Welsh. Mona could see Siân readying herself to intervene but she didn't want any help today. "I'd appreciate it if we can speak in English; I can't speak Welsh." The silence stretched on, and Mona filled it deliberately. "I know you can all speak English, as it wasn't Nesta in the cubicle yesterday but me – the 'Saxon bitch'. So there's no need for any of this bollocks."

"Why don't you try learning Welsh then?" Sioned spat from behind someone else.

"Good point. I may do that, but in the meantime…"

"I'm Dwynwen," came a voice from the front.

"And why are you here?" Mona's voice hadn't softened.

"I want to learn how to fight."

"I can teach you that. But I should warn you not to speak to any of your husbands, brothers, fathers or sons about this." Mona included the rest of the women with her body language.

"Why not?" Sioned demanded.

"Because they don't want you to learn how to fight and if they find out, they will try to stop you." Mona was impassive in face and voice.

"How do you know?" she spat again. Sioned was impressively feisty.

"Because you would already be warriors if they allowed it, and don't ask me why again, Sioned."

Sioned had come here to fight, not to learn to fight, and she broke ranks, edging towards Mona. "I know about your *mark*, I know what it means. Your lot killed my parents." Sioned wasn't far from tears and Mona was ready for something like this.

"I imagine that your mum died fighting. Don't you think she would be disappointed in you, Sioned? How can you sit back and not defend yourself?"

That was too much for the young girl, and she launched herself at Mona. Cai, who had been waiting for this moment, intervened quickly. Whisking his sister away, he attempted to calm her tearful rage. "*Pam na fasa ti wedi'i lladd hi, Cai?* Why didn't you kill her like you were supposed to, Cai?"

Mona heard her yelling, from outside the chapel door. It sounded like Sioned meant what she screamed, but Mona didn't understand, so she continued addressing her small class. "Anyone else care to have a breakdown?" She glared icily at the faces of the women in front of her. "I can fight – and fight well. There isn't a man in this community who can beat me, and it isn't magic; it's just hard work and practice. My parents were murdered and I know you've all lost family." Mona paused to let the information sink in. "And you *can't* leave your destiny in the hands of others, not when you've got the potential to change it yourselves."

Siân broke the atmosphere. "Can you show us? Give us a demonstration of what you mean?"

Mona smelled a hustle, but if it inspired the women, then it couldn't hurt. Mona took off her boots and jacket as Cai handed Siân a much more subdued and red-eyed Sioned to console. At least she was back.

"Cai and I are going to spar. It will be a short fight, the first to three hits. It'll probably be over too quickly for you to see, but afterwards, we'll slow it right down and I'll explain the individual chain of events."

They stretched, acknowledged readiness and took up their stances. The fight was over in less than two minutes and they both turned back to the waiting women.

"Can any of you tell where I made the first hit?"

"Leg?"

"Yes, Dwynwen, the right thigh. Now I'm going to slow the move right down so you can all see how many different separate movements there are in that single kick."

It was a completely different experience teaching women and girls with no combat training at all, and by the end of the session Mona wasn't sure if she'd overcomplicated everything.

Walking back across the quad, she was totally absorbed in how to approach tomorrow's session with the women. Cai caught her by the arm and she looked at it, then back up to him in confusion. "What?" They didn't need to be late for Emlyn; he might ask questions.

"That was great, you were great." Cai smiled, not letting go.

"Mmm." She frowned. "I'm not sure about the approach, it may be too technical. I've got a few ideas for tomorrow but we'll have to talk about it at lunch." Mona kept up her onward march, but when she sensed Cai wasn't following, she halted.

He remained stationary with his arms crossed in a truculent pose. "I don't pay people compliments very often, it would be polite if you could at least accept it gracefully."

Mona walked back to him, bewildered by his attitude. "*Polite!* You arrogant git! Do you think for one minute that I give a shit about getting compliments from you, or anyone else?" His tone had made her blood boil. "The only thing I care about is making sure those women are able to defend themselves. I don't want them to like me, or care about me or give me compliments. It's just a job that needs doing." Cai was reddening with either embarrassment or rage – she didn't care which. "Both our mothers were killed – *murdered*. Knowing that, how could you have let your sister go untrained for this long? You're only interested in fighting to boost your fucking ego. This isn't about showing the ladies your latest moves, you vain bastard." Mona scanned about her, knowing her instincts were right. "Something is coming, Cai – can't you feel it? Colm nearly killed Nia. It's time to stop titting about, and get ready to fight."

≈

The atmosphere remained difficult between Mona and Cai up to and including lunch; he was resentful, awkward and not entirely on the ball. Mona had used Cai as a demonstration model again in Emlyn's class, but he just didn't seem focused. She'd made accidental contact a couple of times, and it hadn't improved his humour.

Though she had apologised, Mona was certain that Cai thought the injuries were deliberate. "Perhaps you should sit the next round out; I can use another victim." It was obvious that Cai didn't appreciate Mona's light-hearted attitude and he forced himself to struggle on through the dead legs.

Mona was sitting quietly at lunch when Nia approached. She was dreading the afternoon session of throwing. The constant physical effort, late nights and early mornings were taking their toll, and she was glazed over. Nia, however, was looking much perkier. "Come and sit down here." Mona patted the space on the bench between her and Cai.

"Just wanted to say that it looks like at least fifteen for tomorrow." Nia's honey-coloured hair fell forward and masked her voice. "Word has spread and we're all so excited. Our own Scáthach!" She seemed to swoon a little.

"Who?"

"The shadowy one! A renowned female warrior who set up her own martial arts school on the Isle…"

Mona was too tired to indulge Nia and cut short the impending history lesson. "Great. I've got a different idea for tomorrow's training." Mona glanced at Nia's disagreeable cousin. "And I've upset Cai, so I'm not sure he's on board for tomorrow," Mona explained.

"But whether he is or not, I'm going to need access to some sort of weapons store. Something no one will miss. Any ideas?"

Nia studied Cai. "What did you say to him? He's livid," she whispered.

"Nothing I wouldn't say again," Mona replied matter-of-factly. "Can you get your mum on the case? We'll probably have to meet later on tonight if we're going to get away with it. Tell her to expect me about eight-ish."

"Isn't it a bit early for the women to use weapons?" Nia asked.

"Probably," Mona admitted, "but my time here is running out."

≈

Mona could feel the excitement in the combat room as the afternoon's throwing got under way. Initially, she'd matched the fighters up to similar sized partners, and let them wrestle themselves into a frenzy. Cai had recovered from his dead leg, and was working out his aggression on Ieuan, who, though broader than Cai, was no match in strength and style. Mona thought she could sense a deep-seated jealousy between the men – two rival stags – and she sniggered to herself.

During the break, Cai approached her, clearly stiff with residual anger. "Aren't you going to fight?"

"No. Why?"

"I'd like to fight you." He enunciated each syllable slowly and deliberately.

Mona cocked her head to the side and eyed him through half-closed lids. "I don't think so. I've got the feeling you want to hurt me."

Emlyn approached. "You've had a long enough breather, Mo, and we haven't seen you wrestle properly yet – not in a bout. I've got a feeling Cai might fancy his chances in this one."

Mona knew it would be unwise to refuse Emlyn now. "OK, I'll wrestle, but not with Cai; I've injured him enough today."

Emlyn seemed ready to accept another choice, but Cai stopped him, forcing a lightness of tone into his voice. "I'm fine, Em. Come on, Mona." He pulled her towards the mats and an audience formed.

Mona didn't want to fight him; Cai was clearly in a belligerent mood and had a hidden agenda. She stripped to her vest reluctantly, unwilling to reveal the *mark* on her chest. She then stretched and shook out her limbs for some time.

"First to three, one slap on the mat to acknowledge submission." Emlyn set out the simple rules.

Mona let Cai come at her with all his rage – this simple move would only work once – and she held on until he was almost upon her. In the final split second, she crouched down low beneath him and exploded up into his chest with full force. Mona caught one arm behind his back and bent him to the ground with a knee. He rapped once on the mat and sprang back up.

Cai was around six foot in height and deceptively slight in appearance. However, his body weight consisted solely of muscle and bone, and he had big mobile hands that she dare not allow to grab her. He was also a quick learner, preventing the use of the same move twice. She therefore decided to attack as soon as he'd straightened up. Dropping a shoulder, Mona rugby tackled him at calf height with pace. Cai hit the ground again, but tried to shake her off. Mona launched herself from legs to chest, pinning him to the floor. He rapped the mat a second time.

Learning from her previous move, Cai didn't waste any time, and dummied her to the right before making a grab for her waist. Mona allowed him to almost make contact, then bent double, grabbing his right shoulder and throwing him over her back, towards the floor. However, Cai had managed to grab the waistband of her leathers and dragged Mona to the floor with him. Refusing to release her on landing, he used her leathers as a lever, twisting out from underneath and almost pinning her arms. The glint of imminent victory glimmered in his eyes. "Nice try, gorgeous," she grunted, and scissored her powerful legs around his, prying him off her and back on to the mat. Cai didn't seem to have the energy to slap the mat for a third time, so she picked up one of his hands and did it for him.

They were both breathing so hard that they didn't hear anything Emlyn had to say about the match. Mona's ears were screaming with her pulsing adrenaline, but she did feel a rumble of deranged laughter in Cai's chest. She disengaged her legs and rolled away.

It took quite a while for Cai to stop laughing; hysteria was such an unusual emotion for him that a small part of his mind marvelled at the freedom it engendered. He realised, of course, that it was an arbitrary release and he could just as easily be wailing tears.

It had taken twelve years to construct and maintain this angry, stunted, selfish man – and only three weeks to destroy him. There was of course no question that Mona had destroyed him. He was gone, completely obliterated, and Cai wondered who he would be, now that all his notions about himself and his life had been blown apart. As he rose to his feet, Cai felt the strange sensation of having been reborn.

Emlyn was looking at him a little worriedly. "*Wyt ti wedi taro dy ben?* Did you take a knock to the head, mate?"

Cai thought back to a glorious Mona, giving him a good dressing down in the quad. "Yes, I think I probably did."

≈

Cai was now able to watch Mona in a way that he would have previously found impossible. There were scratches on her arms and he could see a red weal just above her left cheekbone; her hip was sore where he had twisted the waistband in too far.

From their first meeting, he had deceived her. Since then, all he had wanted was to possess and control her. Mona had protected him, befriended him and saved his life. Shame didn't completely describe the emotion he felt, but he supposed it would do. When Cai finally stood beside her, she looked back at him with nothing but concern in her eyes. "Are you alright?" she asked.

"Are you?" he replied softly. Had he ever asked anyone but Sioned that question before and meant it?

"I've had enough of wrestling," she admitted wearily.

Cai took her hand gently and led her away, motioning to Emlyn that they would be back after supper. "Ah, very good, no witnesses when you exact your revenge," she quipped when they were alone in the corridor.

Mona still seemed happy enough to keep hold of his hand, and hers felt strangely small in his as Cai led her outside to watch the water. He noticed that she winced slightly while easing on to the jetty wall. "How's the hip?" he enquired. She shrugged – it was nothing – and Cai perched next to her as they gazed out over the strait; the lights on the bridges were little twinkles in the summer dusk. "Sorry, Mona."

"What for?"

"I don't know... everything?" he sighed.

"I've got a temper and I shouldn't have said half of those things." Mona paused. "Though I am serious about the other women."

"I know, and you're probably right about that. I'd just never considered it before." Mona shrugged again but said nothing in reply, and they sat for a while in peaceful silence, listening to the evening chorus, until Cai spoke again. "You know, it's a tradition in Celtic lore to receive great wisdom at the water's edge."

"Really?" Mona asked, and Cai nodded his head slowly, looking down at the black water.

"I've lived here all my life and it's only just worked for me." He rubbed his hand gently over hers. "Come on," Cai said, "let's get some of Nia's potions on you before supper. *I'm starving.*" He attempted a dreadful imitation of her Kentish accent.

"Yeah, nothing like being on the wrong end of a thrashing to work up an appetite." Despite the taunt, Cai held on to her hand and smiled.

≈

"Have you found any weapons?" Mona asked and Nia's eyes sparkled. She was daubing Mona with the creams and tinctures.

"Mam had a chat with Taid and he's dug out a whole load of old stuff. It needs looking at, but I thought Cai could take it down to his little hideaway." She'd smeared the cream everywhere she could see, but held the pot aloft, scanning Mona for more injuries. "Where else?"

"Hip," Cai offered from where he lay sprawled on Nia's bed.

"Show me," Nia ordered, and Mona pulled the waistband out, gingerly. "You'll have to pull them down a bit."

Mona unzipped her leathers, revealing stomach, hip and thigh. Cai meant to look away but never actually did. Instead, he impressed himself by maintaining eye contact with Mona throughout the rest of the ministrations.

"What did you do?" Nia accused.

"Nothing, just a bit of a twist," Mona replied, then launched back to questioning Nia. "How are we going to get them from Ifan's to your workshop?"

"Mam's got that covered; it's brilliant," Nia enthused. "Laundry trolleys! It's all arranged with Nesta."

"Genius! Must be where you got your brains."

Siân came in and caught the last comment. "But she gets her looks from her dad." Siân smiled wistfully at her daughter, seeing the man she had lost.

≈

Mona was impressed with Cai's workshop. It wasn't particularly big but the shelves were full of fastidiously organised and interesting projects. His tools were easily accessible and immaculately arranged. "What are you working on at the moment?" Mona asked, letting her fingers trail over an ancient engine.

"All of it," Cai replied simply, as he set up their work areas. "Engines," he laughed, "I really like engines."

Mona smiled back. "Me too." It was good to be getting on with him again. "But I thought you were green?"

Cai grimaced and may even have blushed. "I know – I should be, I am really. Electric engines are the only viable way forward at the moment." He winked at her naughtily. "But I can't resist a combustion engine, it's my guilty pleasure."

Cai's levity was infectious, and Mona liked his naughtiness immensely but nevertheless checked her enthusiasm. It would not do to let him too close; after all, he already had the home advantage.

There was a knock at the door and a woman opened it, pulling a large laundry trolley behind her. Mona recognised the big woman from her first traumatic day here – she had stripped Mona while wearing gloves.

"This is Nesta," Cai announced, smiling at the grey-haired woman. There was a flurry of Welsh and Mona remembered that Nesta didn't speak English. She clearly wanted to say something and Cai translated for her. "She says it's about bloody time someone got the women back fighting." He laughed at the next sentence, "And that she's sorry for not giving you any underwear when you first arrived."

"Tell her all women are welcome, the more the merrier. Tell her I want her to be able to defend herself."

Cai chuckled again as Nesta spoke. "She said thanks, but she's quite handy with a cudgel, though she is sending over her granddaughter." Mona smiled at her, and Cai seemed confused by the next few words out of Nesta's mouth but said them anyway, frowning as he did so. "Thanks, sparkly one."

"It seems odd that she can't speak any English, the rest of you can," Mona remarked after Nesta had trundled out of the workshop.

"Only because we have to," Cai snorted as he rolled up his sleeves, "even to talk to other Druids."

"Oh!" Mona was surprised, "Don't you all speak one *magical* language?" she joked, deepening her voice for effect.

"There is one actually – Brythonic," he replied while scrupulously clearing a workbench. "At one time, we all spoke the one language."

"And you don't now?"

"Only ceremonially," he explained casually, as he started on the adjacent bench. "If I need to speak to another Druid, say from Scotland or Cornwall, it's quicker and easier to use English."

"How awful for you," Mona muttered under her breath, but he didn't smile at the jibe. "So you can't understand each other at all?"

"We can a bit. Welsh, Cornish and Breton share similarities. As do Irish, Scottish and Manx. But they're all too different now and so we have to speak *Saesneg*." Cai had finished clearing up and turned to Mona, dustpan and brush in hand.

"*Saesneg?*" She tried and failed to copy the pronunciation.

"*Saesneg* is Welsh for Saxon, it's what we still call the English language."

The weapons were an old collection of odd short swords, daggers and throwing knives. Mona stared at them. "They're ancient." She picked out a crusty dagger and frowned. "So haven't you moved on? No guns?"

Cai had obviously thought this through himself, as his answer was immediate. "It's difficult enough to stay under the radar without trying to buy firearms and ammunition."

"So that goes for the Irish too?"

"I suppose so, we're all hidden." Cai picked up a weapon from the pile and moved it from hand to hand. "And, besides, we're all Celts; we fight with swords – anything else would be cheating."

"Well, let's hope the Irish aren't cheats," Mona muttered pointedly. "Does anyone know why they keep attacking? What about those Witch doctors in the basement?"

"Healers you mean." Cai giggled at her lack of reverence. "No, they're pretty clueless about the Irish," he replied in a more sober tone.

"So what *do* they do. They can't seem to heal either."

"They *used* to be immensely powerful, back when our magic…"

"Oh come on, not you as well?" Mona rolled her eyes and Cai decided to change the subject.

"Let's get to work on these swords."

Tonight they were concentrating on cleaning the rust from the blades and sanding the handles for a better grip. "I want the women to get used to the weight and feel of them before they're sharpened, but I don't want to wait too long," Mona mused, hefting a sword and then glancing up at Cai in panic. "Shit, I've forgotten about the evening shift. Emlyn is going to be suspicious."

"I had a word with him at supper and I've already arranged an alibi."

"Which is?"

"I explained that we needed a little more time alone, then I waggled my eyebrows like this." He demonstrated and Mona chuckled.

"What did you really say?"

"That we had a meeting with Ifan about what Nia has found out so far."

"Great, what time is it now?" Cai always wore a watch.

"Nearly midnight, just a few more to go. We should be able to get them all in one trolley, as long as we pad it."

Mona grabbed a permanent marker before they packed up. She scouted ahead while Cai pushed the trolley. Luckily, they weren't intercepted, as they hadn't worked out a plausible excuse for moving laundry around at midnight.

When the weapons were all laid out for dawn, Mona whipped out her pen. "Can you lie down on this mat for me?" She was dead tired but had just remembered the prop for the morning session. Cai consented, a little bewildered by the request. "Keep still." Mona started drawing his outline, starting at his head, and explaining while she worked. "I've got ahead of myself with the women. I need to teach them some basic self-defence tomorrow, and you *really* don't want to be on the wrong end of it." She shook her head melodramatically. "Your twin will have to stand in for you." She rearranged his arm, pulling it out from his body to draw all the way around.

"You're a good-looking woman, Mona," Cai said, staring up at her, and Mona laughed so hard that it made her jog the line. "What's so funny?"

"Nothing. That's just a new one for me, that's all."

Cai felt he had to laugh along, if only to disguise his disappointment in her reaction. "So what do they normally say?"

Mona dug around in her memory for a chat-up line. "Nice tits." Cai giggled, too much, and she admonished him with a gentle swipe, but there was a chuckle in her throat. "Don't laugh, they're a nuisance. They get in the way."

"I'd like them to get in my way," he teased suggestively, and Mona rolled her eyes.

"Where did you find a sense of humour?"

"I can't think," he chuckled.

"Keep still, I've nearly finished." Her marker ended at his hip and she pulled his legs slightly apart. Cai held his breath when the marker reached between them and let it out slowly as she finished her work. "I haven't got the energy to pull you up."

He was looking up at the chapel roof. "Come here, you should look at this."

"Do you actually expect me to fall for that old one?" She chuckled again, but more wearily this time.

"It was worth a go," he sighed. "Anyway, it is genuinely interesting." Mona peered up; there *was* something painted on the ceiling. "You need to see it from here," he pushed. Mona groaned but lay down on the mat next to him. "It's your Christ," he pointed.

"He's not mine and, anyway, you make Christianity sound like a whole load of mad mumbo jumbo." She yawned out the last few words.

"Well, Nia's convinced that Christianity is partly responsible for the change in women's status – in Celtic society, anyway."

Mona's eyes were beginning to close. "Yep, sounds like Nia."

Cai ignored her, trying to remember some specifics of that particular rant. "Apparently, early Celtic women were rulers, warriors, landowners, judges, priests, and poets."

"And?" Mona mumbled, not sounding very interested at all.

"*And,*" he laboured, remembering Nia's conclusion. "Christianity came, men took over, and Celtic women lost equality and freedom."

"Are you trying to say it's not your fault?"

"Sort of," he sighed. Mona was lying on her side now but still looking at the ceiling. "I had a friend at university."

"Just the one?" she mumbled, already half asleep.

"Who summed Christianity up pretty well as far as I'm concerned." Cai didn't wait for her to interrupt this time. "Christianity." He coughed. "*The belief that Christ is a cosmic Jewish zombie – who is his own father. That he can make you live forever, if you symbolically eat his flesh, and telepathically tell him you accept him as your master. So that he can remove an evil force from your soul, which is present in all humanity; because a rib-woman was convinced to eat from a magical tree by an infinitely sadistic being, disguised as a talking snake.*"

Cai had been impressed with this synopsis for a long time but hadn't ever had an interested enough audience before now. He waited for some sort of reaction but Mona didn't respond. He hoped he hadn't upset her. "It was a joke," he explained and glimpsed down to see that she had fallen asleep. "Come on, let's go."

There was no reply. Cai tried shaking her gently, but decided there was little point in trying too hard; they'd have to be back here in five hours. His heart warmed with a strange alien emotion as he studied her sleeping face, and after a while, he settled her under an old velvet curtain.

≈

Cai awoke at dawn, stiff from lying on the hard mat and surprised that Mona was in his arms. She must have curled herself into him during the night. He gazed down at her, wondering how she would respond to a gentle kiss. Her eyes opened sleepily, and then closed again almost immediately. "Shit! We must have dozed off. What time is it?"

"Six-thirty."

Mona didn't move anything but the hand that skimmed his chest. "Why did you take off your t-shirt?" she whispered.

"It's under your head." He made good on his kiss, planting it softly on her hair.

≈

Cai's good temper was beginning to make Mona think more seriously about Emlyn's theory. He wasn't any more talkative than normal, but was smiling and happy as the women, fifteen today, congregated inside the chapel.

"We're calling it a dance and keep fit class. It's going to draw less attention," Siân explained to Mona. Both she and Nia were wearing leggings and breathless with excitement. "It fits in well with the clothes and keeps us under the radar. And if you're seen here, we can say we asked for warm-up tips!"

When Sioned arrived, Cai walked straight up to her and held his sister in a fierce hug. Ignoring her giggling friends, the siblings exchanged a few words and she rested her head against his chest as his hand soothed her hair. Siân and Nia turned, open-mouthed to Mona, who looked just as perplexed.

"I know!" she said, astounded. "Emlyn thinks it's brain damage."

"What have you done to him?" Nia slit her eyes and Mona suddenly felt embarrassed by their innocent sleeping arrangements. Initially it had felt quite natural and comforting waking up under Cai's arm, but as she had begun to wake fully, her proximity to his bare chest and smell had ignited a series of chemical reactions. It had taken all her will power not to climb on top of him this morning. "Nothing, I... we did have an argument, I may have shouted at him."

Cai had already started explaining about the weapons, and had given each woman a dagger and a short sword, allowing them to feel the weight. He approached Mona with a dazzling smile and came close enough to hold her by the top of her arms. She flushed deeply. "I've had an idea. I'm getting some stuff from the workshop but I'll be straight back."

Mona felt the burning stares of Siân and Nia on the back of her neck, but strode forward to meet the class. She recognised some of the newcomers from her first day in the training room, and now she could put a face to Cerys from the cubicle incident. "I'm glad you're here, Cerys. I think I may need some help with some basic defence stuff, and it would be great to see if we can sort out a short sequence."

Cerys and Gwen were initially sceptical, but she was used to dealing with that. Either they would come round or they wouldn't. "I saw you beat Emlyn." Cerys's tone was even. "I'd like to fight like that." Her friends nodded their desire to do the same.

"Why don't you come to the main sessions anymore? I could do with backup," Mona retorted. They mumbled something about men and politics. "If I can get you up to speed and into Emlyn's sessions, there'll be five of us to train the women here. Let's get going on the basic defence and weapons this morning, and we'll give the lads a little surprise later." Cerys laughed broadly – so she was the hooter from the loos.

By the time Cai came back with his haul, they had already devised two short sequences; all they needed was a victim.

Cai had suspended his outline on the mat from the rafters, scaling the chapel heights with ease. "Bit lower," Mona called from the ground. He'd attached clamps to the top of the heavy mat with the ropes attached to those. When Cai's outline was at roughly his height, Mona proceeded to draw within the figure.

Permanent marker in hand, she drew a face, with particular emphasis on the triangular nose, a cross in the chest, arrows on the top of each foot and finally a pair of gonads. There was a little tittering, but not as much as she'd expected.

"Where's his penis?" heckled a voice she didn't recognise. There was a definite roar of laughter this time.

Mona cringed at her insensitivity; Cai had slept with most of the women in this room and was related to the rest. "It's not the penis we're interested in," Mona replied too hastily, in an effort to mask her mistake.

"Speak for yourself," came a swift response.

Mona tried to persist with the lesson but the room reverberated with hilarity. "The testicles are the really weak spot," she tried to shout over the din but to no avail. Even Siân and Nia were chuckling, and she glanced at Cai whose face was buried deep in his hands. "I'm sorry; I didn't mean to embarrass you," she muttered sideways.

When he finally looked up, Cai was still smiling. "I had it coming," he groaned.

≈

The added assistance of Cerys and her team improved the session and each woman had her turn at beating up Cai's facsimile. If being attacked from behind, it was a sharp elbow to the solar plexus, incapacitating breathing. A swift, hard stamp down on top of the foot, a fist or backwards head-butt to the nose, and finally a knee or elbow to the groin. "You must never let men get close enough to grapple, even if you're a better fighter. They are stronger, bigger and heavier," Mona stressed.

"Ieuan said you beat Cai at wrestling yesterday. Surely you're strong enough to break a hold?" Gwen asked. Understandably, Gwen had taken the longest to thaw out.

"Yes, I'm strong, very strong, but it was hard work for me yesterday. Cai's an accomplished fighter, and that's more dangerous than strength and bulk. Though if you ever *do* find yourself compromised in a hold, then you can always try..." Mona lifted her eyes in thought, trying to imagine a countermove but failing. "Cai, would you mind." He glanced at the kicks and marks on his doppelganger and seemed reluctant. "I'm just going to talk through how I'd manage it," she assured him.

They walked it through, with Cai wrapping his arms around both of Mona's from behind and pinning them to her side. She struggled but he was too strong. "You see my arms are completely useless." She tried to move them. "But I could still throw my head back." Mona moved her head at a snail's pace to make light contact against the bridge of his nose. "The groin move won't work here, as there isn't enough space between us. The foot stamp would still work if you could raise your leg high enough. But that's about it – I can't even throw him." Mona tried to bend forward but only succeeding in pushing herself back into him. The sensation was powerfully erotic, and she straightened briskly. "He's too tall," she coughed. Cai continued to hold on tightly. "Thanks, you can let go now." He did, and Mona almost wished he hadn't. "OK, that's about it for now. We'll start working with the weapons tomorrow, they'll be sharpened by Friday."

10

Leaving

By Thursday, it was all coming together. The women had been practising diligently, and with the extra training power they would be ready to start with sharpened swords in the morning. Emlyn's daytime and evening sessions were over, and the night work was beginning. Cai and Mona were hollowed out with exhaustion, but set to work, sharpening the weapons in his tiny subterranean workshop.

"Does the radio work?" She was nosing around on the carefully organised shelves while Cai set up the tools. Mona was surprised to see the battered old set there. "I didn't think you were allowed technology."

Cai didn't look up to answer. "We have electricity, Mo." He'd never spoken her nickname before, and it didn't sound quite right. "We're allowed analogue, for as long as it lasts, just nothing with a chip – nothing digital. Ifan reckons it would make us vulnerable somehow." Cai clearly didn't agree.

"And you think he's a mad old duffer?" Mona asked, and Cai snorted in response.

"It's frustrating; I want to move forward. I can see another way for the community to survive – solar, wind, hydro. There are so many opportunities in renewables."

"I felt that way about Brendan, and his obsession with cameras."

The mention of her uncle's name re-opened the healing memory. "Seems like he was right," she added quietly, and busied herself tuning the radio until she felt the pain subside.

"You may not like the station," Cai warned.

Mona didn't like the Welsh conversation programme, and she fiddled the tuner until she could hear music. The only melody she could find belonged to an era of tea dances and slicked-back hair. "I love this one." She swayed daftly, as if in a dream. "By the way, you never did tell me what sort of music you like," Mona recalled.

Cai grinned but ignored the comment. "We have to concentrate on this job, concentrate completely – or we'll cut ourselves."

Mona turned the music down to a background hum, and watched him work. He was using a metal file. "Wouldn't it be quicker with a bench grinder or an angle grinder?"

Cai shook his head. "The friction heats up the blade, destroying the temper and heat treatment. You can lose the geometry too." He sighed at the task ahead. "I'm afraid it's the old-fashioned way for us."

Cai laid a sword on the workbench and propped up the tip, level with a shallow block of wood. He slowly drew the file back and forth, working methodically along the length of the blade, before turning it over and repeating the exercise. "You need to keep the angle at thirty degrees, if you can. We'll work them all up and then start with the whetstone."

Mona turned the music up a little bit and began work at her own bench. Cai checked the first one and then left her to it. After fifty blades, and two hours of toil, they had reached the whetstone stage.

Cai had arranged his finished swords in groups of five. "You like a bit of symmetry, I see," Mona noted.

Cai glanced at her random piles of swords and raised his substantial eyebrows. "Tea." He passed her a grimy looking mug. "It's clean, just stained."

It was hot underground, with no windows, and the necessity for privacy forced them to keep the door shut – it was stifling. "So, is there a gathering every Friday?"

"Not always, but they need a reward after all the torture of this week." He smiled. "Why, are you planning on going?"

"I don't think so. I'm almost too tired to stand, but a few of them have asked, so I thought I might. And they're not a bad bunch – apart from Geraint."

Cai pulled a face then sniggered. "No one likes Geraint." He took a sip of tea. "So what do you think of Ieuan?"

"He's not that bad, his reactions are a bit slow, but apart from that…"

"I think he's keen on you."

"Really?" Mona fluttered her eyelashes comically but Cai wasn't receptive to humour tonight. "Well, he's drop-dead gorgeous of course."

"Not your type?" Cai cracked a smile.

"No, not my type," she laughed. "Is he your big rival then?"

"What do you mean by that?"

"I don't know." She shrugged. "There seems to be some bad blood between you." Cai didn't reply. "Anyway, I've been warned about him too," Mona chuckled, and his eyes snapped up to hers.

"I'm not sure I should be compared to Ieuan."

"No, I heard that you're in an entirely different league." Cai's face fell a little. "Is sex equal for men and women here?" Mona asked without an edge, "Or is there the same double standard that exists with the fighting?" Cai looked uncomfortable. "I'm not prying," she said quickly. "Nia explained about the attitude to sex here, but she doesn't seem to have it, and I wondered if it was just something that Druids spouted. In the same way they talk about women fighting on equal terms." Cai opened his mouth to say something, but he wasn't quite fast enough. "They say it, but it's not true – the men don't want the women to fight, do they?"

How did Mona have the knack of turning everything on its head? Cai had never felt the need to justify his sexual appetite. Nor had he ever even considered a double standard. "I suppose if you're asking could Nia get away with it, I'd have to say no." He weighed up the question in his mind. "And it's more complicated than you think. We're both high ranking, but Nia is an Ovate Druid, and I'm a warrior. Even if Nia were a man, she would be expected to abstain more – in order to get in touch with the mystical realm. Soldiers are expected to have a greater... need."

"So if there are no women warriors there isn't the precedent for sexual equality? It looks like you're almost as bad as those Christian bastards." Mona was making light of it, but Cai was beginning to see her point, and his face twisted in what might have been reluctant agreement. "How would you feel about Sioned making the same choices as you? She's just as gorgeous, she'll also be a soldier, and they'll be queuing up."

Cai was ready for this argument. "I expect her to have a healthy appetite, but I'd prefer it if she had healthy relationships as well." Mona knew instinctively what the next question would be. "How about you, Mona?"

She laughed, and treated him to the full megawattage of her smile; it was like the sun coming out. Mona thought briefly about her sexual past; a variety of short-lived liaisons in the back of wood and metal stores. All very strenuous and exciting, but largely unemotional. Perhaps she and Cai weren't all that different after all. Mona decided not to answer his question. "We'd better get on with it. Have you got two whetstones?"

He did, and Cai applied a thin film of oil to each. "We're polishing now, taking off metal to reveal the edge." Cai began rhythmically and slowly to draw the blade back and forth across the stone. He kept the angle at thirty degrees again, and inspected it from time to time. "This is the second stage; there's one more stage after this. Are you alright to carry on?"

It had started to cool a little as the night progressed. "I'm fine for now," she answered. "I'll tell you if I can't go on." Cai doubted she would tell him anything of the sort.

They worked steadily and in silence, the sound of the fizzing radio accompanying that of the rasping blades. After two more hours, they were both ready to stop.

"The next stage could be bloody; we shouldn't carry on tired." Cai yawned and stretched luxuriously and Mona forced herself to look away.

"But we need them for tomorrow." Mona absolutely needed to stop, but also wanted to meet her deadline.

"It's only a timescale you've created," Cai reasoned. "What's the rush?"

Mona started picking up the oily paper towels from the floor by her bench; she was an untidy worker, and felt that she'd violated the peace of his workshop with her messy abandon. "I want to do everything I can for them before I go. I'm leaving on Monday, my month's up and I want to move on – find my brother. It's all sorted with Ifan."

After a long silence, during which she cleared the bench of debris, Cai cleared his throat. "We should come back here at five in the morning then. That will give us just enough time to arm them for seven."

Cai methodically cleaned his own bench, then joined her by the sink to wash his hands. "There's oil all over your face," he whispered while dabbing her cheek gently with the damp paper towel.

Cai was only centimetres away, and despite the crudity of the advance, she was finding him increasingly hard to resist. "Please don't, Cai." She stilled his hand, closing her eyes, and he backed away slightly.

"I don't want you to go," he confessed, in a voice that hardly sounded at all.

"I need to go now – before I fall for you," she answered honestly. Cai flinched, but it wasn't cruelty. Mona knew she couldn't afford to have her heart broken, not if she could walk away now.

≈

During the hours of the night left to him, Cai wrestled with his choices. He should of course let Mona go, but he knew that she

144

would probably die within days of leaving here. Cai guessed grimly that the Irish wouldn't send less than five men to do the job, and something wrenched in his gut at the thought.

On the other hand, Mona was a massively capable woman. She was forewarned now at least, and she'd survived this long. Once Mona was gone, Cai reasoned that the ache in his chest would leave with her, and he could reclaim the man he'd lost – life would make perfect sense again. Mona opened the door to him at dawn smiling through her tiredness, and he knew he could never let her go.

≈

"So we're going to blend the rest of the metal with the edge." Cai took a postage stamp-sized square of wet and dry paper, dipped it in a little water, and moved his fingers over the sword's edge, with only the paper between his fingers and the sharp blade. "Keep your fingers at thirty degrees."

Mona was dubious. "You've got to be joking?"

"I told you it was a bit tricky. Will you be able to do it?" Cai was unshaven, with dark circles beneath his blue eyes and beetling brows. He seemed a little deranged and dangerous this morning.

"I need tea first," she admitted.

Mona watched him work while the kettle boiled. It didn't look difficult, just potentially lethal. She set herself up at the adjacent bench and started work, glad that he didn't want to talk about yesterday and her decision to leave.

An hour and a half later, Mona stopped. "We've got to go. Let's leave the last few for now, they're spare anyway."

The sudden noise of her voice after such a long silence startled Cai, and the blade sliced a finger, cutting it deep and angled. Dripping blood across the bench and floor, he moved rapidly to the sink, alerting Mona to his injury.

She turned on the tap and went straight to the first aid box, letting him run the blood out underneath the water and down the

145

plughole. It wasn't stopping quickly enough, so Mona sat him down on the stool and applied pressure for a while. Cai let her take his hand, watching hers as she worked. They were strong, square and not at all feminine; and he wondered why the sight of them ministering to his cut made something catch in his throat.

Mona dried and closed the wound firmly with two Steri-Strips. "You're a messy worker, Mona Jones." He frowned at her bench. "Don't you ever put tools back?" It was just something to say, and it was better than asking her not to leave again.

"Yes, I know. I'll tidy up in a minute," she confessed while continuing to bandage him. When Mona had completed the knot she released his hand. As she let his hand drop, Cai propelled his head very slowly forward until it met her stomach, and she ruffled his mane affectionately. "I'm going to miss you, Cai Owens, you aren't such a bad man after all."

"*Paid â mynd.* – Don't go," he whispered into her stomach.

"You'll be fine," she answered softly. But in that split second, as Cai spoke his hopes in Welsh, Mona wanted desperately to stay.

≈

Cai's injury made them a few minutes late, but they were excused when the women received their gleaming blades.

"They're really sharp." Cai held up his wound. "You must be careful today," he warned firmly. "You would normally have longer to practice with them blunt, but we're on a bit of a mission." His eyes strayed to Mona. "Mo and Cerys will give the demo, *slowly*, but if there are too many injuries we're going to have to rethink, so concentrate."

Cai had a good way with the women, Mona thought. Unpatronising and uncompromising. She was sure he'd be leading the entire warrior group before long.

There were inevitable but acceptable injuries. Nia and Siân had come prepared and had set up a little field hospital on a table in the corner. By the end of the session, Mona was facing a group of women utterly transformed in the space of a week.

"I'm proud of you." She felt them flush with pride. "If any more of you want to join the main group on Monday, you should. If you're ready to learn more, ask Cai, he knows his stuff." But when she smiled over at him, Cai wasn't looking at her.

Mona couldn't think of anything else to say, and the women began to disperse. She sat on the steps of the altar, pulling on her boots as Sioned approached. Mona cringed – she was rather hoping to avoid any more confrontation with this family. "Well done, Sioned. You could be a great fighter if you keep it up and lose a bit of the attitude."

The young girl eyed her suspiciously and Mona continued strapping her boots. "You're leaving?"

"What makes you say that?"

Sioned replied petulantly with a question of her own. "What have you done to my brother?"

Mona had had enough, and swung her jacket out, thrusting in an arm. "He cut his own finger; it will heal. I have to go."

"I'm sorry," Sioned grunted, though she didn't sound it. "He looks bad and I thought you might know what's wrong."

"We're both exhausted. He just needs to rest." She flicked Sioned on the arm. "Look after him."

Mona didn't wait to see if Cai was following on, but he reappeared at Emlyn's session, looking even more haggard – if that were possible. "We've only got to get through this last one," she spoke woodenly, without even the energy to look at him. "I'm too tired to fight anymore."

Dafydd started walking over – something clearly on his mind. When he spoke to Cai, the Welsh sounded a little irritable. "There's a shout," Cai translated to Mona, "and Em's left Dafydd in charge."

"Where's Bryn?"

"He's gone too: crew mechanic." There was further discussion between the men, but Mona's fatigue made her oblivious to its importance. "Come on," Cai said after Dafydd had gone, "we've been summoned to Ifan and, apparently, he's not happy."

≈

They trudged up and into Ifan's rooms, ready for a confrontation. "*Eisteddwch i fwyta* – Eat, drink," he ordered them from behind his desk.

Mona collapsed on the huge sofa and Cai slid down to join her. "Will you bloody well speak in English; I *am* here you know," Mona interrupted grumpily; she was now hallucinating with exhaustion. Ifan growled at her blatant disrespect but, bizarrely, Cai began to chuckle infectiously and Mona could not help but join in. "What, Ifan? What have we done now?" she challenged, choking slightly through her giggles. Judging from the grin and twinkle in his eye, Ifan wasn't immune to Cai's contagious chuckling either.

"I just thought you needed a break. Emlyn can be dreadfully demanding, and Siân tells me you've both been missing meals, and getting too little sleep. It's a thank you for training the women… before you go." Mona smiled tightly at Ifan, and he nodded back. "The paperwork is done and we can perform the ceremony on Sunday. What time are you meeting the solicitor?"

"I need to be at the bus stop by nine on Monday morning, or the lawyer will leave without me."

Ifan smiled kindly. "Someone will get you to Moelfre in time." His gaze shifted to Cai, who wasn't looking at anyone, and Ifan flapped his hand at the sparse offering on the desk. "You should eat this banquet and sleep here for a little while. I've got business with the healers, and no one will disturb you. I've let it be known that both of you are officially working here, for me, for the next few hours."

By the time Mona returned to the sofa with tea and sandwiches, Cai had leaned back and closed his eyes. He really was a funny colour – perhaps he'd lost more blood than she realised. "That was kind of him," she said, settling the plate between them. Mona handed Cai some tea but he didn't take any food. "You should eat something."

He cradled his tea for a while before taking the first sip. "Sugar?" his face creased.

"You've lost blood. Don't be a baby."

Mona disappeared for a while and returned bootless, coatless and holding two pillows and a blanket. At her request, Cai got up and she placed a pillow at each end of the sofa.

After discarding his boots and jacket, Cai lifted one pillow and laid it next to the other. "Just let me lie down next to you." Mona stretched out on the sofa and settled under the blanket, before lifting it up for him to join her beneath it.

≈

Ifan wasn't surprised to find them in each other's arms – it was what he had been hoping for. They were much easier to be around when their energies weren't fighting each other. Although even asleep, their combined power filled the room, making his eyes hurt and his head swim.

Ifan wondered if there was anyone left who could really read power anymore, or if it was merely another dying Celtic language. If he concentrated hard enough, he was just about able to make out the slight variation in the power haze. Mona's force pulsed, not metronomically but with random spikiness. Cai's energy seemed to encompass Mona at the moment, and Ifan wasn't entirely sure, but he felt that there might be a cooler, bluer tone to his energy.

They were as still as sculpture in sleep and Ifan shook his head at them. Could these two young people be the answer to the imminent extinction of magic? He wasn't adept at seeing the future, but something about their contented sleep tugged at his heart, and he fancied he saw a new white shimmer around them.

Ifan shook himself out of idleness and reprimanded his romantic notions. Somehow, he didn't think their path was going to be easy.

≈

Cai woke up under her arm, her chin on his head. He had thrown both an arm and a leg over her in sleep, and for a moment it felt like the most uncommonly natural way to wake up – as if they always slept together like this. "You can't lay there all day, lad." Ifan's tone was mellow. Cai checked his watch as he retrieved both limbs from Mona, and she woke, releasing his upper body. "You've slept the whole day away and they're after you," Ifan chided softly. "You're best to go to supper now, and show your faces."

≈

They wandered back hand in hand along the corridors, walking in the dream-like state of the over-rested. Mona had loved holding Cai in his sleep, and wondered if that was what the other women had loved about him – wondered if she had fallen for one of his standard ploys. It was beginning to matter less and less though: she was going on Monday and the die had been cast.

People had begun to swarm past on their way to the canteen, and Cai pulled her protectively to his side to avoid the crush. This close, his smell was a heady perfume and Mona liked the darkness his stubble lent him. She touched it on impulse, smooth one way, so harsh the other. Each short hair pivoted in its own sphere as she rubbed it in a rhythmic circle. Addicted to the novel feeling, she started using both hands, and then moved her lips to his face, brushing them lightly up and down his jaw. They tingled on the upward stroke.

Cai took her hands from his face and held them. That same electric charge was running between each nipple and completing the circuit in her groin. There was a sea of hormones screaming in her ears, so loud now that Mona couldn't hear what Cai said, but knew what he was asking, and she agreed urgently.

Her room was nearest and they fell inside and against the wall. Their kissing became instantly savage, and her eyes teared as his stubble tore at her face. Mona's entire being was lost in his mouth, in the force of his tongue.

Mona had stopped kissing him just long enough to rip off his top. When she resumed, it was not at his mouth; she had pinned his shoulders to the wall and was greedily sucking at one of his nipples while manipulating the other in her fingers. As her hand moved from his chest over his stomach and towards his still-caged penis, Cai thought, for the first time in his life, that he wouldn't be able to hold it together. He pushed her away and took a ragged breath, pulling himself back from the brink.

By the time he was under control again, Mona had lost both vest and bra. Her breasts filled and weighed down each of his large hands. Backing her up to the bed, he dropped his hands from her breasts to unbuckle her trousers, sucking a large hard nipple into his mouth as he bent down to ease them off her hips.

As soon as they were both naked on the bed, the intensity level increased. There seemed to be some sort of pulsing power in Mona's body that was drawing him in. She moved her hips in small circles as he sucked and kissed her chest and throat. She gasped as he slid his hand between her thighs – Mona was opening herself to him, pulling him in, and he had to go.

Cai entered her body as slowly as he could manage, but once she had him there, Mona gradually picked up the pace and in a very short space of time, he could feel and hear her shuddering to an orgasm. Her surge was making him come, drawing it all out. He was coming, coming inside her, he was coming… and then she was gone.

Mona had pulled herself off and away from him, and he was left horribly alone. Cai lay on his back convulsing, as his own orgasm continued to pulse over his stomach. He was appalled that she watched him as he gasped and trembled until it was over.

"That was a close one." She expressed her relief succinctly.

"I'm sorry." He didn't know what else to say.

"I thought you always had a condom with you?" Mona remained reliably matter of fact.

"I did, I do… I just." Words failed him. "I don't know what happened there, Mo." Shame turned his face into the pillow.

Mona poked his chest after a minute. "That's a pity. I rather hoped we could make a night of it." Mona laughed at the eagerness on his face as Cai fumbled on some clothes and raced for his supply. "And have a shave will you, I'm cut to ribbons," she called after him.

11

War

Mona was still asleep. She'd slept right through the tinny bell on her ancient, travelling alarm clock and was lying gloriously naked beside him. It was a small single bed and Cai didn't have to move far to kiss her gently on the lips.

"Morning," she whispered. Cai responded by deepening the kiss. Early on during last night's marathon his body had become addicted to hers, and it was ready for another fix. "Training," Mona muttered half-heartedly between kisses.

"Saturday," he murmured against her neck.

"I promised Emlyn," she added, pushing Cai on to his back. "I'm off…"

Cai didn't let her finish. "No." He sat up and pulled her on to him, so that he could resume the kissing. He wanted to feel her breasts with his lips again, but she sat up.

"No what?" Mona was scrunching her face, trying to decide what he meant.

"No, you're not leaving." Cai sounded pretty convinced of the fact.

"I've got to meet the solicitor on Monday."

"Alright, we'll both go and see him, then we'll spend some time *alone* at the cottages." He waggled his eyebrows with intent and Mona laughed.

153

"Ah, so that's why you kept the cottages at Swnt."

"It's not the *only* reason," he whispered while running both hands along each of her thighs. "I'm not letting you go, not yet."

"Oh, I remember," she smirked, "seven days." Mona's mind ran back to the incident in the loos and Cerys's fateful words. She was one of those women now – addicted, despite her best efforts. Cai was looking confused. "It was just something Cerys said," she explained softly.

Cai stopped smoothing her thigh. "What did she say?" He looked a little startled.

"Nothing really, just that you can only manage seven days with a woman." She was teasing now and kissed his propped up shoulder very lightly. His eyes shut at the contact.

"Not true. I lasted fourteen days with Gwen." He opened them again, smiling. "But I was desperate to leave after seven."

"You are a bad, bad man." Mona kissed him lightly again, in the same place.

"And you are a wild woman." Cai's voice was an awed whisper.

Mona pulled back to take a good look at him, and something in her memory clicked into place. She gasped. "*I knew it!* I knew I'd seen your face before." Mona smoothed his hair away from his forehead, and moved his face this way and that in her hands.

"What?" he wondered at her bizarre behaviour.

"Have you got a brother called Leigh?"

Cai shook his head. "Arwel, and technically..."

Mona wasn't listening, she had covered him with her body, and was whispering in his ear, her hand tracing the muscles in his neck. "What are you like under a high ball?" she teased. Cai's own hands were greedy for any part of Mona's body that they could reach, and he massaged her buttocks as she continued her questions. "How hard?" Mona caught his earlobe and ground it lightly between her teeth, "Is your tackle?" Cai groaned. Mona moved from his pectoral muscles and let her hands drift towards his abdominals. She straddled him with a devilish look in her eye. "How dirty is your sidestep, Cai?"

Cai sat up, and pulled her underneath him. "Filthy," he mouthed and she giggled.

≈

While Mona showered, Cai lay in bed, enjoying the feeling of languid fulfilment. He would have worn a huge grin but a splinter of annoyance was poking into his mind.

Cai had never experienced jealousy before but he suspected that he was feeling something like it now. Mona obviously still had some strong feelings for this Leigh. Her previous relationships weren't really any of his business, and after all, she didn't seem to be too worried about all his conquests, but it niggled him nonetheless.

When a still wet and deliciously naked Mona arrived back from the shower, he lost his train of thought for a while. Having regained it, he asked the question: "So, Leigh? Were you going with him for long?"

"What?" Mona turned in puzzlement as she fastened her bra. Then she understood. "I was talking about *Leigh Halfpenny*," she answered, and carried on dressing.

Cai waited for her to explain but she didn't. "So, what happened?" he asked.

"Leigh Halfpenny, the *rugby player*," she said, as if answering his question.

"I got that," he replied patiently.

Mona sat by him on the bed, in shock. "He's a Welsh international, Cai. You know, Cardiff Blues? Best full back in the universe?" Mona shook her head, and half closed her eyes. "Are you *actually* Welsh?" Cai frowned. "You look like him. A lot like him." She touched a finger to his face. "Though I'd say you're more likely his evil, darker twin."

"I didn't think you watched television," Cai said, hiding his relief by sliding out of bed.

"We didn't." Mona remembered something and laughed sadly. "Brendan was obsessed with the game. We got *Rugby World* every month, no matter where we were. And we listened to the matches on the radio, whenever we could."

Cai suddenly felt a huge well of sorrow for her loss and pulled her against him. "What about the girl stuff?" he asked softly.

"I haven't had a lot of that," she smiled. "We used to take turns at reading the magazine first, though."

"Stay with me?" Cai asked, squeezing her tightly against him.

≈

Breakfast was an ordeal in a couple of ways. Firstly, it seemed they were under a great deal of scrutiny from virtually everyone. Secondly, the public nature of the event prevented them from touching each other. Nia and Siân pounced on them immediately. "Where have you two been hiding?"

The key was to not look at each other. "We... we've been... working with Ifan," Mona replied, sticking to the party line.

The women across the table from her were implacable, their folded arms tucked up under their bosoms. Both mother and daughter were staring at them like stern bookends. "Working on what?" Nia asked.

They had to look at each other then, and Cai flushed a deep scarlet when their eyes met. "Welsh," Mona offered belatedly, but the damage was done.

"Are you blushing, Cai Owens?" his aunt gasped in disbelief. But he had left for the toast machine, and so was out of earshot when the tirade began.

"You could at least be discreet," Nia hissed. "Gods, Mona! I warned you about him. I told you! He's not a good man – he makes Cúchulainn look tame. Please don't say you've fallen for him – not you as well."

When Nia had finished reprimanding her, Siân took over, covering old ground then adding new. Eventually Mona's face fell into her hands, so she didn't see Cai return with a huge plate of toast.

Though she did feel him sit beside her and pull her close. "Leave her alone, Siân," he warned amiably. "At least she was warned about me. Nobody gave *me* fair warning." Cai dazzled Mona with his relaxed smile, and it was Mona's turn to flush.

The emotional intensity of their sexual encounter had completely overpowered Mona. It was evident that Nia was disappointed in Mona's failure to resist her cousin, and Mona wanted to be disappointed in herself as well, but she was just too content to bother. She could already taste the bitterness of the rejection to come, but Mona would gratefully accept a repeat of last night – on almost any terms. At least she had him for six more days.

Putting the plate on the table and taking a slice for himself, Cai motioned to Mona. "Eat up, we've got work to do later." He twitched his eyebrows and she choked.

"That's not funny, Cai," Siân spluttered.

Mona disagreed. "It is a bit funny." Cai's reawakened sense of humour would make the coming week even more delicious.

Nia and Siân then started up on Cai in Welsh. When it became serious enough for Cai to raise his voice, Mona intervened. "What's the problem?" She looked from face to face; clearly there was an issue.

"I'll tell you later," Cai promised.

"If I need to know, I should know now," she replied. Cai raised his voice again to them, more harshly this time, finally taking his arm from Mona's waist and using it to emphasise his argument. "Tell me, Nia," Mona demanded, but it was Siân who explained.

"Cai's family, our family, are part of the dominant bloodline. I'm afraid there are protocols for preserving Druid power – as you know, the magic is failing." Cai shook his head in disgust, but Siân continued with her calm explanation. "All families are supposed to have some power, but there's a gradient, and there are laws that have to be obeyed about passing on that power. Cai isn't completely at liberty to choose who he wants to be with."

"It's not exactly that, Mona." Nia was clearly unhappy with her mother's explanation, and her inner pedant was revealing itself again. "Cai can't just produce children. Space and resources are limited here, and he must attempt to produce a child with the maximum potential for power. Once a mate is chosen he must prioritise them as his legitimate family. Cai's arguing that there isn't a woman here who has anywhere near your power." Cai growled something at the women, which caused both sets of eyebrows to rise in unison.

"I don't understand – I'm not after trying to *produce* any children," Mona said shaking her head, still a little mystified. Cai grunted again, this time in agreement with her.

"I'm sorry, but no matter what you or Cai want, you could never be together." Nia paused to deliver the blow. "You bear the *mark, Mona.* I'm sorry, I tried to warn you."

Mona gently laid her hand over Cai's, which lay motionless now on the table between them. "I'll be happy with my seven days," she mumbled and started to get up. "Come on, we have to train."

Several things happened at once in that moment. Dafydd and Bryn tore into the canteen, a loud klaxon began bleating from the wall, and Siân fainted. She had fallen against Nia, who had gone deathly pale.

Mona launched herself across the table to smooth Siân's hair back, gently calling her name. After half a minute she came to, whispering one word over and over. "*Na, na, na.*"

The rest of the community in the canteen remained remarkably calm. At the sounding of the klaxon there had been a horrified silence, followed by a dignified but hasty evacuation. *A fire drill? A fire?* Mona's thoughts were scattered by the screaming noise.

Dafydd had finished talking to Cai and came over to help his sister to her feet; he enfolded her tightly and she left with him – Nia on their heels. Mona felt Cai boring a message into her soul, but she didn't know what it could be.

The horn continued to blare from the wall above them; he wouldn't hear any question she asked him now, so she followed him from the room. There were alarms spread throughout the institution, so the noise was constant and widespread, but there were pockets of relative quiet.

Cai stopped as soon as he could hear his own voice, though Mona was still forced to lip-read in order to catch all the words. "It's a call to arms, Mona; we have to meet the council."

Mona felt a rising in her chest, and couldn't work out if it was fear or excitement at the prospect of a real fight at last.

≈

They could hear the shouting from the meeting room well before they reached it. Cai paused in front of the door, grasping Mona on each side of her head as if to force his words into her brain. "This will be a hard meeting for you – for us. Sit next to Nia and she will translate. I won't be far away."

Then they entered the maelstrom.

There were only about twenty people in the room, though the noise level suggested at least fifty. Despite the intensity, all eyes turned to Mona and Cai as they joined the meeting. Ifan looked at her as he always did, with something between fear and pity. The others scrutinised them with expressions that ranged from curiosity to hostility.

Mona joined Nia immediately. "Translate it as it comes, don't edit to spare my feelings."

Nia agreed and updated her. "Quite a few of the council are blaming the attack on your presence here, and your *mark*." Mona's hand automatically felt for the zip on her jacket, making sure she was covered to the neck. Nia's eyes flicked to the zip but she carried on. "There's a mass of small boats, from the east coast of Ireland, on their way here, now. We had confirmation from our sources in the coastguard and RNLI an hour ago. They will be here in three hours, but the plan is to send a force out to intercept them."

That seemed a solid plan; attack them before they made land.

Mona ran through the strategy in her head. It would be difficult to fight on boats; they would have to use weapons. "Will they use guns?" she asked out loud.

Cai was convinced that the Irish would follow ancient Celtic rules, but Mona still wasn't so sure. Nobody at the Conway even knew why they were attacking, let alone how. Nia winced at the thought. "Nobody has used guns before. We don't understand the reasoning behind these attacks, but wholesale annihilation has never been their way. There are so few of us left, after all."

"I need to fight," Mona stated.

"That's what Cai is arguing for, but there are several objections. Firstly, that *you* are the enemy and they're afraid you'll attack our fighters once at sea. Secondly, that you cannot fight for us unless you are officially accepted into the community, and lastly, that you are too powerful to be let off the island – no matter whose side you're on."

There was a lot more shouting and standing up all of a sudden, with the focus on Cai and his grandfather Hywel. "What now?"

"Cai's asking that you be made part of the community right now – this minute – so that you can fight with them."

"What's the objection?"

Nia coughed uncomfortably. "Hywel believes that Cai has only suggested that as a way to continue your... intimacy." Mona could hear the creative editing in Nia's pause. "And that he's being selfish, by putting his famous sexual appetite ahead of the well-being of the clan." Nia took a sharp inward breath. "Cai says that he wants to let the council know that he is choosing you – as his life partner." The decibels trebled for a moment. "Sorry, Mona, everyone's screaming now."

While it calmed down, Mona considered how totally insane the situation had become. How far did Cai have to go to allow her to fight?

"Hywel is denouncing him as his grandson, if he chooses you. Cai says that's fine."

"Denouncing?" Mona questioned.

"He gives up the privileges of his birth right and won't become war leader."

"I won't make that much difference in a fight," she muttered, knowing what she had to do, but needing some more information. "Can you tell me who's on Cai's side?"

"Emlyn, Dafydd, Bryn. Ifan wants you to stay here, though for different reasons. He imagines that what you've taught them will be enough, even without you there."

"What are his reasons?" Mona asked, feeling betrayed by the old boy.

"He thinks you are important, and that you may be the target for the attack." Nia listened to the Archdruid's reasons before relaying them. "That it would be safer for you, *and* the warriors, if you remained here with a small contingent. Bryn has been mentioned, and he doesn't like it, but he's the second, so it would seem sensible." The conversation continued in more measured tones. "They're discussing the crew for the lifeboats. Bryn, Dai, Geraint and Dwynwen will also stay – as they're regular crew."

"Won't there be questions?"

"Yes, but we have cover in Beaumaris and Holyhead. They're the nearest stations on the island – we've had to plan ahead." The timbre of the meeting changed again and Nia concentrated on the discussion intently. "Ifan wants Dafydd to stay. He's in line to be the next Archdruid and he doesn't want both sons in the fight." She turned to Mona. "Cai has to go."

Of course, Mona nodded. "When do they leave?"

"As soon as possible."

Mona grabbed Cai's arm while he was in mid-flow, but he turned to listen. "You're running out of time, and I won't make that much difference in the fight." She paused. "I might actually be better off here. Perhaps we should spread our strength?"

"You need to be with me, where I can protect you," he said fiercely, eyeing his grandfather.

"That's not your job now. You're an important part of the chain of command. You need to go. I will stay." Mona glanced up at the still-rumbling discussions. "If you tell them now, it should bring things to a close – before the Irish actually arrive."

Mona re-joined Nia, and she began translating again. "He's told them of your decision to stay. They all seem happier, apart from Em and Cai." Mona didn't need a translation for that; she could feel the tension from the main players. Hywel was furious with his grandson, furious and quite clearly disappointed. "Bryn has been asked to stay as home guard, and he's not at all happy about it. Emlyn is asking you to go with him to the radio room now, to discuss the defences." There were plenty of objections being thrown about. "Apparently you will be Bryn's second, even though you're not officially part of the community. Some people don't like that either."

Nia paused for the shouting to die down. In the meantime, Emlyn had come over. "It's time." The big coxswain smiled tightly. "They'll all still be talking about it as the Irish slit their throats." He turned to Cai. "Be ready at the docks in twenty minutes. We need to talk, Mona; come with me."

She followed wordlessly, with Bryn in tow.

≈

The radio room was as low tech as possible. It housed a bank of old VHF radios, a Morse code machine, a whole set of semaphore flags, and maps – lots of maps. At least it was straightforward. "Nothing with a microprocessor. It's the old boy's most absolute rule," Emlyn answered her bewildered expression.

"Doesn't it make communication with you impossible?" Mona asked, completely non-plussed by the law.

"Yes, but it also makes communication with anyone else impossible. I think that's the point." He flicked a hand towards the VHF radios. "The signal will last up to thirty miles, after that we're on our own. We've got a short-wave radio set here – that's the big aerial you can see. If we make land anywhere, we'll contact you via this machine. You should have someone on twenty-four hour radio duty."

"How about a physical lookout, a boat?"

"We normally rely on our friends in the coastguard and RNLI, but it might be worth it, if you get concerned. The Archdruid will know if you need more information." He put his hand on her shoulder. "I think we've both got some goodbyes to say." He sighed. "I'd rather have you fighting with us."

"Have you got any idea why Em? Why they're attacking now?"

Emlyn narrowed his eyes and Mona thought she might hear something from him other than the usual blank ignorance. But he changed his mind and shrugged. "No, not a clue. But at least we're getting the chance to engage, this time round."

Mona wanted to ask what he meant, but this was no time for idle questions. "Keep safe, Em," Mona said quietly.

Emlyn clasped the ever silent Bryn to his shoulder and left the radio room. Bryn and Mona exchanged the look of helplessness, shared only by those left behind.

≈

Ifan struggled to make it back to his rooms without throwing up. The insipid dread he had felt for the last month was now a monstrous reality. There could be no coincidence between Mona's arrival and the attack. It made him nauseous to even contemplate it, but he was forced to conclude that there was a spy in their ranks. Either that or Mona herself was orchestrating an elaborate plot from here, and communicating with the threat in Ireland.

Mona was the key either way. Brendan must have sent her here for that reason – his last resort. Now they were at war and he was frightened for his boys – for both his boys.

There was a sharp rap at his door. "Come in, Emlyn." Ifan tried not to sound querulous.

"You wanted to see me?" Emlyn was battle ready and eager to go.

Ifan could taste the excruciating and bitter awkwardness between them. They were strangers.

"I wanted to explain, about Mona." Emlyn looked like he didn't have much time to waste, forcing Ifan to blurt out his carefully prepared speech. "She's important, Emlyn; I think the Irish are after her. That's why she's not going – I couldn't risk it."

Emlyn sighed and moved his weight from hip to hip. "You reckon we've been infiltrated?" Ifan was surprised that Emlyn had reached the same conclusion, and he didn't manage to hide it. "I'm not stupid, Father. Mona arrives here and all hell breaks loose. Someone has got past your technology ban to contact them."

"Yes, you're right." Ifan felt suddenly very old and tired.

"Why don't you start looking for the spy?" Emlyn's proposition was stiff but not sarcastic, as so many of them had been over the years.

"How?"

"I don't know. Talk to Bryn. Perhaps you can organise a room search, check the records."

"What am I looking for?"

Emlyn shrugged. "A phone of some sort, I suppose."

Ifan shuffled a little closer to his eldest son and laid a hand on his shoulder. Emlyn flinched but didn't move away. "Let's all do our job and hope for the best. Look after yourself, son."

He smiled tenderly but Ifan was forced to let his hand drop as Emlyn backed away rigidly. The two hardened men stood facing one another as they struggled – if only for the sake of protocol – to formulate a meaningful farewell. The awkwardness was unbearable. "Goodbye, Father."

≈

Cai's hand was trembling as he reached for his full combat leathers, but he couldn't be sure if it was with fear or excitement. He'd dreamt of this moment for more than eleven years, but now it was upon him, doubts clouded his resolve. He'd never even hurt anyone badly, let alone killed. Would he choke? Would he fail on the battlefield?

His grandfather didn't knock on the door – Hywel just marched in. "Were you going to leave without saying goodbye?"

"I've only got twenty minutes, taid." Cai filled the uncomfortable silence with his preparations. Everything was ready though – as it had been since he was thirteen.

"You'll prove yourself worthy, son, I'm sure of that. We'll talk when you return."

"Will we?" Cai's patience with his grandfather was wearing thin.

"You didn't mean what you said in the meeting, surely?"

"Didn't I?" Cai flung back, though in truth, Cai had no idea why he had pledged himself to Mona in front of the committee. He didn't even know her.

Hywel moved nearer, his face conveying a mixture of shock and anger. "You know what she is, Cai, you know what comes out of her mouth."

"Mona can't help…"

"She's an Irish witch with a Saxon tongue. A union with her will poison our bloodline."

Cai closed his eyes against his taid's hatred. Having buckled up the last of his straps, he started to leave the room. He needed to say goodbye to Sioned. "I don't want children, taid. I just want Mona."

≈

All the fighters had convened in the training room before moving to the jetty. Mona cast a critical eye over the gathered troops; some of them could be great fighters – given time. Alun and Glyn were good friends and would work well together – the same went for Cerys and Gwen. Ieuan's reactions could still be sharper, and the young lads were all just a bit green. Cai appeared calm and collected. He was wearing full body leathers, and Mona could see his sword and dagger belt were full.

Her impending separation from Cai was becoming painful in a way that Mona found hard to comprehend. "Don't do anything

165

stupid," she advised, feeling that what she truly wanted to say would be inappropriate somehow.

"That's more your style than mine," he smiled. "Will you stay until I get back?"

"Yes," she replied, and then a little more quietly, "I want my seven days, you arse."

"And that's a promise?"

"I promise to stay, if you promise to come back."

Cai nodded slowly, then held her cheek against his and closed his eyes. "I will."

He seemed to want to say more – stuff she probably didn't need to hear – so she touched the face, held against her own. "I'm going now. Remember the patterns and focus. They're bound to have something up their sleeves."

12

Guilty

Ifan couldn't bear to watch his sons leaving from the dock, so he paced the room ineffectually as the sound of the boats' diesel engines faded into the Irish Sea. Ifan needed help, he needed inspiration – he needed an apprentice.

The traditional twenty-year apprenticeship had dwindled to the odd lesson here and there. Dafydd was next in line but he'd never shown any real appetite for being Archdruid, and Ifan wasn't at all sure that his youngest son really had the stomach for it. After another aimless tramp around his rooms, Ifan came to a decision. He would track down their spy, even if it killed him.

≈

Twenty-four of the twenty-eight fighters had gone to meet the Irish in four vessels. They had taken three ex-coastguard cutters and one handsome old Oakley lifeboat.

Bryn had been ordered to stay, Dai had decided his fighting days were over, and Geraint had been asked to stay – probably so that his own side wouldn't throw him overboard.

That wasn't entirely fair: three of the lifeboat crew had been asked to stay and Geraint happened to be one of them. Though Mona couldn't help but wish that he'd gone – he would be hard to

167

stomach undiluted. She was pretty sure that he'd been the initial cause of the female warriors' exclusion, and was pleased that Emlyn had shown his mettle by choosing Cerys and Gwen to join him rather than such an abhorrent man.

Geraint joined Mona and Bryn in the radio room just as the last crackles of the VHF signal died. She willed him to keep his mouth shut as the minuscule fleet dropped out of range, but he didn't. "Well, that's that then, Bryn – got all the girlies to ourselves." He snorted, rubbing his hands together in exaggerated anticipation. Mona counted to ten. She couldn't afford to lose it with him yet; it had only been a few hours. "We'll have to start straight away if we're gonna give Cai a run for his money, eh Mona?"

Bryn was a man of few words but he seemed to read the electrical firestorm brewing between his subordinates. "Shut up, Geraint." He was brusque rather than rude. "Go and tell Ifan we've lost radio contact." Geraint grunted and left, while Mona nodded her thanks to Bryn. They both settled down in the silence. "We should take shifts here. Someone needs to man this place constantly. We'll divide it into three for now. Come back in eight hours to relieve me." Bryn was more dour even than Cai, but Mona thought she could work with him.

The walk back to the now familiar territory of the institution was bizarre; an aura of barely controlled fear permeated every room and corridor. The hall had taken precedence as a meeting place, and Mona found Siân, Nia and Ifan there.

"We've lost contact." She knew the message had already been relayed, but Mona almost needed to say it out loud to make herself believe it.

Siân appeared calm. "How long, Mona?"

"Bryn's guessing that the fighting will start anytime between five and eight hours from now, depending on how keen the Irish are to engage. Though it could be a trick or a game. We've no real way of knowing yet."

Ifan saw this for the dig it was. "Communication devices make us vulnerable. I'm not discussing it."

"Assuming everything goes to plan," Mona continued starchily, "I'd expect them back in thirty-six hours, give or take."

"Let's hope you're right." Ifan raised himself from the school chair arthritically and creaked out.

Mona gave the women a tight smile. "What else, Mo?"

"I think they may be outnumbered." Understatement, she thought but Siân rallied them.

"They're all accomplished sailors; they know the waters around here."

Mona tried to smile back, but knew that was the same for the Irish and so changed the subject. "How's Sioned?"

Nia grimaced. "Hysterical and angry; not a good combination. I'd steer clear for a while."

As they got up for lunch, Mona realised she had no idea what her role here would entail. The Druids were taking an almighty, inward breath that wouldn't be released until the fighting was over – but she felt the need to act now.

≈

Every aspect of life here had changed utterly in the short time the fighters had gone. It was quieter in the canteen, there was more space but people squashed closer together. Mona ate mechanically, determined to keep Cai and his plight from her mind and to direct her pent-up energy into something positive, but she struggled to find an answer.

There was a commotion at the end of the table; Sioned was storming forward, ready for a showdown. She must have been on the warpath for a while, as she had accrued a sizeable contingent of followers and advisors. "You fucking bitch!" Mona guessed the insult was directed at her and faced the tirade. Nia and Siân were making shushing overtones but the girl did not subside. "Why aren't you out there fighting with them?" Sioned jabbed her head in Mona's direction. "Very clever, Mona. Even you couldn't kill us *all* with the men here to protect us."

"Sioned!" Nia reprimanded.

"How can you be so blind, Nia? She wears the *mark*, she's one of them." Her shout was turning into a scream. "Am I the only one to think it's too convenient that we're left here alone with her?" The entire canteen was at a standstill, waiting to see what would unfold.

"She saved us, Sioned." Nia was quiet but firm, but Sioned already had an answer for that one.

"She's put a spell on you all. All those she chooses. Just look what she's done to my brother; he even thinks he loves her."

"That's enough!" Nia raised her voice. Siân was holding the girl back now, but she broke free and launched herself at Mona across the table, their faces mere inches apart.

"He just fucked you; he doesn't love you. He doesn't love anyone but *me*." Sioned was dragged bodily backwards through the food and slapped soundly across the face by Siân. She began to squeal.

Mona had leapt to her feet in an instinctive response to Sioned's aggression, but she didn't retaliate. Sioned was merely a sad, spoiled brat, and even Mona knew it was best to leave her to it.

≈

There were another five hours before Mona's shift. It would be cold in the leaky, single-glazed radio room, so she packed a few layers. Her minimal wardrobe from Swnt had been augmented by various offerings from Nesta. They were old and faded, but they were all she had.

Mona picked up the shirt she had borrowed from Cai and inhaled its saline aroma, but even as she tucked it back under her pillow, she thought that his sister's description of their relationship was probably pretty accurate.

Mona jogged to the training room, started her patterns and then reworked them. At the end of two hours, she had exhausted her repertoire and her body, but it made for an easier mind. After showering and changing, she used the time to cart her washing down to the laundry.

Nesta was queen of the laundry. She was a big, strong woman of about sixty-five, her beefcake arms constantly on show in the heat of the underground washroom. Mona barely knew the woman, but despite the lack of a common language, she found Nesta to be a warm and solid soul. She was a constant; always busy in her kingdom, humming and singing along to Celtic tunes on the radio.

As Mona entered her domain, it was evident that even Nesta had heard about Sioned's outburst, and the grey-haired powerhouse enfolded Mona in a backbreaking, washing-powdered embrace.

They got to work on Mona's clothes, despite her protestations, and while they were waiting, Mona helped her fold sheets. There was an added comfort in not having to talk, and it ate up the time left before Mona could legitimately get back to the radio room.

≈

As it was, she was still half an hour early for Bryn. "Nothing," he reported wearily. By rights, they should have engaged by now, but nothing had come through on any channel, even from their local contacts with all the monitoring equipment. "I know what you're thinking, Mona, but there's no way of knowing anything, there are just too many variables."

It was the longest sentence she had ever heard him utter. Bryn had a broad, sing-song southern Welsh accent, completely different from the spare, softer accent of Gwynedd. "They've kept supper for you; I'll be fine here."

Bryn nodded. "Geraint's on at three, right?"

Mona groaned inwardly. "Yeah, you go, Bryn."

At first Mona scanned all VHF stations, methodically and repetitively, but in the end, she left the radio to creak and splutter on its own.

171

Then she checked the other machine that Emlyn had mentioned. It was an analogue, solid-state, short-wave receiver and looked like a museum piece. Satisfied that it was on, she settled in to let her mind race ahead to catastrophe. When Geraint came to take his shift, she was too tired to be bothered by him and trudged back to her bed and Cai's shirt.

Drinking coffee during the night had left Mona buzzing with exhaustion and the only remedy was reading or listening to her music. After a fruitless half hour rummaging in pockets and rucksacks for her mp3 player, she decided she must have left it in the radio room. Ifan didn't need to find it there, despite its lack of real technological power, so she set off back to retrieve it.

Initially, the sound of voices in the radio room didn't concern her, though Mona did wonder who might want to visit Geraint at five in the morning. It was only as she moved through the door that she realised something was amiss.

Sioned had been forced back against the wall and was desperately trying to fend off Geraint's unwelcome attentions. Even the Welsh that Geraint slobbered into Sioned's ear sounded slimy to Mona. She heard the word *Cai*, but failed to decipher more of the conversation. His intent was clear though, and he closed in some more. Geraint went for her waist and Sioned chopped down, but he had her.

"Get off me!" she squeaked, and continued to struggle as his other hand reached around her hip. Sioned tried to bring her knee up, but he was too close.

"Heard you were a firecracker," Geraint taunted, moving in for the kill.

Mona didn't want to hit him hard enough to risk injuring Sioned, so she kicked both knees out from behind and he crumpled backwards rather than falling against the girl.

It was a good sign that Sioned seemed angry rather than

frightened as she watched Geraint roll in agony on the floor. Mona was extremely glad that the bastard wasn't trying to negotiate. It was as if he guessed that anything he said now would only cause him more pain.

"Get Ifan, Sioned." It was better that she had a task to do, rather than dwell on her lucky escape, but the girl didn't move. Mona considered that too much overt concern would be counterproductive. "You're alright; nothing happened." Her business-like tone did the trick and eventually Sioned focused on her and nodded. "Then you have to get Ifan; I've got to stay here with him." A final glance at Geraint galvanised Sioned into action and she left.

Geraint carried on moaning for a good while. "I've done nothing you won't walk away from, stop whinging," she barked at him. He stopped griping but didn't try to stand, and Mona noticed with disgust that the fly on his jeans was open and there was spittle in his stubble.

"It was none of your business, bitch. She was up for it."

"She's fifteen!" Mona bellowed, looming over him again. There were no further attempts at communication until Ifan arrived, together with Dai and a couple of the healers.

After being informed of events, Ifan turned to Mona and asked, calmly and rationally, "What would you do?"

She was confused as to why he had asked her, but answered truthfully. "He's a good fighter but Emlyn didn't want him. No one likes him and I think he'll always be a problem in a confined society like this. I would get rid of him – make him leave."

Ifan appeared to consider her assessment. "Thanks, Mona." He nodded stiffly and turned to Dai. "Can you escort Geraint to the cells for the night." He sighed heavily. "And can someone wake up Bryn? We need to keep this place manned."

"I suspect he's done it before," Mona added after Geraint had been led way. "Am I right?" she asked Sioned. The girl looked up hastily, hesitating about whether to tell the truth or not.

"Not to me, but yes, some of the other girls," she admitted.

Ifan closed his eyes, trying to control his temper. However, he couldn't prevent himself from letting rip at Sioned. "Why on earth didn't you tell me... tell someone... anyone?"

Sioned dropped her head and began to cry. "Ifan," Mona barked as she motioned at him to shut up and get out. She took Sioned in her arms. "I'll see her back to bed."

After Sioned had cried it all out, Mona made them both a dissatisfying drink of hot chocolate. It was way past its sell-by date and almost translucent. "I came up here to find you. I wanted to apologise," she mumbled through intermittent sobs.

"That's OK. I know you miss him; I miss my brother too."

Sioned shook her head. "I shouldn't have said that stuff."

"Maybe you shouldn't have said it in the canteen, and maybe not quite so loudly," Mona agreed, not without humour.

Sioned sunk her head in her hands in shame, reminding Mona sharply of Cai. "I'm so sorry."

"What do you want to do, breakfast first then sleep? I don't know about you, but I've had enough of this chocolate." Mona eyed the dregs in dismay.

Sioned agreed but didn't move. "I was frightened you were taking him away from me. I wanted to be the only person he loved, and now he's gone," Sioned confessed, staring at the ground.

Mona choked back the swelling in her throat. "He'll be back, Sioned; you know how strong he is. Come on, let's eat."

≈

Siân took control of Sioned and Mona returned to bed. She woke with a renewed desire to train everyone who was willing and able. Mona had promised to stay until Cai came back, so she might as well make herself useful until then. It also dawned on Mona that Sioned was right: it was awfully convenient that all the fighters bar four – maybe three now – had been called away.

She was pondering her approach, when there was a light tap on the door. "It's me, can I come in?"

"Hang on." Mona dragged on a shirt and opened the door. Sioned was still a little red-eyed but didn't look haunted in any way. "Hi, Sioned, is there a problem?"

There was a pause. "Can I come in?" Sioned repeated.

Mona hopped back on to the bed as Sioned perched on the only seat. "That's Cai's." Mona frowned. "The shirt you're wearing."

"Oh, yes," Mona was suddenly embarrassed by her sentimentality, but Sioned had moved on.

"I wanted to talk to you."

"If it's about yesterday, we should probably wait for a committee meeting."

"It's about my brother."

Mona sighed, she had been hoping they could avoid this topic. "Perhaps we shouldn't talk about him. We might get on a bit better if we don't."

"No." Sioned wanted it off her chest. "That's just it. On the morning he left, he asked me to look after you and I've behaved so badly. He's going to be really angry with me."

"I won't tell him," Mona answered truthfully, though they both knew everyone else would.

"I want to make it up to you," Sioned declared.

"Even if I'm an intrinsically evil bitch?"

Sioned beamed. "We can't all be perfect."

Mona laughed, finding it impossible to resist that familiar smile, and explained to Sioned her desire to train anyone even slightly interested in defending themselves. She also raised the difficulties she foresaw in organising such a training regime.

Sioned was clear how it should work. "It can only be structured on ability. Everyone will have just to take it on the chin."

"You realise, then, that the and fifteen and sixteen-year-old boys may well be better than anyone else. I'm not sure any of us will be able to bear that degree of testosterone-fuelled arrogance."

175

Sioned's face alone told Mona that a pride of pubescent male warriors cruising the corridors would be equally unpalatable to her, and they both sat in silence, trying to digest the problem.

13

Trial

Monday morning at nine, the sleek car pulled up at the bus stop. The solicitor motioned her inside and Mona sat down against the cool leather. "Are you coming with us?" he asked dispassionately.

"No, I've found..."

The solicitor put up his hand. "No information please." He handed her an envelope. "This is your inheritance, to be shared with your brother – if he ever returns."

Mona ignored the cold, dry tone of his voice and opened the envelope. Inside was a cheque for a surprisingly large amount – surely much more than the small house in Kent had been worth. "I haven't got a bank account," she thought out loud.

"Not our problem. I suggest you remedy that within six months or we'll have to reissue." The solicitor appeared impatient to leave and checked his watch.

"I'm probably leaving here in about a week; do I have to do anything else?" Mona enquired, and the solicitor seemed vaguely amused.

"No." The reptilian look in his eyes said it all. Mona was on her own again. He opened the door and she started to ease out of the seat.

"I'm sorry you came all this way for nothing," she apologised civilly.

"I'm surprised you're here at all, actually. I never normally see them again – once the connection has been made." Mona wanted to ask him what he meant, but the door had already clunked shut.

≈

Geraint's trial had been organised for noon in the hall. As the majority of the committee were away fighting the Irish, there had been a hasty investing of replacements: Bryn replaced Emlyn, and Nansi was standing in for Dafydd. Mona was stunned to discover that not only were Nansi and Dafydd married, but had several young children.

Nia was acting as counsel for Sioned, and Geraint sat alone in the middle of the circle. Ifan began proceedings, which, being in Welsh, were summarised for Mona by Nia.

Geraint was accused of attempted serious sexual assault. Everyone who had anything to say, including Geraint, was free to express themselves, but after a while Ifan began to ask direct questions. Sioned answered without hesitation. Bryn tersely confirmed his reservations concerning Geraint's conduct with women. Mona told him all that she had witnessed upon her return to the radio room.

Ifan asked finally if Geraint had anything to say in his defence. He did, claiming that Sioned had been used as the bait to set him up for a fall. He raised the point that Mona had just left, so why on earth had she returned so quickly and conveniently? Geraint seemed very pleased with himself as Hywel, Ifan and Nansi deliberated.

Dai interrupted proceedings with a question from the door, and Ifan beckoned him forward. Geraint's face blanched as four young women were led through to join the committee. "Would you like me to ask these women for accounts of their dealings with you?"

Geraint didn't look down in shame, but ahead with belligerence. "No."

The girls were ushered out and Ifan's attention turned back to the accused. There was a moment of heavy silence before he pronounced the court's verdict.

"Geraint Rhys Williams, you have been found guilty of the crimes levied against you. You are to be banished from this community forthwith, and I send no forwarding letter with you to any other kingdoms. With regard to releasing any information to the wider world about our existence, I must inform you that your life is forfeit in this instance. Do you understand the judgement?"

Without looking at anyone in particular, Geraint blinked lazily and mumbled, "I do."

Ifan had tried to keep the disgust from his face, which he'd barely managed, by focusing on Bryn. Now though, he let go. "Get him away from here. Take him to the mainland on the next tide, or overland straightaway. I don't care which."

Geraint avoided any eye contact until he reached Mona. At that point, he wrenched himself from Bryn and spat a rabid sentence at her in Welsh: "*Y ffwcin butain, yr ast Saesnag.* You fucking whore, you Saxon bitch."

The intensity of loathing in his voice made Mona feel physically sick. Fear clenched her heart and she slumped backwards in her plastic chair, almost passing out.

Geraint was soon bundled on his way, and Mona reasserted her grip on reality, hoping that no one had noticed her moment of weakness. It had happened again; the language had pummelled the loathing Geraint felt for her directly into her soul, and she'd been badly bruised by it.

Someone *had* noticed it though, and that person watched her with a cool eye as she excused herself.

14

Tribes

Mona spent the interminable hours at her post in the radio room, devising ways to organise the upcoming training sessions. She had sketched out various combinations of mixed-ability groups, but none of them were going to work. It was still three hours until Dai's stint. Although she hadn't expect anything to happen, she was constantly disappointed when it didn't.

There was a knock on the door and it opened immediately. Sioned came in hauling someone behind her. "I've brought somebody to meet you, Mona. He's a sort of relative." That wasn't surprising, given the nature of the community at the *Conway*, but Mona was curious. She knew Sioned wouldn't bother her with nonsense at this time of night.

Her companion was a tall, gangly, teenage boy, whose body had yet to work out where it ended. Wild, light hair fell in his eyes, which stared resolutely at the ground as Sioned nudged him. The boy's colouring made him unique in the community, and Mona wondered why she hadn't noticed the white blonde hair and light blue eyes before now. How could he possibly be related to Sioned?

Mona said 'hello' and waited. Sioned elbowed the boy again in the stomach and muttered at him until he straightened and replied. "Hello, I'm Arwel. I like the way you fight."

"Thanks, Arwel," Mona answered with a smile for his compliment.

"That's *Arrr-wel*, Mona," Sioned emphasised her rolling R's.

"I thought that's what I said?" Mona replied, but her visitors both shook their heads in solemn unison. She tried a few more times but received the same feedback at every failed attempt. "Have you got a nickname that I can use instead?" Mona asked, too defeated for another attempt. She was shocked to see a look of pain and shame pass over the boy's young features, and Sioned tried an obvious cover up.

"No, not really."

"How about if I call you Al?" Mona improvised to relieve the tension.

Sioned didn't look convinced, but the boy in question smiled shyly from underneath his fair mop. "Ok then."

There was a loaded sigh from Sioned for some reason, but she continued with the rest of her introduction. "Arwel is mad keen on battles and things like that."

The boy grumbled at the inadequacy of Sioned's explanation. "Military tactics and strategy," he corrected, and his meek frame seemed to grow in stature at the utterance.

Sioned appeared more than a little irritated by him. "Anyway, he's come up with some pretty good ideas about training in groups."

Mona had been thinking of grouping by age, ability or gender, but all of these had pitfalls, and she'd been chasing her tail for days. Arwel's idea was based around a sort of house or squadron system. "That way we can mix the whole community up." He looked down at Mona, expecting her to understand. Instead, she urged him to continue. "OK, so you have your young studs - good fighters, competitive but nauseating." Mona was beginning to warm to this boy. "And you have your old men, who could be quite useful in a fight, but aren't willing to be embarrassed by the youngsters in training."

She was getting it now. "We split our fighters into teams of three." Mona finished for him.

"Four might work better, employing strengths and diluting

weakness." Arwel moved his hands around enthusiastically. "That way everyone on one team would be forced to mix: old ladies, young bucks. The theory is that if they work together, respect will come." Mona understood immediately that it was inspired. A little healthy competition would create a diversion from fear and worry; he was a genius.

"I've even created names for them, based on Celtic tribes in the Bronze and Iron Age in Wales." Arwel was on a roll, and Sioned look pleased with the result, as if a gamble had paid off. "I chose tribes that lived in present-day Wales. The Gangani, from the Llŷn Peninsula; the Ordovices, Gwynedd; the Demetae, Dyfed; and the Silures, South Wales." He was beaming now, but appeared a little bashful when he added, "I was going to name one of the tribes Cantiaci – from Kent – but we haven't got enough for five tribes."

Sioned saved him from further embarrassment by leading him away and waving goodnight. The smile slowly withered on Mona's face as she turned to face the still-silent equipment banked up before her. Six days was far too long to have not heard anything; everyone knew it but no one was saying it.

≈

Emlyn squinted against the sun's sharp glare off the water. They'd rushed out to meet the Irish head-on, but their quarry had melted away. He began to wonder if there was a strange magic at work; that at least would explain how so many boats had vanished in such a short space of time.

The VHF crackled again, and it was clear that Dafydd had found nothing either. It had been three days now and they should be returning to base. Emlyn knew all the warriors were thinking it – and that they were fearful of a trap.

He picked up the binoculars and scoured the horizon one more time. Returning home empty-handed felt like failure to Emlyn. He didn't have anything to prove to his father – not any more – but still, a few more days searching couldn't hurt.

Emlyn and Dafydd nursed a shot of rum each as the old Oakley lifeboat rocked and lapped at anchor. The silence between them was easy; it was always words that had been more difficult.

"Who's on first watch?" Emlyn asked.

"Cai," Dafydd answered dryly, and his brother chuckled.

"He's not that bad, just needs a few corners knocking off him. Who's with him?"

"Ieuan," he answered, and Emlyn's eyebrows rose.

"Now he *is* a knobhead," Emlyn spoke evenly and without malice.

Dafydd sniggered quietly at his brother's bluntness. "Maybe." There were a few more healthy sips taken before Dafydd spoke again. "Cai reckons the *Conway* might be in danger, and that this is some kind of wild goose chase to keep us away."

Emlyn sucked his teeth. "Possibly, but I don't see how." The coxswain rubbed the back of his neck and moved his head to one side to ease a twinge. He grinned. "Cai just wants to get back to his woman."

"You might be right," Dafydd agreed. He paused to ponder this. "I'm still not sure about Mona." He rolled the dregs of rum around in the glass. "Whatever side she's on – and I'm not convinced it's ours – she's trouble."

"I can't work her out at all," Emlyn agreed with a nod. "She's either really thick or really smart," he added, as he threw down the last of his drink. "But she's some fighter," he whistled out.

"Dad seems to trust her," Dafydd muttered, and waited for his brother's anger to erupt, as it so often did at the mention of their father.

But Emlyn closed his eyes and the anger remained within. "We'll have to wait and see. In any case, we can't stay here indefinitely. I'll get Cai to contact them from the Isle of Man tomorrow, then we'll know the score."

≈

Cai hadn't known quite what to expect as they'd scrambled the boats out of the strait and into the Irish Sea, but it definitely wasn't boredom. The enemy boats that the coastguard had flagged up were either fictitious or had melted away into various cracks in the distant coastline, disguised by the myriad of summer sailors flailing around in the water.

This was the sixth night at sea, and the small flotilla dare not moor, as it would make them vulnerable to attack. They rafted the boats together each night, dropping the anchors and leaving two on watch at all times. Anchors invariably slipped, and there was always some repositioning to be done.

Ieuan wasn't part of the crew on Cai's boat, but they had drawn watch together tonight. Cai joined him in the cockpit with a heavy heart, as Ieuan *did* like to talk – incessantly and invariably, about himself – though he was normally easier to stomach without his faithful hounds.

"We'll have to make a decision soon; the supplies are getting low." Ieuan began the conversation and merely Cai nodded. There was no need to reply; the situation had been discussed endlessly. "I'm all for heading back myself – bit of a red herring don't you think?" Cai passed Ieuan a black coffee, hoping that if he drank he wouldn't talk.

Cai didn't want to answer, because he knew very well that Emlyn planned to stick it out until something was resolved. Telling Ieuan that would be tantamount to talking through a loudspeaker to the rest of the crew, so he just shrugged.

"Come on, Cai, you must be desperate to get back. I hear you've thawed her out." Ieuan gave him a lascivious wink, and an unbidden image of Mona writhing astride him hit Cai's mind and groin simultaneously. This was what Cai had truly been dreading. Ieuan often initiated little chats like these about women when they happened to be alone, and it always made him cringe.

Ieuan was ignorant of the discomfort he was causing Cai, and blundered ahead. "I'm always pleased once you've started on them." Cai looked at him and Ieuan acknowledged the query in his face despite the low light. "Oh yes, it's great." He chuckled at his own joke.

"It never takes me long to get in there once you've finished with them. All they need is a shoulder to cry on." And still he blabbered on. "I feed them all that emotional bollocks." Ieuan finally took a sip of coffee. Cai begged inwardly for the conversation to end, but Ieuan just kept gabbing on. "So what's she like?"

The thought of Ieuan and Mona having sex enraged Cai in a way he'd never before experienced, and he vaguely fantasised about smashing the mug in his hand and using it to destroy the smug face opposite. Instead he sipped the drink and coughed. "I'd rather not talk about Mona." Maybe Ieuan had finally got the message, because there was not much more conversation that night.

15

Visitors

Shift work was not agreeing with Mona, and she'd fallen asleep against the desk again; pulling herself upright just as Dai made it through the door to relieve her at 3 a.m.

She was getting into the habit of sleeping in until after lunch, and was often dragged from her room by Sioned and Arwel, who had been busy organising the political minefield of the tribal houses. "It means you can start training us straightaway," Sioned enthused.

Mona attempted to snap out of her exhausted stupor by trying to ask intelligent questions. "What's the breakdown for each group?"

Arwel consulted his paperwork. "Twenty-five individuals in each group, consisting of three broad age ranges: over sixties, forties to sixties, and under seventeens. We've divided them all up."

"Are there any exceptions? Anyone missing?" she asked.

He nodded efficiently. "The healers don't want to know, and they'll get Ifan's backing to stay underground. No one can understand them anyway. And Hywel."

Sioned made a face at the mention of her grandfather, but Mona didn't ask. "Anyone else?"

"No, but you and Ifan have to remain impartial, as the judges for various competitions. Sioned and I would make the teams uneven, so we will have to join the judging committee." He beamed and Mona returned it.

"Great," she said. "Let's put the plan to the Archdruid." At that, Arwel stopped smiling.

≈

All three of them paused in front of the door to Ifan's rooms, and Mona raised her hand to knock.

"Here's the paperwork, Mona. You and Sion can do it. I'm… I've just remembered, I've got someone…" Arwel blurted out nervously.

"Not so fast, you little toe rag." Mona grabbed him by the arm before he could bolt, and Sioned glanced at him with rare sympathy. Ifan shouted that he was on his way, and after what was a protracted wait, the door eventually opened.

Arwel appeared reluctant to talk, so it was Mona and Sioned who outlined their proposals. "So, what do you think?" Mona asked at the end of their summary.

"Excellent. Go ahead, and the sooner the better. We need to keep the people occupied and happy. But leave the healers." Sioned smirked to herself. "You know how they get," he added by way of explanation.

Arwel collected the paperwork under Ifan's cool gaze, and they exchanged a few curt words in Welsh. Arwel kept his eyes fixed firmly at his feet, and Mona thought the teenager might fizzle up with embarrassment.

There was a sharp rap on the door, saving Arwel from complete humiliation. Bryn poked his head around it and growled at them. "These two were asking after you at Swnt." Ifan beckoned Bryn and the two newcomers into his rooms.

Mona had never seen a Hollywood film star in real life, but she imagined that this was near enough the same experience. Bryn introduced two men, but only one drew her attention. He was big, blonde and handsome, had a dimple in his chin and designer stubble; in fact, he was a real Disney Prince Charming. Mona was trying to absorb the full extent of his splendour, when Sioned shared a wide-eyed gawp with her. Immediately, both women were infected with a fit of the giggles. It wasn't attraction exactly, but more the reverence one pays to an exquisite sculpture or painting in an art gallery: polite awe.

Bryn broke the silence. "This is Rob." He dismissed the god with a wave of the hand. "And this is Gareth." He gestured equally nonchalantly to a smaller man.

Though not small or particularly plain, Gareth could not compete with the radiant magnificence of his companion. Ifan seemed to peer into their souls, and Mona wondered if they might also be subjected to a trial.

"Did you come together? Are you from the same tribes?" Ifan was talking in Welsh and Gareth answered. Mona didn't know what he'd said, but she felt she could listen to him saying it all day. He had an amazingly deep and resonant speaking voice, and for a moment, her attention was diverted from the blonde god beside him.

"I'm sorry, I don't speak Welsh." Rob's voice on the other hand was soft and light, gentle even, and in an accent that wasn't Yorkshire, but something close. "I'm from Cumbria," he said, "I've got this letter – it's for you, I think." He handed Ifan an envelope.

Mona was inordinately pleased that Rob couldn't speak Welsh, though it certainly looked as if Ifan didn't share her opinion. "And you?" Ifan turned his now aggressive stare at Gareth. "Where are you from?"

"Pentre Ifan. Here, I'm just passing through." He handed over his own document. Gareth had a very broad southern Welsh accent, which Mona found it hard to believe that the old man had missed.

Arwel was enormously interested in the newcomers and treated them both with overt suspicion. Bryn was utterly bored by the proceedings and no one had made the introductions, so Mona took the initiative. "Hi, I'm Mona, this is Sioned and Al. I expect we'll see you at supper."

As soon as they were outside the door, Mona and Sioned dissolved into laughter. Hands clamped over their mouths, they sprinted away, with a perplexed Arwel at their heels. "What was so funny?" he asked as they rounded the corner.

By now, both women had calmed down and stopped laughing – that is, until Sioned tried to answer his question. "I'll tell you when you're older," she cackled.

That set them both off again, and tears rolled down their cheeks as they staggered off to the hall. Once the sniggers had subsided, Mona asked Sioned, "Isn't it unusual for two strangers to arrive together from different tribes?"

The question sobered her. "It is a bit."

≈

Sioned spread the gossip about the visitors while they set up the hall for the first meeting of the tribes. Just before supper, the vast majority of the community had congregated there.

As discussed, Ifan took control of the meeting; blending lore with tradition and experience, he controlled his people with the strength of his speech and deportment. The community of the *Conway* were spellbound by the innovative challenge of the tribe system and the new training regime. They were determined that the sacrifice of the warriors would be equalled, here at home.

Mona passed Ifan the lists of the new tribal mixtures, and integration began in earnest. Each tribe gravitated to a corner of the hall, leaving Mona, Ifan, Sioned and Arwel alone by the stage. The transformation was remarkable to witness. Tribal tables formed at supper, across the boundaries of family and friendships. Arwel had been right; the barriers were being broken down.

He sat next to Mona at supper. "The next step is a bit trickier."

"Really?" She watched him shovelling great forkfuls of food into his mouth, barely waiting until he'd swallowed to explain.

"Each tribe has got to elect a leader."

"Ah, what if they can't?"

"I haven't thought that through. You have to let them grow up sometime." Arwel rolled his eyes parentally, making Mona chuckle. "The most important thing now is to get the work rotas sorted out. If you're going to take a tribe for training both mornings and afternoons, you won't be able to carry on with your stints on watch. In fact, I think that watch duty should be incorporated into the new rota and split into four rather than three."

Mona agreed, happy to be drawn back into the land of the living. They continued to plan and organise until the newcomers joined them. Rob had his head bowed, trying to deflect some of the female attention he was receiving, but Gareth appeared relaxed and smiling as they both sat down to eat. "We meet again," Gareth beamed. Whereas Rob lifted only his eyes in salutation and began his meal.

"So have you settled in?" Mona asked politely.

"Yes, thank you, though apparently we need to be assigned a tribe." Gareth's voice was like velvet.

Arwel grabbed his paperwork. "That won't work; it would make the teams uneven." He was quite terse in his reply, but Sioned, who had emerged from nowhere, contradicted him.

"Not if you and I are assigned to a tribe Al, then they'll be one extra for each tribe." Mona hadn't known the boy long, but took his silence for disagreement. She doubted Sioned would take much notice though, and she pressed home her advantage. "What do you think, Mo?"

Not wanting to upset Arwel, Mona prevaricated slightly, but concluded by agreeing with Sioned; it would be better to train as many people as possible. "The more the merrier. Arwel will allocate each of you to a tribe."

Gareth smiled expansively, Rob less so, and after ten minutes of pencil chewing and deliberation, Arwel announced his decision. "Sioned, Silures; Rob, Gangani; Gareth, Demetae; and I will be Ordovice."

Rob spoke to Arwel directly. "Is it only fighting or are there other intertribal matches?"

This question seemed to delight the young man. "No, there's going to be music, poetry, comedy, art and boat handling."

"How do you choose a winner in any of these?" Rob asked, his voice barely above a whisper.

"Mona and Ifan are judge and jury; they have the final word."

Gareth took up the challenge, on the charm offensive. "So it's worth getting on your right side, Mona." He flashed her some teeth. Perhaps Mona had become too accustomed to Cai's reserve, but she felt that Gareth smiled too much, and he definitely overdid it on the aftershave.

≈

Ifan was festering with worry for his boys, and Siân could see it was making him physically weaker. "Come on, Dad, calm down," she said softly, as she passed him tea in his favourite mug.

"I shouldn't have allowed Dafydd to go." He'd been repeating this same sentiment for over an hour now.

"It wouldn't have made any difference; you know how close they are."

Ifan sat down briefly, then stood again, too agitated to remain in one place for any length of time. "He's the last of the line. If anything happens to Dafydd, we'll be leaderless when…"

"Not the last Dad; aren't I your child too?"

Ifan met his daughter's eyes with shame. He wondered how primogeniture had inveigled its way into this Celtic stronghold – of all places. "Siân…" he began. She stood and took his hands, rubbing her fingers over his inflamed joints.

"I don't want it, but I'd accept the responsibility if I had to."

"Your mother would be appalled at what I've just said," Ifan whispered, and he finally allowed Siân to take him in her arms.

"A clip around the ear, at the very least," she chuckled sadly, remembering her mother's strength and temper.

"Come on," she continued, "let's sit down. I want to chat about Mona."

"What about her?" Ifan became suspicious.

"She didn't go with the lawyer."

"We gave her that option, remember."

"Yes, I remember, but perhaps that was a mistake."

Ifan raised his eyebrows. "You distrust her still? Even after she saved Nia and Cai." He rubbed his eyes. "And Sioned, to a certain extent." The Archdruid could clearly see his daughter's anguish.

"I don't distrust her. I just... she's..."

"Dangerous," Ifan finished.

"And it's not only that. I'm worried that she's stayed for the wrong reason." Siân buried her head in her hands, then lifted it quickly. "She's fallen for Cai, she's staying for Cai," she said irritably.

"Surely that was to be expected, I mean..."

"You don't understand. He feels the same way, I'm sure of it."

It was Ifan's turn for calm now. "This is Cai we're talking about, my love. I wouldn't get too concerned about his heart."

"And what if I'm right? You were there at the committee meeting; you heard what he said about choosing her."

"He was trying to get her to *fight*."

"They can't be together. Mona bears the *mark* and, anyway, his mate has already been chosen." Siân finished with an air of finality, and Ifan smiled gently at his daughter's cross-armed belligerence.

"What do you reckon your mam would have said to that?"

"I'm just saying..."

"I know, I know," Ifan said, trying to mollify her. He did not want to meddle with that particular hornets' nest. "So what shall we do with Mona? Ask her to leave?"

Siân shrugged before answering, but was interrupted by a light tap at the door. "Come in," Ifan bellowed, and Arwel shuffled in, head down and mumbling into his shoes. "What did you say, boy? Speak up!" Siân's heart reached out to her strange blonde nephew, but she didn't intervene.

"I... I just wanted to ask about the visitors, Rob... and Gareth," the youngster stuttered.

"What about them?" Ifan's tone was astringent.

"Well... isn't it a bit strange?"

"What is?"

"That they both turned up together, from completely different communities, and I'm not entirely convinced about Gareth's..."

"The letters were in order, I've had them checked."

"Are you sure? Just because something's written down, it doesn't make it true." Arwel's quick words seemed to pop out of his mouth unbidden, provoking an apoplectic reaction from Ifan.

"How dare you?" he thundered, but the boy had backed out of the door and vanished into thin air.

"You shouldn't be so hard on him Dad, it's not his fault," Siân admonished but Ifan didn't hear her. He was staring out through the door and into the past.

≈

When the attack came, it was rapid and brutal. Four fifty-foot, big-engined VSVs crept up to within ten metres of the rafted flotilla. Only the slap of water on hull and the purr of the boats' engines gave Cai and Ieuan any time at all to wake the crews.

After that it was a blur of slipping ropes, and engines firing up, as the boats began to disengage. There was a rasp of blades, flashing in the moonlight, and then the fighting began.

Cai powered the boat away from the flotilla, taking it in a large arc and slamming it into neutral. He then launched himself at one of the Irishmen, who was brandishing a short sword at Ieuan and Cerys.

Alun was already dealing with an opponent, and the small craft rocked violently with the rhythm of combat as he dodged and weaved on the small decks. Alun lost his footing and took a blade deep in the shoulder. His cry alerted Ieuan, who'd lost his composure and concentration for a split second. It was long enough, though, for the other attacker to knock the sword from Ieuan's hand and into the sea. Cerys plunged her blade in from behind, taking the man's weapons before kicking him overboard. Alun continued to counter blows one-handed, but he was tiring quickly. As Cai reached the duel, he grappled the Irishman's arms behind his back and Alun dispatched him from the front.

Ieuan had finally taken the initiative and was moving the boat back to the rest of the fleet. The fighting was heaviest here, as only Cai and Dafydd had managed to free their boats before the bulk of the Irish had boarded. There was carnage on the decks of the still-tethered vessels. Thanks to Mona's training, the Welshmen were now superior fighters, but they were considerably outnumbered. Cai and Dafydd arrived back at the boats simultaneously, and they boarded from opposite ends, fighting their way through to the middle.

The attack ended with an almost choreographed abruptness, with the Irish leaping back to their vessels as one. Their spectral boats whisked them away at incredible speed, as if they had been summoned.

Shaky relief that he was still alive replaced the adrenaline in Cai's system. The attack had been brutal and efficient, but there was a worrying nag at the back of his mind. The Irish had numbers, why hadn't they done more damage?

Cai watched the vessels disappear to the south-west. The speed of their retreat was breath-taking, and the moonlight illuminated a single symbol on the boats' slender hulls: a design identical to that on Mona's chest. Cai shuddered as he turned his attention back to the chaos, hoping that no one else had seen the symbol.

A brisk scan told him there were many more casualties than Alun. Cai needed to reach Emlyn and Dafydd on the middle boat, to talk about the next move. The boats were tethered up temporarily, with crew holding the lines rather than making off on the bollards.

Cai hopped from boat to boat, stunned by the attack but more shocked by the speed of the Irish boats. They would never be able to outrun them if it came to flight. Six serious injuries, four superficial. Cai was mentally cataloguing the human damage as he reached the deck of the lifeboat.

It was the silence that warned him first, and then the look on Dafydd's face as he stared directly into Cai's.

Emlyn was still alive but fading fast in his brother's arms. Cai sunk down on the deck, supporting Emlyn's bulk from the other side. Cai didn't search for the injury; he could only look into his uncle's face. "Em," he rasped. Emlyn didn't speak, but there was a plea in his eyes and Cai knew what the man was asking. "I'll look after him, Em. I'll take care of Arwel, I promise," Cai said without hesitation.

Even after Emlyn had died, the men continued to hold him up, bound together in a family tragedy that had finally played itself out. There was a solemn pause, as if they were waiting for some momentous symbol of his passing. It did not come.

A long time later, they pulled apart and the talking began.

16

Trial Run

Gareth seemed to be there every time Mona turned around. She didn't mind though; he was good looking, charming and funny – even if he did use too much aftershave. Gareth and Rob hadn't really hit it off as far as she could tell, and Mona couldn't blame him for seeking out the company of another outsider like herself.

"Can I give you a hand with that?" The rich tones of Gareth's rolling accent made Mona smile, as he strolled over to help her manhandle the last of the heavy mats into place. "Are you alone?" he asked, giving her a flirtatious grin.

"Not for long." Mona glanced up at the time; the Ordovices would be arriving any minute. She looked back to Gareth to ask if he wanted anything in particular, but the mood had changed.

Gareth was talking to her in soft Welsh now, and he was moving closer. Mona watched his full lips utter the beautiful sounds, and she was entranced. With a small and increasingly insignificant part of her brain, Mona knew that the language was ensnaring her again – pulling her in with its rhythm. Gareth was offering her the innermost desires of her heart. He was offering, and she leaned towards him to accept. Mona's lips grazed his, and he gasped – he stopped talking and the spell was broken.

Mona stared up at him, suddenly clear-eyed but confused at her momentous lack of inhibition. She sprang away from him as Arwel led the Ordovices into the hall. Arwel's eyes narrowed at the lack of space between Mona and Gareth. "Sorry about that, I don't know what came over me," Mona babbled contritely.

"No problem." Gareth winked and turned from her in waft of fragrance.

Mona shook her head. Gareth was an attractive diversion but she couldn't understand what had made her react to him that way. Something nagged at the back of her mind, but she was a practical woman, and deliberately shut her mind to the niggling notion of magic. Mona chuckled at herself for even considering it – she'd clearly stayed here too long.

≈

It was the second day of training for the Ordovices, and Mona had started teaching the young bucks about pattern and line work. Some of them were pretty experienced anyway and eager to fight – ready for the chance to prove themselves against their friends in the other tribes.

Sioned and Arwel had shared out the combat-trained women among the groups, and they were taking the self-defence lessons with the remaining women, young and old. Everyone was given a weapon, even if they couldn't walk.

Mona was intrigued initially that Arwel didn't want to train with the lads of his tribe; he didn't even gravitate to the older men of the group. As the afternoon progressed, Mona watched a pattern emerge; people didn't shun him, they just didn't see him. He wasn't included because he wasn't there. Nesta was one notable exception to this rule, and Arwel stayed close by her. They both sat with the very old and the very young, chatting away, while reading books to toddlers or wiping snotty noses.

Arwel was an enigma that Mona wanted to solve, so she knocked on Nia's door after supper. There was a now familiar singing voice coming from underneath the door, and before it was opened, Mona remembered the hymn. "Didn't think you *did* God?" Mona asked as she settled upside down on Nia's bed and slid her legs up the adjacent wall.

Nia looked guilty and switched off the creaky old cassette recorder. "It's Bryn Terfel," she replied tartly.

"Same thing eh Nia?" Mona joked.

Nia ignored her with a roll of the eyes. "Why do you always do that?" She flicked a hand at Mona's unusual pose, merely to get an inverted shrug in return.

"I thought you only did the *diddly-diddly* music?"

Nia frowned, and Mona knew she had stepped into one of those cultural trip wires."*Diddly-diddly*?" Nia growled.

"Well you know what I mean, it's the…"

"If you're referring to the fiddle, mandolin and harp then yes…"

"Calm down, Nia, I was just making conversation."

Nia opened her mouth to say something, but decided that it wasn't worth her breath and turned back to her book.

"What are you reading?" Mona asked casually. She wanted to ask about Sioned's friend, but Nia seemed much more prickly than normal.

"The Mabinogion."

"The *whaty whaty what*?" Mona teased frivolously.

Nia's back stiffened in unfeigned irritation. "Don't you ever take anything seriously, Mo? Have you got *any* idea how important these myths and legends are to us?" She settled back in the chair slightly, still grumpy, and Mona asked the question before she did any more damage.

"I came here to ask about Al, actually."

"Al?" Nia replied, clearly perplexed by the name.

"Yes, you know that blonde kid, Sioned says he's her brother but…"

"*Arwel*, you mean." Nia injected both vexation and venom into her rolling R's.

"Yes, well, I couldn't say that properly so I..."

"So you changed it," Nia finished for her, the aggravation ramping up to anger. "That is *so* bloody typical of you! What gives you the right to change his name?"

Mona opened her mouth to explain, worried about the depth of Nia's irritation, but she was cut off before she could speak. "The English have never bothered to learn *Caergybi* so it becomes Holyhead, *Abertawe* becomes Swansea, *Ynys Môn* becomes Anglesey. The list is endless." Nia had risen from her seat and was flapping her arms up and down in fury.

"He doesn't seem to mind," Mona tried in her own defence.

"That's not the point."

"I know, I'm sorry, I won't do it again, promise," Mona murmured, and Nia sank back into her chair, a little mollified.

"Let's try again with the Welsh lessons, Mo. I'm sure..."

"No!" Mona answered firmly, "Our friendship can't take another beating like that."

Nia considered arguing the point, but thought better of it. The lessons had been excruciating, and Mona had learnt absolutely nothing. "Anyway, who is he?" Mona changed the subject ineptly.

Nia sighed and studied Mona's disconcertingly upside down face. She'd been waiting for this and could guess how Mona would react.

"Arwel is Emlyn's son," Nia said softly.

A quick calculation in her head made Mona raise her inverted eyebrows. "How old is Em then? He can't be much older than thirty."

"Emlyn *is* thirty," she sighed. "He was fifteen, they both were." Nia frowned at the distant memory. "His mother was from the north, Northumbria somewhere, I think. It was a summer holiday romance but she became pregnant. I was too young to understand all the details. I only know that Arwel was left at Swnt when he was one, and has been brought up here."

Mona was caught up in the story and had righted herself on the bed. She frowned at Nia. "That doesn't explain why people ignore him."

Nia didn't provide an explanation immediately, but eventually clarified the community stance. "His mother was not one of us; she was just English, or worse."

Nia's extreme views still rankled, though by now Mona was able to make a joke of them and understood better the historical perspectives underpinning her prejudice. Pulling a face of mock horror, Mona exclaimed, "Worse than English!"

"Viking," Nia mouthed, scandalised.

"You are having a laugh."

Nia obviously wasn't, and Mona guessed, rather than knew, that along with the Romans, Saxons and Christians, the Vikings had done their fair share of Druid bashing. Though Nia's tone sobered her. "He's not registered in the book."

"What book?" Mona asked, side-tracked.

"We have a book; a ledger of births, deaths and marriages – just like in the outside world. But…"

"Don't tell me! There are all sorts of dodgy rules about getting into it."

"There are rules. A tiny community like this needs rules to survive. They are important."

Mona rolled her eyes in blatant dismissal. "So you're saying that he's not officially part of the community?"

"That's right," Nia mumbled waiting for the outburst.

And although Mona felt the injustice, she kept her tone civil. "What about his father? Emlyn's the Archdruid's son. Surely he's half Druid – at the very least?"

"I don't know all the details; only Emlyn and Ifan know the truth. Even after all this time it's a taboo subject. They're no longer close." Nia spoke into the silence. "I know you think it's harsh, but there are strict rules here; sometimes it's the only way to ensure survival."

"What's his nickname? He got upset when I asked."

Nia did look uncomfortable now. "*Bwgan*. It means ghost."

Of course it did. Arwel was a true outsider, and his colouring would forever reinforce that difference, forcing him to glide around the perimeters of the community all his life. Mona was surprised to find a lump in her throat. To have never had a mother was unimaginably painful to her – at least Mona had her precious memories. "Sioned said they were related."

Nia smiled sadly. "Rhiannon and Gwilym took him in." Mona creased her brow, never having heard the names before. "Cai's mam and dad," Nia explained. "They all lived at Swnt for a while, Emlyn as well. When they died, Sioned and Arwel were four, Cai was thirteen. The community did their best to help but they all just stuck together. It's sort of been that way ever since."

Mona remembered her brother through the bond of loss and grief. "And Ifan's never got to know his grandson?"

"Emlyn keeps them apart; there's been too much damage done. Arwel's much less fragile with Em and Cai around."

Amongst all the mixed emotions, a huge swell of pride bloomed in her chest for Cai and Sioned. It also explained the close relationship between Emlyn and Cai – they'd been children bringing up children. Nia seemed to pick up on Mona's mood. "Have you fallen in love with him?" Nia winced, knowing the answer but not wanting to hear it.

"Don't be daft, he was just a good shag," Mona blustered.

Nia was sceptical, but she responded at face value. "Good. That's not a situation you want to find yourself in. Not with all that nonsense about Cerys still unresolved." Nia went back to her book, leaving Mona to wonder.

Mona wasn't under any illusions about Cai, but she was quite fond of Cerys and didn't fancy any conflict with the woman. "What about Cerys?" Mona asked simply.

"I knew he wouldn't have told you." Nia slammed her hand against the open page and gave her an incredibly pointed look. "Cai is not to be trusted. At all, *ever*."

Mona nodded – she had worked that out. "Cerys?" she prompted. Nia gasped slightly, her hand moving to her abdomen. "What is it?" Mona asked.

"Time of the month," Nia reassured her with a dismissive hand, before continuing. "Cai and Cerys have been intended for each other from the beginning. It was decided a long time ago that they should mate. The healers chose Cerys because of her lineage, the magical potential I was talking about before. Hywel's especially keen on the union."

That in some way explained Hywel's attitude towards her, Mona thought. "So are they both err – magical?" Mona asked tentatively.

Nia laughed, and then held her belly again with a frown on her face. "No one knows." She sighed wistfully. "Though they used to. I've read about people being able to *see*, or almost *taste* the magic in others. But now it's all worked out on the family tree. We've even lost the ability to see it now, let alone use it."

"Do you *really* believe all that nonsense?"

Nia gawked at Mona in disbelief. "How can you, of all people, say that?"

"The more I think about it, the more I think there must be a scientific solution. You know, spontaneous combustion or something," Mona answered, perfectly seriously.

Nia was rocking a bit on her chair and Mona could see she was in pain. "And how does that explain…"

However, Nia couldn't finish her sentence; she was now rigid and moaning in agony. Mona stood up. "What shall I do?"

"Get Mam," Nia hissed through gritted teeth, as she succumbed to the next wave.

Mona ran from the room, bumping into Gareth just outside the door. He looked aghast at her panic. "Help me with Nia," Mona ordered, dragging him into the room with her.

In the end, it was easier for Gareth to carry the woman to her mother's rooms, as she couldn't straighten herself long enough between the attacks to walk. "Thanks," Mona said, touching Gareth gratefully on the shoulder. He seemed to flinch slightly but Mona didn't think any more of it because Hefin, the witch doctor from the depths of the *Conway*, appeared in the doorway with Siân.

Mona hadn't seen Hefin since Nia's near-death injury, and he blanched at the sight of her. The eccentric healer's eyes darted then to Gareth, where they stayed a little too long for comfort. Siân broke the moment, urging the Druid to tend to her child. As Hefin set to work, Gareth made to leave. "It's getting a bit packed in here. I'll save you a space at supper," he said, smiling at Mona.

"Thanks, but I'm staying here with Nia."

"Breakfast then!" Gareth's eyes spoke of more than breakfast.

≈

It was none of her business, but Arwel's past dogged Mona's thoughts, every time she saw him. The more she watched, the more she saw that people's eyes slid over him constantly. Her regular table in the mess hall was outside the tribal setup, and was frequented by all the other outsiders: Arwel, Rob and Gareth.

Sioned visited occasionally, but now she was a proper Silure, her loyalties were becoming divided. Nia would be out of action for a while; the word was that she might need tests in a real hospital. Siân was worried that the unbearable cramping was a direct consequence of the black poison, but in truth no one knew for certain.

Gareth struck up pleasant conversation at the breakfast table. "I hear there's a music competition in a couple of days." He directed his question at Arwel but it was meant as a more general conversational opener. Mona listened half-heartedly about plans for the evening, but her mind was on both Nia and the young boy, and she felt the need to ask Ifan a few questions.

≈

"Come in, Mona." She frowned as she walked into Ifan's suite of rooms.

"How did you know that was me?" She secretly suspected magic and it showed on her face.

"Not magic, just attention to detail. No one knocks quite like you when you've got something on your mind."

Ifan had put her on the back foot but she forced the question out anyway. "I wondered if you could explain about Arwel."

"Explain what?" he snapped, on the defensive immediately.

"Why you treat him so badly for starters," she retorted.

"It's none of your business, you're just…"

"Just what? English? An outsider? Or just not in your sodding book."

Ifan realised he wasn't going to get away with shouting at her to leave, and he sighed dejectedly. "They were only fifteen; I believed I was doing the right thing." The regret in Ifan's voice was tangible. "Emlyn came to me when they found out she was pregnant. He begged me to let her live with us. Ingrid didn't have much of a home life, and they had it all planned." He glimpsed up at her with a plea for understanding in his eyes. "When I refused him, he tried to run away with her." The old man struggled to say the words out loud. "I locked him up." Mona's gasp said it all. "He was next in line, too important to the community. I thought I was doing the right thing. I thought that he would get over her eventually."

"What happened?"

"A couple of years later, her father left the baby at the Lifeboat Station. Ingrid had got mixed up with the wrong crowd and they couldn't cope with the baby." Mona's hands were instinctively clenched as she waited. "Ingrid died of an overdose, at seventeen." His sigh was a little lumpy. "Emlyn adores the boy, but he's riddled with guilt and hate. There have been plenty of women, but any love he had died with Ingrid."

Mona broke the stunned silence with a small question. "Have you tried to apologise?"

Ifan exhaled fifteen years of regret. "It's way beyond apology now. Emlyn gave up his birth right in favour of Dafydd years ago, and now we only ever speak in anger."

"You could try to get to know him whilst Emlyn's away." Ifan looked at her in surprise, but she pushed. "He's a genius tactician, and he has a great sense of humour. I promise you won't regret it." Ifan shook his head, either in fear or defeat. "You could try apologising to Arwel; it might be a start."

But Ifan was already back on his feet, all defences back in place. His body language told her the chat was over, and Mona turned to go. "Why didn't you leave on Monday with the lawyer?" he asked suddenly, and Mona shrugged, not really knowing herself. When he continued, Ifan's voice had lost its edge. "You know Cai's…"

"I know what Cai is," she interrupted quietly.

"He's promised to Cerys. They're to handfast." Ifan amended his words: "Cai and Cerys will *marry* at Lughnasadh."

Mona shrugged again, knowing she should have gone when she had the chance – before she'd tasted that sweet drug. "Perhaps you should have gone earlier," Ifan murmured, seeming to understand where Mona's recent thoughts had taken her, and she smiled with a hint of regret.

"Perhaps."

"There are some here who want you to leave."

"If you want me to, I'll go." Mona turned again for the door. "But not until I've trained this community to defend itself." The door slammed behind her and he sank back in his chair. Left alone with his guilt and worry, Ifan's mind wandered back to the plight of the fleet.

17

Ingrid

The crew sat in a broad ring around the fire, their thoughts on Emlyn. Cai felt Dafydd's pain – they were as close as brothers could be. His own memories were sharp and clear: a skinny kid hanging on the coat-tails and words of his young uncles. Emlyn and Dafydd were cruel in the tradition of older boys, but he had still worshipped them as gods.

That autumn fifteen years ago was marked indelibly on the minds of the community. Cai could remember vividly the endless screaming and sobbing from the dungeon. Sneaking down to see if he could help, he'd found Dafydd staring helplessly through the bars at a broken Emlyn, curled in on himself in his grief. Cai had watched Emlyn piece himself back together, only to be shattered again at seventeen. Cai had been just eleven when Ingrid died, but he knew Emlyn would never be the same again.

And later, warm memories of their days at Swnt. He and Emlyn, lying in the hot summer sun, while Sioned and Arwel attacked their slumber with buckets of water until the chase was on and the babies were tickled mercilessly to the ground. Screaming with hysterical joy, they were chased again and again into the sea, with Mam and Dad laughing in the background. And all around them, the sounds of happy music from the portable radio.

Cai remembered Arwel lying asleep in Emlyn's arms by the

firelight at the end of the day, his uncle gently kissing the bright white hair. It had been Cai's last good summer. After his parents' death, nothing had ever been the same, and Emlyn changed again. When they moved back to the *Conway*, it had been together. Emlyn became more than a big brother; he became more than an uncle. Emlyn had taught Cai never to give his heart away, and he had been a model pupil.

≈

The Druid community at Douglas on the Isle of Man, had let them carry out their passing rites for Emlyn. He had been burnt and the people of the island had sung for him, but the song wasn't in their souls.

For the men and women of Ynys Môn, their lives had been marked and measured by song. It was as constant as food or drink. Not everyone in their community had a good voice, but many did, and even those who didn't could hold a tune. It was inevitable that their voices lifted in song to their fallen leader, as they drank the pain away with donated rum.

Each warrior knew instinctively when to join in and when to leave the singing to a solo performer. The folk songs of the sea and the fields turned to songs of love and longing. Cai coughed, expressing his desire to sing.

He knew now what he had to sing for his uncle, the mixed language of the verse as apt as the sentiment. His voice was not pure and powerful like Alun's, but it had a husky quality, which enhanced the solemn intimacy of the fireside vigil.

A ei di'r 'deryn du
To my dearest love.
O cais fy nghangen gu,
For I'm so deep in love.

Ni welaf yn unman
Such a damsel in my sight
Â'r ferch mor lân o liw
She is a beauty bright.
Mae'i gwallt yn felyn aur,
Just like a ring of gold,
A'i phryd fel eira gwyn
The truth it must be told.

Cai had only seen Ingrid once – when he was nine years old. With his child's eyes, the girl had seemed to him like a living faerie, an alien creature of pale, fragile beauty – just like her son. "Emlyn and Ingrid," he toasted into the silence. "That they meet again."

≈

It was five days since the attack and Emlyn's death. The community at Douglas were dumbfounded with the Welshmen's lack of technology, and their aversion to using it when offered. The small community here had been civil, but Cai suspected their fear of the Irish trumped any druidic loyalty.

Cai had enquired about a short-wave radio and had eventually been given access to one. The set had been stored for over twenty years in the bowels of their station and was in dire need of repair. However, Cai was pretty confident that he could mend it and started work immediately, glad of the solitude he found in the corner of a little workshop.

Dafydd knocked lightly on the opened door. "How's it coming?"

Cai breathed out. "Slowly, but surely," he answered and continued with his tinkering.

There wasn't a need to fill the silence, but Dafydd brought him up to speed. "They're all out of danger, but recovering slowly – we won't be able to attempt a return for a couple of weeks." Cai wasn't surprised by the news. "What do you reckon they'll do, Cai?"

"We're trapped here, and with boats like that we're scuppered anyway – they can travel in excess of fifty knots."

Dafydd whistled. "I've never seen anything like them. Have you?"

"VSVs," Cai answered. "I've read about them." Dafydd frowned at the unfamiliar acronym. "Very slender vessel," Cai explained. Dafydd allowed himself a wry smile; Cai was as famous for his interest in machines as his luck with women and his taciturn nature. "They're wave-piercing, based on the military boats used by the SBS. They have a massive range, they're extremely fast, and able to cope with the roughest of seas." Dafydd couldn't respond and merely gawked as Cai continued. "Well, at least we know one thing about our enemy."

"What?"

"They're incredibly wealthy. Each one of those boats would cost over one and a half million." Somehow that information hadn't alleviated Dafydd's anxiety, and he no longer wondered why his nephew had kept the information to himself. "The only possible way home is to leave in dribs and drabs – to hug the coastline and hope for the best. I don't mind giving it a go," Cai volunteered hopefully.

"I'll think about it, but our real concern is the *Conway*. We need to get some fighters back there, and soon. I've asked three of the young lads to take the ferry." Dafydd paused. "When will that be ready?" He pointed at the radio.

"In a couple of hours. Do you want me to contact the *Conway*?"

"Keep it short – I'm getting as paranoid as Dad about technology." He ran a worrying hand through his hair. "I've been called up to meet the Archdruid here," Dafydd sucked his teeth and shook his head, "seems we've attracted too much attention. I've got a feeling they want us gone."

"Mind your P's and Q's" Cai quipped sarcastically, though Dafydd hardly cracked a smile at the jibe. It was a galling irony that he would have to speak to the Manx Archdruid in English.

Cai was still at it five hours later, when there was another knock on the door. He looked up from the innards of the ancient machine to find Gwen standing by the bench. "How's it going?" she asked – her eyes red with grief.

"Nearly there." Cai only needed another hour or so.

Gwen moved up next to him and put her hand gently on his back and rubbed it. "I just can't believe he's dead." Gwen's voice broke and she turned her body to Cai's, crying into his chest as she weaved both arms around his neck.

Cai put down the screwdriver and stoked her hair. "I know, nor can I." Gwen wiggled herself backwards on to his lap and her sniffling turned into kisses at his neck and chest. Cai eased her hands away from his neck. "No, Gwen. I don't want this."

Gwen ignored him and felt for the hardening muscle in his leathers. "Liar," she taunted, feeling it grow through the material. "I know you, Cai Owens," she whispered at his ear. "We'll both feel a lot better soon." Cai leant back involuntarily as Gwen's strong little fingers found their rhythm. Gwen knew her way too well around his body – she knew what he liked. "Forget about Mona," she breathed, unbuckling his sword belt. "She'll be giving Bryn a good going-over as we speak."

Ice rushed into Cai's groin and bile into his stomach. "No, she won't. I asked her to stay," Cai protested.

Gwen was exasperated rather than annoyed at his sudden loss of interest. "Do you really believe a woman like Mona would stay? Wait around for you like the rest of us idiots?"

Cai hadn't ever doubted it, but began to at Gwen's attitude. "Why? Do you think she'll leave?" he asked, incredulous.

Gwen climbed off him and just shook her head in answer. It was time to admit defeat; she was clearly going to be denied tonight.

Cai rushed to finish the job after Gwen left, and his heart was in his mouth as he found the frequency and began transmitting. He wanted Mona to be waiting at the other end. She wasn't; Dai took the brief message, and reassured him that everyone was fine. He confirmed that Mona was still there, and Cai arranged to send another transmission in a few days' time.

≈

Mona's body was taking ages to adjust from her shift patterns. She'd started to take sneaky naps in between the morning and afternoon training sessions, and as she wandered back from her room, she could hear the sound of her mother's voice ringing in her head. *You'll sleep your life away, Dozy Doris.*

The Silurians definitely had the best fighting squad, and Sioned led from the front. The older folk seemed to be veterans and even the young children were eager to enter the fray. Mona was pleased with the training programme and her spirits were up – until she saw the look on Dai's face as he approached.

Mona knew this was his shift and that he wouldn't have left his post without good reason. *Not Cai, not Cai, please god, not Cai,* her mind screamed.

Dai kept his voice low, though everyone in the room waited silently and expectantly. "They were attacked a week ago; there are several badly wounded." He lowered his voice even further. "Emlyn is dead."

There were gasps, followed by some soft sobbing, and Mona tried to contain her rising apprehension. "How was contact made?"

"Short wave, from Cai." Mona didn't show her relief, but she felt Sioned breathe out shakily beside her. "They're on Man. He's going to make contact again in a few days, or as soon as he can."

"Who knows?"

"Bryn's on his way to Ifan." He turned to Sioned. "I'm looking for Arwel right now."

It was clear that Dai didn't want the job, and Sioned offered. "I know where he is."

"You'd better get back, in case there's more contact," Mona added numbly.

Dai glanced at both women before he turned away. "Dafydd's sent three warriors back by ferry, we should expect them soon."

≈

Arwel was tucked away in his office, inside Nesta's subterranean laundry. The washerwoman read the bad news on their faces immediately. She switched off the radio and watched in agony as Sioned spoke quietly to the boy.

Witnessing Arwel's grief was excruciating, because he didn't break down. He just stared at each woman in turn until Nesta swept him up in her enormous arms. Even then there were no tears, merely glazed silence and whispered denial. Sioned finally started sobbing and Mona held her in a tight grip.

Arwel sat against Nesta for a very long time. They had all drunk several cups of tea but hadn't yet spoken a word. "Will you come with me, Al?" Mona held out her hand to him and he just took it woodenly, not looking at her again until they had reached Ifan's room. When they arrived, he blinked at her in slow motion. "You need each other now," she said, squeezing his shoulder.

Mona had no idea how Ifan would react, but Bryn opened the door, looking extremely taut. She pushed her way passed him, pulling Arwel along by the shoulder. Ifan stood as his grandson approached. Not wanting to witness any more grief, she dragged Bryn outside with her, leaving them to it. Mona could see the big man was struggling with his own emotion, and she left Bryn with his head in his hands.

Mona made it all the way back to her room before the tears began. She hadn't cried since before her parents had died, but tears came freely now, and she cried them all into Cai's shirt before falling asleep, clutching her ironwork against her. He was still alive.

≈

Mona didn't know what she had expected, but she was humbled by the extraordinary composure of the community. Work went on as normal, people turned up for training, and life carried on. There was no mass weeping and wailing. Even Siân was functioning.

Nia was on the mend, and had just confirmed that the music competition was going ahead as planned tonight. It was rumoured that Gareth and Rob were quite the golden boys of entertainment, and each tribe had been practising their party pieces in private for the last five days. The evening ahead promised to be a musical high point, and Mona was appointed both judge and jury.

Ifan hadn't been seen out of his rooms, but Arwel had appeared at training for the first time this morning. There had been a subtle change in the attitude of the community to the newly orphaned boy; people now acknowledged his existence with a slight nod of the head and a soft touch on the shoulder.

Arwel had sought out Mona at lunch. "Will you be OK to judge tonight, Mo? I thought you might like a help with the translation."

"I do hope you're not trying to nobble the judge?" Mona attempted a little joke, and Arwel glanced up hastily, ready to refute the accusation. But he saw the attempted humour in Mona's expression.

"It was worth a try for the honour of the tribe." He tried out a smile, and it sort of worked.

"Have the lads arrived yet, from Man?" Mona asked. Arwel shook his head extremely slowly and Mona changed the subject. "Actually, I think I'll take you up on your offer, as long as you don't resort to bribery."

Mona and Arwel sat with the rest of the outsiders, and Nia had joined them from the Gangani table. "So you're off tomorrow, Gareth?"

"Yes, alas." The whole table was treated to a magnificent grin. "But I'm planning to go out in glory." His eyes moved to Mona but it was Nia who rose to the competitive taunt.

"I hear you have a voice, Gareth." Nia smiled, glancing at the ever-bashful Rob. "But we also have a secret weapon." Rob seemed to sink further down, but snorted an affable noise back at her.

Mona put her hands over her ears melodramatically, and *la-la'd* loudly. "I can't believe you lot. No one will sway my judgement."

18

Music

Arwel knocked on Mona's door, startling her awake. *Shit!* She had only meant to have a five-minute nap. Perhaps she was coming down with a bug. "Be out in two minutes, Al." She called from the bed.

Arwel looked extremely smart, for a Druid, and he eyed Mona's clothes and bed hair. "Don't you start; I'm not into fashion," she grumbled, missing her bed already. Arwel led them off down the corridor, and Mona took advantage of the fact that he wasn't looking at her. "How are you, really?"

"Better. You were right about Taid. I've moved in with him for a while and we've been doing a lot of talking." He turned to her just before the hall. "Thanks."

She shrugged, and decided not to ask if there was any news on the missing lads. "You *do* know that I can't sing for toffee. How am I supposed to judge this?"

"Just go with your heart," he answered simply, lifting his slight shoulders.

All four tribes were squashed into the hall. Everyone who wasn't on stage was in the audience, so there was a great deal of upheaval in between events. The Silurians were up first, with an ensemble piece. They had gone for laughs as, according to Arwel, no one in the Silurian tribe had an outstanding voice.

It was an evidently humorous song and was helped along by

some of the antics of the young boys in the tribe, which the audience found hilarious. "It's about multi-coloured goats." Arwel advised with dead pan delivery, and Mona stifled a fit of the giggles.

As the other tribes warmly applauded, Mona murmured to Arwel. "You're a clever chap." She didn't need to add that his brainchild had lifted the entire mood of the mourning community. Arwel knew what he had achieved, and acknowledged the compliment graciously.

Next up were the Ordovices; they had a few excellent musicians and had decided to go with an all-instrumental attack. Mona knew that she was listening to exceptional music. People here didn't watch television or play computer games; their precious leisure time was spent in the pursuit of excellence, and they were showcasing it tonight.

As the clapping for the Ordovices died down, Gareth took the stage alone and sat down with a guitar. Arwel explained that it was a testament to his talent that he had been allowed to represent the Demetae – they wouldn't have done it out of kindness.

As soon as Gareth uttered the first note, Mona was caught. He sang of the seashore and of love, and she was there with him, sharing in the innocent wonder. "Mona," Arwel was nudging her arm, bringing her back to reality. "Are you alright, Mo?"

"No," she admitted, still stunned. The truth was that the Welsh was affecting her in the same way as it had in the chapel, over six weeks ago.

Another strum on the guitar announced Gareth's next offering. "*Paham mae dicter, O Myfanwy ...*" Mona was dragged in again, this time into a story of unrequited love. The sense of loss and longing was unbearable, and her heart broke for the young man. She found herself slumped against Arwel's shoulder, sobbing as the strains of the guitar faded into the silence of the stunned crowd.

The applause was tumultuous, and it gave Mona time to dry her face and rearrange her expression. Arwel eyed her anxiously. "That's not a normal reaction, Mo," he whispered in her ear. "Though I don't think anyone has actually noticed; a lot of people have been genuinely moved."

They looked nervously at each other as Nia and Rob made their way to the front. Nia took centre stage. "Tonight we're singing in English as Rob isn't a Welsh speaker." There was a murmur of discontent, but Nia was equal to it. "And our esteemed judges have worked very hard already tonight." She flashed a wicked grin in Mona's direction and sat down in front of an enormous harp.

Mona suspected that, like her, everyone was anticipating a duet. However, it became clear when Rob stood up and addressed the audience that he would be singing alone, with the harp as accompaniment. "This is a tribute to the Buckley family." Rob's soft Cumbrian accent was continually at odds with his film-star looks, and Mona smiled in anticipation of the song. It was one of her dad's favourites and she would know immediately if he sang it well or not.

Arwel touched her hand, afraid that she might overreact again. "I'm going to be fine." She patted his hand back.

Rob's voice wasn't laced with strange Welsh magic; it was clear and soft, but he sang from his soul. He dragged the audience into a whirlpool of emotion as he sang of bitter, broken love and fruitless longing.

Eyes closed, and head slightly bowed, Rob was obviously a true entertainer, and Mona found herself mouthing along to the four hallelujahs in the simple chorus. If any of the women in the audience weren't in love with him already, she thought, they would be by now. His performance had obviously made up for the fact that he had sung in English, judging by the rapturous clapping and wolf whistling, which went on and on.

Rob's singing had moved Mona, but not in any way that left her feeling out of control or helpless. There was only one possible champion, and she strode forward to attach the small cardboard facsimile of the Eisteddfod chair – *y Gadair* – to Rob's chest.

By eleven the party was starting to wind down. Mona said her goodnights and left for bed, her eyes almost closing as she took the last few steps to her door. Someone called from behind and her heart sank as Gareth bounded forward. She caught a whiff of something chemical and familiar, but the memory faded as he started speaking to her in Welsh. "I wanted to say goodbye properly, Mona. I'm really going to miss you and I'm away on the morning tide." He moved nearer, wielding his silken voice. "Won't you miss me just a little bit?" His hand cupped the side of her face and Mona realised that Gareth was right: she didn't want him to go and, yes, it was a good idea that he came in for a drink before bed.

≈

Alarm bells rang in Arwel's head as he saw Gareth stalk after Mona – the musician had watched her like hawk all evening.

Observing them from a safe distance, Arwel saw Mona fall under his spell and invite him into her bedroom. With his brain screaming magic, Arwel sprinted off to his grandfather – the only person who would truly believe such an outlandish notion.

≈

Rob wasn't enjoying the attention that his success had brought. It was stupid really, because he loved it when he was on stage and the music worked through him. On stage he was someone else, somewhere else.

"You sing well." As always, Rob was scrutinising the floor, and murmured embarrassed thanks. But when he realised that neither the feet nor the voice were female, he glanced up. It was the big man from the Moelfre Lifeboat Station, Bryn.

They were about the same height, but Rob hardly ever thought of himself as a big man. Bryn was probably about twenty-eight, but the beard added a few years. "Do you sing?" Rob actually looked at Bryn as he asked the question.

"A little… anyway, I'm on duty, so… well done."

Bryn stalked away and Rob watched him go, cursing himself. It was always a mistake to make eye contact.

≈

Gareth continued the seduction in Welsh as they walked into Mona's bedroom. She couldn't entirely remember why he was here, but when he suggested that she take off her jeans, it felt like a genuinely good idea. Mona didn't want to upset or hurt him; she'd misjudged him before.

Despite being captivated by his delicious promises, Mona understood on some level that Gareth's Welsh had changed. He was speaking now in another equally captivating tongue. Gareth was talking in a beautiful, lilting Irish Gaelic. But the spell wasn't broken with the language change – if anything, it had intensified.

Still murmuring about her body, he began kissing her neck, and Mona was suddenly positive that she wanted to have sex with this man; she needed him, all of him, and now. Gareth, though, seemed hesitant at that moment. His hands started trembling, but she held them steady in her own.

It was all the encouragement he needed, and Gareth moved forward, pulling her against his body at the waist and driving her back against the wall with his mouth and hips. Their breathing was hard and shallow, and as he moved his mouth from her neck to her shoulder, Gareth slipped his hands below the waistband of her pants and began kneading her naked bottom.

At his touch, she pressed her hips forward into him. He wasn't responding quickly enough to her need, and she eagerly unzipped his jeans, rubbing her hand lightly against his testicles. Gareth groaned with pleasure, and for that fraction of a second, he was unable to speak. As he stopped talking, Mona froze briefly, but immediately thawed as his voice began again, its delicious sounds stroking and stimulating the erogenous zones of her body. There was a sharp stab of discomfort as he rammed himself into her, but pain didn't matter now, only sex.

Gareth's thrusting was frenzied, his speech slowing and faltering as he worked himself to a climax. When he came, the words stuttered to a halt, his mouth stilled in a yawn of ecstasy.

A feeling of horror suddenly washed over Mona in that silence: Gareth was ejaculating inside her and she had to stop him. As he jerked to a stop within her, anger pulsed from her hands and she pushed him violently away.

There was a strange look of victory in his eyes, but the smile on his lips didn't linger long. It changed rapidly to shock, then fear, then nothing, as his body incinerated into hot ash, all over her.

≈

The door was locked from the inside. Arwel shoved feebly against it a couple of times, calling Mona's name, as Ifan rooted around in his pocket for the master key. There was an awful smell of burning coming from under the door. The Archdruid was painfully slow and Arwel made claws with his hands as he resisted the ferocious urge to grab it from his taid's fingers.

When the door was eventually cracked open, Arwel slipped through the gap and into her room. Scrunching his nose against the acrid stench, Arwel skimmed a glance around and was reassured to see Mona alive and sitting up against the far wall. Relief turned to horror, though, as he pieced together events from the clues around him.

Mona was wearing only a shirt with most of the buttons missing. Her knickers lay in a ripped heap beside her, semen leaked from between her thighs, and she was covered in a greasy black ash, some of which still floated in the air.

Ifan hobbled to the bed and dragged off its duvet to cover her. Arwel fell to his knees beside her and took her blackened hand in his. "Mona…" Her expression of confused vulnerability stuck in his throat.

220

"Gareth…" She frowned with child-like bewilderment. "Gareth…" But she was incapable of finishing the sentence.

≈

It had been at least two weeks since they had left the *Conway*, and Cai had passed beyond frustration. Dafydd had allowed him only two forays into the Irish Sea before ordering the vessels to remain ashore.

Ieuan had whinged constantly about the closeness of their last call, and not just to his faithful followers. Cai could barely look at him now without feeling a seething sense of resentment crawling up the nape of his neck.

Try as he might, Cai couldn't work out how the sleek Irish boats had managed to intercept them so easily. There was something he was missing, and it gnawed at him that his home coastline was so tantalisingly near. In broad daylight, the design on all four boats had been unmistakeable, and Cai had felt the glare of accusation on Mona's behalf.

Performing the patterns was the only thing keeping Cai sane, and he had begun practicing them religiously, as soon as they'd landed on Man. Initially, he'd tried to coax the others to join him. Some of them did, some of the time, but he was glad that he'd been left alone today as he climbed the hills above Douglas Bay.

He worked slowly through the moves Mona had taught him. It seemed to bring her close while he was performing them, and he found himself correcting and adjusting as if she were there, scrutinising his progress.

Dafydd waited until Cai had finished his ritual before interrupting him. "We're off to Maughold Head; apparently we're causing too much interest from the government. They've said we can stay at the lighthouse up there." Cai didn't feel like being pleasant, so he acknowledged Dafydd's words with a barely perceptible nod and followed the war leader back to ready the boats. "Try not to kill Ieuan, he's not so bad," Dafydd urged, sounding more like family than authority now.

Cai disagreed with that judgement, but didn't contradict his uncle. "Best not let us crew together then," Cai replied evenly. Dafydd could never tell if Cai was joking.

Motoring east to Maughold felt appallingly wrong. Cai's whole being ached to travel west and south, to Mona. When they arrived at the entrance to Port Mooar even its beauty couldn't quell his unease. After mooring the boats, they settled into the lighthouse keeper's house, which nestled safely among the cliffs, well away from the prying eyes of the authorities. Cai, though, slept aboard: the ropes would need adjusting during the night, and some nameless worry kept circling in his mind.

≈

Relationships between the crew were starting to break down. Dafydd struggled vainly to maintain control, but he was fighting a difficult battle and many of the crew were now openly mutinous.

Ieuan had spread word of the Irish insignia he'd seen painted on the hulls of the ships. It increased the paranoia and fear that surrounded Mona's presence back home, and defined groups formed, with dissension alive in their mutterings. Realising the danger, Cai had started to support every decision Dafydd made in public.

Now that they were alone, he needed to let his uncle know what had been playing on his mind. "We need to experiment, Dafydd; it's the only way."

"They nearly got you last time, Cai, and I don't think Ieuan's going to let you forget it." His tone wasn't as negative as the last five times they'd had this conversation, and Cai grasped his chance.

"If we try several different directions at once, we might be able to split them up. Maybe one of us can get through." Cai saw that his uncle was running out of alternatives; staying here at Maughold was not a long-term option.

"We need a contingency, if you fail," Dafydd hedged.

They both moved to the charts, and Cai trailed his finger over the paper. "You lead the others north around the east of the island and I'll try to sneak south. I've got a nasty suspicion they're trapping us." His fingers strayed to the Menai Strait. "The *Conway* will be horribly exposed, I know the lads will have arrived back home by now, but the Irish have numbers."

There was no surprise on Dafydd's face, just stress. "Then we have to try."

Cai had won the round, but he continued to press home his advantage. "If they stop me, I'll follow you up. Keep on going until Mull and we'll try for the Caledonian Canal. It's too public for them to take us on there at least."

"It will take weeks to get back, if we have to circumnavigate clockwise," Dafydd answered glumly.

"Could be months," Cai corrected. "The Caledonian Canal is a short cut but it's still northern Scotland; if we don't get a move on the weather will close in fast." Dafydd was forced to agree and Cai spoke again. "We'll have to let Bryn know, and we should at least debrief the lads, they might have something to report. There's a short-wave set in the lighthouse."

"OK, just keep it short."

Cai understood Dafydd's reticence about making contact. But they both knew it wasn't this ancient radio that was giving them away – it was some sort of technology beyond their comprehension. He thought back to the Irish attack and why it had ended so suddenly. Perhaps the sole intention of that skirmish had been to plant bugs. Could they have done that within those ten awful minutes of brutality? Perhaps, he concluded, and Cai vowed to scour the boats for bugs the following morning.

Dai took the message again. He had hesitated when asked about Mona, but promised to pass on the entirety of Cai's message. Mona would take the warning seriously – if she hadn't already left.

Cai lurched back towards the lighthouse to give Dafydd more bad news. None of the three young warriors had made it back to the *Conway*.

His uncle seemed unable to process the information. His face drained to a grey sheen and he clutched at the desk in front of him. "No…" he shook his head from side to side, clearing the awful news from his brain. "What…how…?"

Cai ran both hands through his hair and down his face, he was out of rational ideas, everything he had left was veering towards science fiction. How could those three young lads have been recognised and eliminated? Perhaps they had been traced, but how, and when?

"How, Cai?" Dafydd pleaded, "I don't understand…"

"Me either," Cai admitted numbly, "but we have to try again. *I'll* try again. Maybe they weren't careful enough?"

Dafydd was shaking his head again. "No, Cai, I won't lose you too. We stick together from now on."

"I could try another route," Cai stabbed a finger on the chart, "get to the Scottish mainland and catch a train, it's…"

"No!" Dafydd shrieked. "No, we keep together and keep to the water –it's what we know."

Ail Ran

Part Two

Cai's Journey

Outer Hebrides

Moray
Firth   Whitehills

Peterhead

Caledonian
Canal

Eigg
Inner
Hebrides

Eyemouth

South Shields
Hartlepool

Isle of Man

Anglesey

Nefyn

Cardigan
Bay

St David's
Head

Pin Mill
Southend

Bristol Channel

Dover

Beachy Head

Isle of
Wight

Mullion   Mevagissey
Falmouth

Isle of Man - Ellan Vannin

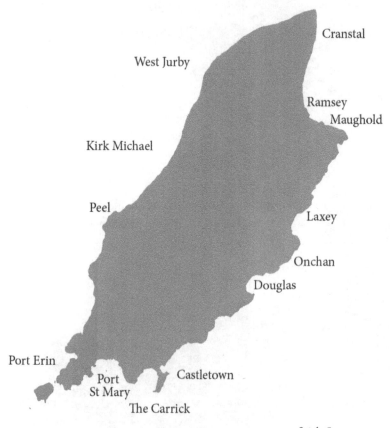

Cranstal

West Jurby

Ramsey
Maughold

Kirk Michael

Peel

Laxey

Onchan

Douglas

Port Erin

Port
St Mary

Castletown

The Carrick

Irish Sea

Scottish Hebrides

Lewis

Outer Hebrides

The Minch

Harris

Skye

Eigg

Mingulay

Inner Hebrides

Tobermory ·

Loch Linnhe

Mull

Islay

Jura

Cornwall - Kernow

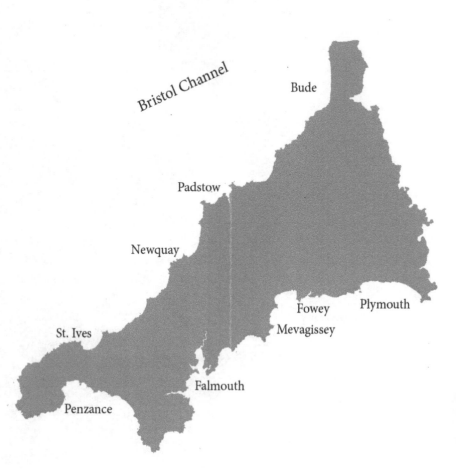

Bristol Channel

Bude

Padstow

Newquay

Fowey

Plymouth

Mevagissey

St. Ives

Falmouth

Penzance

Contents

Mae hen wlad fy nhadau

Mae hen wlad fy nhadau yn annwyl i mi,
Gwlad beirdd a chantorion, enwogion o fri;
Ei gwrol ryfelwyr, gwladgarwyr tra mad,
Dros ryddid collasant eu gwaed.

Cytgan
Gwlad, gwlad, pleidiol wyf i'm gwlad.
Tra môr yn fur i'r bur hoff bau,
O bydded i'r hen iaith barhau.

Hen Gymru fynyddig, paradwys y bardd,
Pob dyffryn, pob clogwyn, i'm golwg sydd hardd;
Trwy deimlad gwladgarol, mor swynol yw si
Ei nentydd, afonydd, i mi.

Cytgan

Os treisiodd y gelyn fy ngwlad tan ei droed,
Mae hen iaith y Cymry mor fyw ag erioed,
Ni luddiwyd yr awen gan erchyll law brad,
Na thelyn berseiniol fy ngwlad.

Cytgan

Land of my Fathers

The land of my fathers, the land of my choice,
The land in which poets and minstrels rejoice;
The land whose stern warriors were true to the core,
While bleeding for freedom of yore.

Chorus
Wales! Wales! Fav'rite land of Wales!
While sea her wall, may naught befall
To mar the old language of Wales.

Old mountainous Cambria, the Eden of Bards,
Each hill and each valley, excite my regards;
To the ears of her patriots how charming still seems
The music that flows in her streams.

Chorus

My country tho' crushed by a hostile array,
The language of Cambria lives out to this day;
The muse has eluded the traitors' foul knives,
The harp of my country survives.

Chorus

Newgrange – Brú Na Bóinne – Ireland.

Diarmuid couldn't fit his big fat fingers into the mug's handle, and he hoped that none of the other visitors had seen him struggle. Apart from the two girls behind the counter, there were no other Druids in the building, but Seamus had been right; the strawberry blonde girl was powerful, she pulsed with green light. Diarmuid could taste the healthiness of it on his tongue; tender green vegetables, lettuce and crisp celery. She was a healer then, like her aunt Molly.

Taking another sip of coffee, he made a sweep of the visitor centre, trying to look interested in all the Celtic memorabilia that swamped the cafe whilst tracking the movements of their prey beside the till.

It hadn't taken a lot of research to anticipate the girls' routine, and in fifteen minutes he knew their fate would be sealed. Niall should never have chosen this moment to stand up to Seamus. The drunkard should have allowed his father to take the girl – he should have made the deal. It was too late now for bargaining.

Diarmuid pushed the repulsive thought from his mind, and eased his bulk forward to lean across the table. His half-brother was stretched out along two chairs with the nonchalance of the very slim, his capped head bent over the game he was playing on his phone. The twins either side of him had already crushed their cans and were eager for action; he could tell by the feverish darting of their pale eyes. "Only the older girl," Diarmuid warned, looking at the plastic clock above their sandy heads. "The other one is too young."

"You're fucking joking, fatso."

"No, you heard me. Just the one, just Aislinn."

Diarmuid's authority was waning – he knew it – and these little rats were only interested in Cian's opinion. They looked at him now for support but he continued with his game, seemingly oblivious.

"One," Diarmuid repeated as he rose from his seat. Despite his bulk, Diarmuid knew he no longer impressed them; they'd all seen him back down and suck it up in the face of authority too many times. "I'll be by the van."

At exactly 5.45 p.m., Diarmuid heard the rap on the Transit's rear door. The two girls were bound and gagged, slung like sacks over the shoulders of the twins, but he didn't need to see them struggle and scream to know how deeply scared they were. "The little one hasn't got any power at all, he won't need her." Diarmuid struggled to keep the pleading from his voice as Cian sauntered into view.

"She's still got tits and holes," Cian whispered, finally making eye contact, and Diarmuid's head filled with the black buzzing from the boy's awful power. "You know how the lads like to play." His phone snapped shut. "Drive," he barked, making for the passenger side as the twins dragged the girls into the back.

19

Action

Arwel wasn't keeping a bedside vigil exactly. He was too busy maintaining the smooth running of the tribal system, as well as fielding all the concerns and questions about Mona's mystery illness. He'd only been able to keep her friends away by fabricating the need for a working party to Swnt.

Mona had slept, almost continuously, for the first week after Gareth's death. She was still there now on day ten, lying on Ifan's sofa, not asleep, but staring into space. She had moved to drink and visit the loo, but had eaten very little, and spoken not a word to either of them.

Ifan was so worried about her that he was even considering outside help. Arwel and his grandfather had spent hours discussing the attack, and they had conflicting opinions on the action they needed to take. Arwel wanted to cross question Rob, after all, both men had arrived on the same day. His taid, however, was convinced they couldn't risk it – no one could know of the attack.

Mona wasn't forthcoming, but she had told them three things: First, that Gareth had smelt strongly of chemicals – sulphur, she thought – and that he had tried to cover up this smell with aftershave. Second, that he wasn't Welsh but Irish. And third, that Irish had the same catastrophic effect on Mona's brain as Welsh. Apparently, Mona could recall every second of the attack.

Arwel sat beside Mona on the sofa now. She had flinched away

237

from any physical contact, no matter how slight, so he didn't try to take her hand. Arwel was hoping his news would snap her out of her lethargy. "I know you can hear me, Mo, and you don't have to answer. But please, just listen carefully to what I have to tell you." There was no reaction, but he didn't expect any yet. "I've just come from the radio room. Cai has made contact again, a short-wave transmission. He said they're being pushed back every time they try to come home. He suspects the Irish are trying to keep them away from here. They're trying to find another way back." Arwel paused to check for a reaction. "He said it could be months; the injuries mean they can't move quickly." Mona had turned to look at him, and he forged ahead with new hope. "He said to make sure you could defend yourself properly." She was staring straight at him. "And that he sends his love."

Mona closed her eyes, but it didn't look like sleep. There was a knock on the door and Arwel went to answer it. He was needed in the hall.

≈

Rob had decided that he liked Mona; she was refreshingly honest and it was easy to be around her. She was quite ill at the moment though, with suspected glandular fever. Every other sensible person had gone off to refurbish a row of cottages in Moelfre, and Rob found himself left to the mercy of simpering teenage girls and their jealous suitors.

He was looking for escape in solitude and music, and Nia had said he could use her library as long as he didn't disturb her filing system. There didn't seem to be an obvious system, but he avoided all contact with anything book-like, making up a lounging area on the floor and plucking at his mandolin for hours at a time.

The old girl needed a bit of work, but though he had his tools, the library wasn't a suitable area for tampering with such a perfect instrument. Perhaps he would ask someone about borrowing a workshop for a couple of hours. The thought of doing so made his stomach churn, but he strummed it away.

The door creaked open hesitantly, and Bryn filled the doorway. Rob stopped playing. "I'm sorry, I'll get out of your way, I was just…"

"No." Bryn moved slightly inside the door, gesturing for Rob to sit back down. "I heard the music; I was curious – mandolin isn't it?"

Rob was colouring up as usual, and stammered slightly before answering. "Yes." He was on solid enough ground here though. "She's an old A-style arch top, in need of a bit of TLC I'm afraid." He offered Bryn a closer look.

"She's a beauty," Bryn whistled out.

"I inherited her." Rob gazed down at the instrument as one might at a loved pet or child.

"I play percussion; we have a bit of a jam from time to time. Perhaps you'd like to join in. Nia's in charge really."

"Yes, I'd like that," Rob replied quickly. Maybe *too* quickly. Did he sound overly eager? Rob could never tell, but he suddenly felt alive at the prospect of making music. There was a spark in his eyes that wasn't there earlier.

Bryn was already backing away to the door. "Tomorrow night, training room, about nine… see you then." And he was gone again.

≈

"Mona?" She could just about hear Arwel's voice over the shower. The decision to move from the sofa had been one of the hardest Mona could ever remember making, but now she was up, the possibility that she could become a functioning human being once more seemed less far-fetched.

Mona felt vulnerable. Gareth had defeated her in a way that she had never thought possible, and it was through a weakness she couldn't even understand, much less control. She was glad he was dead and that she had killed him herself, but she was frightened for the first time in her life. Strangely, it wasn't another attack she dreaded; Mona feared her own awful, destructive power. She gazed down at her hands. They had incinerated two men now, and had acted almost unilaterally both times. Whatever this power was, she knew it wasn't a gift.

It felt odd, having to use her voice again; it sounded strange to her ears. "Can you bring maps, any charts you have, back up here?" Mona paused so that Arwel could reply, and when he did, she added to the list. "And food, a lot of food."

Once Arwel was gone, Mona continued to scrub herself clean, rubbing her skin raw as she did so. There was a strange fizzing sensation in her nipples, which she ignored.

Between them, Arwel and Nesta had provided clean underwear and combat leathers; they were stacked in a neat pile by the sofa. Mona had lost weight over her ten day leave of absence and the clothes were a little baggy. Yet facing herself in the mirror, she felt satisfied by the lack of femininity and vulnerability in the figure that confronted her; she now looked like the machine that she needed to become.

Arwel was disturbed by her appearance as he set out food on the small kitchen table, though he attempted to hide it with a forced cheeriness. Mona had shaved her head entirely, leaving only a thin, uniform layer of stubble across her scalp. The lost pounds showed starkly in her face – her cheekbones were sharp and the hollows deep around her eyes. There was no colour at all in her complexion.

"Can you show me on a chart where they are and where they were attacked?" Mona asked as she started eating. "Then I want to see any other possible routes back and any problems you've foreseen."

They worked for several hours, and Mona asked questions that were mostly pertinent to the plight of the warriors. But her mind had begun fretting again over the reason for the Irish attacks. No one had yet given her even a half plausible answer. She'd asked Ifan, Nia and Sian with no joy. She'd even dared to query the truculent Bryn, but to no avail.

"Tell me why you think they're attacking us?" Mona asked Arwel, completely out of context.

"I…it's…" He coloured up, and Mona knew they were all hiding something.

"I've a right to know," Mona stated quietly. "Tell me."

"There's nothing to tell," Arwel answered quickly and shot from his seat. Mona rose slowly and took one deliberate step towards him. Arwel shot out both his arms at her, palm outwards. "No, sit down. I'll tell you."

She sat and waited. "The truth is we *don't* know." He looked Mona straight in the eye. "But we *do* suspect."

"Why didn't anyone…"

"Because it's you. We suspect you. All of us – Ifan, Nia, Cai, even me." He dropped his head.

"But that was when I first came here. Surely…"

"Your uncle triggered the first attack, and you have triggered this last attack."

"And what about the other times?"

"The other massacres occurred because we were brave enough to go looking for a fight." His voice trailed off. "That's why there was so much argument about the fleet engaging this time. We'll never be that brave again. But you… you and your family are the only common link anyone can find."

Mona felt dead inside. "And what about now, Al?" she asked sadly. "Do you think I planned Gareth's attack?"

Arwel met her hard stare with complete sincerity. "No, Mona," he said. "I don't."

She closed her eyes, shook away the numbness and rummaged around for some resolve. "I'm going back to my room now. Tomorrow we need to start work. This place should be protected at all times. If Cai reckons they'll attack, we should take note." She began collecting her clothes. "Can we work from your office?"

From the forced, fragile smile on her face, Arwel could see that Mona didn't want to deal with anyone else. "I'll meet you in there with breakfast."

"Bring lots of food." Mona hiked the bag over her shoulder and ruffled his hair; she seemed to remember that was a good way of showing affection.

≈

Cai decided to take a sweep of the boats on his own; no one else needed to know his fears about the surveillance devices – though even that wouldn't explain how the young lads had been intercepted. After hours of searching, he found nothing on any of the four boats: an irritation in one way and a relief in another.

Cai's mind now turned to the task ahead. He and Glyn were prepared for the worst as they idled the *Marc'h* in readiness for the big escape. There was to be no radio contact with the rest of the fleet unless there was a genuine emergency. Glyn knew what to look out for, and he scanned the pre-dawn horizon obsessively, watching for the tell-tale bow wave of the Irish crafts.

All the other Welsh vessels had left together, in another direction, leaving the *Marc'h* alone to make its solitary run for home. The *Marc'h* was Hywel's boat and Cai had handled it since he was a young boy. It was small but he knew how to use her agility to the full – and beyond. If anyone had a chance against the enemy fleet, it was Cai in the *Marc'h*. Glyn wasn't the best sailor in the fleet, but he was probably the bravest, and the boat didn't need two skippers.

"*Dyma hi yn dod.* Here she comes," Glyn warned in a half-breath. They had rounded the Calf of Man, heading south-west, and Cai could see the sleek vessel bearing down on them. It had picked them up faster than he would have thought possible. Holding his course and nerve, Cai steered her over the treacherous tidal races of Calf Sound.

They were heading for *The Stack*, a tall rocky outcrop some forty feet offshore. Millions of gallons of sea water were forced through the narrow gap at every tide, creating an immensely powerful surge between the steep cliffs on either side.

Cai had done his homework, and had practiced this manoeuvre

time and again over the past few days. At a certain distance from rocky pillar, it was difficult to resist the current – and beyond that point, there was no going back. The VSV was fast and stable, but Cai knew it lacked the agility of the *Marc'h*. He also doubted whether its skipper had ever needed to get out of trouble before now.

The sleek vessel was upon them in a flash, and Cai reached the mouth of the slim channel just feet before the bigger boat. Using his gathered momentum, Cai skipped the *Marc'h* over the current and out through the other side. Glyn turned in time to see the helmsman of the Irish boat panic as his bow was caught by the fearsome race. The VSV was now drifting across the mouth of the gap – a gap that was not wide enough to allow it through at that angle. Glyn's eyes closed in relief as he watched the stern catch as well. The current now held the boat fast between *The Stack* and the cliffs, wedged firmly between the two rock faces.

Cai didn't look back but opened the throttle up fully. They could just about see the green fields of Ynys Môn when Glyn screamed the warning. Cai turned to see three of the knife-edged bows carving through the waves on their stern. He held on, desperate to see the curved brickwork of Amlwch Harbour – the closer they could get to land, the safer they would be. Even the Irish couldn't risk the exposure of a double killing in the full glare of mainstream society.

The speed at which the boats were intercepting them was mind-boggling, and even with fear clutching at his heart, Cai was able to estimate their speed to be a staggering sixty knots or more. They were never going to make it.

With all other options closed down, Cai executed an extremely sharp turn at full speed. Glyn was braced and ready, realising that their only hope now was to retreat past the Isle of Man and on to Mull. The three boats slowed in their pursuit when it became obvious that the *Marc'h* was in retreat. It seemed that the Irish weren't any more inclined to engage than the Welshmen.

The message was clear though: they could travel north, but every attempt at returning home through the Irish Sea, would be prevented.

≈

Ifan hobbled back from his arthritis treatment with the healers. It was only August, but the Archdruid was already in difficulty and dreading the pain that would come with the damp November air.

Another dread clutched at him the nearer he got to his room. The image of Mona, forlorn and silent, filled his mind. Ifan hadn't stopped berating himself for his patent lack of judgement, and he also felt guilty for consistently ignoring Arwel's warnings. He had noticed Mona's susceptibility to the language a long time ago. If he'd done something about it then, maybe she wouldn't be lying in that defeated stupor on his couch. Their resident spy had certainly noticed, and acted on it swiftly enough.

Gareth hadn't been chosen at random to attack Mona; he had been chosen because he held a powerful magic of his own – in his voice. Ifan recalled that it had even affected him at their first meeting, his initial suspicion of the newcomer wiped clean by the fake Welshman's soothing tones. The old man paused in his shuffling as an icy hand gripped his heart. Gareth could have made her do *anything*; he could have harnessed her immense power.

Ifan was trembling as he lurched into the room, and his old heart missed a beat when he saw that Mona was missing from the sofa. "Where is she?" he screeched, desperate for his grandson.

Arwel appeared promptly from his room, smiling. "She's better, much better." The look on his grandfather's face made him pause. "I think she'll be fine. She's up and showered and she's eaten loads of food." He grinned.

The good news didn't seem to be affecting Ifan the way Arwel had hoped it would, and the Archdruid sank down into the chair, unable to stand any longer. "Mona could destroy us all, Arwel." He spoke into his hands. The boy seemed at a loss, and Ifan began to explain what he had only just realised himself. "The spy knows of her weakness. If they found a way to harness that power..."

He let Arwel come to his own, awful conclusion, and the boy gasped at the expression in his grandfather's eyes. "What are you planning?"

Ifan looked away, ashamed at what his grandson may have seen in his face. "I don't know," he lied.

"You can't hurt her, Taid. Please don't say you'll hurt her."

"Not even to save the community, Arwel? Sometimes we have to make really hard choices."

"You don't always make the best choices," Arwel whispered, and Ifan felt the knife of recrimination in the words.

"We need to find out who it is, this spy," Ifan mumbled to himself, screening out the pain of his regret.

Arwel knelt at Ifan's feet, taking his hands. "I know you've got your doubts, but Mona is a good person, Taid; I'll keep an eye on her, just promise me that you won't hurt her."

Ifan agreed with a nod of the head, and stroked back his grandson's fine blonde curls. Arwel was all he had left of his own dear boy, and there was a brief whiff of hazy, golden power around the lad. Ifan smiled. "I'll root out the spy, I promise."

Ifan had always hoped, rather than believed, that Geraint had been the culprit. After Geraint had been expelled, he'd put the issue of the spy to one side. Once again, Ifan had proved himself to be lazy and short-sighted. "What shall we do?" It was a soft, rhetorical question, but to his surprise, Arwel had an answer.

"We trust no one; anyone could be guilty. We get that Rob in here for starters; I know he seems harmless enough, but so did Gareth." Ifan was shocked by the confidence in his voice. "I suggest we also conduct a room-by-room search."

"How?"

"Something valuable has gone missing." Arwel's brain was rippling with ideas, and Ifan got caught up in the energy of his thoughts.

"A text?"

"No, something saleable." His eyes brimmed with the answer. "How much gold have you got?"

"None." Ifan sighed.

"Does anyone know that?"

Ifan shook his head. "I rather like keeping my shortcomings quiet."

≈

"*Wyt ti'n barod?* Are you ready?" Ifan hissed to his grandson when they heard the tentative knock.

The teenager nodded and Rob's head appeared around the partially opened door. "You wanted to see me?" he asked, already apologetic.

"Yes, come in, we need to ask you a few questions." Arwel's job was to watch and analyse Rob's reactions to his taid's questions. He just smiled up at the big man, who held his mandolin protectively against his chest. It was clear that Rob was already nervous, his eyes following Ifan's to the letters on the desk.

"This letter," Ifan picked up the paper and waved it, "you say it's from your grandmother?" Rob nodded rather than answering. "Is she still alive?"

"No," there was pain in the young man's voice.

"So she wrote this shortly before she died?"

Rob gave a little shake of his head. "About a year and a half before she died. It was cancer, she knew what was coming. Is there a problem with the letter?"

"Well, I'm a little baffled. I wasn't aware that there were any of us left in Cumbria, and you speak neither Cumbric, Brythonic nor Welsh." The Archdruid's voice was softly accusing.

"No, the language has been dead a long time. We are the last." Rob sighed, stroked the curved wooden body of the mandolin, and revised his words. "I am the last of us."

246

"So you've come here, why? To breed with one of us and repopulate?" Ifan's question sounded like a fairly reasonable guess to Arwel – attempted repopulation had been successful in the past. Yet Rob seemed extremely uncomfortable about the prospect.

"No... no. That's not why I'm here. Did the letter give you that impression?"

Ifan glanced briefly at the letter, sucking his teeth and shaking his head. "So why are you here, son?"

Rob closed his eyes and shrugged. "She thought I belonged here I suppose. But I don't know if she was right."

Ifan took a long hard look at the nervous musician, and changed tactics. "Some gold has gone missing." Rob's eyes widened, and his mouth began to open in protest, but Arwel intervened.

"Everyone is under suspicion, but being the most recent newcomer, you have been singled out. Your rooms are being searched as we speak."

Rob took the intrusion fairly well and asked his own question. "When was it taken?"

"Just over a week ago," Arwel improvised without conferring with Ifan. "Have you got any suspicions yourself then?"

"Well no, not really but Gareth left about then. Could it have been him?"

"Possibly," Arwel mused. "What did you think of him?"

Rob shrugged noncommittally. "I thought he was a bit of a prat if I'm honest."

"In what way?" Arwel and Ifan leaned forward in interested unison.

"I don't know, just something about him... too smooth maybe, I don't know. He didn't strike me as a thief though."

"And you'd never met him before coming here."

"No."

"And yet you arrived on the same day."

Rob weighed up the evidence and saw that he was implicated in some way. "Well, all I've got is my word. I didn't take your gold, Ifan."

Ifan relaxed back in his chair, lost in thought, so Arwel concluded the meeting. "Thanks, Rob, you can go now."

Rob straightened out his tall frame and turned to go.

"How is she?" he asked from the door.

"Who?" Ifan asked, distractedly.

"Mona. We're all getting a bit worried."

"She's on the mend," Arwel pitched in, smiling at the big Cumbrian.

Once Rob had left, Ifan waited until Arwel had filled the kettle before turning to him. "Well?"

"I think he's pretty genuine actually."

"Me too," his taid agreed gently. "But there is *something* he's not telling us, and we'll need to find out what it is."

≈

Rob rubbed the neck of the mandolin absentmindedly as he made his way to the rehearsal. The instrument reminded him of his gran whenever he played it – which was all the time. His nerves had been jangled by the meeting with the Archdruid, but he kept his nagging fears at bay with the promise of imminent music making.

Nia was back from university again. She was the life blood and energy of the musical soul here, always finding more material to play, though pieces like their mandolin/harp combos were not for the faint-hearted. Dai, Bryn, Rob and Nia were the backbone of the group, but Nansi played a mean fiddle, attending every session the children allowed.

Rob was early as usual for the get together; he didn't have enough to fill his day and lived for the next musical interlude. He'd tried to ask for a job but had always been directed to Ifan, who was usually too busy or too sad to see him – and it just hadn't seemed appropriate to ask today.

Nia arrived shortly after him and Rob seized the moment. She was easy to talk to and he explained his predicament. "Bryn could sort you out with some manual work – big strong man like you…" she answered straightaway.

Realising that he would have to come clean with her, Rob spoke up. "I know I look it, but I'm not much of a labourer," and hastily continued before she asked why. "I've always worked well with children and babies; they like the music."

He was colouring up again and looking at the floor, but if Nia was shocked that he should enjoy such a traditionally feminine role, she didn't show it. "Taliesin!" She almost sang the words. Nia's excited reaction was definitely not what Rob was used to. "You're a true Bard, Rob," she sighed, and he knew from the glazed look in her eyes that he was on the verge of another long history lesson.

Rob couldn't decide if textbooks or music were the most important part of Nia's life. Together, these two loves didn't seem to leave any room in her life for romance, and he admired that sort of dedication. But he needed an answer and Rob steered her gently back to the present-day. "So, is there a nursery where I can help out?"

"Of course there is, just ask Nansi."

Rob determined to do that, but later. Everyone had finally arrived and there was music to make.

To her delight, Nia had discovered that, of the seven main vocal types, she had five in her little group. Tonight would be an experiment, but she had great ambitions for the group's future.

Dai had a rumbling bass voice, whose vibrations overflowed his diminutive frame and caused the ground to shake beneath them. Nia placed him in the middle, with the baritone and tenor combination of Bryn and Rob on his left, and the contralto and soprano mix of Nansi and herself to his right. They played around, backing up Dai's voice with a hummed melody, but eventually settled on the combination of Bryn and Rob, with all the singers coming in on the last stanza.

Bryn's voice was the steady rock in the two men's melodic stream.

At first, Rob's voice followed Bryn's closely. As the song progressed, however, it began to rise, soaring high above it before dropping once more into the tonal warmth of Bryn's mellow baritone. Rob revelled in that warmth, even as he prepared to be engulfed by the tide of approaching voices. As these musical waters rushed over him and receded, Rob clung fast to the rock of Bryn's voice; never wavering, it provided the necessary focal point in the powerful maelstrom of voices around him.

As the last of the a cappella notes died away, each of the singers knew that true magic had been made that night. They hadn't needed an audience to confirm it, and every one of them secretly feared it could never be repeated.

For once, Nia was stunned into silence – and it was Bryn who broke the spell, glancing at his watch and mumbling something about his shift as he stumbled out of the room.

It was a poor excuse, but Bryn needed a reason to escape before Rob turned to look at him. He'd felt that radiance only twice before, and each time had been rendered incapable of thought or action.

After the intimacy of their duet, all Bryn's defences were down. If he were forced to confront Rob now, he would fall and drown. Better to run and hide, he thought, as he gulped in the night air and placed a shaking hand against the boathouse wall.

20

Mutiny

The lifeboat station at Tobermory on Mull consisted of a row of converted cottages. Cai and Glyn knew where to go, but they were nevertheless met by an anxious Dafydd as they docked in the harbour.

The news of their failure had further increased tensions within the Welsh party, and it was obvious that there was not enough room for them to stay more than one night.

The squabbling and fault-finding continued for some time. Cai waited until his ship-mates had blown off some steam, before putting forward his idea – this time to the whole crew. "We should cut through the Caledonian Canal and attempt a circumnavigation – while the weather's still good." It got their attention at least.

"Are you mad? That would take weeks."

Cai wished it wasn't Ieuan who'd spoken; he would have answered less harshly to anyone else. "A month if we pushed hard," he corrected. "It's August now; we should go while the weather is with us. There's no way back through the Irish Sea."

All eyes turned to their leader. "I've been thinking the same, but only as a last resort," Dafydd replied evenly. "I just never imagined it would come to this."

Lack of rest and constant travel had prevented injuries from healing quickly. The crews just wanted to go home now, and the thought of another month at sea was hard to digest.

There were more mumblings from Ieuan's corner and his pack of followers bristled with discontent. "What now?" Even Dafydd's equable temper was beginning to fray, and Ieuan, who seemed like he wanted to say more, merely shook his head.

≈

After refuelling and filling the water tanks, the four small boats left the Sound of Mull at dawn. Their destination was Loch Linnhe and the sea lock at Corpach. From there, the Caledonian Canal would provide a short cut between the Atlantic and the North Sea: a journey of between two and three days, depending on how hard they pushed.

None of the crew had any inkling of how magnificent the route would be. Forested hills climbed steeply each side of the canal's clear, blue water, and as they glided along it was impossible to ignore the awe-inspiring presence of Ben Nevis.

Not wanting to draw unwelcome attention, the small flotilla pushed up to, but rarely beyond, the five mph speed limit, forcing the boats' crews to unwind and relax in the warm summer sun. Cai wondered how many of the holidaymakers and sightseers even considered their strange little convoy.

The uncomfortable atmosphere between Cai and Ieuan persisted, but it was lifting with each mile homewards. It might take them a month of early mornings, late nights and of scratch living, but they would be back in the *Conway* by September.

Cai's pulse quickened at the thought of seeing Mona again, surprising him with the intensity of his feelings. He fantasised about jumping back into bed with her; about talking to her, laughing with her.

Such emotions had a depth and tenderness that he had never experienced before, and Cai marvelled at how rapidly he had become infatuated with Mona. When he'd first spied on her at Swnt, Cai had thought her a large, plain tomboy. But now, every memory he had of her made him inexplicably happy. Whatever Mona had done to him, Cai hoped it was permanent.

In her absence, however, he was slowly slipping back into his previous sullen introspection – that dark, gloomy state that Mona had so successfully dispelled with her light. If Mona was here, Cai knew there was a good chance that he would be smiling, possibly even laughing. If Mona was here Emlyn may never have died.

≈

"Sioned's getting suspicious, Mona, you're going to have to face her soon." They'd been strategising in Arwel's quadrant of the laundry for a week now. Nia, Sioned and Siân had returned last night, and were itching to catch up.

"What are we going to say?" Mona asked. At least it wasn't a point-blank refusal, this time.

"Glandular fever. I've looked up the symptoms and some of them are viable." Arwel counted out the possibilities on his fingers. "Exhaustion, nausea." He peered closely at her. "Depression. You'll have to add on flu-like symptoms if they ask. You look bad enough for anyone to believe it."

The fizzing in her nipples had progressed to a dull ache over the last week, but this was probably information that Arwel would prefer she didn't share. "Thanks for that."

The boy was aghast. "I didn't mean…"

"I know."

It was too late for any more conferring, because there was a knock on the door, followed immediately by the entrance of her friends. It had been three weeks since she'd seen any of them, but it could have been a lifetime – Mona had changed irrevocably.

Both Ifan and Arwel had cautioned her not to mention the attack, and she had agreed, but only because she wouldn't be able to bear the pity. Mona relived the horror each night; why talk about it during the day?

Her friends were profoundly affected by her physical appearance. Even Sioned was dumbstruck, but not for long. "I like the *Gráinne*

253

Mhaol look," she muttered and Nia elbowed her. "What! I said I liked it!"

"Who's…?" Mona scrunched her eyebrows in a question.

"Gráinne Ni Mháille was a sixteenth-century Irish pirate; you might know her as Grace O'Malley," Nia explained patiently.

"She had cropped hair too," Sioned added helpfully with a big, innocent smile. Then Siân and Nia attacked from both sides, taking a hand each.

Arwel flinched in sympathy, knowing Mona's recent aversion to physical contact. "Come on, you two, don't crowd her; she's been really ill."

Mona flexed a muscle in her mouth, giving him a half smile to let him know she was coping. "So what's new in Moelfre?" she asked, putting them off the scent.

"Just running repairs, odd jobs – that sort of thing," Siân replied wearily, though Sioned was full of it.

"I stayed in *Lifeboat House* and there are some tasty new lads in the crew." She winked at Mona and both Nia and Siân rolled their eyes.

"Old Pricey died," Nia said sadly after a moment.

Mona didn't think she'd heard of him before. "Was he from here then?"

Nia shook her head. "No, he was *Old Moelfre*. He knew all the village histories, but now he's gone," she sighed sadly, "and the stories have died with him."

Nia seemed to treat her books and stories like living people, friends almost, and though Mona thought it was odd, she accepted it as one of her friend's foibles. "Didn't he leave a family?" she asked.

"He did, but they live in Liverpool now; his grandchildren don't even speak Welsh." Mona kept quiet, having learnt by now not to upset Nia by trivialising her language. "I should have recorded his stories; I should have written them down," Nia grieved.

"Perhaps some of his mates might know them?" Mona offered but soon realised she should have kept her mouth shut.

"They've all gone, Mo. He was the last of the old Welshmen left in the village."

"The last? They're all dead?"

Nia sighed. "No, not dead, just gone." Mona obviously looked puzzled enough to cause Nia to explain further. "This is a beautiful part of the world, and it's near enough to several big English cities." Arwel, Sioned and Siân nodded in tacit agreement. "They come here on holiday when they're young and retire here when they're old and rich. There's not much work locally, not now that the fishing is gone, and tourism alone can't support all the Welsh youngsters – so they go."

"They don't even try to learn the language," Siân remarked wearily.

"It's a difficult language, to be fair." Mona tried to defend not only her country, but also herself – and it sounded pretty lame.

"The English-speakers come, and the Welsh-speakers go – that's how a language dies."

After they'd breathed a sigh of grief for the loss of the man and his stories, Arwel picked up the mood with a newsflash. "Mo's starting the training programme again tomorrow." Mona frowned at him but he didn't even glance in her direction. "I've got the schedule; we'll hand it around at supper."

"Aren't you coming, Mo?" Sioned asked.

"Well, I'm not really…" Mona looked to Arwel for support. "I'm not actually…"

"You've got to do it sometime." Sioned insisted. She had already linked arms with Mona and was steering her through the door and up the stairs.

≈

The crews had got as far as Fort Augustus, slipping through the last lock before it closed at 6 p.m. The facilities at the lock were excellent, and after Cai had showered and visited the laundry, he joined Glyn, Cerys, Gwen and a couple of youngsters on the deck of the *Marc'h*.

Cai guessed the women were here to avoid Ieuan's attention: the idiot had probably made a play for each of them or pushed them away with his constant sniping. Cai was glad that Gwen had decided to keep her distance. He didn't want her, but he didn't want to hurt her feelings.

Their meal was straight out of a can, but as compensation they got to sit around on deck afterwards, soaking up the long evening sunshine. "Watch out, Cai, you're doing it again," Cerys teased, interrupting a delicious train of thought concerning Mona.

"What?"

"Smiling."

"A man can smile, can't he?"

Cerys nodded. "It's just we've never seen you smile so much before." Cai frowned. Surely that wasn't true.

"Don't get me wrong, it's good to see, it's just …"

"What?"

"You only do it when you're thinking of Mona." Glyn's laugh was filthy.

"How do you know?" Cai chortled back as Glyn pointed at his crotch. "Very funny," he said, settling back in the sun.

"You really like her, don't you?" Gwen asked quietly.

Cai sat up and replied simply. "Yes, I really like her."

Both women reacted as if he'd confessed something monumental, and they exchanged a look he didn't fully understand. "Make sure you don't hurt her feelings then," Gwen chided, without malice.

Glyn giggled. "I'd like to see him try."

They all agreed, good-naturedly, that it would take more than a lothario like Cai to undo Mona. Though when the taunting had died down, Cai was left again with thoughts of the Englishwoman.

Cai was no stranger to sex, but what he'd shared with Mona still felt astonishingly vivid. Mixed with the passion, stamina and total abandon had been a surprising amount of comedy; they had both spent much of that one day together laughing.

Mona had said she wanted her seven days, but Cai was pretty sure that seven days with Mona wouldn't be enough to satisfy him. But how many would be enough? Seventy, seven hundred? A lifetime?

"*Ti'n gwneud yr un peth eto.* You're doing it again." Gwen's voice was a sing-song, until he threw his teabag at her.

≈

The boats' crews stuck to strict shifts at the helms to allow for naps during the voyage, but sleeping on-board was awkward, cramped and uncomfortable. They motored just over the speed limit, desperate to make the Clachnaharry sea lock.

From Inverness they carried on into the North Sea until dark. The flotilla regrouped in the Beauly Firth to discuss the charts; both Dafydd and Cai had been looking for the buoys that marked the channel out to sea. Picking up the binoculars from the chart table, Dafydd scanned the horizon. Within seconds he wordlessly handed them to Cai and pointed, his expression wooden.

The three VSVs weren't steaming towards them, but loitering, their engines ticking over. The message was clear: not this way either.

≈

Rob was pretty sure that Bryn was avoiding him. The memory of their duet haunted his every waking hour, its precision pestered his sleep. He had never felt so literally in tune with anyone in his life – yet Bryn had withdrawn from all musical sessions since.

Rob asked Dai the odd question about the shifts in the radio room, and it seemed that Bryn virtually lived there. Apparently, he didn't trust anyone else enough to monitor the equipment, or field any potential contact from the fleet.

It had been a week since their voices had met, and Rob had been looking for excuses to reacquaint them, so he jumped at the chance to carry a message up to the radio room for Dai – mandolin case in hand.

Bryn appeared deep in thought, listening through a large set of earphones, and didn't notice Rob until he was standing beside him. "Rob." Bryn's voice sounded bored and irritated, but he looked like he'd seen a ghost.

"I'm sorry, I should have knocked louder," Rob apologised. "Dai's ill and wondered if you could carry on for a couple of hours. He's arranged for Nansi to take over, once the kids are in bed."

"No problem," the big man replied, and turned away to fiddle with a setting.

Taking courage, Rob held up two beers and his mandolin. "I'll keep you company, if you like."

"No thanks, Rob. It might not look much, but I have to concentrate on this."

Rob hid his disappointment admirably, but felt that this might be the only chance he would ever have to bring up the singing. "I've never sung a duet like that with anyone. Our voices…"

"Really?" Bryn answered briskly. "I didn't think it was anything special." Rob found himself unable to respond adequately and admitting defeat, he abandoned Bryn to the company of his machines.

It had taken all of Bryn's considerable willpower not to accept Rob's company, but he was certain it was for the best. His unnatural desire for the beautiful Englishman was overwhelming, and nothing good could ever come of it.

≈

No one spoke at all. The order was given to moor at an anchorage, as near the tourist cruisers as possible. At least that might prevent another attack. Cai's mind was working feverishly. How had they known when to make the interception? It was almost as if…

"We need a word." Dafydd's voice broke across his random theorising. There was nowhere to have a private conversation, so his words were muttered. "We're heading back to Tobermory. I'll decide what to do from there."

The voyage back along the canal was grim. No amount of magnificent scenery could dispel the deep gloom that had settled over the boats' crews. Cai wracked his mind and memory to solve the riddle, and lost in thought, he failed to notice the atmosphere of suspicion that had spread throughout the crew. Until the meeting.

≈

A sympathiser from the Mull clan had lent them the keys to a musty village hall. Cai sat next to Dafydd, who he presumed would be running the show. However, the meeting quickly turned into the free-for-all that Cai had feared, with Ieuan and his protégés making most of the noise.

"Well, it's obvious, isn't it?" Ieuan spat. Cai watched him talk, not really wondering if he had the wit to work out the mystery, but desperate enough to consider anything at this point. "There's a spy," Ieuan exclaimed to a chorus of loud agreement. So far, so good, Cai thought. "Someone has been passing information to the Irish. How else would they know? Isn't that right, Cai?"

Ieuan wasn't after agreement and Cai realised, too late, that it was an accusation. "You're right, Ieuan, there *is* a spy," he replied evenly. There weren't any gasps; just the noise people make when they try not to react. Cai continued. "And they could be here, but more likely, the spy is still on Ynys Môn."

Dafydd was aghast, but Ieuan began smiling broadly; Cai was playing directly into his hands. "Ever since Mona arrived in Gwynedd, we've had nothing but grief. Have you all forgotten about her *mark*?" Ieuan glared intently, from face to face. "The very same symbol is painted on the side of those Irish hulls." Of course they hadn't forgotten, of course they'd noticed. "Can't you remember what it stands for? For fuck's sake, it was engraved on the blade that killed Emlyn – that killed the young lads." Dafydd sank lower in his chair as Ieuan held forth. "Mona's orchestrating the whole show. Why did she train those women in secret?"

Cai stared at Cerys and Gwen but they couldn't meet his eye – both women had clearly caved to Ieuan under questioning. "It wasn't like that," Cerys replied hesitantly, "Mona just wanted them to defend themselves."

"That's what she told you," he pointed at her, "but what if it that wasn't her intention at all? What if she's trained up a pretty handy army by now, all led by the Saxon slut's dark magic?" Ieuan's nodding head was drawing the Welsh crew in. "She's sent us off on a fool's errand."

Doubt was nagging at the entire crew now and none of them were looking at Cai – they all knew what was coming next. "All but one. Her own little spy, seduced by the power of her body and magic. A fucking *turncoat*, who contacts the Irish whenever he can – whenever he's told the plan by his uncle."

"*Ieuan.*" Dafydd's tone was pleading rather than admonitory, and his lack of resolve fuelled Ieuan's fever.

"What will we find when – *if* – we ever get back? Will everyone we love be dead, or turned into Mona's zombies?"

Cai endeavoured to reason with Ieuan, but he feared the damage had already been done. "Yes, there's a spy, and I don't know who, but I think I might know how…"

The relentless momentum of Ieuan's accusations steamrollered through all opposing thought or speech. "We should lock him up somewhere, while we discuss our options." Ieuan looked hard at Dafydd, aware of his new power and ready to embrace every opportunity to exercise it.

"Come on, Cai," Dafydd mumbled towards the floor.

Cai knew that if he didn't go now, with Dafydd, he would be restrained, and was still calm enough not to want to hurt his friends. Dafydd fumbled in his pocket for the set of hall keys. "Good idea. Stick him in the khazi and lock him away," Ieuan gloated.

Dafydd obediently took hold of Cai's arm and led him away. They walked slowly, their heads close together. "Look ahead."

Dafydd's lips were barely moving. "You need to get away from here. Now."

"If I run, they'll think I'm guilty."

"If you don't, you could die. Ieuan has tipped the balance of power and I won't be able to stop him." No one was following them but Dafydd made a show of jangling the keys. "Find me when you've worked it out." Cai took a breath to reply but Dafydd cut him off. "Don't tell me now; just hit me and go." It was a good idea, but not one Cai looked forward to executing. "For fuck's sake, Cai, hit me and hard. I don't want any explaining to do."

Afterwards, Cai checked Dafydd's pulse and mentally apologised to his unconscious form, before sprinting for the jetty. He found the tiny rowing boat under the pier, right where his uncle had said it would be. He lay down flat in it.

The ensuing manhunt was half-hearted at best – most of his countrymen didn't want to believe him guilty, and they were probably relieved at not being party to a trial.

The search was called off about midnight, giving Cai plenty of time to contemplate his next move. He had studied the chart of the Inner Hebrides stashed in the supply bag, but the only name that rang a bell was Eigg. There was some kind of renewables project there, and he tried to recall more details. However, the rage pulsing through his body made it difficult to think coherently.

Casting off, he moved silently out into the cold waters of the Atlantic, hoping to have remembered more by the time he reached the tiny island.

21

Eigg

Arwel plodded into their rooms, walking more like an octogenarian than a teenager. He flopped on to the sofa and stared straight ahead. "Well?" his grandfather asked, despite already sensing failure from the boy's body language.

"Nothing. We searched every single room," he growled in frustration. "I don't even know what we're looking for."

"Did Bryn ask any questions?"

Arwel pulled a face. "He's been like a bear with a sore head all day – not that he's ever any different."

"But you don't reckon he suspects an ulterior motive for the search?"

"He suspects I've lost my mind, and I'm beginning to agree with him."

"So," Ifan asked, "what now?"

"Paperwork," his grandson conceded resignedly. "I'll start searching documents. It's the only place left to look."

≈

For the first few hours, Cai just rowed, keeping his rhythm by reciting the sea shanties his dad had taught him. He glanced from time to time at the compass, but focussed his anger on the job in hand. If he slowed, he would get cold, even August wasn't particularly warm here, and he was cruelly exposed. Cai wanted to be out of the water before the sun rose, and the CalMac ferries started their daily journeys around the islands. The swell alone might tip him overboard, and he had no life jacket, no radio and no flares.

Cai held the rhythm of the stroke in his head, spying the headland of Ardnamurchan on his right at about 3 a.m. He prayed that he'd make Eigg by dawn and before he ran out of energy. It had only been a journey of about thirty kilometres, but for a long time he had been forced by swells and tides to row with all his might just to make any gains at all.

With biceps and back screaming in agony, he shuffled the tiny boat up the shale beach. Cai knew he mustn't stop moving until it was safely hidden. When they stopped, his muscles would seize up, and there was no telling when they might start to work again.

After stowing the rowing boat well above the high-water mark, he collapsed against it. The rising sun warmed him through and he drifted easily into sleep.

≈

Cai was startled awake by wet, cold-nosed snufflings – dogs, he thought straightaway, but they were extremely pointy and thin. The fawn and white one sniffed at his face once more and moved away casually, but the grey-coloured dog lay down right next to him and started shivering. The dogs had collars and therefore owners, but they seemed dangerously undernourished. Cai stroked the head of the nearest animal, and it closed its eyes, snuggling a little nearer, in search of body warmth he guessed.

It was warm but the wind had picked up and was coming onshore. Even the small movement involved in stroking the dog's head had been difficult, and Cai braced himself for the forthcoming pain of standing.

He heard shouting in the distance, and Cai decided to test his muscles out gradually by extending his stroking movements along the length of the dog's back. The stiffness in his shoulder was unbelievable, but began to ease with the gentle activity. The calling drew nearer and the dog got reluctantly to its feet and mooched off towards the caller.

Using the half-hidden rowing boat, Cai managed to pull himself upright and adopt a nonchalant demeanour before the dogs' owner appeared. "Hello there!" The voice was very English. "Sorry if my dogs were bothering you; not awfully obedient I'm afraid."

Cai didn't particularly want to talk to anyone, but he needed help and put as much effort into being affable as possible. "No problem. I think he's a bit cold." The trembling grey dog had slunk back into the shelter between Cai's legs and the boat.

The man laughed. "He's hamming it up a bit, but maybe I should have put his coat on."

The dog-walker eyed the rowing boat and Cai's dishevelled state. Knowing there'd be questions he had prepared a story that stuck as close to the truth as possible. "I had a bit of a falling out with my friends last night; you know how it is, too much to drink… Anyway, I thought I'd just get away from them for a while." He glanced at the boat ruefully. "It's a long way from the peninsula with a belly full of beer."

"That it is." The man shook his head. "Do you know where you are then?"

"Eigg?" Cai prayed his navigation skills hadn't completely failed him.

The other man nodded. "The next ferry isn't until this time tomorrow – you've just missed it. But there's a shop and a pub. I can point you in the right direction if you want?" He beamed jovially.

Cai tensed as he wondered if Dafydd had stowed any money in the bag. "Thanks," he said, turning to check. He found £20 and a loaf of bread, but even while giving silent thanks for his uncle's foresight, Cai knew that longer term survival here, without help, was going to be impossible.

"Actually, I need to pick up a pint of milk myself. I'll wander down with you," the Englishman announced. The dogs sniffed along beside them as they walked and talked. He was around forty-five, tall and broad, and his head was shaved. He and his wife had lived here since 2007; they loved it, despite the challenges of the weather. The dogs weren't malnourished, they were whippets, built for chasing rabbits.

"Do you know anything about the off-grid electricity project at Glebe?" Cai's memory had saved him. The plan had been to ask in the shop, but that was a sure-fire way of advertising his whereabouts.

"A bit, why?" the man replied.

"I did some research on it for my masters. I'm thinking about a PhD, and it's the sort of stuff I'm interested in – renewables, you know."

"Which university?"

"Bangor."

"I thought that was a Welsh accent."

They approached the shop, and though Cai was desperately thirsty, there was no way he was spending precious cash on bottled water when it would be plentiful in the hills. "Do you mind?" The man pointed at the dogs, and Cai assumed he was to keep an eye on them.

As soon as the man disappeared into the shop, Cai rooted around in the overflowing rubbish bin for empty water bottles. He snagged three large plastic containers and had them neatly stowed away by the time the man emerged with his milk, a bottle of water and two chocolate bars.

"I'm going near Glebe. Get your shopping and I'll show you the way."

Cai tapped his backpack. "I've got plenty of supplies." The dogs' owner scrutinised the pack, the look lasted a lot longer than was comfortable, and Cai got the distinct impression that he wasn't fooling anyone.

Cai didn't need the Englishman to guide him to the site; he had already seen the blades of the four big wind generators from the beach. "So tell me what you know and I'll fill in the rest," the dog walker said. He pointed vaguely at a green container, which was obviously the control hub for the project.

Cai was happy to oblige with as much as he knew. "The islanders clubbed together to buy their island in the nineties and decided to do something about the electricity supply; wanting to go as green as possible." The man nodded, but Cai couldn't gauge anything from it. "There's a twenty-four kilowatt wind farm, a photovoltaic solar installation of about ten kilowatts, some hydro systems." He scanned around, unable to see them immediately, but he'd hit his stride and was becoming enthusiastic. "In there," he pointed and moved towards the container, "you'll have a large battery bank, inverters and chargers. There will also be a pretty powerful generator, to charge the batteries and to act as fall-back just in case the wind doesn't blow and the sun doesn't shine."

The man seemed to be suppressing a chuckle. "Follow me," he smirked, "I'll introduce you to the boss; they might let you take a peek inside."

"That would be great." Cai couldn't believe the change in his luck, and he followed the man for a short distance until they reached a long, L-shaped tin shed.

The man opened the door and beckoned Cai inside, glancing at his watch. "Boss will be along in about ten minutes."

The Englishman closed and locked the door from the inside. Cai tensed but the man walked past him and filled the kettle. "You've got that long to tell me that you're *not* the wild young Welshman who stole a boat and rowed here from Tobermory last night." Cai backed up towards the door. "You could have a go at telling me the truth. I'm not completely unshockable, but you'd have to go some to upset me. Come on; sit down." He handed Cai the water and a chocolate bar. "Eat that; you might be able to think a bit straighter. But hurry up, we haven't got long." The man eyed the far end of the shed, from where they could hear the sound of grinding and loud music.

The water was wonderful and the sugary chocolate rushed to Cai's head. "I *have* had a falling out with my friends; but it's serious, deadly serious. I can rectify the situation, but not until I've solved a problem. I haven't got any money or anywhere to stay." It was all near enough the truth. "What gave me away?" he asked earnestly.

"Well..." The man smiled. "I saw you scavenging the water bottles from the bin and I reckon if you were really just a hung-over lout, you might ask to borrow some money." He studied Cai, trying not to laugh again. "And the blades at your hip are decidedly dodgy." Then he frowned. "They're not real though, are they?"

Cai shook his head vehemently. "No, of course not." He blanched and felt for the sword and dagger dangling from his belt, but the man was talking again.

"OK. This is the story we tell the boss." He glanced at his watch and began to speak even faster. "You're part of a medieval re-enactment group, travelling the Highlands. You've had a row with the leading man because you've shagged his girlfriend, and he's after you. I've offered you a job here until it quietens down. Deal?"

It was the best offer he was likely to get. "Deal." Cai agreed rather lamely.

"Right, stick to the story."

There was some clattering at the far end. Someone walked in, swearing as they took off their welding mask. "That's two discs in twenty minutes... Who are you?" The woman was short and stout, her face dirty with grinding dust. Dragging off her leather gauntlets and apron, she glared at Cai.

"This is Steve," the Englishman volunteered, too quickly. "He's going to be helping me with that little project we talked about." She eyed the man but seemed confused for a second, so he helped her out. "Mini off-grid?" he reminded her.

"Oh... oh, yes." She thought about it for a while, then smiled at the man. "Very good; I like it." She had no smile for Cai. "Where did you come from?"

Between them, the men regurgitated the impromptu cover story, and when they had finished, the woman took a long sip from her mug of tea. "So you're not the young Welsh fugitive that Angus came by to warn me about?" She glared at Cai again. "You know, the armed and dangerous one?"

22

Berys

By late September, everything had changed. Nia had gone back to university, taking the music with her, though the get-togethers had faltered even before then. With Nansi's children sharing their chicken pox around, and Bryn's increased shift work, the magic had never been repeated.

Rob felt it like a hole in his chest. Sometimes he and Dai got together for a little musical fix, but it wasn't the same. Rob realised that he'd misinterpreted his connection with Bryn, and on the few occasions that their paths had crossed since then, both parties had been careful to avoid each other.

Life in the nursery had kept his mind focused during the day, but the early mornings and late nights were times of loneliness and longing. Rob felt that a dreary pall had fallen over the grey buildings as the weather worsened and the year wore on. The torpor was unending and punctuated only by a couple of events that were out of the ordinary: Mona's long illness and a community-wide search for the pilfered gold – though he'd not personally been subjected to any more questioning.

Rob had roamed the shoreline at dawn about a month ago, unable to sleep, when he'd stumbled across Mona, clearly on the mend and dancing in an excruciatingly slow and deliberate way. "Exercise will set you free," she misquoted at him. Rob had explained that all sport was anathema to him, bar swimming. At this point she'd ordered him down to his underwear and into the Menai Strait.

He had taken to the cold waters regularly since then, swimming his lengths, while she killed imaginary people, slowly. It was clear to Rob that Mona had her own demons, but they appeared to trouble her less as they bantered. "You sing pretty well, Rob; you're a sort of mixture between Bryn Terfel and Cerys Matthews." Her eyes lit up with mischief. "I've decided to rename you Berys; it's *so* much more Welsh."

"That's not a real name, and anyway, what's wrong with 'fish boy'?"

"I like both. How's it going at the nursery?"

"It's good; I know what to expect from children."

"Poo and sick." Mona pulled a face and Rob pretended to laugh at the cliché.

"No; they're just uncomplicated, I suppose."

Mona grunted. "Still, you should interact with other adults at some point."

"Not that you count," he fired back. "You're like a teenage boy: all you do is fight and pretend to fight."

"Which reminds me, no one gets out of combat stuff, even the little brats you look after are better with a knife than you." Rob started to protest, and she became slightly serious. "If there's an attack, we'll all need to fight."

Mona was always a little too intense when they discussed this topic, and he artfully diverted the conversation. "So, I hear he's a bit of a god, this Cai."

Mona couldn't stop her heart racing at the mention of his name, but she didn't have to let Rob know that. "He's OK; not a bad fighter, as it goes."

Rob tried, really tried, to keep a straight face at her forced nonchalance, but it was no good, laughter bubbled up uncontrollably from inside him. "*Oooh*, Mona Jones, you've got it *bad* for that man."

His smile was infectious and she had the good sense not to try to defend herself.

"Shut up, Berys, I'm starving."

≈

The woman stood up slowly and glowered at Cai, but she spoke to the Englishman beside him. "What the bloody hell are you playing at, you daft bugger. You can't trust every Tom, Dick and Harry you meet on the footpath."

"But Liz…"

"Don't you *Liz* me. Angus said he'd knocked his mate unconscious."

"He told me that himself. I just thought…"

"What's the real story then?" The woman ignored her husband, directing a deepening frown towards Cai.

"I can't tell you," Cai grumbled.

"Can't or won't?" she said, picking up a cordless phone.

"Can't," Cai spat. "There'd be consequences."

"Are you threatening me?" she growled at him, and he shrugged. "I'd like to see you try, sunshine," the woman countered, leaning forward and gritting her teeth.

This woman looked nothing like Mona, but the Englishness of her delivery and the jut of her chin suddenly reminded Cai of the gurning moment at the party, and he began to laugh. He was vaguely aware that his giggling had enraged the woman, but couldn't seem to control himself, and the situation wasn't helped at all when her husband joined in, his shoulders lifting in subdued mirth.

"Give me strength," Cai heard her mutter, but felt there was a distinct softening in her tone.

≈

It took an entire week for Cai and John – as he discovered the Englishman was called – to broker a deal with his wife , and Liz drove a hard bargain. At the end of negotiations, Cai was employed as electrician's mate and general muscle, but also head chef and laundry maid. Liz had been adamant in gaining the cooking concession, but Cai secretly enjoyed working his way through her collection of cookbooks, and had started to produce some excellent food.

Laundry duties had happened accidentally, when Cai had caught Liz forcing his combat leathers into the washing machine. His leathers were his most important and valuable possessions, apart from his father's sword, and he had been taught how to care for both from a young age. Boiling them was not part of that regime.

It also took several days for his body to heal itself, but crushing damage had been done to his soul, and that would take much longer to mend. The men and women who had betrayed him weren't just friends or even just his countrymen. They were companions of the heart who had lived and breathed in each other's company from birth: training, fighting and even dying side by side.

As the days passed, Cai found it more and more difficult to reconcile himself with what had happened and forgive those responsible. He was connected to the Druids by a complex root system; one that he had assumed was unbreakable. But he had been proved wrong; it had only taken one loudmouth idiot to snap those fine threads – he found the effects of this amputation devastating. Logically, Cai knew he should put the incident behind him, and set his mind to discovering the truth about their plight, but he could not. Very gradually, he closed his mind and heart to the Druid diaspora at Tobermory, and soon enough he didn't think of them at all.

Despite the fact that John referred to her as the boss, Liz wasn't in charge of the electricity project on Eigg. John wasn't either, as far as Cai could make out, but was rather a sort of renewables consultant who monitored the system, while working on his own related ventures.

John was on a mission to complete his own project before the weather stopped him, and Cai was the answer to his prayers. The work was absorbing and exhausting, and Cai began to lose himself in it gratefully, finding a refuge from the demons in his head. He and John were up early each day and late to bed each night, putting together this off-grid microsystem in a race against time. Work took the place of thought and of memory, and Cai existed in the present tense only. He barely noticed that the summer had passed.

The English couple had two children; boys around Cai's age – Arthur and George – and he had become Arthur for the benefit of the local community. Liz had given him a serious haircut and dressed him in some of Arthur's clothes. There had been a well-publicised arrival date, and Cai had even obliged them by walking out of the CalMac ferry terminal to greet his eager parents. Later, Cai was paraded around, as Arthur, at the local social hotspots of the cafe and the post office. After that, he kept his head down and out of the way – not that they had very many visitors.

"Arty, come here. I found this website last night. These are just what we need." John was speaking from his study and pointing to one of the many computer monitors.

Their tin shed had been divided up. It was mostly a communal living area, with two bedrooms and a study. The study was larger than both bedrooms combined, and it was where John did all his cogitating, and played his guitar.

"See." He pointed at the image on the screen. "Lithium ion batteries. There's a twelve per cent increase in yield, they hold the charge better, are lighter and would last a lot longer." Cai knew there was a 'but' coming. "Expensive though; it's always the same with new technology." John sucked his bottom lip under his teeth, in thought. Technology and renewables seemed to be John's raison d'être, and he was never happier than when surfing the Internet in pursuit of items to build the next prototype. Cai guessed that, despite the price, lithium ion batteries would become an integral part of the microsystem scheme.

The couple gravitated to the kitchen when the food started smelling good. Liz came out of the shower, pink and shiny, having scrubbed away the day's metal work, and John from his study, iPad in hand.

The strange English couple had hardly anything to do with each other during the day, each of them lost in their own little universe. Yet every evening, at around this time, they greeted each other with an enthusiastic kiss and cuddle and caught up with each other's day over a bottle of wine. To begin with, Cai had shunned the offered drink, thinking it somehow too decadent, but two months on and he was looking forward to a glass of Rioja with his meal just as much as his hosts.

"Smells amazing, Arty." John smiled over his glass, upheld in thanks. "You'll make someone a wonderful wife one day," John teased.

A sudden blast of emotion caused Cai to drop his knife. He hadn't mentioned his past and they had never pried. Over the past few months he'd somehow managed to live in the moment, shutting away memories of the world he'd left behind.

In everyday life, he no longer ached for Mona; he had no reason to believe she would have stayed. Gwen had ridiculed him for even thinking she might. Cai had weaned himself off her memory – he had been doing well, and couldn't work out why the innocent comment should have affected him so badly.

≈

Liz washed and Cai wiped, while they listened to John's guitar playing through the thin study door. "Sorry about John earlier; he didn't mean to upset you." So they had both noticed.

"I'm not upset," he reassured her quietly.

Liz sighed, as if she had made a difficult decision. "Are you out?"

Cai glanced around. "Of what?"

She'd stopped washing up, and was staring deep into the greasy water. "Have you come out?"

Cai creased his brow again. "I don't know what you mean."

Liz grunted, as if he were being purposefully obtuse. "Are you gay?" Cai was totally stunned. "It's OK, Cai, there's nothing to be ashamed of."

"No, I'm sure there's not," he replied, finally drying the plate, which had stood idle in his hands during the last part of the conversation. "But why did you ask? Do I act gay?"

"Well, you're hideously good-looking for a start."

"Oh."

"Jesus, Cai; that was a joke."

Liz was wiping down the worktop now. "I only meant that you're unnaturally quiet about your personal life, and you'd mentioned that a good friend of yours was a welder. I know you like the smell coming from my workshop, and I just thought it was because it reminded you of him." Liz waited for Cai to confide in her, and when he didn't, she concluded. "And you don't seem interested in any of the women on the island. I'm sorry, I should mind my own business."

≈

Mona had followed the instructions and was now waiting for a result from the urine-soaked gadget in her hand. The unbearable tenderness in her breasts had been replaced by a blue-veined solidity. She had missed at least two periods, and so there wasn't any doubt in her head that she was pregnant.

However, the blue line in the little window bolstered this knowledge with a new reality and substance, shattering weeks of denial. The constant nagging fear had been replaced by a waking nightmare. She was pregnant with Gareth's child, and it was too late to abort.

True to form, Mona felt an initial instinct to run – but where to and what from? This time she carried the enemy within her; this was something she couldn't outrun. Crying seemed useless, so Mona wandered out into the cold dawn air – it was pattern time anyway.

"I don't know how many more times I'm going to freeze my arse off in here." Rob's teeth chattered as he hobbled up the beach to meet her. "I only keep doing it so you won't take the piss... What is it?"

Mona was deathly white, and staring through Rob to the horizon. She didn't answer but held up a small white pen, which he took from her. "*Ah.*" She didn't respond. "I suppose that would account for the amount of food you've been eating."

Mona focused on him then, but there was no humour in her eyes. All he could see there was panic and fear, and when he enveloped her in a cold, wet embrace she crumpled into him like a rag doll.

Tea and toast made her feel better, if only slightly. "I've never even picked one up." Rob was confused. "A baby, Berys; I've never picked up an *actual* baby."

"Babies are easy; people are hard. Besides, it will all just happen naturally; your motherly instinct will take over." Rob didn't even sound convinced himself, and tried a new tack. "We'll all give you a hand until he comes back," he continued, a little gentler.

It was Mona's turn to be confused, but not for long. Cai. Rob was talking about Cai. She would lose Cai. "No one must know." Mona leapt to her feet, mortified. Rob didn't want to state the obvious, so he gazed pointedly at her still flat belly. "Not yet, please," she begged.

≈

Arwel and Ifan were both in varying degrees of undress when she battered on their door. "You're a bit keen, Mo. I know we're trying out a battle simulation today but..."

"I'm pregnant," she blurted out.

Arwel froze but Ifan spoke portentously. "Gareth." Mona didn't need to confirm this and neither of them asked; they both knew how and when the child had been conceived.

The men talked in circles. Mona had come here for advice but was appalled by what they had to say. "Why can't I tell the truth?" She looked towards Arwel, but it was his grandfather who did the explaining.

"Mona, we've already gone through this." She hated that tone. "Gareth, or whatever his real name is, was sent from Ireland to kill you: we found the knife, all his papers were false, he is the enemy."

"But…"

"You could admit to a one-night fling with him, if you really want to. But no one would believe that he could have overpowered you conventionally, and you *must* not, under *any* circumstances, let your weakness be known." To her disbelief, Arwel was nodding in agreement.

"My friends would understand." Her voice had become a little whiny.

"No. They would fear you and with good reason." Ifan stated matter-of-factly.

"Perhaps we could say you were drugged?" Arwel tried, though he knew Mona would view this option with equal abhorrence.

She shot him a filthy look, confirming his suspicion, but Mona soon realised that the two men had something new to tell her by the way they eyed each other. "What? What aren't you saying?"

Ifan plonked down onto his chair and massaged his eyes, covering them as he spoke. "It has become obvious to us that there is a traitor, here, in the *Conway*."

"It's not *me*. I'm not a fucking traitor," she screamed shooting to her feet. Shock and impotence had finally turned to anger inside her and she vented it at Ifan, who remained stoic at her outburst.

"I know," he replied calmly.

"You do?" she whispered, her fury morphing into incredulity as Ifan dipped his head in an honest reply.

"Someone within the *Conway* has betrayed us, Mona."

"Geraint?" she asked feebly.

Ifan shook his head. "No, I'm afraid not." Mona's mouth opened to deny it, but nothing came out and Ifan continued. "Someone knows of your unusual reaction to spoken Welsh and has used it to threaten your life – through this Gareth."

"A spy?" She spoke the horrible thought out loud and Arwel nodded. "But..." Mona was dumbfounded. "Have you got any clue..."

"Listen to me," Ifan insisted firmly. "I have no doubt that this person's primary purpose is to leak information, but what if they are capable of using you as a weapon?"

Mona recognised immediately that Ifan was right to be worried. She remembered the power of Gareth's commands. Yes, she could be turned against her friends – easily. Seeing the desperation in her eyes, Arwel moved to sit next to her, reaching out to rub her shoulder. "We're doing all we can, Mo."

"But it could be anyone..."

"Any one of us," Arwel agreed sadly. "But there's also a good chance that the spy is within the fleet."

Mona gazed blankly from grandfather to grandson – she didn't know what to say. Breaking the silence, Arwel began addressing more immediate concerns. "As soon as Cai comes back, we'll tell him the truth. Until then, we won't have to say anything; people will just assume the child is Cai's."

It was easy for them to sit there and postulate, but this was her body, her future. The thought of explaining to Cai that she'd somehow given birth to a stranger's child filled her with despair and rage. She shook off Arwel's hand. "And what about when the baby's born? As far as I can remember, Gareth had dark brown eyes." She was standing now, fists clenched tight.

Ifan's supercilious glance only aggravated her desire to hit him, but Arwel intervened, speaking quietly and kindly. "It's not as straightforward as that, Mo; there is a possibility that the child will have blue eyes anyway."

Her mind struggled back to GCSE biology. "I thought that brown eyes were dominant." Arwel nodded. He was a lovely boy, but he was also beginning to adopt an irritating habit of condescension, and she began to direct her vitriol in his direction as well. "Explain quickly," she spat.

Mona's tone distressed Arwel, who hastily blurted his answer. "Put simply, blue eyes are homozygous, but brown eyes can be either homozygous or heterozygous." He beamed at her, delighted with his concise explanation.

"Simpler," Mona grunted.

"Two blue-eyed parents will *always* have blue-eyed children. With one blue-eyed and one brown-eyed parent, it will depend on the brown-eyed parent's genes. If he or she has a parent with blue eyes, his or her eyes will be heterozygous; but if both parents have brown eyes, then their child's brown eyes will be homozygous." Arwel hoped she'd understood this time, as he would struggle to find an easier explanation. He was relieved when she began working it through.

"So, if my baby has blue eyes, people will believe it's Cai's. If it has brown eyes, there's a big problem. Explain how we get out of that one."

Arwel said the word so quietly that she didn't catch it immediately. "Rob," he had said, before flinching out of her way.

After Mona had calmed down, she tried to explain. "I don't have any feelings for him other than friendship, Al."

"But you and Sion said he was gorgeous."

He was too young to understand, so she tried another tack. "I'm only really interested in Cai like that, to be honest," Mona mumbled. Speaking the truth was embarrassing, and she knew that Arwel would launch into another bout of "*It will all be fine when Cai comes home,*" but she feared the boy was mistaken and told him so.

Arwel disagreed. "We'll just have to explain the situation carefully first – it will be fine." Mona was pleased with Arwel's naivety in a way – it was as it should be for such a young boy – but her face told Arwel she didn't believe him. "Do you hate it?" He pointed to her stomach, which at present seemed to be getting denser rather than larger.

279

At first, Mona thought that Arwel was talking about her foetus. But soon realised that he was thinking about how his mother had felt about him, when she was pregnant. "Your mum and dad loved each other, Al; of course she wanted you. It's not the same for me."

"So how would you feel if it was Cai's child?"

Mona answered Arwel's question as best she could. "It would be easier, but I'm not ready for this and nor is he. I don't even know if he feels anything for me at all."

≈

John's throwaway comment had opened the floodgates on Cai's emotions: troubling memories of Mona, the battle and his crew came pouring through. It had all threatened to overwhelm him last night, but he was now ready to confront the reality he'd been hiding from.

There was still a problem to be solved. His fellow Druids had made a mistake, but that was all. Cai needed to find a solution and get back. He wanted Mona, and he wanted her to stay with him.

When Cai joined the couple for breakfast, he smiled as Liz nudged her husband under the table. "Cai, I'm sorry if I upset you last night, mate," John said after the unsubtle prompting. "I can be such a duffer sometimes."

It was odd how they had reverted to his real name now. "I can't talk very much about my life, it's… complicated, but you're right, I am in love with a welder." Liz coloured at the memory of her clumsy probings. "And I may lose her forever, if I can't get home."

Cai couldn't confide the truth to the English couple. Druidic secrecy had been the number-one rule for millennia; it was the only reason they'd survived. Also, he'd grown extremely fond of them both, and exposure to the harsh realities of his life could put them in harm's way. However, if he wanted John's help, he had to tell him something – however vague – about the enemy ships' uncanny ability to locate

280

their fleet so accurately. "I think the boats were bugged," Cai admitted, hardly believing himself as he uttered the words. The thought of a traitor in the *Conway* was almost physically painful.

John nodded then put a finger to his lips as Liz bustled out of the door for her morning walk with the whippets. "Watch this." He opened an application on his iPad, which was still nestled among the toast crumbs. Cai was fascinated as he watched three red dots move around on the screen, and it only took a few seconds to realise that it was Liz and the dogs – he felt vaguely appalled. "Don't get your knickers in a twist; she's got the most awful sense of direction, and when the weather closes in around here it can be dangerous."

John picked up some plates and carried them to the sink, but Cai had caught a quick glimpse of the couple's strong love for each other – a love usually hidden beneath a layer of light-hearted repartee. "How long have you been together?"

"About twenty-five years." John made a face. "Oh my god, I'm so old." He was laughing but Cai couldn't prevent a sweet but searing memory of his own long-dead parents. He turned back to the image on the screen.

Cai could see the Liz dot marching up towards *An Sgurr*; she probably used the rapid trek to the highest point on the island as a bit of a workout. Cai had been up there a few times with her, and the panoramic vistas from the summit were astounding; on a clear day, most of the Inner and Outer Hebrides were visible, together with a remarkable view of mainland Scotland. The two other dots mostly meandered fore and aft of her, sniffing and stopping in unison. "So how does it work?"

John had cleared the table and was keen to share his knowledge. "She'd kill me if she found out, so I knew they would have to be almost invisible. The radio transmitter is easy to keep small, it's the energy supply that's hard to disguise." John beamed at his own cleverness. "I got these from Sweden; they're driven by kinetic energy. Liz's is attached to her coat and when she moves she creates the power source herself – same with the dogs' collars."

John's voice faded away as Cai's mind grappled with the sophistication of the technology. If the radio transmitters were that small, they could have been planted, not only on the boats, but the clothes of the three missing lads. Standing suddenly, Cai began to feel around in the fabric of his clothing. They had all been bugged.

John's voice came back again. "The intelligence services in the U.S. have started making transmitters that look like part of the object they're monitoring, making them undetectable even to a trained observer. If they're sophisticated enough, the bugs will be impossible to find."

Cai drooped visibly as John disappeared into the study. He had planned to track down each boat in the fleet and make a more thorough search for the bugs this time, until each one was clean. Now that applied to their clothing as well, and it seemed like a gargantuan task in the light of what John was telling him.

Cai had his head in his hands as John re-emerged, holding a walkie-talkie-like device. "Unless you've got one of these puppies." He beamed, victoriously, and Cai's heart swelled with sudden hope. Rushing to his room, he grabbed the combat leathers and offered them up for John to test. As John passed the wand over the clothes, the device lit up and beeped. "Bingo!" John whispered.

Cai, though, felt sick. Their discovery meant that, without doubt, the *Conway* harboured a spy. The bug had been hand-sewn into the leather.

23

Salt

Bryn didn't admit, even to himself, that he was spying on Rob and Mona. He just happened to have been looking out from the control tower when she'd ordered him into the water that day. Rob had a swimmer's body, broad-shouldered and slim-hipped. He had deceptively defined musculature, which had tensed as he'd laughed and flirted with her.

Bryn gazed in morbid fascination as they met each morning, as regularly as clockwork. He watched with gut-rotting jealousy as their relationship blossomed, culminating in that wet embrace a few days ago.

He ventured less and less from the radio room now, and when concerned people forced him to rest, he took to his room, consoling himself with rum. Life had lost all shape and meaning, but it was better this way, much better.

≈

Mona was working hard, and the simulated battles were progressing well, with each tribe taking the role of an invading force while the other three defended. Arwel and Mona had devised many possible scenarios, and while there was always room for improvement, they were both excited with the developments.

She was also pleased that Arwel and his grandfather seemed to have given up on the Rob solution, allowing nature to take its course.

People would just have to gossip when the child was born with brown eyes – they would anyway.

Mona had decided to wait until Cai came back, tell him the truth, and go from there. She'd heard that there were always kind people, ready to adopt babies, especially new-borns. If it went as she expected with Cai, she would leave immediately; her bag was already packed. Mona would have the baby in Kent, give it up for adoption, and then go searching for Idwal. The plan didn't fill her with happiness, but it was a way forward.

≈

The Gangani had just defended the shoreline admirably. Eventually though, the Silurians had fought through to victory, and Mona was about to compliment their leader, Sioned, on their success when she was interrupted by Rob, who came loping up behind her. "Can I have a word?" He seemed uncharacteristically serious. "After supper, in the library?"

"Of course." Mona spoke to his back as he turned away hastily. He probably wanted to nag her some more about making the pregnancy common knowledge.

Rob was already there when she opened the library door, but this wasn't the funny, confident man she'd got to know over the last three months; he had reverted to the painfully awkward boy who had first arrived at the *Conway*.

"What is it, Rob?"

"I've been talking to Arwel, and I know." Mona breathed a sigh of relief. They had come to their senses at last; she could finally speak to him about the baby's father without lying. But Rob hadn't finished speaking. "Arwel's right; you shouldn't be on your own with depression." His eyes were full of understanding rather than pity. "I know how it feels, Mo."

The damned teenager had outwitted her. "So what did Arwel suggest?" she asked, already knowing the answer.

"That we should move in together."

"And what do you think about that?" Mona tried to keep the acid from her tone; he was only being kind.

Rob coughed, still awkward. "I think it's a great idea; we'll be able to keep an eye on each other. Nights are always worst for me, and they're drawing in quickly now." Mona waited. "It would be helpful for me in another way too... and I need to be upfront about it... before we decide what to do." Rob ran trembling fingers through his golden locks. "I'm gay. And it would get the girls off my back without me having to come out – again."

Mona didn't imagine she reacted in any way that Rob could have possibly foreseen. Hysterical laughter probably wasn't a normal reaction, but the situation was so bizarre that it tipped her over the edge. Arwel, the supreme strategist, had pulled it off again. Mona was Rob's beard, and he would unknowingly become a candidate for the paternity of her child. Genius.

However, it was Nia's reaction that was the most remarkable. When they decided to forewarn her and Sioned of Rob's news and the altered sleeping arrangements, Nia became unexpectedly dreamy-eyed and distant.

"*Cúchulainn and Ferdia*," she sang under her breath. All three of her friends shared the same lost look between them. "One of the greatest Celtic love stories," she insisted. Mona was completely lost but Nia challenged Sioned. "Surely you must have read the Irish saga *Táin Bó Cúailgne*."

"Yes, but I thought Cúchulainn was a real ladies' man?" Sioned asked, a little confused.

Nia sighed. "He was, but his soul belonged to *Ferdia*; they were both friends and lovers. Eventually though, they were forced into a battle to the death."

"What happened?" Sioned asked.

Nia smiled sadly, "Cúchulainn killed Ferdia – it broke his heart."

≈

285

Their slightly larger combined room had one of the few double beds in the *Conway*. It became a regular meeting place, where tea was drunk, strategies were discussed, and music was played. "Why haven't you told Sioned yet?" Rob asked as he strummed and tweaked, directly after Arwel and Sioned had left for the night.

"I will. It's just…"

"She'll be pissed off if she's the last to know; she'll be an aunt." He eyed Mona's slightly enlarged belly.

≈

Convincing Liz to allow John on the debugging mission was proving to be an almost impossible task. It was now October, the weather was turning grimmer by the day, and even the ferries would stop their daily service on the twentieth – as she repeatedly told them both.

In the time that he'd spent there, Cai had never heard the couple argue, but now he heard raised voices from their bedroom every night. That it was about him was sickening. "You said he was a great sailor!"

"Be reasonable, Liz. It's madness to go out around the islands alone at this time of year."

"Exactly," she screeched. "Why can't you just wait till the spring? There's loads to do on the microsystem and Cai said he would help out with the new extension to the workshop."

There was silence for such a long time that Cai thought the fight was over. "I'm sorry, love, but he's in serious trouble. I've got to help the lad. We're off in the morning."

When they met at dawn, John wasn't wearing his customary grin for the first time since Cai had met him. They had trailered the rigid inflatable down to the shore, slid it on to the shale beach, and returned the Land Rover to its place outside the shed. The equipment was stowed and both men were waterproofed and life-jacketed to the nth degree. Liz was nowhere to be seen.

John was performing a final check before launching when they spotted her barrelling towards them at speed. With red eyes and a wet face, she grabbed hold of her husband by the waist and buried her head in his squeaky yellow chest.

"I love you so much, you silly bugger. *Do not drown.*" Cai thought her words were supposed to sound like an order, but they came out a bit wobbly. John linked his arms around her and Cai walked round to the other side of the boat to give them some privacy. "Not so fast, Cai." She approached with arms outstretched and gave him an extremely powerful squeeze. "Keep him safe!" This time, it was definitely an order.

≈

Bryn didn't get to hear much gossip, and he certainly didn't want to hear this particular update, but the news was all over the canteen. It was an impressive step forward for him to be seen in public. He'd pulled it together enough to recognise the need to start looking after himself, and this was day three of solid food and no alcohol.

Discovering that Rob and Mona had moved in together sent Bryn running back to the sweet oblivion of dark rum. Once he was nestled within its warm embrace, he decided never to attempt escape again – reality was too painful.

≈

The night before Samhain was Sioned's sixteenth birthday. Mona had bought her a fine-looking set of throwing knives from the second-hand shop in Holyhead. She'd sharpened them in Cai's workshop, breathing in the poignant memories as she worked on the blades.

Sioned's popularity had grown since being elevated to Chief of the Silures; she had been matured and honed by the additional responsibility into an astonishing young woman. Sioned looked so achingly similar to her brother as she unwrapped the knives. "Only *you* could give someone knives for a birthday present," she beamed.

"I bloody well told you," Rob giggled from the bed, as he dodged Mona's swipe.

"No, I love them; I absolutely love them. Thank you, Mo."

"We'll practice after the partying's over," Mona promised.

Nia had explained the traditional wildness of the festivities around this time of year. Samhain was a time of no time, when the veil between the worlds of the living and the dead were thin enough to pass through, and chaos reigned. These days it was celebrated in the form of drinking, dancing and music – like almost every other festival in the pagan calendar. Though the dark nights and bonfire preparations added an atmosphere of Gothic morbidity to the three days of anticipated fun. "So, what have you got planned tonight, Sion?" Rob asked with a glint in his eye.

"Who told you?" she challenged, but there was laughter in her question. Mona wasn't in on the joke but got caught up in their teasing tone.

"Well, he *is* a Gangani, and you know how it is with us blokes." Rob yawned and stretched dramatically.

"Ooh, the little toad," Sioned chuckled.

Rob was quick to defend the toad. "No, I just guessed from the look of ecstasy on his face, after your little chat."

Alarm bells clanged distantly in Mona's mind, and she stared at them in confusion. "Sioned's planning on seducing Iestyn tonight," Rob explained, taking the ensuing punishment quite well, and managing to shield all major organs from Sioned's tickling attack.

"What?" Mona hadn't meant to shout, and it brought all frivolity to a full stop. "I mean, aren't you a bit young?"

Sioned sniggered. "No, I'm sixteen, and frankly it's well overdue as far as I'm concerned." Rob remembered he had to help set up and left hurriedly. "It doesn't just happen; you choose someone beforehand. Don't worry, Mo. It's all above board," Sioned explained patiently.

Mona felt like an old woman suddenly, but she was frightened for Sioned. Would he hurt her? Would the young girl end up pregnant like Mona, her life going nowhere before it had begun? Sioned picked up on her distress. "I'll be alright, Mo. I'm looking forward to it. He's a bit of an idiot, but the best of a bad bunch. Mo, what's wrong?"

Mona had sunk on to the bed, head in hands. "I'm pregnant, Sioned. That's what's wrong."

≈

Rob didn't think of himself as a coward – leaving Mona to deal with Sioned – but he was glad to be out of the firing line. Anyway, there were music chores to be arranged for tomorrow.

Nia wasn't back until the morning and Rob knew she'd appreciate a little preparation before she arrived. Dai was in the hall, fiddling about with chairs and music stands – he was clearly peeved. "This is Bryn's job," he muttered. "You haven't seen him, have you, Rob? He's missed several shifts, and if he's in his room, the bugger's not letting on."

"Might he be ill? Perhaps he's got whatever Mo had," Rob offered. It was unlike Bryn to shirk his duties. "Perhaps we should check on him?"

Ifan had a master key, and though he seemed sceptical that it could be glandular fever, he released the key into Arwel's care, asking him to open Bryn's door for Rob.

The stench of vomit, rum and unwashed body filled the small dark room. Rob saw Bryn propped upright on the floor against the bed. The sitting position may have saved his life; had he vomited this much while lying on his back, Bryn might well have choked to death. "Go to the canteen and get beakers and salt – a lot of salt." Arwel moved to obey. "And tell no one." Rob hadn't needed to tell him that – no one should see a tribal chief in that state.

Bryn's pulse was weak and erratic; the alcohol had done untold damage. Arwel returned promptly, out of breath and carrying all the salt he could find. Under Rob's supervision, they dragged the big man into the shower cubicle.

"Hold his head back against the wall and keep it up." Rob poured an entire salt shaker into a beaker of water before forcing it down Bryn's throat. After much choking and gagging, he'd swallowed enough of the saline to induce more vomiting. When he thought Bryn could vomit no more, Rob asked Arwel to turn on the shower. "You can go now, Al; he'll be fine. Thanks." Bryn didn't look fine, but he took Rob's word for it. "Remember, no one – not even your granddad." Rob reminded the boy. Arwel agreed immediately, but left thinking that it might just be possible to know too many secrets.

Rob held Bryn in the shower until the water ran cold and he'd started to come round. He then began to peel the sodden clothes from Bryn's body and helped him to stand. "Can you wash?" Rob was matter-of-fact and Bryn was truthful.

"No," he rasped through an acid throat.

Rob started with his hair and beard, scrubbing out the dried-on debris, then proceeded to sponge the rest of his body, where the urine and faeces had burned and stuck. Bryn somehow managed to remain standing throughout the ordeal, and afterwards, Rob wrapped him in a towel, propped him on the loo, and changed the sheets.

After Rob had eased Bryn into bed, he stripped off his own soiled clothes and showered. He noted how orderly Bryn's room was as he dressed himself from the minimal wardrobe; it was a pleasant change from the mayhem he endured living with Mona.

Bryn slept now; his pulse was stronger and stable. With plenty of water on hand, Rob settled in for a long vigil in the chair, knowing that every drop would be needed before the night was through.

24

Bugs

"*The Mission*" – as John had dubbed it over the past week – was to be carried out under the auspices of a last-minute supplies run. That way, they could visit all the islands with the same story, and just be thought foolish rather than suspicious.

The couple's sons had hardly ever visited and John doubted that anyone would remember their faces. However, as a precaution Cai wore a cap low over his eyes. He was pretty sure that the rest of the crew would have stayed within the Inner Hebrides, probably finding work in any sympathetic druidic networks.

The plan was simple: cruise all the moorings, find the fleet boats, get on-board and relieve the batteries of their radio transmitters. It would be essential to replant the bugs close by, with a new power source, so as not to alert the Irish to their removal. When each of the boats had been 'cleaned', Cai would attempt to contact Dafydd. There wasn't a strategy in place to deal with the bugged clothing – as yet.

Tobermory was their first port of call, and Cai scanned the boats at the jetty as soon as they came into sight. Only one, Dafydd's boat, was moored here, and they would wait until dark to free it of any bugs. John decided that they should do some sleuthing while shopping for supplies.

Ever anxious about being recognised, Cai kept a low profile, but there was no sign of any of his compatriots in the small supermarket, the post office or the pharmacy. Cai peered into the windows of some of the smaller shops but saw no one he knew. He was eager to find out where his uncle was staying, but was desperate to avoid Ieuan.

"I'm sure Dafydd will be with the RNLI crew," Cai repeated. John had already checked at the station, but it was barred and bolted.

"Let's check in the pubs. I fancy a beer and we can wait in comfort."

"A lemonade, you mean," Cai muttered, remembering his promise to Liz.

"Absolutely," said John, grinning cheekily back at him.

The pub on Main Street was the nearest, and they walked in as unobtrusively as they could wearing their bright yellow, wet-weather gear. As heads turned towards them, John put up a hand and shouted in his very best, and loudest, idiot English, "Hullo, everyone! What weather we're having, eh?"

The strategy paid off: every local in the pub turned away from them and began sniping to their neighbour about "*the bloody Sassenachs*". Cai already had a huge regard for the man, but this little stunt raised the bar again, and he was forced to suppress a smile.

Some familiar-sounding guffawing from the bar caught Cai's attention. Looking up, he saw Ieuan appear from behind it, big arms encircling the waist of an unimpressed barmaid. Anger slid into Cai's belly – and its aftertaste registered on his face. "Friend trouble?" John asked subtly. Cai nodded, unable to speak through his bile, and John ambled up to the bar, sporting a moronically friendly grin.

He chatted for a while with the men at the bar, but Cai could tell from their body language and grunting that they didn't want his company. He returned with two shandies and a packet of peanuts. "Your mate Ieuan lives here, upstairs. He's been here since August and is not popular with the ladies, as you can see."

As they sipped their drinks, John removed a pen and pad from his pocket. "Write a letter to your uncle, making sure he knows it can be from no one but you." Cai tore his eyes from the bar and started writing. He folded the letter and left it on the table between them. "Drink up, take the shopping to the RIB, and I'll meet you at your uncle's boat with the tool bag. I'll give Dafydd the note when he comes in." As Cai picked up their supplies, John let out a theatrical sigh, winking at him simultaneously. "I don't care what your mother said, I'm bloody well having another drink." John ambled to the bar as Cai closed the pub door behind him.

≈

By four in the morning, Mona was fretting. Sioned had said she'd be back for a chat later, which Mona had thought would be two at the very latest. She was considering a search and rescue exercise when the knock came, and she wrenched the door open in relief. Sioned waltzed into the room, flinging herself nonchalantly on to the bed. "Rob not back yet?"

Mona tried to keep her cool. "Well?"

Sioned made a face. "Bit of a disappointment, really. Awkward and messy."

Mona couldn't resist a chuckle. "It'll get better."

"It did." Sioned chortled, delighted by the shock on Mona's face.

"And you were…"

"Careful? Yes. You sound like my mother." Sioned sighed.

"Sorry, Sion, I'm just worried about you making the same mistake I did."

Sioned gently moved her hand towards Mona's abdomen, her eyes asking for permission to touch it. "It's not a mistake for you two; he'll be over the moon." Sioned had a sudden thought. "Can you imagine what a good fighter she'll be? I claim her for the Silurians. In fact, I claim my brother too – he could come in handy."

Mona desperately wanted Cai to come home, but she wasn't relishing their first conversation. "Don't worry, Mo, they've got to be back soon."

Standing up abruptly, before she succumbed to tears, Mona forced a bravado she didn't feel into her voice. "I suppose this means everyone knows by now?"

"Everyone apart from Nia," Sioned declared unashamedly. "And as soon as Siân gets hold of you, you're going to be nagged to death."

Mona paled at the thought of the impending fuss. "So no one's shocked or angry?"

"No – a bit surprised, though, as Cai's always been super careful."

"Mmm," was all Mona could manage in reply.

≈

Arwel opened the door to the hammering as Ifan could only just find the energy to open his eyes.

"Mona's pregnant!" Siân shouted from the door, and Ifan sighed.

"It's four in the morning, Siân. Perhaps we should wait…" Arwel tried and failed to block the woman's path into the rooms, and she stood expectantly at the end of Ifan's bed.

"Get up, Dad, we need to talk."

"I understand your concern, Siân," Ifan replied sleepily, "but Mona isn't going to be any less pregnant in the morning."

Siân had no time for flippancy. "Hywel's here too, and he's not happy."

Arwel offered to make tea while the elders discussed the pregnancy. Hywel was incandescent. "Sioned thinks the child is Cai's."

Ifan didn't get the chance to answer. "Of course it's Cai's," Siân huffed out, exasperated with her careless nephew.

"I wouldn't be so sure," Hywel growled. "I've seen her flirting with that big Englishman, or it could even be that other lad, the singer. *Gwraig llwyn a pherth!* Dirty old slapper!"

Arwel forced a laugh from the kitchenette, despite the cruelty of Hywel's abuse. "Gareth? Hardly – they couldn't stand each other." Hywel glared at the youngster but said nothing more, and Ifan was impressed by his grandson's quick thinking.

"How far along is she?" Siân asked her father.

"Too far."

"Not necessarily," Hywel said darkly. "I'm sure the healers…"

"No, Hywel, it's too dangerous for Mona."

"I don't understand," Arwel asked, as he passed his betters their tea. "I know it's not ideal, but if it's magic you're after, surely this baby would have an excellent pedigree."

"Cai was supposed to handfast Cerys; we all agreed," the old man fumed. "That bitch has cast a spell on my Cai, but she's not a Druid, so what is she?"

"Of course she's a Druid…" Ifan argued wearily.

"She can't even speak our language," Hywel shot back. "It's English that comes from her Irish mouth. That woman bears the *mark*. She's a monster, and that baby will be the same. It shouldn't be allowed to live." Ifan was staggered by his old friend's vehemence.

"*Yr un fath â fi?* Like me?" A little voice said, and Arwel's young bright eyes stared straight into Hywel's dark old ones.

"*Ia, yr un fath â ti.* Yes, like you," the old man replied evenly.

≈

Rob dragged all Bryn's dirty washing down to the laundry. He'd struck up a good rapport with Nesta, who seemed to appreciate his sartorial cleanliness. The odd impromptu tune on the mandolin hadn't harmed their relationship either.

It was Arwel who was holding the fort now though, as Nesta was involved in more pressing work. At least he didn't have to explain the state of the sheets. "I got these from the healers." Arwel grinned. "Bryn will need them after a dose of diarrhoea and sickness like that."

"Good lad." Rob winked and took the offered herbs.

"Cat's out of the bag about Mo," Arwel mentioned casually.

"Sioned," they agreed in unison.

"She'll hate all the fussing," Rob sighed in mock sympathy. "I'm steering clear of our room in that case. After all, I might be infectious."

"Indeed. You'd better get everything you need from the room now, before the invasion."

"Good point," Rob shouted back through the swinging doors, in a race to avoid the inevitable clucking.

Mo was still asleep when he crept in; she looked like a child herself as she clutched Cai's shirt, the earphones from the ubiquitous mp3 player stuffed into each ear. Rob wondered if Mona was aware that she wept in her sleep, almost every night. He didn't have any siblings, but suspected he'd found a combined brother and sister in Mona.

He almost had a clean getaway, but she woke just as he was pressing down on the door handle. "You moving out?" Mona's hair had grown since that strange, shorn phase. It now stuck up in all directions with comic randomness.

"There's some sickness bug going round and I was in the thick of it last night. You don't want it." He thought it only fair to give her warning: "And besides, you're about to be invaded by an army of Welsh women."

Mona paled and allowed her head to drop back to the pillow. "Please don't abandon me now!" she pleaded to no avail; he was already edging through the door, musical instruments and carrier bag in hand. Outside, Rob chuckled as he felt the thud of the pillow hitting the door.

≈

Breaking into Dafydd's boat was easy; Cai knew all its nooks and crannies, and waited below deck in the dark. John hadn't explained how he knew that Dafydd would turn up at the pub, but he seemed pretty confident. An hour later, Cai heard footsteps and the sound of his name being whispered.

"I'm down below," he replied, the Welsh sounding odd in his throat. Cai held his breath until he actually saw his uncle's face.

"Cai!" Dafydd pulled him into a tight embrace immediately.

"Thank the gods you're alright." He didn't let go for a long while. "I couldn't bear it if anything…"

"I'm OK, I'm fine. We've worked it out; the boats are bugged."

Dafydd sighed, putting his hand over his eyes. "No, I had the same thought. We've been over them all with a fine-tooth comb, and we found nothing."

There was a clattering from the wheelhouse. "Is anyone at home?" John sang down the stairs in a half whisper. It was almost comical, and Dafydd raised his eyebrows in amused disgust.

"He's a genius," Cai explained simply.

"He's English."

Cai agreed. "But still a genius."

John trundled down the stairs. "Hello. Dafydd, isn't it?" He held out a huge yellow paw and Dafydd shook it in bewilderment. Cai, meanwhile cleared a space to gain access to the engine and battery compartment under the floor. John removed his gloves and peeled off a layer of waterproof clothing, then knelt down beside the two other men.

"You see, just a normal battery terminal," Dafydd explained, and Cai had to agree it rather looked that way.

John fiddled with the detector and passed the gadget back and forth above the battery. Within seconds, a small red dot and an insistent pulse had appeared. "She's there all right – just beautifully hidden. Can you pass me that small needle-nose?" Cai passed him the pliers, while Dafydd directed a torch on to the spot between the two battery terminals. The radio transmitter had been cast into a paper-thin resin plate bearing the name of the manufacturer. As John gently lifted the plate, Cai and Dafydd were able to see clearly the thin wires trailing between the negative and positive terminals. "Very clever," John whispered with admiration.

Cai knew the next part was tricky and had the small replacement battery ready. "We need to do this as quickly as possible, and hope they're not monitoring when we break contact." All three men took an inward breath as the connections were broken, remade and tested with the detector. Cai secured the new battery to the side of the jetty, hiding it safely out of sight.

While he was occupied, Dafydd thanked John. "How did you know I'd turn up?"

"If I had a loose cannon like Ieuan around, I'd stick close by."

"He's not a bad lad, actually; young and full of it, and I think he regrets what happened with Cai."

Cai returned below deck just in time to watch John pass the machine over Dafydd. The screen lit up. "But this must mean... it means..."

"Yes," Cai agreed gravely, "a spy. Ieuan was right."

John tried to ignore the expressions of horror on both men's faces and started to formulate a solution. "You'll need to let the rest of your friends know. I'm pretty sure they will all be bugged."

Cai was nodding, but Dafydd was stuck with his dark thoughts. "The three lads..."

Cai glanced at John; he'd been careful about not revealing too much about their past. "So what shall we do about these?" Cai pointed at Dafydd's chest.

"It will look fishy if you all dispose of them at once." John shook his head, a plan still forming in his brain. "We need to change things gradually – just let them know, Dafydd."

"OK, I will, but after we've cleared the boats. I'm coming with you."

"More the merrier," John grinned and wandered away with device in hand.

"What about Ieuan?" Cai asked his uncle cagily.

"Leave him to me. He's got plenty to do over the next few days; he'll be fine."

Cai scowled then slowly rubbed his hand down his face. "It's Sioned's birthday today. She's sixteen and I'm not there for her, of all birthdays." Cai's voice was desolate and small.

Dafydd didn't play down the event's significance, but did try to soften the blow for Cai. "She's got Arwel – you know how close they are – and there's Siân..." He was struggling.

"Arwel is a child, how can he possibly prepare her? And you know how difficult she can get with Siân. The only sound advice she would get is from Mona, and they detest each other."

Cai stowed the tools while John ran the detector over the face of the battery again. He didn't look convinced. "I'm still getting a faint echo." He screwed up his face, thinking hard.

"Could it be coming in through the hull?" Cai offered. "I placed it as near to this position as I could."

"Yes, that's probably it. Still, I'll have a once-over while I'm at it. This is sophisticated stuff – expensive. And they've gone to the bother of bugging everything and everyone. If it were me, I'd have put a back-up system in place."

≈

Sioned made sure that there was a minimum of touching and fussing, and only allowed the women to stay for an hour – though Mona thought this was the least she could do, considering her part in the rumour mill.

Finally alone, she left to perform her patterns in the training room. Mona's centre of gravity had changed marginally, and it required extra concentration to alter her moves while remaining completely balanced.

A noise from the door broke that concentration and brought her face to face with a man she had met barely a couple of times before. Hywel Owens was spare and bony; his eyes were blue, but not the deep, bright blue of his grandson. "I thought I'd find you here." Hywel wasn't used to speaking in English and his accent was strong. He walked towards her with slow and deliberate menace, pointing at her *mark*. "You have that atrocity on your chest and my grandson's child in your belly." He continued to advance. "You've played your hand exceedingly well, but someone like my Cai isn't easily caught."

"I don't want to catch him…" Mona was taken aback by the accusation.

299

"You won't in the end, of course. How will you manage to maintain the interest of a man like him, especially with a baby to take care of?" The old man helped her to an extra portion of disgust. "You're not even Welsh."

Hywel had cut right to the chase: Mona had never truly believed that they'd had anything more than one good night together; the rest had just been wishful thinking. He continued, relentlessly. "They smile to your face, Mona, but everyone's blaming the power of your *mark*. After all, no one in this community wants to see their favourite warrior destroyed, however you do it." The old man turned from her slowly and just as slowly turned back, pointing at her stomach again. "That child is an abomination."

His words lingered, long after Hywel had left, and the urge to run returned in force. If she went now, Ifan could tell Cai that the child wasn't his. She could write a note and never have to face him again.

25

Samhain

Dafydd had judiciously spread his charges throughout the Inner and Outer Hebrides – wherever there was sufficient work to sustain them, in fact. But even asking for bed and board only, the pickings had been slim. With the tourist season now over, there were bound to be lay-offs.

Having made his excuses to Ieuan and the RNLI coxswain, Dafydd joined the other two in the RIB. They were fully equipped and ready to endure whatever the Scottish weather could throw at them – though sailing an open boat around the Hebridean islands was never going to be fun at this time of year. There was a nasty weather front moving in from Iceland, but there was still enough time to debug the other boats and be on their way within the week. Dafydd was a more cautious sailor than Cai, but even he was willing to brave the November gales to get back to his family – and deal with the spy.

With a population of nearly 10,000, Skye had been the largest and easiest of the islands on which to find work for the crew. Cerys and Gwen had secured jobs at the college, while the Talisker distillery had taken on a couple of the eighteen-year-olds. However, it had been necessary to place three of the more seriously injured crew members in rented accommodation, wearing Dafydd's resources as thin as their sanity.

It was very late by the time both the transmitter was removed and relocated, so they made their bed on Emlyn's old Oakley, keeping light and activity to a minimum.

At dawn, it was on to the penultimate boat on Islay, where eight of the men had found work as manual labourers. The work changed regularly, but Glyn seemed to be doing a good job of keeping them focused and busy.

Glyn had made the decision to moor the boat on one of the floating pontoons just outside the harbour wall in Bowmere. This relatively obscure position had the advantage of avoiding the ferries and tourist vessels of Port Ellen, and it also made the clandestine mission of Dafydd, Cai and John that much easier.

The wind was blowing nose-on as they headed for the Isle of Lewis. No one said a word, but the men all knew they could expect an average of five to nine gales a month between now and the end of March. The seas continued to grow larger, but they were on the return journey before the worst of the weather hit.

Even in good weather, with decent visibility, it would have been a push to get back to Eigg in daylight hours. In darkness and storm-force conditions, the journey home was horrific. John took the helm while Cai held the compass, the boat's sophisticated GPS having failed hours ago. All three men were dangerously cold and exhausted by the time Eigg and the little jetty became visible. Liz was waiting in the Land Rover, and silently helped them haul the RIB on to the trailer.

≈

Bryn wasn't asleep, his breathing was too controlled, but Rob let him carry on the pretence for a good while before striking up a tune. "Feeling better?" he asked after Bryn inevitably turned to face him.

"No."

"Try this then."

Bryn took the herbal tea, drank it, then lay back down to watch Rob play. "Thank you for last night."

"You're welcome," he replied with such a sunny grin that it forced Bryn to turn his face up to the ceiling.

"You've moved in with Mona." It was more than a whisper but not much more.

"Mona's having a baby and she's really unhappy about it. She needs me to take care of her, even if she doesn't know it." Bryn had gone incredibly still and Rob continued with his matter-of-fact explanation. "You're not upset about Mona: you're frightened about what might happen between us." Bryn said nothing, allowing Rob to continue. "Can't we just say hello to each other when we meet, talk about the things we're both interested in, and try to be friends?" Rob got to his feet and began the long-winded process of putting away his mandolin. "I'm going to bed now, but I'll see you in the morning, and then we'll start rehearsing for the concert."

Bryn eventually turned to face Rob again, this time studying his attire. "Are they my clothes?"

"Yes, I'm going for a new military look." Rob executed an extravagant parody of one of Mona's more aggressive moves. Bryn laughed – not much, but it was enough.

By morning, Bryn was able to understand clearly that he had reached a crossroads in his life. He had the choice of getting up and returning to the closeted darkness of the radio room, or of turning the other way at the threshold and walking towards the light and Rob. Either way, he knew the decision would be irrevocable.

≈

Liz expended a great deal of time and energy stoking the fire and bringing in warm clothes and blankets. Cai could see that her worry for John had morphed into anger – now that he had returned safely. They had been gone for the best part of four days, and he wondered how long she had been keeping vigil in the Land Rover.

The three men had showered and were thawing out on the sofas, all dressed in the warm pyjamas and dressing gowns they'd been issued. Her ministrations finished, Liz left with a slam of the door that shook the plywood walls. Cai and Dafydd busied themselves with starting on the food, though their eyes slid towards John, who was staring at the recently slammed door. "I'm in deep, deep trouble, chaps."

The two Welshmen couldn't help but laugh at the expression on John's face, both sniggering simultaneously into their stews. Cai tasted a mouthful; it was some sort of lamb dish and it was delicious. "I thought Liz couldn't cook."

"No, she can, she just doesn't. Something to do with a waste of creativity." John had shuffled over to open a bottle, his voluminous dressing gown hampering his progress. "May as well be hung for a sheep as a lamb."

"I hope that's not some sort of sheep-shagging joke." Dafydd tried to frown at John, who merely grinned back.

"Wine?" By the time he had returned to the sofa, Dafydd and Cai had already helped themselves to seconds of stew. After the third bottle of wine, Cai crept off to his bedroom, leaving Dafydd and John to continue bonding.

Cai guessed that they'd probably succeeded when he found them both passed out on the sofa in the morning. Liz was bustling about intently in the kitchen. "Thanks for the meal last night, it was delicious."

"Don't try to get round me with your boyish smile; I'm immune," she pointed at the sofa. "I've got three of my own." Though Liz was thawing, despite herself, and Cai knew she was desperate to know what had happened.

"All the boats are clean of bugs. It means we can go home." She seemed surprised, and he explained, "John's got some extremely sophisticated weather software. If we wait for a good break in the gales, we'll have a chance to make a run for it." With a decent weather window, a direct voyage home via the Irish Sea would only take two days.

"What about the bugged clothes?" she asked.

He frowned. "Not entirely sure yet."

≈

Mona had planned to spend the entire three days of the Samhain madness locked away in her room, listening to her music and working out any possible loopholes in their defence. The plan had worked splendidly until the final night, when Sioned had virtually kidnapped her, dragging Arwel along for the ride.

She had missed the previous night's major musical offering on purpose, fearing that the Welsh singing might overpower her. By all reports it had been a cracker. "*Suo Gân*" had been sung a cappella, with Rob and Bryn performing an amazing duet.

The band members now sat together having a quiet drink. Tonight's entertainment was the equivalent of an open mic night, with everyone free to have a go. The band was only there to fill in any awkward silences and to provide instrumental backing if required.

Nia made room for Mona to sit beside her; at least she hadn't burst into tears this time. Nia seemed incredibly moved by the idea of Mona and Cai producing a child, despite it being a political scandal. Her reaction was starting to get on Mona's nerves, and not only because it needled at her deception. Nansi chatted for a while, congratulating her awkwardly before leaving to check on her brood.

Bryn and Rob were deep in conversation about modifying musical instruments, so Mona asked Nia about the gossip, telling her not to spare her feelings. "Some people think you're a tart for moving in with Rob, and speculation has already started about him being the father." Mona glanced at Arwel, who smothered his grin by placing a drink between his lips. "We're trying to quash that rumour by exaggerating how close you and Cai were before he left. Sioned's helping with that."

"Great," Mona muttered into her orange squash. It was too late to be upset about the problem, or the remedy.

As more and more alcohol was consumed, the quality of the musical offerings degenerated markedly. Rising to his feet, Rob decided to take matters into his own hands. "What are you going to play?" Arwel asked, enquiring subtly if the song would be Welsh.

"I fancy a little bit of country music. What do you say, *pardner*?" Rob affected an American drawl and peered at Bryn, who groaned but joined him on stage.

"I'll see what I can get out of this fiddle."

Mona suspected that the long instrumental intro was a way for Rob and Bryn to get the mandolin and fiddle attuned to each other. It was obvious their voices didn't need to be introduced.

The room erupted into clapping and hooting as Rob hammed up 'Jolene', accompanied by Bryn in the chorus, who was clearly enjoying himself immensely. The crowd bayed for more as Rob dived into his country repertoire. He crooned many of her mum's old country favourites – it wasn't a coincidence, Rob knew Mona's music intimately, and he gave her an extravagant wink before plunging into the next song. The men's voices really did harmonise delightfully, and Mona was glad that she had missed the Welsh lullaby – it would have been too far dangerous.

Rob's excellence seemed to have frightened away the last of the die-hard revellers. Mona scanned the hall; most of the community would have a sore head in the morning. "Good job the Irish didn't choose tonight to invade," she joked.

Mona had meant to make a throwaway remark, but she was not the only one to feel a sudden lurching sense of horror at the truth in her words. Five heads flicked up, and suddenly they were all running to the control room. Bryn got there first and demanded to know if there had been any recent activity. Dai, who was on duty, appeared to have just woken up. "Nothing," he replied groggily. "Is there a problem?"

Bryn was already quizzing the coastguard. "How many?" He closed his eyes as the answer came. "When?"

"What?" Mona demanded.

"Four VSVs were spotted a couple of hours ago, just beyond the Swellies." Mona sighed.

"What's a VSV?" Rob asked.

After checking the time and the tide timetable, Bryn answered. "They're wave-piercing military boats, very fast, very stable and very unusual in these waters. The tide's turned so they won't attack tonight, but we'll need to be ready."

Mona was furious with herself – and Arwel to a degree. The Irish had come within half an hour of their jetty. Mona vowed that they wouldn't be caught off guard again, and went to bed relieved but suspicious that the Irish hadn't pushed home their advantage.

≈

It was Mona who called the meeting early next morning. She had asked Ifan along, not expecting him to turn up but gratified when he did – she was even happier when he agreed to all her recommendations.

The close call was a catalyst for the start of a new regime, with Sioned taking the first waterborne patrols in the single seaworthy vessel left by the absent fleet. Bryn accompanied her on her first trip, guiding the young warrior through the perils of the Swellies.

Arwel had explained to Mona and Rob that without knowledge of the tides and races around the narrow strait's perilous rock formations, Sioned would undoubtedly come to harm in a small boat. He stressed that the Swellies should *never, ever* be attempted at high water, leaving Mona feeling deeply apprehensive until Bryn and Sioned's safe return.

"She's a natural," Bryn said with a rare grin, ruffling Sioned's hair, and she beamed like a child at his hard-won praise.

26

Forgiveness

The colour of the world had changed for Bryn. If he could describe his happiness, it might be in those terms. His friendship had deepened with Rob over the last few months and, through him, the members of the band became friends he cared about, rather than mere colleagues.

Mona's new regime had placed additional demands on the inhabitants of the *Conway*, and this had had a detrimental effect on the ability of the band to rehearse. Nia was away again, but there was enough momentum now for them to keep going without her, and today they'd managed to find time for a rushed rehearsal around noon. Nansi had brought the kids along and stuck four-year-old Emyr on Bryn's lap while she tuned her fiddle.

Rob was holding nine-month-old Bethan and they grinned at each other over the children's heads. "We should swap jobs for a week," he teased.

"No thanks. Give me a sword and a boat any day – at least they can't talk back. Do kids ever stop asking questions?"

"No," he replied, giving the baby a little squeeze. "Not really." Rob smiled and Bryn's chest tightened.

≈

Bryn watched as Rob lovingly repacked the mandolin after the session. He never tired of observing the quick precision and delicacy of Rob's fingers as he folded the cloth and closed the latch on the case. "Lunch?"

"Good idea. We're on patrol until eight; I'll need something to keep me going," Bryn replied with a sigh.

Without ever openly discussing it, Rob and Bryn had implemented a strict 'no touching' rule in their relationship, something that Bryn was finding more and more difficult to adhere to. Standing beside Rob in the lunch queue was pleasurable torture; beneath the smell of soap and deodorant were subtle hints of male body odour, a fragrance that Bryn found himself inching ever closer to inhale.

The spell was smashed totally by an enthusiastic Arwel, who bounded up to them with his usual boyish exuberance. "I've just had the most brilliant idea."

Arwel explained over lunch that the idea was a signal mechanism. Apparently, it would show not only *when*, but also *where* a breach in the perimeter had been made. He roped them both in for the brief experiment. "We're on duty at two," Bryn reminded him as they hurried out, the young lad leading them towards the shore.

Arwel stopped at some relevant point, asking them to stay put until he gave the signal. He then moved back towards the boathouse. "OK, now make an attack," he called from his vantage point.

They both fell into the attack position easily, having rehearsed it ad nauseam to keep Mona happy during pitched-battle practice. Both men jogged up from the beach, as Arwel had asked, but soon found their legs folding underneath them in a cat's cradle of fishing wire. As the wire became taut, it triggered a whooshing noise, and a red flare exploded above their heads.

They landed in a tangled web, about two feet from one another. As soon as Rob started to laugh, Bryn found it impossible to muster up any anger towards Arwel, who was rushing over to evaluate the damage. "If we colour coordinate the flares for each area, we'll be able to see, at a glance, which side they've approached from," he explained patiently. He did not think it important to ask whether they were alright.

"Yes, yes, well done. Go and get Mona so you can gloat," Rob chuckled.

It was hard work to untangle the fine wire, especially while still in the throes of hysteria. Rob escaped first and extended his hand to help Bryn, who accepted it without thinking.

At the touch of their hands, all pretence of a platonic relationship vanished instantly. Even after Bryn had made it to his feet, neither could let go. Bryn could feel his heart racing, producing a pounding in his eyes and head. He tried to swallow, but something about the way Rob was gazing at him had completely dried out his throat. Once more, it was Arwel's chatter that broke the spell. "I'm going to leave you to it; I've got an army to lead," Bryn stammered.

Late for duty, he jogged off to train the Demetae.

≈

Waiting for a break in the weather was excruciating. Dafydd had been gone for two weeks now and Cai had become obsessed with John's forecasting software. He experimented with its accuracy, but its ninety-eight per cent hit rate continued to depress him, confirming as it did the ever diminishing chances of escape.

John tried to keep Cai's mind off the weather by teaching him the odd application or programme. Outside activity on the grid system had come to a standstill, and in between bouts of worry, Cai attempted to make the best use of his time by learning all that John was willing to teach him.

"How about if your mates plant their bugs on other people – co-workers, flatmates, people with the same shift patterns?" John asked, still attempting to crack the bugged clothing conundrum without alerting the perpetrators.

"No." Cai didn't even glance up from the screen, and John breathed out noisily, exasperated by Cai's stubbornness.

"Well it's the best I've come up so far, everything else is too dodgy. If they're looking out for mass movements…"

"No," Cai reiterated, giving no other explanation.

≈

Cai was waiting on the jetty when Dafydd's boat came into sight. Out of nowhere, a possible three-day weather window had emerged, and via a coded VHF message, John had managed to get the prearranged signal to Dafydd on Tobermory.

Cai's excitement was soon replaced by feelings of irritation as he recognised Ieuan's outline at the bow. Catching the rope and making it off, Cai tried his best to keep both alert and calm at the same time. He had assumed that he and Dafydd would make the experimental run alone.

They'd been planning to wait until the last of the swell had died down before attempting the journey. If they left at dawn tomorrow, they would be guaranteed good weather and a quick passage, but this meant an awkward overnight stay beforehand. Dafydd seemed as if he wanted to explain Ieuan's presence, and Ieuan appeared apologetic, so Cai kept a lid on the emotions bubbling inside him. Cai had cooked spaghetti and John used the excuse of company to keep the wine flowing, though Cai didn't feel much like drinking.

Liz and John had both retreated to their bed by the time Ieuan attempted his apology. Several glasses of wine had not improved his sense of tact, and Cai could sense Dafydd gauging the tension.

"You see if I'm not right about Mona though." Ieuan nodded sagely, and Dafydd began a cautionary sentence, but Ieuan was in full swing. "Calm down, Dafydd. It's been over four months since we left. If I know Cai, he's well over her by now." Ieuan accompanied this assertion with a salacious wink.

Trembling with suppressed emotion, and not knowing what else to do, Cai began to clear away the remains of the meal. "I was going to ask about the local talent here – we should compare notes." Ieuan laughed convivially, and on some level Cai was aware that Ieuan was merely trying to engage with him on a subject of mutual interest. "The pub's been a great place for me – almost a new girl each week. I've even had two Americans." The table was nearly cleared now, one more return journey and he'd be able to leave the room. "I like the way normal girls smell, all that lipstick and perfume; they're softer somehow. Don't get me wrong, I'm sure Mona was a great shag, but you wouldn't want to handfast a woman like that. I mean, just look at the way she's built. It must have been like fucking another..."

Cai didn't register exactly when it happened, but before Ieuan could finish his sentence, he was dangling from Cai's pinched grip, halfway up the wall. The table was overturned and the remaining crockery smashed to the floor. Dafydd had been ready for the explosion, but was too slow to defuse it. Ieuan was making an unhealthy gurgling noise, so Cai let him drop.

≈

Cai was lying awake in bed when Dafydd knocked and entered. "He's sleeping on-board; no harm done." Dafydd didn't expect an answer. "I didn't know you felt like that about her."

Cai shrugged. "Is it a problem?"

"I don't know." Dafydd could feel his nephew bridling again. "Let's cross that bridge when we come to it," he added diplomatically. "I'm going to try to keep an open mind, but we both know there's a breach on the *Conway*, and Mona does seem to be a common denominator." In a way, all the signs did point to Mona but they would learn the truth soon enough, either way. "But just so you know, Cai, we're not contacting the *Conway* at all from now on. We've been playing into this spy's hands for far too long."

≈

As the weather deteriorated, Mona's belly began to swell, requiring regular adjustments to the waistband of her combats from Nesta. She still performed her patterns every morning before breakfast, though no longer outside, now that it was getting much colder.

Mona was waiting for one of her minders to pluck up sufficient courage to tell her to stop exercising. Arwel had given her all the information she needed as ammunition for when the time came, and she was determined not to be bullied.

Women who she barely knew wanted to talk to her about the "*pregnancy*" and the "*baby*". As far as Mona was concerned, it wasn't something that she needed to spend time thinking about. It would happen, and she would deal with it – there was no point fretting until then.

To his credit, Arwel hadn't nagged her at all, but Mona knew he was responsible for the leaflets on pregnancy and childbirth that had suddenly started appearing in her room. The size of her belly was becoming an inconvenience though, and she had to constantly readjust her line work to accommodate it.

"Hi, stinky," she greeted Rob as he returned from the nursery.

"Hi, fatty," he answered by rote, but the regular taunt sounded hollow, as if his heart wasn't really in it. Mona guessed he was susceptible to a darkening of moods as daylight hours shortened.

"You can get special lights, you know. We should ask Dai to get a bulb when they do the big shop for the solstice."

"Maybe," he agreed half-heartedly, flopping down on the bed next to her. Rob had learnt very early on not to mention Mona's pregnancy. If Mona wanted to pretend it wasn't happening, then so be it. The fatty joke was admissible, as it made her laugh.

"You smell pretty ripe. Perhaps you should change your clothes before supper."

"Perhaps we shouldn't bother with supper. What do you reckon the chances are of getting room service?" He closed his eyes with a deep sigh. That was better, at least he was making an effort to joke. She was struggling to think of a witty retort when something strange happened in her lower abdomen. Mona gasped and froze simultaneously. Rob sat up as the sensation occurred again, and slightly stronger this time.

"What's wrong?"

"I… I don't know."

"Are you in pain?" It happened for a third time, but she was ready for it this time, and put her hands against her tight stomach.

The sensation of being kicked from the inside, and feeling it through her hand on the outside, was surreal, and it finally drove home to her the terrifying reality of her pregnancy. There was a child growing inside her and it had just moved around. There was no way she could fight a pitched battle against the Irish: if Mona died, then her baby would die too.

Rob was worried now, Mona was pale and trembling. "Oh my God, Berys, I'm going to have a baby," she whispered, hands still clutching her fluttering abdomen.

≈

As they stood, the current battle plans relied heavily on Mona being present in the teeth of the fighting. She spent an uneasy night wrestling with viable alternatives.

All four chiefs, together with Arwel, Ifan and Mona, had started to meet up early each morning to discuss the impending attack. They feared it was only a couple of weeks away; the Irish had come within a couple of miles of the *Conway* during the last big festival, and no one, not even Arwel, had figured out a plausible reason for their last-minute withdrawal.

The winter solstice was a huge event in the pagan calendar, and the smart money was on the Irish attacking again, when they would expect their Welsh counterparts to be largely inebriated. The committee had decided to speak publicly about the expected date of the attack, to ensure that the community was ready to go into battle, given ten minutes' notice.

It was impossible to second-guess the actions of the spy in their midst. Ifan and Arwel had been ceaselessly poring over documents for months, but to no avail. Mona had come to the conclusion that if they were always ready for an attack, the existence and actions of the spy were inconsequential. Arwel disagreed but he couldn't say why.

As the flow of talk in the meeting whirled around her, Mona continued to ponder the ramifications of her dilemma. Arwel wanted to address the signalling from the patrol boat and Mona vaguely registered the rumbling discussion about the code-words and flares, but the baby inside her was active and the movement seemed to have sparked some sort of a relationship between them. She snapped out of her reverie to find everyone staring at her. "Sorry?" Arwel repeated a question he must have posed to her before, but she cut to the chase. "I can't fight them hand to hand."

The faces in front of her weren't registering disappointment or anger, but relief. Sioned broke the silence. "We're so glad you came to that decision yourself. Arwel's been considering secretly administering a sedative right before the battle."

They all laughed nervously, but Arwel was extending an apology. "It would only have been a last resort."

Mona smiled at their concern. "I'm not fighting hand to hand, but I will be involved in the battle." Someone sighed. "We'll stick to the plan, but Sioned will play my part and I'll back her up – just not from the front line."

Despite her concern for Mona, Sioned erupted with pride at the thought of being her understudy.

"So how will you fight? What with?" Bryn was direct and concise, as always.

"I'm going to learn how to throw knives. Reckon I've got a couple of weeks to become an expert." She smiled at the confused faces. "How hard can it be?"

≈

John answered the door to Dafydd at dawn and accepted the cup of coffee. Cai had packed and was ready to go, having cleared up the mess and apologised to John for the breakages.

"Where did you and Ieuan leave your bugs?" John asked Dafydd as he joined the men on the path to the sea, clutching the detector and frowning.

"At the pub in Tobermory – we spend a lot of time there." He grinned at John, who appeared preoccupied. "What is it?"

"I don't know," he mused as he gave Dafydd's boat a final check over. "Sometimes I get a faint echo, but it's gone now." He turned off the detector as the Welshmen boarded, but was still lost in thought as he threw Cai the stern rope.

"Thanks, John." Cai hoped that the Englishman understood that he was thanking him for more than just the rope, but he seemed too engrossed in his machine to notice.

To prevent any lingering ill feeling, Dafydd decided to grab the bull by the horns and tackle the issue of Cai and Ieuan's falling-out head-on. The matter had been raised before he'd even started the engine. "I know you two have had your differences, but we've got to stick together now – I can't have any more of it."

They both understood, and Ieuan was the first to admit his guilt. "I'm sorry, Cai. What can I say? I'm a complete prat."

Cai shook the offered hand. "I haven't exactly showered myself in glory," he admitted with a grim smile.

Dafydd took the helm with a look of satisfaction, while Ieuan and Cai deliberated over the chart. They needed to decide whether to hug the coast or take a direct line on full power. Time was the issue, and they all agreed on the latter. As Dafydd fired up the engine, the sun came out and Cai and Ieuan picked up the binoculars.

They'd been motoring for a few hours, but the traffic was light and they were making good time, having already exchanged the Sea of the Hebrides for the open waters of the Atlantic. Cai was trying to keep his burgeoning hopes at bay, when they were completely sideswiped by the sight of a signature bow wave bearing down on them.

He quickly raised the alarm. They were isolated in open water; retreat was their only option, and Dafydd immediately performed a U-turn.

Cai expected the VSV to back off, as it had before. The Welshmen had been warned and were taking heed. However, instead of slowing to watch their retreat, as had happened previously, the VSV's skipper accelerated towards them at an incredible speed, placing his vessel on a collision course with their own.

Dafydd glanced at Cai. "Hold your course," he advised. Dafydd's boat lacked the manoeuvrability of the *Marc'h*, and Cai had no idea what to expect from the latest Irish ploy, but it was the only possible action to take. The magnificent vessel was upon them within a minute.

Ieuan and Cai had their swords out, but they would have to wait for their attackers to slow and board before they could use them. As the vessel veered around into an elegant sweep, Cai realised that they were being corralled. "Ease up, Dafydd," he warned.

The grey boat continued to circumnavigate their cutter, and Cai saw men emerging from inside it. They seemed to brace themselves against the turning force and point at them – with guns.

"Guns!" Cai bellowed, snatching Dafydd from the wheel and throwing them both to the deck. "Ieuan, get down," he bawled, pulling at the man's leg from the ground as the bullets thudded and twanged into the fibreglass and metal of the boat around them. Ieuan hesitated for a moment before falling to the deck.

The velocity of the powerful machines' withdrawal had churned the waters up into an incredible swell beneath them. The men rolled on the floor, desperately attempting to grab hold of each other to regain some sort of balance.

Dafydd waited until there was complete silence before inching upwards to assess the situation. He could see the corridor of frothy water left behind in the VSV's choppy wake, and pulled back on the throttle, slowing the boat, and leaving it to tick over in neutral. He was shaking with adrenaline as he turned to the two men on the deck.

Cai was sitting upright against the hull. He had dragged Ieuan onto his lap, as was apparent by the large swathe of blood left behind on the planks. The men were talking as Cai pressed down on Ieuan's abdomen. The boat's deck was awash with so much blood that there could be very little left inside Ieuan.

≈

Rather than just teaching herself to throw knives, Mona had decided that two other members of the community should learn alongside her. Being equally clueless about standard combat, Rob and Arwel had both been volunteered as students. All three now stood shivering in the cold of the empty boathouse, a building of sufficient length and dilapidation to fit their purpose to a T. Arwel had drawn a fairly competent facsimile of a human being on the far wooden wall, and she appreciated that he had taken the time to paint the eyes an obvious brown.

They all held three throwing knives. Mona had borrowed Sioned's and Ifan had purchased a set each for Rob and Arwel. Rob was the least enthusiastic of the trio; his dark mood was lingering and Mona suspected there might be something else underlying his seasonal depression.

Predictably, Arwel had sought out reference material on the subject and was reading it aloud to them while holding his first dagger aloft.

"*Your feet have to form a forty-five degree angle. The left in the twelve o'clock and the right in the one o'clock position. Both knees are bent, especially the front one. The weight rests primarily on the ball of your back foot.*" He contorted unnaturally.

"You look ridiculous," Rob sniped, but Arwel ignored him.

"*Next, you make sure both arms are straight and pointing towards the target, which should be at chest height.*" Arwel was finding it hard to enact the requisite movements while holding the book. Taking it from him, Mona held it so he could continue to read. "*The right arm now makes a round and smooth swing to the back; the knife is even behind the head.*" He made the action and beamed at them. "*Then it swings forward towards the target, like so.*" Mona was getting impatient to start but stilled a sigh. "*While swinging forward, the weight is shifted to rest on the front foot; the chest follows this movement. The right shoulder does not move – it remains in a tilted line with the left.*" Arwel deliberated

318

on that point then nodded to himself, waggling his shoulders a bit, and Rob groaned. *"For the throw, the weight is shifted to the left foot, while the right arm, with the knife, is brought to the front. As the knife arm is roughly in line with the left one and points exactly to the target, quickly let the knife go and snap your fingers back together. Do not stop the swing of the knife; go on with the movement. This is called 'follow through' and considered very important for a good stick."*

Rob rolled his eyes at Mona. "Come on then, sunshine, stop talking and give it a go. I'm freezing my nuts off here." Arwel took a deep breath. Trying to remember all the instructions, he let fly.

All three blades failed entirely, the first and third never even reaching the target at all. He retrieved the blades with a certain amount of chagrin. "It's much harder than it sounds." Mona stood up by the first marker and raised her arm to begin. "Your feet are all wrong, Mo."

Mona shot him a warning glare and he shut up. She held the knife rather as if she was holding a hammer; it felt quite natural and she thought she'd just give it a go. All three knives landed on the target with a satisfying thud. She was delighted.

"Bloody typical," Rob grouched. "Please don't tell me you've never done this before."

Arwel was gazing at her as if she'd changed water into wine. The *mark*, his eyes said, even if his mouth didn't. "I'm just good at this sort of stuff. Now shut up and have another go."

After three hours, they had all improved. Arwel was hitting the target, though a lack of power through the forearm prevented his blades from sticking. Rob had plenty of power but lacked motivation or accuracy, while Mona had discovered two or three further techniques that she could apply in various situations. "Same time tomorrow then?" she asked breezily.

As they trudged off to lunch, Rob and Arwel were acutely aware that it was going to be a long, hard course. Their arms began to ache merely at the thought of it.

John watched from the jetty as the engine gurgled into life. Still holding the detector in his hand, he waved and wished the young men luck. As the boat vanished into the Sea of the Hebrides, the sun suddenly made a long-overdue appearance, and his spirits lifted.

Raising his eyes towards the light, John's mind – which never wandered far from the business of renewables – turned to the PV solar cells up on the hill, and all the free electricity they would now be producing. Suddenly the machine in his hand flared into life, showing an insistent but receding red dot. There *were* back-up bugs on the boats – and they were powered by the sun.

Cursing Dafydd's aversion to communication devices, John sprinted to the shed, bellowing for Liz as he made the door. "We've got to go after them; they're still being tracked."

≈

The RIB was on the water in twenty minutes, but by that time the cutter was out of the tracker's range. Luckily, John had half listened to the Welshmen's planned route, and so was able to plot their likely position on his chart while Liz took the helm.

Even though Liz was gunning the RIB, it would still take time to catch up with the cutter. The water was relatively calm after the previous fortnight's gales, but she knew that there would be more storms waiting in the wings at this time of year.

The sun had disappeared, but they knew they were too late when they heard the unmistakable sound of rapid gunfire and the roar of a powerful engine. The exact location of the sound was difficult to pinpoint, so they continued on their current course while John scanned the horizon with his binoculars. Having spotted something, he tapped Liz on the shoulder and pointed her in the right direction.

The RIB gained rapidly on Dafydd's stationary boat, despite the sudden localised swell. There had been an extremely fast boat here recently – but it was gone now. Liz slowed as they pulled alongside the bobbing vessel. A spray of bullets had ripped a jagged pattern along the entire length of the superstructure.

Dafydd emerged on deck above the RIB. He looked extremely drawn, and from the pain in his face, Liz worried that he'd been hit. John climbed on board ahead of her, then turned back instantly, to prevented her from joining him. "It might be best to stay there, love." Liz knew John was protecting her, but she nevertheless hauled herself up to stand beside him. On the deck in front of her, Liz saw Cai holding the other Welsh boy in his arms and sitting in a lake of blood.

As soon as Ieuan fell, Cai knew he'd been shot. He'd grabbed out and pulled Ieuan close until the violent pitching had slowed to a gentle rocking. The blood was already beginning to pool as he dragged Ieuan on to his lap; it was coming from below his chest, and Cai tried to staunch the flow with his hand. Dafydd passed him a towel to increase the surface area of pressure. As the blood leaked from his body, saturating the towel, Ieuan began to talk. "I just wanted to be your friend. I wanted you to like me." His voice was quiet, but clearly audible.

"I know; I'm sorry."

"When we meet again then…"

"I'll remember."

Ieuan's eyes continued to stare up at Cai after he had died. Closing them, Dafydd managed to bring Cai back to the present. "There was a solar-powered back-up transmitter; John's just found it," he uttered vacantly.

Cai nodded, strangely lucid. "We have to burn him. He's not going to the sea."

"No," Dafydd agreed wearily, knowing that the young man deserved a proper passing.

"We can't burn him on Eigg; we'll make for a smaller, uninhabited island." Cai wasn't looking at him and Dafydd couldn't understand his logic.

"Why? It would be…"

"I don't want them involved. We can't lead the Irish to their door – what if there's satellite surveillance we don't know about? They could be watching us right now."

"Cai, we haven't got time for all this."

Still holding Ieuan in his lap, Cai finally gazed up at his uncle. "I couldn't save my mum and dad. Let me protect John and Liz, please." Dafydd moved away to the chart table, where he discussed the situation with John.

When it became apparent that he wasn't going to move away, or let go of Ieuan's body, Liz sat down next to Cai. "I never liked him, not since we were kids, and I pretended not to know why." Cai brushed an errant hair back off Ieuan's forehead. "He was popular, he knew how to talk to people…"

"Come on now, love…"

"Mona knew; she was right about me."

"What did she know, Cai?" Liz's voice was unbearably maternal.

"That I'm an arrogant, selfish bastard, who thought that my birth right put me above people like Ieuan." The wind blew Ieuan's hair around and Cai smoothed it back. "He thought we were alike, he wanted to be my friend… but I was too good for him." The engines of both boats had come to life again and they were on the move.

"You were his friend at the end, he knew that."

Cai dropped his forehead to Ieuan's. "Did he?"

When they landed back on Eigg, Cai gave Dafydd a filthy look. Catching it, John quickly intervened. "It's all right, Cai, the boat is clean of bugs. There were solar stickers on the windscreen; they're all gone now, I promise you."

They drove as near as possible to the cave mouth at Talm, then carried Ieuan's body the rest of the way. It took hours to transport the wood, but the fire was ready by dawn and Dafydd began chanting the passing rites, to the best of his ability. Cai was still covered in Ieuan's hardening blood when he spoke for the dead man.

The two Druids had allowed John and Liz to stay for the ceremony; they were beyond caring about the enormity of the transgression. The couple watched in quiet solemnity as Ieuan's body burned. It was a strange rite, in a strange language, but the depth of emotion drew them in as both men faltered through their words.

Cai concluded the rites with a song, coughing a little to clear his voice before beginning: "*Holl amrantau'r sêr ddywedant, / Ar hyd y nos.*" Dafydd joined his voice with Cai's, Liz recognising immediately the tune of 'All through the night'. John put his arms round her shoulders and she cried quiet tears into his chest.

By the time Cai had finished singing, John and Liz had gone. Both men stayed, however, until nothing was left of Ieuan – nothing but ash. Cai picked up Ieuan's short sword and added it to his belt.

≈

A new weather front of torrential rain met them on the slow walk back to the tin shed. Liz was prepared for their arrival with hot water, clean clothes and food.

They talked about repairing Dafydd's boat, retrieving the back-up transmitters from the other vessels, and de bugging the clothing. The first task would be completed tomorrow, allowing Dafydd to return to Tobermory before any awkward questions could be asked. The others would have to be done by Dafydd alone, during breaks in the weather.

"I'm not trying the Irish Sea again." Dafydd's decision sounded final. Cai had been silent for most of the discussion; there was a heaviness in his chest that was affecting his breathing, his brain pounded against the inside of his skull, and he just couldn't get warm. "At the first real break in the weather, we're trying the Caledonian Canal again."

Cai was too weak to argue but wanted to know specifics. "What are you classing as a real break?"

Dafydd looked at John meaningfully. "Good enough so that the next time we leave, it's for ever."

27

Winter Solstice

Bryn wasn't avoiding him exactly, but Rob had noticed how he kept a good metre of personal space between them and that he was careful never to find himself alone in the same room. Something had changed last month on the shoreline and Bryn was terrified by it.

Rob lay playing the mandolin on the bed. Mona was beside him, plugged in to her mp3 player and scribbling ideas on a pad. As he strummed another chord, Rob put his free hand on her stomach, absent-mindedly gauging the baby's reaction to the minor key. Experiments had already showed a liking for the major key.

Mona enjoyed the way Rob was behaving towards her unborn child, and she hoped that he might prove to be a reliable father figure. It was abundantly apparent that she wouldn't be able to make a run for it now.

Despite the experiments, Rob was still distracted and grumpy. "If someone's pissed you off, you should deal with it – confront them." She carried on scribbling while she talked.

Mona's advice came out of nowhere, and Rob put it down to the fact that she was getting a bit nervy about the impending invasion. Mona and Arwel were convinced of the date, and as it drew nearer, they were all feeling the tension. He strummed again, filling the room with melancholy. "Really? Is that what you do?"

"Always."

"And does it work?"

"No, but it always changes the situation."

Her last point had merit, and Rob decided to take the advice.

≈

The doctor on Eigg told them that Cai had a bad chest infection and that if the second course of antibiotics didn't shift it, John and Liz would have to take him to the hospital on the mainland.

Cai had fallen ill the day after Ieuan's passing. The heaviness in his chest had morphed into laboured breathing. He blazed and froze alternately and lost pints of water through sweating. Liz had found him thrashing and delirious in the early hours of the following morning, his body racked by dry sobs and incoherent ramblings.

After a week of worry and indecision, they had called the doctor, but it had taken him three days to get there through the atrocious weather. The rain and wind were relentless, but snow was also rumoured to be on the way, and the doctor had left two courses of antibiotics in case he couldn't make it back.

≈

Two weeks after the doctor's visit, Cai finally got out of bed. "At last!" John beamed from his monitors. "Sensible conversation."

The comment was aimed at Liz and she countered it wearily. "Good luck with the interminable technology, Cai." She squeezed his now bony shoulder on her way to the workshop and gave her husband a final warning. "Do not *bore* him to death or tire him too much. I will see you both at supper."

Cai wasn't taken in by their breezy talk. He knew they'd sat in shifts at his bedside through the worst of it, cooling him with wet flannels to keep his temperature down, and piling on the blankets when he froze.

The effort it had taken to shower, change and walk into the living

325

area had sapped his strength, and he had to sit down on the only sofa that the dogs hadn't commandeered. Cai leaned his head back for a five-minute nap, waking to the smell of food and the sound of people trying to talk quietly.

"At least the boys will be together for Christmas." Liz always talked quite loudly – hearing damage from the power tools he guessed. Cai didn't have to see John to know that he'd motioned to his wife to keep her voice down. She continued in slightly lower tones. "It'll be our first Christmas without them, you know."

"I know, love, but you've always got me."

Through half-opened eyes, Cai saw John slide his arms around her waist as she cooked and nuzzle into her neck. Liz giggled and elbowed him lightly in the chest. After putting down the spoon, she swivelled around and into his arms.

The kissing went on for some time and Cai began to wonder if he should wake up a little more noisily. He decided against coughing – a uniquely unpleasant and painful activity at present. Fortunately, the little grey dog, who had been curled up against him all day, decided it was time for his supper. Wandering into the kitchen, he managed to prise the couple apart through the sheer force of his pathetic stare.

The food must have been delicious, but Cai still couldn't stomach it. He had a funny taste in his mouth and a constant nausea in his belly; he'd never had antibiotics before – in fact, had never been this ill before. "You're going to have to eat." Liz was no longer cajoling. There was a hard edge to her voice, and, not for the first time, Cai caught a glimpse of her strict maternal streak.

"See what I have to put up with?" John cocked his head in her direction: good cop, bad cop. It had taken Cai some time to figure out their relationship, but now he had, it fascinated him. John and Liz were a team, not a couple. Their relationship had been forged through years of working together and raising children, but it was the fierce friendship beneath that Cai envied.

There may have been the first glimmerings of something similar between him and Mona, though he would never know now. It was almost the winter solstice – five months since he'd last seen her. She'd be long gone.

≈

Rob had no idea how he would start the conversation. Even so, he braved the arctic conditions and climbed the stairs to the radio room, walking straight in without knocking – before he lost his nerve.

Bryn was there, of course; he had a glass in his hand and there was a half-empty bottle on the table. Nerves forgotten, Rob felt the bile rise in his throat and erupt in a wave of furious anger. "What the hell are you doing?" he bellowed, striding towards the offending bottle.

Bryn grabbed it first, staring straight ahead. "Leave me alone," he insisted calmly.

"Give it to me and I'll go." Rob snatched at the exposed neck of the bottle and pulled. Bryn hadn't expected him to be so strong and quick, and was unable to prevent him from snatching it away.

"Give it back," he growled.

"No, you've had enough."

Rob turned towards the door, but Bryn was no way near drunk enough to let the bottle go. Intercepting Rob before he reached the door, Bryn seized him by the scruff of the neck and began shaking him by it. "Give it back."

"What are you going to do, hit me?"

These last words brought Bryn up short. He lessened his hold on Rob, but found himself unable to release it entirely. His hand stayed resting on the bare skin of Rob's neck, where he had pulled away his shirt.

Unable to help himself, Bryn gently rubbed his thumb up to the line of Rob's jaw and then back again. It was almost as if he were watching another hand, one that belonged to someone else. Rob closed his eyes and turned his head away. Instinctively, Bryn raised his other hand to pull Rob back to face him – until he was holding Rob's beautiful head in both hands. Rob opened his eyes slowly, and Bryn knew that there could be only one conclusion if he allowed himself a taste of those trembling lips.

Without warning, Bryn jerked himself away, sickened by his own excitement. "Get away from me. You're disgusting, you pervert. Get out."

Rob still held the bottle of rum by its neck, and as Bryn backed away from him he raised it level with his shoulder. Fuelled by Bryn's vicious rejection, he simply let it drop – to spectacular effect. "You're a bloody coward," Rob choked hoarsely.

≈

Rob must have returned while she was sleeping – late, she guessed, as he was refusing to get out of bed, claiming sickness. Unusually, Mona hadn't been able to cajole him out of it, and she went to breakfast alone for the first time in ages.

There were only two days until the winter solstice, and Mona constantly fought the urge to call it Christmas. The aroma of evergreen sap was everywhere, and the smell triggered memories of her lost family.

The defence plan had been fashioned in meticulous detail, but depended on every single member of the community to play their part, and the margins for error were minute. Even Bryn was distracted and jittery at the final meeting; understandably so, as the majority of the leadership responsibilities were falling on his shoulders.

"No throwing today then, Mona?" Arwel asked hopefully.

"Rob's not all that well, but you could certainly do with the practice. Come on, matey, no time like the present."

He sighed and fastened the knife belt around his skinny hips. It held nine blades now, as did Rob's and Mona's.

≈

At Mona's request, the very young, the very old and the very sick had been carted off to Swnt, and were awaiting the outcome of the attack under the watchful eyes of Nia and Siân. Owain and Osian were the only half-decent warriors she could spare to protect them, and Mona doubted whether either of them were much older than twelve. All that was left to do now was wait.

≈

The snow had arrived and looked unlikely to disappear any time soon. It was unusual for the Inner Hebrides to have snow at sea level, but Cai was unsurprised by it. This latest catastrophe was just about what he had come to expect from their doomed voyage.

As the illness had left his body, it had been replaced with an equally debilitating torpor of the mind. He didn't sleep all the time now, but did very little apart from sit stroking the whippets and staring into space.

Cai was contemplating how easy it would be to come back as a whippet, when John strolled over for a chat. "They've really taken to you." Cai cracked a small smile and carried on stroking. "I know you're disappointed that you didn't get away." John's voice was calming, like a doctor – like a dad. "All indications suggest that the weather isn't going to let up till spring." Cai knew that, and he was surprised John had mentioned it again. "We can get a lot done in three months, Cai. There are things I'd like to teach you before you go."

John's gentle tones were crushed by an almighty huff from the kitchen. Liz had been listening to her husband pussyfoot around Cai in his efforts to motivate him, and could take no more. Marching from the kitchen, she stood defiantly in front of Cai, dishcloth in hand and hands on hips. "This woman of yours, what's she like?"

Cai didn't even consider not answering. "She's strong, a good fighter." He stroked the dog, "She saved my life." Even his voice was croaky from lack of use.

"And do you think she'd approve of you, lolling around feeling sorry for yourself?"

"Liz!" John's muttered warning went unheeded.

"What would she do, Cai?"

Despite himself, he felt angry at the interfering woman, who was now glaring at him with accusation in her eyes. "It doesn't matter now; she's long gone," he replied, tersely.

"Would you want her to see you like *this*?" Liz answered her own question. "I don't think so. When you arrived here you were strong and fit. Take a good look in the mirror, Cai, you're fading away. *So what* if she's gone when you get back? Isn't she worth searching for, fighting for?"

Cai hated Liz in that moment, so intensely that he wanted to attack her. He hated her because she was right.

≈

"If Arwel's right – and he always is – they should be here in four hours: dawn on the winter solstice. Unnecessarily melodramatic if you ask me, but that's Druids for you." Mona gabbled on breezily, trying to corral her own emotions before the fight.

Rob was sitting up in bed now as Mona forced some soup down him. He certainly didn't look well, and she chastised herself for not believing him earlier. "You can sit this out in the chapel. You're no good to me anyway unless you can do your job."

"No, don't worry, I'll be fine. I'm over the worst of it now." His voice was thin and small, as if the volume had been sucked out of it.

≈

At the appointed time, every Druid in *Conway* dressed themselves from head to foot in protective leather. The community had been stitching and altering since Samhain; and it was hoped that the leather might form some sort of barrier against the tainted blades, though Mona thought it was probably just a placebo.

Success depended on the clockwork precision of Arwel's plan. At a signal from the patrol boat, the klaxon would sound. The young children and the elderly would be rounded up and led to the chapel by four 'shepherds': Rob, Arwel, Nesta and Nansi. Everyone else was expected to fight.

≈

About twenty Irishmen landed on the snowy beach. Mona had forty active warriors and only a handful of them were experienced men, but she waited patiently as sequence after sequence unfolded according to plan.

Ready, on either side of their route were the Gangani and the Ordivices. This passage was already laced with the fishing wire that, when broken, would activate flares.

Once the fireworks began, a cacophony of beating saucepans on either side created a wall of sound that further disoriented the attackers. As they stumbled free of the wire, the Irish were forced into the path of the best of the fighters. In the front line of defence were the Demetae, led by Bryn, and these were backed up by Sioned and her Silurians, ready to mop up any invaders that got through.

The Irish had just finished engaging with Bryn's troops, when Ifan shuffled up behind her. This was not in the script. "Problem?" she demanded brusquely.

Ifan grimaced. "Come with me." With the enemy already so close, it was the last thing she needed to do. Although a bit roughed up by Arwel's beach games, they were still big, powerful men wielding swords. How could her gaggle of women and children possibly hold out?

Turning her back on the action, she followed Ifan back the way he'd come. He explained that Emyr, Nansi's middle child, had vanished and taken his baby sister with him. Rob, Nesta and Arwel had gone in search of them just before the klaxon had sounded. It took Mona and Ifan much more time than they could afford to waddle to the chapel.

Nansi stood distraught at the entrance, clasping the hand of her eight-year-old and repeatedly scanning the snowy horizon for signs of her missing children. Near hysterical, she ran to Mona immediately.

"Emyr," she choked. "He hates loud noises... the klaxon... and when I looked around for him..." She broke down. "He's taken Bethan with him."

Mona could see that Dylan, her eldest, was fighting back tears; watching his mother's pain was almost unbearable.

He spoke to Mona instead of his mum. "I think I might know where they've gone. Emyr goes there a lot – the noise doesn't go there."

Nansi was all ears. "Where have they gone, Dylan?" Mona could see she was trying to contain her shrill terror.

"Where the boats are kept," he replied solemnly.

"The boathouse?" Mona wanted to be certain before she moved anywhere.

The young boy nodded. "There's a cupboard in the corner."

Nansi pushed her boy towards Ifan and started to march forward, but he stopped her. "Nansi, you need to stay here; we haven't got anyone else to protect them."

Mona backed him up: with the three other shepherds missing, Nansi was needed to protect her charges in the chapel. "You're a better bet than me at the moment, there's just no one else."

Nansi accepted Mona's point with stoic resignation. "Please... get them, Mona," she begged.

"I will. Get everyone inside now and lock the door. You know the signal."

Mona trudged back up through the slush to the main battle, where she could see that Bryn and Dai had dispatched more than six men between them. Most of the youngsters had to fight in pairs against the invading men, and they were exhausted.

Sioned stood alone and at first acquitted herself well, but things changed rapidly when a late arrival from the shore pitched his bulk into her side, forcing her to the ground. Fighting on two fronts now, Sioned would not be able to last long.

Mona knew she could alter Sioned's plight if she could just reach her in time, but her body refused to move quickly enough up the hill. The faster she waddled, the more she slipped on the hardening slush. The anguish of impotence dragged her eyes again to the young woman.

Strangely, neither man went for the kill. Instead, they began to bind Sioned with a length of rope. Anxiety chimed in Mona's head as Sioned struggled violently with her attackers. Rope? Her blood ran cold.

Sioned managed to connect a brutal kick with a stomach. The man doubled over, leaving an open target for Mona who had finally reached the summit. She threw two knives, but one would have done. According to Arwel's manual, a knife to the jugular was always the most effective, and she'd practiced the relevant throw obsessively.

Recovering quickly, Sioned kicked out again, knocking the second man unconscious this time. Once she was free, Mona sent another four blades flying in the general vicinity of the melee, this time injuring rather than killing. Though the panic and confusion caused by the flying blades provided an immense boost to her battling troops, who steadily but inexorably began to turn the tide of battle in their favour.

Bryn was grim, bloody and panting as Mona reached his side. "It's kidnap," she shouted as he wiped his blade. "They're after the girls."

Bryn immediately grasped the implications. A lot of the saucepan caterwauling had come from the weaker girls in the Gangani and Ordovices; they would be easy pickings so close to the shore. Sioned and Dai had rallied their tribes and were already in pursuit of the would-be abductors. Bryn started to follow but Mona stopped him. "You need to come with me." Already she was struggling to catch her breath.

Once apprised of the situation, Bryn set off at a sprint; if he could find the two lost children, Mona would take them back to the chapel. She followed on as fast as she was able, only pausing once she had reached the front of the boathouse.

There was no activity outside, but her heart sank at the tableau on the other side of the rotting doorway. Nesta and Rob had taken up defensive stances in front of the cupboard, and they faced two rabid men. Rob would have known where Emyr's bolthole was, and Mona guessed that Arwel was holed up in there as well, protecting both children with his life.

Rob had used up all his throwing knives, except the one he held in his hand, like a miniature sword. Mona could see blades dotted around the floor, and a glance at both the attacking Irishmen told her that Rob had found his target at least once. Nesta was fury itself as she cursed them profusely in her native tongue, holding her huge cudgel aloft.

Where was Bryn?

A tiny flicker of movement from the water side of the building warned Mona that Bryn was about to attack. To maximise his chances, she needed to create a diversion.

Holding two of her three remaining knives, she stepped noisily into the fray, throwing them simultaneously at each man. It wasn't a move she'd practiced, and her left-handed throw didn't stick very deep in the Irishman's arm. The throw from her right hand was better, and deflected the attention of the other Irishman towards the blade sticking out of his leg.

Bryn now made his attack, virtually flying through the air as he tackled his man to the ground. Straddling him, he efficiently slit his throat, then moved to assist Nesta. Mona got down on her hands and knees and scrabbled around on the floor, searching for Rob's fallen blades. She had gathered up four by the time the shouting began.

The bulk of the attackers were running for their boats, and the fear of being left behind had galvanised the injured Irishman in the boathouse into calling out pitifully. Bryn shut him up with a single thrust from his blade, but the shout had been heard, bringing reinforcements.

The next man in was consumed with bloodlust, and Bryn was tiring. Rob threw his remaining blade but it was swotted away. Bryn engaged but Mona saw the tell-tale signs of fatigue weighing down his sword arm and making his foot work sloppy. "Take the kids and run," he commanded Rob with as much breath as he could spare. Scraping together the last dregs of his vitality, Bryn overpowered the attacker, diving his sword home with a troubled grunt.

Nesta had worn herself ragged with her labours, and could now do nothing more than lean on her cudgel. She didn't even see the sword as it was driven into her back. The blade went straight through her heart, causing Mona to scream out in a mixture of anger and impotence. Pulling the blade from Nesta's body, the newcomer continued his advance on Bryn. The intruder was fresh, Bryn was exhausted – he was going to lose this bout.

A chord of adrenaline sang in Mona's chest, and the familiar throb of power thundered through her bloodstream. She peered at her hands and remembered the hot grit of death on them. Mona didn't ever want to feel that energy again– the intoxication frightened her – so she opted for conventional weapons.

Her scavenged blades bounced off the back of the Irishman's toughened jacket; Mona needed a sword if there was any hope of helping Bryn. She turned her back on the action, and crawled away in search of one.

Nesta's weapon of choice had always been the cudgel, but she had been issued with a sword as well. Fumbling to unclasp it from the dead woman's belt, Mona felt a desperate pang of loss as she breathed in the familiar scent of soap powder.

Mona's swollen belly impeded her progress as she groped her way along the floor, Nesta's sword held ready at her side. Finally standing, she saw Bryn cast an eye towards the corner, checking if Rob had followed the order. This momentary lapse of concentration gave Bryn's assailant the opening he needed. Mona and the Irishman struck their opponents simultaneously and all three fell to the floor in unison.

Mona had used all her momentum to force Nesta's blade into the man's back, but he wasn't dead yet, so she pulled out the blade and dispatched him with a savage blow across the neck. Bryn was conscious and nursing the dagger that was wedged in his chest. "I'm fine; you stuck him first." The pain caused him to speak through gritted teeth. "He got me across the ribs, not through them."

Mona was panting and bloody. "Shall... shall I pull it out?"

He moved his head. "No, wait for the healers." Bryn knew the answer, but asked anyway. "Nesta?" Mona shook her head ever so slightly, and Bryn lifted an arm. "Come here. We'll need to keep warm." Mona eased her bulk to the floor and inched through the pooling blood towards him.

They lay motionless for a while – until the pains in her abdomen began. The cramping caused Mona's fists to clench. "Lie still, just rest now," Bryn soothed.

There was another sharp twinge. "If I have the baby now," she swallowed, "will it die?" Bryn pulled her closer but didn't reply.

≈

It couldn't have been very long before Rob and Arwel clattered in again through the opening, but time had become difficult to judge. There were a few seconds of excruciating silence before Mona heard the sound of Arwel's heart, breaking at the sight of Nesta's prone body.

Tears that he'd never shed for his mother or his father now flowed from him. Arwel sobbed and howled over the body of the big woman, kissing her face and calling her name, over and over again. For a long time he sat with her head in his lap, smoothing her grey hair back and crooning to her in Welsh. Mona was too far away to hear properly, but it sounded like a lullaby. As she was carried past on a stretcher, Mona put her hands over her ears. She couldn't bear to hear any more.

28

Mourning

Bryn had lied; the knife hadn't grazed the front of his ribs but had smashed through, breaking two of them and puncturing his right lung.

Rob had carried one end of the stretcher back to the infirmary, and remained in the room while the medic checked Bryn's breathing and inspected the wound. The small hospital was full to capacity and the *Conway's* only trained doctor was grateful for Rob's help. "We have to insert a chest tube."

Rob nodded, not understanding what that would entail, but ready for anything. "There will be a lot of blood when I draw out the knife. Do you understand?" He did. Bryn's breathing was slow and grating and Rob didn't know if he was just asleep or unconscious. "He's had a sedative, but I'll need you here if he struggles with the pain." Rob assured the doctor that he could help, hoping it was the truth.

As the procedure got underway, Rob concentrated on Bryn's head and chest. The warrior's eyes flew open as the medic grasped the hilt of the dagger, and he bucked upwards with the pain. Rob pushed his body weight through his hands against Bryn's powerful shoulders. "It's all right. It's going to be OK."

Bryn gritted his teeth and relaxed into the pain as Rob smiled into his eyes, sending him reassurance and comfort, until Bryn tensed again and squeezed his eyes shut. Rob guessed that the tube was being inserted and glanced from patient to doctor. Sure enough, there was a tube in place of the dagger, and the doctor was cleaning around the open wound. "It will have to stay exposed like this for a couple of days. I'm afraid he's going to be vulnerable to infection until I can withdraw the tube and the wound heals." The doctor examined his handiwork. "I've given him a shot of antibiotic that will last a couple of days." He scanned the packed ward. "Any chance we can move him into a room on his own? I think that might minimise the chances of contamination."

There were two small rooms, facing each other, at the extreme end of the ward. Mona had been installed in one and together they hauled Bryn into the other. Once they had heaved him onto bed, the doctor left Bryn in Rob's care. He had another ten people to patch up before he was done. "I'll come and check up on him when I can. Keep an eye on his breathing – and call me if he deteriorates." Rob pulled a chair up to the top of the bed and concentrated on Bryn's breathing rhythm.

≈

The pain in his chest was immense, but Bryn felt much better on seeing Rob's head resting at the edge of the bed. The sight produced a slight shift in Bryn's breathing pattern, disturbing Rob. "Are you alright?" he asked but Bryn could only nod. "Shall I get someone?" He shook his head, and there was a profound sadness in his eyes. "Mona's fine; she just needs to rest," Rob reassured him.

Inexplicably, Bryn's eyes filled with tears. "I'm so sorry." His voice could barely be heard over his rasping breath. Rob gave him some more drugs, and wiped his eyes with a tissue before he fell back into a drugged sleep.

≈

Cai had to summon up all his courage to knock at the workshop door. He couldn't knock loudly enough to be heard over the grinding, and waited patiently until there was a break in the work.

"Come in." Liz's voice was muffled behind her visor.

Cai had expected to come clean straightaway, but was struck dumb for a moment by the sight of Liz's work. It was the scale that surprised him most; he had expected something substantial, but the shed was populated with metal sculptures well over seven feet in height. At first, the figures weren't recognisably human, but on examining them closer, he began to decipher limbs and features from among their twists and curves.

"Stainless?" he asked.

"316, marine grade. No point in mucking around." Cai remained mute, forcing Liz to fill the silence. "It's the human condition; life and death, sex and love." She waved a gloved hand in the direction of her current work. "It's all that matters in the end." Liz shrugged – not embarrassed, just not able to explain adequately.

In her sculpture, Liz had captured the essence of everything Cai understood about paganism. He had only known how to express it in song, but here was another way.

"It's like magic," Cai said finally, but their different understandings of the word were millennia apart, and Liz laughed.

"No – it's welding," she joked. Cai wanted to explain, but he didn't know where to begin, and anyway, she had become normal Liz once more. "What can I do for you?"

"I'm going to start my patterns again. You were right, I'm being pathetic – and I just wanted to thank you."

"And?" She'd seen right through him, and he smiled at being caught out.

"Can I do them in here? There's too much snow outside."

They spent all morning lugging heavy lumps of metal around, but on the strict condition that he be out of her hair before nine each morning, Cai was eventually granted a square of space in the corner of Liz's workshop.

≈

It was the kicking that woke Mona, the kicking from inside her, and she was filled with a strange joy that she found difficult to understand. Losing this baby should have been the best possible outcome for Mona – she'd thought so often enough before. Yet somehow it didn't matter to her now who its father was, or how it had been conceived. The baby was the most important person in her life and she would always love and protect it.

Finally opening her eyes, Mona recognised the infirmary and remembered the battle. *Nesta. Arwel's grief. Bryn's bravery.* She needed information, and scanned around for people who might have some. They had stuffed her away in a room on her own, but she could hear the sounds of care being administered on the main ward, and considered getting up to investigate.

"So! Awake at last." Hywel's wasn't the voice she'd expected or wanted to hear.

"How's Bryn?" Mona asked mechanically.

"Alive and well, thanks to you." The thanks didn't sound sincere. The old man sat in the recess of the high-backed hospital chair. "Another great move, Mona. You really are playing the long game, aren't you?"

She was beginning to suspect the man was cracked. "I'm not playing a game."

"What do you think will happen when he comes home?" Mona tried to answer, but the question was rhetorical. "Let me tell you a few things about the father of your child." Mona doubted that shouting at him to leave her alone would make the slightest difference, so she prayed that someone would come and interrupt him. "Do you know why Cai was so keen to be the one to deal with you? No? You can't guess?" His tone was slow, deliberate, mocking. "Revenge, Mona. Even before your *mark* was confirmed, we knew what you were, and he was desperate to kill you. He's harboured that hatred for years. What makes you think a bastard child will change his mind, especially if it's born with brown eyes?" There was real loathing in his voice, and Mona's heart skipped a beat. Had he guessed about Gareth? Had Ifan let it slip? "He'll kill your Saxon lover too, Mona; I know what's in his heart."

The door opened and Rob poked his head around the corner in such a casual manner that she knew it had become routine for him. His eyes widened at seeing hers open at last, and he rushed over to her side, kissing her head as he held it between his hands. "The baby's fine, Mo."

Rob either hadn't seen the old man in the chair or didn't care, and though Mona was moved by his joy, she felt a twinge of worry. Rob wouldn't stand a chance against Cai – not much more than a baby would.

When next she looked, Hywel had vanished.

Rob was reliably thorough at providing Mona with all the missing information. Of the twenty invaders, twelve were dead and burnt. Several of the Irish survivors had been injured, and their getaway had been laboured and messy, but they had all escaped.

Many of the girls had been caught and bound, but between their two tribes, Dai and Sioned had prevented any from being kidnapped. Ifan had already visited the local council offices and smoothed over the complaints about the 'noisy re-enactment' on the beach.

Only a few of the Welsh Druids had suffered severe injuries and they were now on the road to recovery. Their huge but sole loss was Nesta. It was a remarkable victory – one for Nia's storybooks.

"And Arwel?" Mona asked.

Rob sighed and shook his head. "No one can get near him. Ifan was hoping you'd have a go," he smiled broadly, "as soon as you get your fat arse out of bed."

Mona cackled at the outrageous insult.

29

Christmas

The next time Bryn awoke, there were two people by his bed. He guessed the man standing next to Rob was a doctor.

"I'm going to take out the tube and close up the wound." He smiled reassuringly, and Bryn knew he was in for more pain. "I've applied some local anaesthetic around the wound, but the tube will hurt on the way out. Rob's offered to help." The doctor turned to Rob, who seemed nervous, with another encouraging smile.

At Bryn's signal, the procedure began. As the doctor started to pull at the tube, Bryn reached for Rob's hand, locking their interwoven fingers as the pain climaxed and ebbed. Once the worst was over, Rob disengaged his hand gently. But Bryn wouldn't let him release his hold altogether, grasping him stubbornly throughout the remainder of the operation – keeping his eyes screwed shut all the while.

≈

Somehow, the struggle in the boathouse had already become mythologised and exaggerated out of all proportion, and the constant stream of well-wishers was beginning to tell on both Bryn and Mona's nerves.

"I need to get out of here." Mona popped her head round his door. "Fancy making a run for it?"

To his credit, Bryn attempted a laugh. Rob was less amused. "You know he's out of action for six weeks, and anyway, what are you doing up?" Rob was as stern as anyone holding a mandolin could be.

"Sounds much more fun over here," Mona said as she heaved her body on to the end of Bryn's bed.

"That child is going to be huge," Rob muttered.

"I bloody hope not," she countered.

She was still trying to get comfortable when Arwel knocked. The grief was raw in his face, but he'd started visiting Mona yesterday – two days after the battle; two days after he'd lost Nesta.

"Sioned's organising a party," he said by way of conversation.

Both Mona and Bryn groaned, and Rob looked up in surprise. "I thought you loved parties."

She pointed to her stomach. "Not when I can't dance or drink." Mona patted a portion of bed next to her, and Arwel sat down. She took his hand and rubbed it between hers. "OK, tell us everything."

Nia and Siân were coming back the following day with all their charges, and things were slowly getting back to normal. Arwel doubted the Irish would attempt another attack, but just to be sure, Sioned and Dai had taken up the slack left in Bryn and Mona's absence, and there was always a skeleton defence on patrol.

"If only we'd caught one." Arwel spat with bitterness. "I would have enjoyed asking him some questions."

"It was the girls – kidnap? Wasn't it?" Mona asked, not entirely convinced now, by the doubt in Arwel's eyes.

"Probably," he sighed, then kneaded his eye sockets irritably. "Possibly... I just don't know. If I'd had my wits about me..."

Mona ruffled his blonde mop. "Hey, come on, Al, don't beat yourself up about it. It's over."

"Is it?" he asked solemnly.

≈

Cai was enjoying his first ever Christmas, though the whole present giving routine proved something of a farce. In the weeks running up to Christmas, Cai's opinion had been sought regularly, and he'd lost count of the number of times he'd been sworn to secrecy. In the end, Cai deduced that the whole rigmarole was a game of bluff, and was unsurprised to discover a pile of presents underneath a tacky, tinsel-draped pine tree on Christmas morning.

Cai was basking in the extra warmth of their camaraderie as he cooked the 'Christmas breakfast'. This was an ordinary full English/Welsh, depending on the chef, with champagne instead of tea. John and Liz sat next to each other on the sofa, taking turns to open their presents.

"If you think I'm wearing *that* then you're very much mistaken mister." There was a twinkle in Liz's eye as she reprimanded her husband.

Cai couldn't see the opened present, but John had already shown him the lingerie he'd bought her, and he suppressed a grin at the memory. "Hurry up, you two – it's nearly ready."

They brought their champagne to the table, but before sitting down to eat, John passed him a small flat parcel. "Happy Christmas, Cai."

"But I…" What was he going to say? That he didn't believe in Christ or that he had nothing to give them in return?

"Just open it." Liz's words were curt but her tone was gentle. Cai fumbled with the Sellotape and paper to reveal a tiny blue machine, which he knew to be an iPod. "Happy Christmas, love." Liz smiled at him through moist eyes.

"Don't get too excited, Cai," her husband added. "It's part of your homework. I'm enrolling you on a new course tomorrow, so enjoy your freedom today."

On that cryptic note, they began to eat, and didn't completely stop until late into the night. Cai was pleased to note that with regard to eating and drinking yourself into a stupor, there was very little difference between the practices of Christianity and paganism at this time of year.

≈

Bryn was trying desperately hard to concentrate on the book that Arwel had lent him. However, *The Decline and Fall of the Roman Empire* couldn't possibly compete with the way Rob's eyelashes brushed the top of his cheekbones when he closed his eyes, completely absorbed in his music practice.

This was Bryn's fifth day of enforced incarceration, and Rob was not only making it endurable but enjoyable. "Wouldn't you think a fifteen-year-old might be interested in more than just military history?"

Rob put his instrument down. "I've been waiting for you to crack." His eyes were smiling as always. "How about we ask if Nia's got anything more up your street? What do you fancy? Stories from the Ulster Cycle or the *Mabinogion*? I doubt she's got any Len Deighton or Patricia Cornwell."

"It actually does hurt when I laugh. So stop it, now."

"OK." Rob checked the time. "She's bound to be there; I'll pop down and beg for something."

As Rob began the ritual of bedding down the mandolin, Bryn had an idea. "Forget it. I'll have a look myself." He pushed the covers back, and began to inch his body upright ready to swivel out of the bed.

"Wait." Rob clicked down the latches. "Let me help." He moved to the other side of the bed and crouched forward, so that Bryn could pull himself up using his shoulders. Bryn was still having difficulty swivelling, so Rob pulled Bryn's thighs around and forward until his feet touched the floor. Bryn gasped, but it wasn't in pain. "Sorry. Let's take it slower. Here, lean on me."

As Bryn slowly moved his arm over Rob's lowered shoulder, he felt the stray hairs from Rob's chin tickle his cheek; their faces were unbearably close now. Bryn was staring, not into Rob's eyes but at his mouth, and he licked his lips self-consciously. There was a knock on the door, and Bryn hastily stood upright, supported by Rob at a suitable distance. "Are you supposed to be up?" Sioned was characteristically direct.

"Yes," Bryn lied.

"The funeral is tomorrow. Ifan asked if you could sing, Rob."

≈

Nia didn't seem too annoyed by their request – more bemused. "I'm not sure I know what you mean by light reading." She blinked over the top of an enormous tome.

Bryn felt Rob trying to stifle a giggle but couldn't risk an elbow jab. "Do you mind if we just have a look?"

Nia bridled slightly at that. "No, but you can't take books out of here. If you want to read any of them, you'll have to come here to do it." Rob felt a little deflated, but not surprised – he knew how she felt about her books.

"Don't worry, I'll get Dai to have a check in the charity shops," Bryn said, and Nia felt immediately remorseful.

"I'm sorry, Bryn." She glanced at the time on her wrist and sighed. "I've got to dash, but have a look around and if you find something I don't need, then I'll consider it." She was late for a meeting and vanished in a swarm of book dust, leaving the men alone to browse.

"You start at that end." Bryn did his best to point without raising his arm too high. With his other hand, he held on to a bookshelf. "Call them out to me."

Leaning back against the shelving, he started to relive that sweet moment in the infirmary when they had almost touched lips, had almost kissed. Bryn's body and mind ached for release. He couldn't risk being alone much more with Rob: his strength of will was not strong enough for it.

"So what have we got?" Rob's Welsh had greatly improved, but there were some sounds his mouth would never be able to make. Rob's mouth.

"*The Vegetable Gardener's Bible*?"

"No."

Bryn smiled at Rob's mock disappointment. "But that's a classic! Oh, OK," he continued, pretending to be excited, "how about the *UK and Ireland Circumnavigator's Guide*?"

"Already read it," replied Bryn straightaway, chuckling lightly as he did so.

Rob laughed in return. He was a couple of bookshelves nearer, and Bryn closed his eyes so that he wouldn't get distracted. "*War and Peace*?" Bryn groaned, and Rob moved to another stack, even nearer, running his finger along the spines. "I'm afraid we're getting into taboo territory as far as Nia's concerned. *The Holy Wells of Cardiff*?"

"Afraid not." His mouth was drying in anticipation – this was the last aisle.

"Not even *A History of the Order of St. John of Jerusalem in Wales and on the Welsh Border*?" Rob would be able to see him now.

As Rob stepped in front of him, Bryn held his breath. He knew the kiss was coming, and when it finally did, he was overwhelmed by its tenderness: only their lips touched, softly. Rob had been careful to avoid any more contact and was already pulling away.

It was sweet, almost chaste, and Bryn knew immediately it wasn't enough, would never be enough. He used his left hand to cup Rob's head towards his mouth again.

Rob exhaled noisily and Bryn felt hot sweet breath on his lips

Their kissing became more and more insistent, and Bryn yielded slowly to Rob's demanding tongue. Responding passionately to this surrender, Rob let his body fall against Bryn.

Before he knew it, Rob had pushed him back against the shelving. "Sorry – your chest," he apologised quietly. They were both panting and Bryn shook his head; Rob had only stepped back a pace, but he was too far away. "You need a shower," Rob smiled tenderly.

Bryn had to answer, but the pounding and aching made it hard for him to talk. "I don't think I'll be able to do that on my own."

≈

The lessons that John had alluded to on Christmas morning began on Boxing Day – a day which promised to follow a similarly gluttonous pattern to the previous one. John had been setting up a computer and monitor in the living room, while Liz and Cai did the dishes. "It's a ritual; he does it every year with the boys." Her tone was explanatory rather than mocking, though she whispered under her breath. "They swap music, it's his favourite part of Christmas," she sighed nostalgically. "Just humour him for a while; I think he's missing them as much as I am."

"What are they like?" Cai asked. The boys Skyped their parents fairly regularly, but Cai had always made himself scarce on those occasions.

"It's a straight split actually: Arthur's me and George is John," Liz said matter-of-factly.

"Is that how it happens then?" Cai thought back to his sister and parents, and was pretty sure that they were both a mixture.

"What about you?" Liz asked.

"My sister and I look alike, but thinking about it, I'm much more like Mam and Sioned's more like our dad."

"They must worry themselves sick about you, Cai."

Sometimes he forgot, and let things slip from his real life. "They've been dead a long time now," he said softly. Still holding the wet dishcloth in her hand, Liz squeezed him around the waist. It wasn't pity, more comfort, and Cai squeezed back.

John said nothing by way of explanation, but led Cai to the monitor and sat him down in front of it. "Enjoy." John smiled as both he and Liz flopped down on the opposite sofa, hands held and eyes closed.

There was the sound of soft piano notes from the impressive array of speakers in the room. Cai closed his eyes and waited. The voice was compelling from the first sung word: warm, deep and complex. Cai knew the genre fairly well, but had never heard this song or this voice before. By the end of it, the singer had wrung every drop of emotion from within her soul and given it as a gift to the music. For some reason, the pain in her voice sent him back fifteen years, to the cell underneath the *Conway* and Emlyn's desperate sobs.

"Here beginneth the first lesson," John breathed. Cai guessed that John was enjoying himself by the way he rubbed his hands together. "When it comes to Northern Soul, you can't beat Lorraine Ellison." He sat down next to Cai and moved the mouse on the screen to reveal a catalogue of genres.

There may have been over a thousand – Cai couldn't be sure – and looked askance at Liz, who smiled and shook her head gently. Cai glimpsed again at some of the offerings on the screen. They spanned Indonesian Campursari to stoner metal, but he was relieved to see that John had also refined the categories into a more manageable group.

"So, here we have all your basic Western categories." It was a much smaller list, but Cai was sure that hidden away in the hard drive of this computer, John had thousands of examples of each, all of which he was desperate to share. "Classical and art music traditions: European, classical, religious, folk, popular, blues, country, electronic, funk, hip hop, jazz, reggae, rock – heavy metal and punk, traditional…"

Cai had an intense but private love of music. He hadn't wanted to talk to Mona about his musical tastes, partly because they were so wide-ranging. The breadth of John's music collection was wider still and it gave Cai new directions in which to explore. By the new year, he had learnt a great deal more about music and had an iPod packed full of perfect tunes.

≈

Arwel had asked Mona not to come to the funeral. He had told everyone else that after her exploits in the boathouse, it was unadvisable for her to stand for too long. Neither of them wanted to witness Mona's reaction to such an outpouring of grief – spoken and sung in Welsh. Rob had popped by to make sure she was OK, before setting up with the band. He tried to convince her to go to the wake but she declined that too, blaming tiredness.

Mona didn't sleep though; her mind and thoughts were with Nesta, just as much as those attending the funeral. Arwel had wanted to speak for the dead woman, but hadn't been allowed – he wasn't a registered member of the society and therefore ineligible. The astonishing young man was almost a non-person, despite the fact that it was his talents that had saved the community from annihilation. These Druids were an odd bunch of people, Mona mused.

Nia and Sioned tapped on her door later; the wake hadn't lasted long into the night and both women were red-eyed. Sioned curled up next to Mona for a cuddle. "How's Arwel?" Mona asked.

"Better than I thought," Nia answered vaguely, smoothing Mona's hair back.

Mona found that one of the more irritating phenomena of pregnancy, was that her body had become public property. People felt compelled to feel her stomach and touch her in a way that they never would have dreamed of previously. She had long ago given up trying to stop them though, and it was undeniable that Nia's soothing touch was a great help with her headache. The baby gave an almighty boot, and Sioned immediately put her hand on Mona's bulge.

"I saw that! It poked right up." Sioned gasped and gawped at Mona in total amazement. Then both women were feeling her stomach. "Ifan wants to have a ceremony for you," Sioned said as she waited for the next kick.

"Why?" Mona asked.

Sioned pulled a face that left Mona in no doubt of her stupidity. "Because you're a hero," she said with slow and deliberate patience.

"I think he wants to put you in the book," Nia added, as if this was controversial news.

Her theory was confirmed by Sioned. "Taid won't like it."

Mona knew Hywel wouldn't like the idea. "Because of the *mark*?"

Nia nodded. "Partly, though after the invasion there isn't much currency in doubting your allegiance. I think it's because you and Cai can handfast if you're registered – without him losing his status."

Mona put her hands over her eyes; perhaps she should mention another possible future to these women. "What if Cai isn't pleased about all this?" She pointed at her own belly.

"Don't be daft, he'll be ecstatic." Sioned smiled as she felt a kick under her hand, and Mona tried again.

"Cai... we never intended to have a baby." Mona didn't want to say the word accident – it seemed too cruel somehow. "What if he's moved on, met someone else?" That eventuality was eminently possible and all three of them knew it. "I don't want him to feel he has to stay with me. That wouldn't be fair on either of us."

Sioned looked shocked as a new possibility dawned on her. "You can't leave, no matter what happens."

Mona didn't answer, leaving Nia to intervene. "Cai loves you, Mona. It will be all right."

Mona was already well aware of it, but Nia had just proved that she was a totally unconvincing liar.

≈

Ifan *did* want Mona in the book and he wanted Mona to agree to it as soon as possible. "Only if Arwel gets registered at the same time; he's the one we should thank," she argued.

It was clear from his face that Ifan wasn't surprised by this demand, and that there was something else he wanted in return. "Only if you agree to Welsh-language lessons." Mona was appalled at the prospect, but Ifan's reasoning was undeniable. "You're vulnerable." He glanced at her massive bulge. "Now more than ever. You can't expect Arwel to always protect you. Besides, I've got a theory that if you *learn* the language, you can also learn to *fight* its effects on you."

"That's all very well and good, but won't I need to learn Gaelic too."

Mona meant it as a joke, a way to squirm out of the lessons but Ifan nodded sagely. "Good point. But let's start off with Welsh and see how we go, eh?"

It wasn't as if she was allowed to do much else anymore, and so Mona reluctantly agreed to the deal. Though she had the distinct feeling she'd been tricked.

≈

The ceremony itself was much more moving than Mona had expected, despite the fact that Nia had tried to put a dress on her. She was given a cloak, symbolising her high rank as a warrior, and Arwel was not only invested as an Ovate Druid, but apprenticed to his grandfather. Both their names were added to the book; Arwel would be Archdruid someday, and something about that made Mona feel warm inside.

There was a good old knees-up that night. Arwel ensured the band played an all-English repertoire – and that's when she saw it.

Bryn and Rob were a big part of the band. They were obviously having a whale of a time with the other musicians, but within that, they inhabited a separate universe of love. It seemed difficult for them not to touch each other in public, and their shared expressions of tender yearning tore at her heart. Because Mona could just about remember that feeling, and the loss of it.

When Rob eventually came back, she sat up and turned on the light. "Sorry, Mo, I was trying to be quiet," Rob apologised in a whisper, though she was wide awake.

"What are you doing here, Berys?" His brow screwed up – had he upset her? "Bryn," was all she said in reply, and Rob's face dropped and coloured simultaneously.

Mona wiggled her toes in delight and giggled at his discomfort. "*Ooh*, Robert, you've got it bad for that man." Rob ran his hands through his hair, his expression pensive. "I'm not going to breathe a word," she reassured him. "But you're going to have to try a bit harder to keep it under wraps. It's written all over both of you." Rob gave her a look of helplessness. "Why don't you stay there at night?" she asked, intrigued. Then Mona considered the narrowness of the single beds and the sizes of the men involved. "You could always put the mattress on the floor." Rob laughed out loud. "What?"

"I don't know; you're always so practical. Anyway, that's not why I don't stay with him." It was Mona's turn to be perplexed, especially when he seized her hand. "I don't want to leave you on your own, Mo."

Mona became immediately tearful – an alarmingly frequent occurrence these days; the little creature inside her was taking over her mind as well as her body. Rob's arms were around her in a second; the depth of his kindness constantly surprised her. Mona would miss him, but if she had a chance at a love like that, she would take it with both hands. "Life is sorrow and the joys are brief," she quoted at him, a little bizarrely.

"What's that from?" he asked into her hair, rocking her gently.

"Some soppy song; my mum liked it. You never know how much time you have with anyone, Rob; you should be with him. And, anyway," she said, finally smiling, "this bed isn't big enough for both of us anymore."

≈

Winter deepened further on Eigg. Wind and snow prevented any prolonged activity outside. Cai, John and Liz even took it in turns to drag the dogs out into the whiteness to relieve themselves.

Cai had regained weight and muscle thanks to his revived pattern work. His body wanted to run, but it made do with the chin-ups, press-ups and sit-ups now included in his morning routine. The more Cai did, the more energy he had, which was useful, because John had devised a new way of draining him of it. "How much computer science have you done?"

"I'm really an engineer." Cai knew this wasn't the right answer, and John waited. "I picked up a bit of C and C++ at university."

John's face was expressionless. "How about binary?"

"Some."

"Binary maths?"

Cai made a face. "That's hard."

John laughed. "At last; I find something he can't do." Liz nodded at John, as if granting him permission to share a secret with Cai. "We don't want you to take this the wrong way, Cai, but we've been thinking that you may have fallen in with the wrong crowd – made some bad choices in your life."

Cai wondered what assumptions they had made about his life, after witnessing the sharp end of it. "I don't have a choice."

"We just want you to know there's an alternative. I'd like to show you some programming; you're a bright lad, and with what I can teach you, you could be a very high earner." John and Liz were talking about something that Cai had never even considered before: life outside the community.

"You could get your girl out of there and start a new life for yourselves." He paused. "You could bring her here to live with us – until you're on your feet." It had been an effort for John to remain serious for so long. "If she's as good as you say, we can have that new workshop up and running in days."

Cai didn't speak for a long time. The concept was too new and enormous to be easily digested. "Yes," he said finally. "I want to give it a go."

30

Imbolc

Ifan was a diabolical teacher: strict and demanding. The situation was not helped by Mona's inability to pass a single test; a failure that made her feel stupid even without Ifan's constant carping. The lessons had been underway little more than a week when Mona threw a heavy volume off the table and on to the old man's lap. He swore at her and she stormed off, slamming the door as she left.

Arwel had the sense to let things alone for a few days before offering to teach her himself. He was much more patient and kind than his grandfather, provoking Mona to tears of frustration rather than rage.

After even his attempts failed, it became clear to Mona that there was something fundamentally wrong with her – though Arwel put it in a slightly kinder way. Her brain seemed incapable of accessing language and music at a conscious level – which perhaps helped to explain why her singing was so bad. But neither Arwel, nor his grandfather, could get to the bottom of her dangerous susceptibility to the sound of Welsh and Gaelic, deepening her sense of isolation still further.

≈

Cai's body knew it was Imbolc, it knew that lambs were being born and that snowdrops were emerging. Maybe not here but certainly on

Ynys Môn, and these first stirrings of spring were at odds with the continuing freeze. Imbolc was the first of the three spring festivals in the pagan calendar, and it filled him with a renewed yearning for home. He had started to glance at the long-range forecasts, but they all suggested a thaw no earlier than mid-March.

His studies kept him from despair, and Cai redoubled his efforts. Having just about mastered binary, he had done what he could with binary maths, but soon abandoned it for the siren call of AutoCAD, SolidWorks and Inventor. These drawing programmes came easily to him, appealing to both the technical and creative aspects of his personality.

"Happy Imbolc." Cai had been working on repaying the couple's kindness since Christmas, and he handed Liz a printout of his 3D designs for her new studio annex.

After enthusing over the plans and kissing him, she took another look. "You've got an eye you know."

"Watch out, matey, if you think binary maths is hard you should try still life." John grinned boyishly before adding, "And she's a crap teacher."

≈

Liz didn't make Cai draw but she gave him a sketchbook. "It's not just for drawing; you should keep a record – it's surprising what you forget." John muttered playfully about the Stone Age and analogue tools, but Cai was already pondering what to fill it with. Perhaps even some memories to share with Mona: the grid system, the whippets, Ieuan's short sword.

The sketchbook took on a comforting importance in Cai's life, and filling it became his evening activity: the perfect antidote to the intensity of the daytime screen work. It was at such times that he felt part of a family again, with John strumming away and Liz in her own little world.

The first stirrings of spring had filled his mind with erotic thoughts of Mona, and these found expression in a number of sketches he made of her.

"Is her chest really that big?" Liz was looking over his shoulder. Embarrassed, Cai quickly slammed the book shut, and Liz ruffled his hair. "Sorry. Inappropriate. Sometimes I forget." She sat next to John, who tutted at her extravagantly, and Cai forgot his awkwardness.

"I don't know; I can't actually remember. But I hope so," he sniggered. John was currently into 'Blues' in a big way, and he twanged a bar or two of something before asking a proper question. "What do you reckon you'll do when you get back? Have you decided?" The couple's offer hadn't been mentioned again, though Cai thought of little else while lying in bed and waiting for sleep each night.

"I want her to marry me," he declared quietly. "If she has to stay, then we stay. If she's gone, I'll find her. And if she wants to – we'll come here."

John didn't allow Liz to become emotional. "Excellent – time for the next phase then." He played a few more delicious, toe-tapping bars before suddenly glancing up. "What's her name? You never did say."

"Mona," Cai replied, enjoying the sound of her name again in his mouth.

John beamed and burst into song. The title and refrain bore Mona's name, but it was the song's wild, relentless rhythm – not its nonsensical words – that made it the perfect fit for her. Cai was still humming the tune when he awoke the next morning.

≈

The 'next phase' included the manufacture of a flashy business card emblazoned with Cai's name and credentials:

Cai Owens BSc, MSc
CAD Consultant and Programmer
07889 457976

"Consultant?"

"Well, you'll have to keep abreast of all the new versions and updates, but I can't teach you anything more." John scrutinised the forecast again, and mumbled distractedly. "I've got a bit of time left before you go. A little microchip programming work will go quite nicely with the offgrid work; I think there's a good potential market in that. Though the 3D CAD work will be your bread and butter, and you're good enough at that to get a job tomorrow."

Cai didn't know what to say; they'd given him so much already. He studied his business card again. "But I can't have a mobile phone."

"I don't pretend to understand your phobia about certain types of technology." John shook his head. "So don't take it with you now. You can use a landline to phone me and I'll send it in the post. Simple."

The couple had thought long and hard about everything, including his wardrobe. "Try this on." Liz was holding an expensive-looking grey suit in one hand with a shirt and tie in the other, and she laughed at Cai's shock.

"You can't go into a boardroom dressed like some scruffy nutter."

≈

"Mona." There was a quiet but insistent knocking on the door. And again. "Mona, are you awake?"

She was awake, as there was no way her baby was going to allow any sleep tonight. "Come in," she called through a yawn. "What time is it? Are you OK?" Mona panicked a little on seeing Arwel. The teenager was rarely fazed by much, but tonight he appeared shocked and drawn. He slumped onto the chair at the end of the bed. "Arwel?" Her mind raced. Was it Ifan? The Archdruid was old, and no one lived forever.

"I was looking for a book," he said, finally focusing. "I had an idea about the spy and I went to Nia's library." Mona checked the time on her travel alarm clock: 2 a.m. "Rob and Bryn were in there. I thought... I thought they were fighting."

"Ah," was all she said, allowing him to carry on.

"They were kissing, Mo. I mean, really seriously kissing."

Mona would have to take this gently; homosexuality wasn't something that she'd ever heard discussed in the community, apart from Nia's ancient references. "They love each other, Arwel. And even if they didn't – it's just sex. I though you Druids were a broad minded lot." The boy seemed even more shocked, annoying Mona. "I never had you down for a bigot, Al. The way you looked a minute ago, anyone would have guessed they had a *mark* or their parents weren't up to scratch."

Arwel knew where she was going with this. "That's not the same, Mo."

"Isn't it? Sex is only selectively applied friction after all."

Despite himself, Arwel chuckled, and it made Mona pleased with her witty remark. He didn't often laugh but she supposed this was scientific enough to tickle him; at least it broke the tension. And maybe Mona shouldn't have asked, but it was the perfect opportunity to broach something she'd been wondering about for a while. "You can tell me anything, you know. I mean, is there anyone you're attracted to?"

That comment wiped the smile off his face. She was right; there was someone, and Arwel began pacing around the room. "I won't say anything about Rob and Bryn," he assured her, in a business-like manner. "You know I can keep a secret, and anyway, we've got to preserve Rob as a possibility for the child's father." He explained calmly. "In case of the brown-eyed scenario."

It was a diversionary tactic, but Mona marvelled at how Arwel's brain continued to work strategically, despite his obvious discomfort around the issue of sexuality. Mona had her own suspicions regarding Arwel, but decided she was probably out of her depth. "If you need to talk anything through, Rob would be the best person – if you can't face talking to me. He's very kind."

"Yes, I'll remember that," he replied hurriedly then said his goodnights and left.

Cai was expecting the fleet to arrive on Eigg around the middle of March. The conditions were still foul, but he knew they were going to improve, and the plan was to leave the moment the weather broke.

John and Liz had already started preparing the locals for the arrival of twenty young warriors. The imminent gathering was disguised as a party for all Arty's uni friends – a big birthday bash. The English couple played the overindulgent parents well, making plenty of noise about the forthcoming celebration, and ordering huge quantities of food and drink from local stores for the occasion.

≈

Dafydd's was the first boat to arrive, with Cerys, Gwen and the youngsters on board – along with the now fully recovered group from Skye. Both John and Cai met them on the small jetty, one holding the detector, and one holding a plastic bag with '*Dafydd-Tobermory*' written in black scrawl on its side.

"What's the plan then Chief?" Dafydd asked John, holding up his own small bag, containing the bugs from his boat and those of its crew.

"Throw them in here," Cai flapped open the bag and his uncle obliged.

"Then what?" he asked.

"Then we start the game!" John beamed and Dafydd couldn't help but smile – his mood buoyed with hope. "Once all the boats and bugs have arrived, we'll collect all the little buggers into the appropriate bags. I'm hoping it will look like you've all come together for a spring equinox piss up. But as the bugs were only planted in your kinky leathers," he winked appreciatively at the leather-clad women, "they may suspect something is a-foot."

Dafydd nodded, but his mood had started to deflate as he carried on listening to John's plan. "I'm going to leave them here for a few days, until you're well on your way."

"And then?"

"Once you've scarpered, Liz and I will take a mini cruise around the islands, dropping off each set of bugs back to the corresponding isle. It will hopefully seem like you've had a bit of a get together, and then gone back to daily life. We'll drop the boat bugs at the various harbours and the clothing bugs as near to your old digs as possible," he glanced at Cai, "without putting any of the locals in danger."

Dafydd nodded again, it sounded like a solid sound plan. "Will it work?"

"It will work for a while. I reckon after a week, maybe ten days, they'll get suspicious. So you'll need to get a move on. Get down into the east coast of England as quickly as you can."

"Right," he frowned. "Where are you off to?"

John had clambered aboard the boat. "Giving them all one more sweep," he muttered belligerently.

Glyn and Alun came hot on Dafydd's heels from Islay and Lewis, and Emlyn's lifeboat was the last to arrive from Skye. Cai was sad to see Dewi skippering his uncle's boat, but the pleasure at being reunited with the crews, and the fresh hope of a return to Ynys Môn was too overpowering for much sadness. Liz had ingeniously created enough space within the shed to sleep all the guests, and the partying began almost immediately.

Once everyone was wrapped up warmly around the bonfire, and their hearts and throats loosened by rum, the singing began in earnest. John was beside himself with enthusiasm for the music and brandished his guitar at the earliest opportunity.

With all the Welsh being spoken, Cai sat near Liz, interpreting and explaining. "What are the songs about?" she asked.

"The sea and love, the land and love. It sounds pretty straightforward, but it's not: it's *hiraeth*."

"*Hiraeth*?"

"It's almost impossible to translate into English, and definitely not in one word, but the closest would be homesickness, I suppose, or longing.

It's not just a longing to be back home, but more a grieving for the loss of our land and how it used to be. Some people translate *gwlad* as Wales, but it's more than that, it's land, country, nation. We miss it as we miss a person." Cai grinned. "They say that if you have Welsh ancestry but have never set foot there, you can experience *hiraeth* as an indefinable lifelong yearning. I wouldn't know much about that – but I miss my home."

Alun's haunting song had finished and he held his glass high. "*Gwlad y Medra*," he called out, and his compatriots returned the toast with gusto.

"What does that mean?" Liz asked, intrigued.

"It's a toast to our homeland, to Ynys Môn. There's a saying about the people of the island: that if ever asked, the answer is always *Medra*, I can."

"So the translation is 'The land of I can.'"

"Yes, I suppose it is," Cai agreed slowly.

Her curiosity piqued, Liz was ready to ask more when Cerys and Gwen bounded up exuberantly. Cerys plonked herself on Cai's lap, causing Liz to worry for a moment that the old garden chair might break beneath them.

"We've missed you, Cai *bach*, haven't we, Gwen?" exclaimed Cerys, draping her arms around Cai.

Both women were a little tipsy. Cai introduced them to Liz, whom they treated extremely politely, knowing from Dafydd how much help she and her husband had given the Welsh Druids.

Glyn came over looking for Cai. "Dafydd wants you to clear something up – one of Mona's moves." Glyn helped Cerys from Cai's lap, lingering a little longer than necessary around her waist.

After Cai and Glyn had left, Cerys plopped into the vacant chair. "I'd forgotten how gorgeous Glyn was," Cerys said, studying his retreating backside.

Their English had improved considerably and Liz laughed. "What about Cai?"

Cerys and Gwen thought that was immensely funny. "Well, you know Cai." Gwen rolled her eyes.

"Not really." Liz was old enough to know when to ask questions and when to shut up and listen.

"Sex and engines, that's Cai. Hasn't he worked his way through the female population here yet?"

"Bit of a reputation with the ladies then?" Liz asked innocently.

"You could say that."

They all sipped their drinks simultaneously. "What about this Mona then?" Liz had touched a nerve, but it wasn't jealousy. She sensed some sort of secret, one that the girls were initially reluctant to share with her. However, their love of gossip soon quashed any misgivings, and they leaned towards her, whispering.

"We think he loves her." They both seemed scandalised.

"I think so too. Is it a bad thing?"

"Cai doesn't love people, Liz, apart from Sioned."

Liz had heard Cai talk about his sister, so didn't allow the name to distract her. She wanted to know more about the mysterious Mona, the woman that no one wanted to talk about. "Cai says she's strong," Liz probed.

"She's..."

They wanted to talk about her but they weren't sure how much to reveal. Using what she already knew, Liz helped them along. "That she's a good fighter."

They both nodded. "Like you wouldn't believe."

"But what sort of person is she?"

That appeared to stump both women. "Difficult," Cerys managed eventually.

"What? She's difficult or she's difficult to describe?"

"Both really." Gwen struggled to articulate her thoughts. "It's not that Cai's not good enough for her, but maybe he's just not... enough." Cerys nodded in agreement.

"And does he know this?"

"Probably not – he is a man." The women giggled in a girlish way.

Liz found it hard to imagine that Cai might not be good enough for any woman, but then she realised something. "He's never had that before, has he?"

Their heads shook solemnly. "It took Cai over *three* weeks to get Mona into bed." The women seemed in awe of this fact, and Liz felt extremely old. "How long was it with you, Gwen?" Cerys asked, as if out of interest.

"I don't know. Maybe three hours."

They both guffawed when Cerys held up both hands and wiggled her fingers. "Ten minutes," she squealed. "But then again, I was supposed to marry him in August."

The man in question returned before Liz had a chance to learn anymore. He and Glyn were holding up an extremely happy-looking John between them. "He might need a lie down." Cai grimaced at her. "Sorry."

"Rum's great, Liz, you should try it," her husband beamed.

≈

Cai gave up his bed to Cerys and Glyn, who were in dire need of privacy towards the end of the party. But despite the heavy heads, an awful lot of organising took place the following day.

Cai wanted the boats checked and packed that day, so that they could leave for the Caledonian Canal at first light. He and Dafydd had been up since dawn, carefully working the detector over every millimetre of surface area, on every boat – yet again.

As an added precaution, they also repainted each wheelhouse roof a different colour, in the unlikely case of aerial reconnaissance detection. Cai had been obsessively planning the details of their departure for months. As a result, the men rattled briskly through their tasks, getting everything done by lunchtime.

There was only one thing left to do. Cerys and Gwen had agreed with Liz that the men's unkempt hair might attract attention, and that they should all get a haircut. By nightfall, each male warrior sported an extremely modern-looking short back and sides.

Rather than leaving en masse, John advised a staggered departure. The *Marc'h* was the last to leave. Cai had said his goodbyes the night before and tried to make his final farewell quick and painless, but he knew that a large chunk of his heart would be left behind on Eigg. There was a lump in his throat as he watched the two figures on the jetty dwindle into the early light.

≈

After the snow had gone, it had rained and gusted across the Menai Strait for all of January and February. Mona became even slower as the baby got heavier and more difficult to lug around. Walking was the single exercise the baby allowed now, so she did it as much as possible, even if it was only inside and around the corridors.

Siân started to flex her maternal muscles around about the spring equinox, and cornered Mona at breakfast one morning. "So, how much do you know about what's going to happen?" Avoidance hadn't worked so far and there was no way she could run. "Um, well, Arwel has given me some leaflets about breathing."

Siân wasn't fooled. "And?"

"Well, in and then out... slowly?"

Siân lost her temper. "For goodness' sake, Mona, you need to get prepared. I don't want you getting hysterical on me, when the time comes."

Mona took the scolding. "I'm just trying to avoid thinking about it for as long as possible." She hadn't wanted to admit this to anyone. "Truth is, I'm scared, Siân. Scared I won't be able to handle the pain – that I won't know what to do with it after it's born." And her biggest fear. "I'm frightened that there's something wrong with the baby – after what happened at the solstice."

Big fat tears plopped into her tea and Mona realised that Siân, who had pulled her into a tight hug, was also crying. "I know, it's what we all fear, but you'll be alright." Siân kissed Mona's hair. "I'm so sorry."

"What for?"

"Doubting you, distrusting you." She sighed deeply. "Even after you saved Nia, I still had doubts. I was angry about this baby, Mo. I was angry that you'd messed up our bloodline." Her laugh wasn't a happy one. "And now you're carrying all that's left of Cai's blood."

≈

Early the following morning, Rob and Bryn arrived at her door bearing bags containing musical instruments and manuscripts mostly, but also some clothes. "I'm moving back in, fatty, so deal with it."

Mona glanced up sharply to see if Bryn was showing any signs of distress. He wasn't, but Bryn was a closed man to her. "Are you two OK?" Their shared gaze reassured her that their love was intact. But the question remained, "Why?"

Both men stared at the mountain her stomach made under the bedclothes. Bryn's expression wasn't disgust exactly, more like morbid interest, and she knew why. How could anything that big come out of her body without it killing her? She'd had the thought often enough herself over the past few weeks, and she was only getting bigger.

Rob became exasperated. "Do you even know when your baby's due?"

Mona knew this one; Arwel had told her. "April."

"Good. And what date?" This stumped Mona, and Rob shook his head. "I'm reliably informed by Sioned that he left on the fourteenth of July, Mo."

She was stuck now: the earliest date that the baby would come was some two weeks later than the date Rob had in mind. "But they can come at any time, sometimes much later than you think, can't they?" she confirmed nervously.

"Or earlier." There was tremendous sympathy in his voice – he knew she was petrified. "The baby could come at any time now, day or night. And I want to be here when it happens."

"Or I could come and get you," she suggested.

Rob made an exasperated huffing noise and glared over at Bryn. "What did I say?"

Mona realised she was performing entirely to type. "But don't you mind, Bryn?" she asked.

Bryn looked as if he might say something serious but instead broke into a rare grin. "He'll just worry himself sick if he's not on standby."

Rob smiled his gratitude as Bryn left. "Budge up then, fatso."

"I've missed you, Berys," she laughed.

They weren't alone for long; a slight knock was followed by the rapid entry of Nia, Sioned and Siân, all holding bags. Before she could ask, Sioned explained. "We didn't want to freak you out before, but as it's so close now, we thought you might need this stuff."

Mona picked something at random from a bulging carrier: a tiny sleep suit, one of what looked like many. There were also nappies and wipes and balls of cotton wool. She dug a little deeper to find ointments, bottles, a changing mat and sterilising equipment. Mona gawped at Sioned who was holding up a wicker basket, complete with miniature duvet and pillow. Rob must have guessed how Mona would react, because he squeezed her arm subtly.

"I've got exams from the eleventh to the fifteenth, so you can't have it then. Wait until I'm back," Nia explained in all seriousness.

Rob put her right. "If you're here, you can be her birthing partner; if you're not, it's me. Alright?"

"What do you mean, birthing partner? I thought you were going to deliver the baby, Siân."

"I am – at least I will if it's straightforward – but the doctor's on standby just in case." Mona swallowed, thinking she ought to ask what might go wrong, though it all seemed too little too late now. "But you'll need someone special there with you; it would be Cai if he was here."

"I'm sure I'll be fine on my own."

"Tough." Nia was surprisingly firm. "We've sorted it all out. Sioned will be trying to calm Arwel down, and it will either be Rob or me with you."

Mona's friends were staring at her, and she wasn't entirely sure how to react, but gratitude was always well received. "Thanks, everyone."

They mostly ignored her after that, and began rearranging the room to accommodate a new person. Rob orchestrated proceedings and Mona was left to wonder what on earth she would do with a new-born baby. As if in response, she got a boot in the ribs.

31

Gift

The weather was better than it had been for at least four months, but the forecast suggested that they should still expect a rough ride along Scotland's exposed north-eastern coast. On John's advice, they'd all bought a full set of waterproofs, and these proved indispensable as they advanced through the canal towards the North Sea.

The crew of the *Marc'h* held their breath at the Clachnaharry sea lock, almost afraid to look up for fear of spotting the distinctive profile of an enemy boat bearing down on them. Thankfully, there was no sign of the sleek vessels that had foiled their progress last summer. They continued without incident as far as Lossiemouth, where the relatively sheltered waters of the Moray Firth were exchanged for the stormy open waters of the North Sea.

John had spent time with each of the skippers, explaining about their various options for port, and it had made for a depressing conversation. The lack of natural harbours on the east coast had made it necessary to build some for Scotland's fishing fleets. But because of the power of the seas, the entrances to the ports were skinny and often involved a dog-leg design to slow the rush of water. These ports were never to be tried at night, when the combination of a high sea, low visibility and a concrete wall could spell disaster. In fact, John advised them not to attempt landfall until Eyemouth. The man-made harbours along the east coast were the preserve of the commercial fishing fleet, or what was left of it, and not particularly welcoming towards pleasure craft.

Cai had switched on the VHF radio when they left Eigg and it had now become his obsession. He not only listened to the local inshore transmission sent out every three hours, but also had his ear pressed up against a little transistor radio for the twice-daily offerings from the BBC at 00.53 and 05.26.

The entire crew heard the gale warnings for Forties, Cromarty, Forth, Tyne and Dogger, and they braced themselves for a rough twenty-four hours.

They were battered at Whitehills in a boiling sea, and a glance back at his crew told Cai that he should have taken John's advice and waited for a longer break in the weather. It was too late now, and he set up a rota for helm duty with two on watch at any one time. Maintaining course was physically exhausting – the boat pitched and rolled as the sea tried doggedly to drag the wheel from his grasp.

Cai gladly handed control over to Glyn at the end of his first stint, but the storm abated as they rounded the corner and passed Peterhead. With wind and tide behind them, they made good time, soon passing Stonehaven, Arbroath and the mouth of the Firth of Forth.

Along with the rest of his crew, Cai was looking forward to the promise of a hot shower in Eyemouth, the port now beckoning on the horizon. The storm would keep them captive in this quaint fishing village for at least three days, but they were too relieved to have come through unscathed to grumble.

Life on a cramped boat was not easy after the freedom of shore, but even given the vagaries of weather systems, they shouldn't have to put up with it for much more than a month.

Six people in a confined cabin certainly kept them warm, especially when two of them were finding it hard to keep their hands off each other.

Cai could feel the tension building in Gwen; disgruntled that she had been displaced in Cerys's affections by Glyn. "Come on lads,

Gwen, let's go into town. I'll buy you a coffee." Some of the youths whinged about the rain, but they were soon out and shuffling into the town centre.

After Gwen had hopped on to the pontoon, Cai told the young lovers to get it out of their system in the two hours of privacy he'd secured for them.

On the walk into town, Gwen grumbled about Cerys to Cai. "Come on, Gwen, we're just jealous," he told her truthfully. The wind and rain was blowing directly into their faces, but he thought he heard her laugh.

It was too early in the season for pleasure boats, and the women in the cafe seemed happy enough for them to keep ordering tea and coffee. The lads had some money of their own and began flirting with the young Scots waitresses, while Gwen and Cai sat as far away from them as they could in the small shop.

"I actually miss Ieuan," Gwen muttered softly. Cai grimaced; it was getting easier, but he still didn't feel ready to talk about Ieuan, so he changed the subject.

"I thought you and Alun might be getting reacquainted back in Eigg." He gave her his cheekiest grin and she slapped his arm in warning.

"I'm working on it," she teased back. "Anyway, you're right, I'm dead jealous of Cerys and Glyn." Cai nodded over-vigorously, making her smile again. "That was a kind thing you did for them, back there at the boat."

"I'm just happy for them, you know, that they've got each other." Cai fiddled with the sugar jug.

"So what are you going to do about Mona, when we get back?"

Cai glanced up and briefly considered fobbing her off, but decided to give Gwen the truth. "I want to grab her, keep hold of her and never ever let her go." Gwen studied him sceptically, she'd know him for too long, and Cai pulled a face at her cynicism. "It's more than sex with Mona; I'm in love with her, Gwen." Cai reached into his jacket pocket, pulled out his iPod, and placed it on the table between them. He stared at it.

"And what if you can't have her? We all know what your taid thinks."

Cai pointed at the small blue machine on the table. "I want to give this to her." He filled up with emotion, and his smile almost made Gwen gasp. "As a handfasting gift."

A tiny part of Gwen grieved that she'd never been able to make Cai smile like that, but a larger part of her was both happy and concerned for him.

"Do you think they'll let you? You were supposed to handfast Cerys at Lughnasadh?" As Cerys's friend, Gwen had been party to all the political intrigue. "She's the one you're supposed to have children with – the council worked it all out, remember?"

"I don't want children. I just want Mona," he replied evenly. Gwen now gawked at him. What he was saying was tantamount to treason – high-ranking warriors like Cai had a duty to reproduce. Though she was even more surprised by his next words. "Was Cerys upset?" Cai had been impressed by the resilience of both women on this cursed voyage, and his new found compassion was finding a voice.

Gwen shrugged. "Not really, they don't offer a two-week handfasting option," she chuckled dryly. "Anyway, she's much better off with Glyn." Cai had to agree and they were quiet for a little while before Gwen softly asked. "What if Ieuan was right, Cai? What if Mona's on the wrong side?"

Cai replied just as softly. "I don't care anymore, Gwen. Come on, I'm going to cook some fresh fish for supper." The discussion was over. They dragged the youngsters away and made for the harbour.

A plastic box of mechanical scrap was sitting on a chair outside the hardware shop, and Cai couldn't resist a trawl through it. The box was full of all the normal junk he would expect to see, but an old clock mechanism caught his eye. Cai was drawn to the layer upon layer of intricate engineering within it. The shopkeeper said he could have the whole box for a fiver, but he only wanted the mechanism, and gave the man fifty pence.

≈

Endless walking had taken over from Mona's patterns as her primary means of distraction. She couldn't rest unless she had circumnavigated the entirety of the *Conway* – its interior if the weather was bad, but increasingly outside now as well.

The April weather was lemon-sharp and invigorating, bringing with it the smell of spring on the wind. Mona had woken early with a touch of heartburn, but the exercise was seeing it off.

As she rounded the boathouse, Mona remembered Nesta. She also thought she saw Arwel disappearing into the boat shed. She hadn't seen him for over a week – it may even have been longer – and thinking that she might be able to catch him, Mona upped her pace.

Ignoring another twinge of heartburn, she waddled into the gloom. "Arwel," she called out, when she couldn't see him. There was a bit of shuffling and whispering from a nearby corner and Arwel emerged, looking flushed and decidedly dishevelled. "Sorry, Al," she whispered, so that his co-conspirator couldn't hear.

Putting a finger to her lips and mouthing her apology once again, Mona retreated. She had only gone a couple of steps, however, when she was struck by a severe clenching sensation deep in her abdomen. The pain was beyond anything she'd experienced so far, and it didn't take Mona long to realise that she was going into labour. Her discomfort must have been evident, because Arwel was immediately at her side. "Has it started?" he asked in a panicky voice. "The baby's not due for a couple of weeks."

"No, it's far too early," she agreed. "I've just pulled something in my leg." Mona ruffled his already wild mop of white hair and winked before she turned away, to Arwel's obvious relief. "See you later."

The journey back was slower. Each time her muscles clenched, the pain was a little more intense, but Mona was sure she'd easily make it to the infirmary – before anything important happened.

≈

The weather fought with them again as they dodged the sandbars off the east coast, but it improved dramatically the further south they got. Boredom and a numbing sense of isolation were their main enemies now. To the Welsh sailors, England's east coast seemed dull and alien, lacking the beauty and Celtic connections of Britain's western seaboard. Only the majestic Thames barges sweeping past Pin Mill in full red sail, were briefly able to rouse them from their apathy.

Cai spent his time sketching and listening to the music he couldn't wait to share with Mona. The sketchbooks were filling up and he had a plan for the clock mechanism that had fired his imagination. There were also several pages of sheep-shagging jokes – he'd heard them at the various boatyards, where they'd stopped to refuel. Cai felt compelled to write them down, if only to remind him why he hated that Saxon arrogance so much.

They were just off Southend when the VHF crackled into life. The engine was running super-hot on Emlyn's old lifeboat, and they had to pull in. It was also emitting white smoke and a 'funny noise'. Cai's heart sank: white smoke meant water, which meant trouble in an engine that old. He kicked out at the deck and thumped the steering wheel in frustration. What else could possibly go wrong on this bloody journey?

They all hove to outside Southend, and Cai jumped aboard the lifeboat. He could smell the damage straight away. A quick glance told him all he needed to know: water had entered the combustion chamber and the engine would have to come out and be replaced. Repair might be possible, but this would involve a long search for discontinued parts.

Cai was unfairly furious with Dewi; Emlyn wouldn't have let this happen, his uncle would have heard the changes in the engine noise and nursed the old V6 back home. "She'll have to be slipped; there's bound to be a boatyard around here somewhere."

Dafydd rubbed his chin. "We have £250 left in the world, Cai, we cannot afford it. The slipping charges alone will leave us penniless."

Cai was pacing up and down, thinking. An idea had occurred to him, but it was not something he wanted to do, except as a last resort. "Let's slip it, perhaps they'll let us repair it ourselves. I'm sure we can bodge something together that will get us home." Dafydd agreed they should try, though neither uncle nor nephew had much faith in their success.

In the end, it was the worst of all worlds. The charge was £100 for getting the boat in and out again. The old GM Diesel had long since become obsolete, and the manager at the boatyard estimated a four-week wait to get the parts and £200 a day to repair it. The alternative was a new engine: £2000 to fit a reconditioned engine of appropriate size, and all the work to be undertaken by the yard.

≈

They were sentenced to a month on Canvey Island, where most of the moorings dried out at each tide. So they found some deeper water at Ray Gut and used the *Marc'h* as a ferry to the mainland.

Cerys and Gwen found work in pubs, while Glyn accompanied a few of the lads back into the labouring trade. Job opportunities were limited, though, by the simple fact that they could only accept cash as payment: the crew didn't have a P45 between them.

"How much money do we need to get hold of?" Cai asked as they sat contemplating their current calamity.

"We need two grand straight away, so that we can order the engine." They had discussed the possibility of selling the boat, but the remaining three vessels lacked the capacity to take on the extra crew members. It was also one of the few remaining assets of the *Conway*.

"How much money do we need to get home, comfortably?"

Dafydd laughed wearily. "If we could get £4000 together, I would be a happy man."

Cai made his decision. He unpacked the grey suit and business card and made a phone call from the yard's landline. It rang for a long time before someone picked up, but eventually a woman's voice answered.

"Hello, Mum, it's Arty. Can I have a word with Dad?"

≈

When Cai appeared next morning, he was wearing the grey suit and feeling extremely constrained by the tie round his neck. He had shaved and combed his hair, so he didn't understand why he was receiving so much scrutiny from Cerys and Gwen, who were on hand to give advice about dealing with the English public.

"What?" he demanded, smoothing down the front of his jacket, and trying to flatten out any remaining wrinkles. "Is something wrong?" Neither of them answered directly.

"What sort of job are you going for?" Gwen asked.

"IT. I'm going to try the Job Centre first. Is this OK?"

"I don't know what it is," Cerys said, keeping her voice low, "but there's something about you in that suit that's extremely attractive. It looks very expensive."

She was incredibly matter-of-fact, and Gwen joined in. "If anyone asks – you're married." They scouted around for a ring; Dafydd was the only one of the group who wore one. Cai didn't see the point – it didn't mean anything in his culture – but the girls were adamant.

"Look after that, Cai." Dafydd was reluctant to give up his wedding ring, surprising Cai with his reticence. His uncle didn't talk much about Nansi, but then he didn't talk much about anything.

≈

Cai had worked out that he needed a job with an annual salary of £50,000 plus. On this amount, he would be able to earn enough money to quit after a month.

The cards in the window of the Job Centre didn't look that promising, but the woman who took his details seemed fairly cheerful.

"You're a bit overqualified, really." She peeped over the forms at him. "I suppose you've tried modelling?" she flirted. Cai answered "yes" before realising that she wasn't referring to his Airfix collection. "I'll get my supervisor; he deals with executives. Hang on."

Colin was only a little older than Cai, but had an unhealthy, pasty look about him. His handshake was cold and clammy, making Cai want to recoil from his touch. "I've got nothing around here, I'm afraid, but there's a company in Billericay that needs a 3D drawing expert. I don't know whether that's up your street?"

≈

The problem was that Mona had forgotten where everyone had said they would be. The ward was deserted, and she didn't think it would be a good idea to stay there on her own, so she waited for the next contraction to pass and made for Siân's room.

The pain wasn't unbearable yet, but she'd had a taste of what was to come, and Mona's initial desire was to leave her body to deal with it and run. After another contraction and a serious talk with herself, she tried to think about it in different terms: like a complicated pattern or a horribly difficult move. However, fear of dying from the pain was starting to infiltrate her mind. The duration of each bout of pain increased with their intensity, and she was quite exhausted by the time Siân's door number came into view.

There was no answer at the knock and her anger rose. Normally, she couldn't walk down this bloody corridor without bumping into five or more people. Where the bloody hell were they all?

It was another two contractions before Mona reached her own room, and she crawled on to the bed exhausted. It was better if she concentrated on the pain, attacked it rather than let it control her, but in between the pains there was enough time to worry that no one would ever come to help her.

Eventually people came. Other people must have come, but the only person, the only face she saw, was Rob's. He was her constant in the excruciating pantomime. Even through the agony of not being allowed to push, he distracted her with words, soothing the urge away and readying her for the next bout of denial.

When the order to push finally came, the relief was almost pleasurable. Everything stopped in that instant: she couldn't feel and couldn't see what was happening. Rob had turned away from her, and Mona feared that something awful must have happened.

There was some sobbing among the other noises, and she willed Rob to turn back to her. His eyes would tell her all she needed to know. When finally he did turn around, it was with a wet face, screwed up with emotion.

Mona was concentrating too much on his face to see what Rob was holding in his arms – until she felt the hot slickness against her chest. The body was wet with bloody slime, and she must have said out loud what she'd been thinking, because Rob laughed. "It's a baby!"

≈

Cai was interviewed in a glass meeting room, that was situated within the large, open-plan office. There were about twenty people beavering away beyond the fish bowl, at computers, or speaking into phones. Malcolm was the boss, he owned and ran the business, and seemed like a straight-talking man.

"You come highly recommended by Energy Systems UK." He scanned the page. "The MD can't speak highly enough of you. Not related, are you?" Cai laughed weakly at the quip, not altogether convinced that his false documents would fool anyone. "The problem is, that you haven't got any real experience," he shook the dossier, "and I'm after quick results. I need someone who really knows their stuff." He shrugged his shoulders. "I can't waste time training you up. Not being funny mate, but I can't afford to lose this contract – sorry."

Malcolm stood and started to rearrange his cuffs, but Cai didn't move to join him. He needed this job; it was the only way they'd get back home now. "Just let me show you what I can do," he insisted forcefully.

The man studied his watch, and after a little while he pointed to a screen and keyboard. "You've got fifteen minutes," he said wearily, sitting down beside Cai this time.

≈

The child was bigger than the clothes that had been bought for it, but it still looked like a very small thing. Its eyes were open and staring sombrely into her own, but it wasn't the composure in them that stopped the breath in Mona's lungs: it was the colour. The child's eyes weren't brown or blue, but an astonishing shade of violet. She hadn't heard it cry, and Mona asked Rob. "Is it all right?"

That made him weep again, but he was smiling as well. "It's a boy, Mona. What will you call him?"

She hadn't been able to look away from the infant's intense stare, but as her gaze deepened, she recognised a long-lost face among the new-born's features. "Tom," she said, and knew it was right. Despite the unearthly purple of his eyes, the baby looked just like her dad, and Mona loved him with her entire soul.

Siân appeared at the other side of the bed. "I have to take him away to wash him, Mona; he's getting cold." She must have seemed reluctant, because Siân smoothed back her hair. "I'll bring him straight back. I promise."

Rob was much more composed now. "How do you feel?" he asked tenderly.

"Not bad. A bit peckish, actually." She was sore and tired but Rob knew that. "I could murder a cup of tea."

The doctor arrived and, after examining her, gave Mona a clean bill of health. He also left her with instructions, but she felt safe in ignoring these, because she knew that Rob wouldn't.

Tom hollered quite magnificently when he was being bathed, and the sound brought Sioned and Arwel bursting into the room.

Arwel's concern was for Mona, but Sioned made a beeline for the baby, only pausing briefly to check that his mother was still alive.

Mona became instantly worried about the alien colour of Tom's eyes, until she heard Sioned's loud gasp. "He looks just like Cai!" At which point Arwel gave Mona a subtle victory smile. However, when Sioned brought the baby over, Arwel caught a glimpse of Tom's violet eyes, and his eyebrows vanished into his hairline.

32

Employment

The demonstration lasted just over an hour, by the end of which, Cai had managed to secure the job. "I can only offer you a six month contract," Malcolm said apologetically. "That's the policy at the moment, I'm afraid." He pointed at the screen, "But you're exactly what I need, and you should fit right in here. Go and see Barbara, she'll sort it all out." Both men stood and shook hands. "See you on Monday."

Using his false documentation, Cai opened a bank account. His wages would be paid automatically into this – though not until he had completed a full month's work.

≈

The boatyard wouldn't budge on ordering the engine ahead of time, but they did allow him to live on board the slipped lifeboat. He ran to the station at Southend each morning, and then from Billericay to the industrial estate, showering and changing at work before 8 a.m. He had no time for patterns.

After the first week, Cai realised two things: firstly, that no one in the company knew what he was supposed to do, and secondly, that working in an office was much like warfare.

Life in the open-plan workplace was merely a scaled-down version of the *Conway* – with its bullies, romances, gossip and power struggles. One of his colleagues, Craig, didn't like Cai from day one, but it didn't matter; the work was easy, and interesting. Following Gwen's advice, he kept his head down, and chose to work through his lunch break rather than socialise.

After the second week, Craig felt he knew Cai well enough to start the sheep jokes. They weren't as original as those he'd already heard, and Cai was almost disappointed that they didn't make the cut for his sketchbook repertoire.

"You talk funny." It was the office junior, who might have been pretty if she hadn't disguised herself as some sort of strange doll, complete with false eyelashes and skin. She had enormous gold hoops in her ears that must have been extremely painful to wear. Whenever she spoke, Cai was mesmerised by the chewing gum that rolled around in her ever-open mouth.

"He's a sheep-shagger," Craig offered as explanation.

"I'm from Wales," Cai corrected, ignoring Craig and addressing the young girl.

"Is that near Scotland?"

"Not really," he replied distractedly. Cai was clearly more interested in his work, so she drifted downstairs for a cigarette.

≈

Stacey and Paula were both about thirty-five and married. Cai knew this because they did nothing but complain about their husbands to each other, all day, every day. Stacey had been interested in Cai from the moment he walked into the office – in a similar way that a spider is interested in a fly.

It crossed Cai's mind that the women might be related. They had the same dyed and straightened hair, wore excessive amounts of foundation, and possessed the sharp nails that he'd come to expect from most women outside the *Conway*.

Stacey wore exceptionally tight-fitting skirts and sheer blouses through which her delicate underwear could be clearly seen. Cai got the feeling she spent a great deal of time and money on her appearance.

In the first week she had sneaked up behind him and felt his biceps. "Someone works out." She had flashed a practiced smile and Cai had thanked her politely. In Cai's second week at work, Stacey had leaned against his desk, caught hold of his tie and stroked it suggestively. "Nice tie. It brings out the blue in your eyes."

"Thanks, my wife bought it for me," Cai replied politely, floating in the heady scent of Stacey's perfume.

"Well, she has good taste." She winked and walked away, but Cai hadn't had sex with a woman for ten months and despite his best efforts, his body had risen to Stacey's proximity.

After that, Cai went to great lengths to avoid her, but she finally caught up with him again in the office kitchen. "A group of us are going for a drink on Friday. Do you fancy it?" The double entendre wasn't lost on him.

"Thanks, but I'm out with my wife on Friday."

"What's her name?"

"Mona," he said without thinking.

"Mona," the woman repeated the name in her ugly accent. "What's she like?"

"Kind, brave." But Cai was beginning to forget what Mona was actually like, and he struggled to form an image of her in his mind.

"Kind! That's not very sexy." Stacey vamped out of the room, giving her hips some extra rotation for Cai's benefit. His eyes were reluctantly drawn to her figure, as she knew they would be.

≈

On his last day at the company, Cai had his pay-slip in one pocket and his letter of resignation in the other. Before leaving, he handed the letter to Barbara in HR, explaining to her that he needed to return home – there was a family emergency. Barbara was kind and concerned; they had been extremely pleased with his work and were sad to lose him so soon.

As he passed the stationery cupboard, Cai heard Stacey swear and some files spilled out on to the corridor. He picked them up automatically and handed them back through the open door. As she took them from him, Stacey somehow managed to press herself closely against Cai. Using the files as cover, her hands deftly fondled the front of his suit trousers.

"Mona's not taking very good care of you at night, is she?" Stacey spoke in a throaty whisper and he closed his eyes with pent-up desire. As she continued to wiggle her body against his, Cai groaned involuntarily and licked his dry lips. "Are you sure you don't want to come over tonight?" Her lips were at his ear. "My husband works shifts."

≈

A strange circus of breastfeeding instruction and visitors began almost immediately. Mona had anticipated reclaiming her body after giving birth, but felt like she was being handled more than ever.

Tom seemed desperately keen to get to grips with breastfeeding, but he sucked so hard that Mona was in constant pain and dreaded each attempt. However, they both persevered, and through a process of trial and error, soon had it cracked.

When Tom fed, he did so with a powerful intensity, staring up at Mona unblinkingly and even fighting sleep when it threatened to overwhelm him. Rob had started to strum during his feeds, and though Mona had no way of telling for sure, she thought Tom liked the music.

≈

Arwel arrived at their door on day five, unannounced and wearing his Ovate cloak. "Nice hoodie, Al. Got a hot date?" Arwel blushed profusely and found something very interesting about the floor. He *did* have a hot date.

"Actually, I've come to take you and Tom up to Ifan's; he needs to be registered in the book." There wasn't to be a ceremony, just a signature and a witness. "You ought to put on your cloak, too."

Rob held Tom while Mona prepared. Smiling and cooing was a full-time occupation for Rob, and he still became moist around the eyes occasionally. He was the perfect father.

"Sorry about that, I didn't mean to embarrass you."

Arwel dismissed her apology, changing the subject as they walked to Ifan's rooms.

"Everyone thinks he's Cai's. It's lucky their colouring is so similar."

"Yes," Mona admitted. "Though haven't most Welsh babies got dark hair and blue eyes?" Showing off, she added, "Heterozygous brown, then?"

Arwel smiled. "Yes, I'd say you're right. Either Gareth's mother or father has eyes that are almost *identical* to Cai's." He paused to see whether Mona would pick up on the implicit question. She didn't, so he asked her directly. "So, is there a chance he *is* actually Cai's son?"

Being forced to reflect on the most passionate night of her life, out of the blue and in front of a teenager, made Mona blush. Arwel misinterpreted her response and gasped. "It's much, *much* more likely that he isn't," Mona blurted out.

"What does *that* mean?"

"I don't want to talk about it with you, Arwel." She baulked at the thought.

Arwel stopped walking to stare at her. "Even if there is a small chance, he should know. I would want to know."

Mona also stopped and turned. "There really isn't any chance that Tom is Cai's." She pressed her lips to his fragile skull. "And you must *never* tell him that there might be. Promise me, Arwel." Mona was well aware that the boy didn't want to be the keeper of any more secrets or promises. "If I tell him that he could be Tom's father, it will be like blackmailing him to stay with me, don't you see that? And anyway, I can't see the likeness. I think he looks the spit of my dad – apart from the purple eyes."

"They're not purple anymore, Mona. They're blue – very blue."

Mona gazed down at her gorgeous son to find that Arwel was right. She'd been gazing into his eyes so often that she'd failed to notice the gradual change. "That's lucky, then." She smirked and Arwel finally laughed.

Ifan was waiting for them. "He's a bonny boy. How much did he weigh?"

"Nine pounds."

"Did you have any problems with the delivery?" The Archdruid had the knack of making the most personal conversations feel like interviews.

"Not really." Mona peeked sideways at Arwel before joking. "Though I can't believe no one prepared me for it." Arwel performed on cue, opening both mouth and eyes in mock accusation.

There was a plain hardback book open in front of Ifan, and he turned it towards her. "Just put in your full name, Tom's full name, and the father's."

"I don't know his full name."

"Yes you do. It's Cai Gwilym Owens."

"I'm not putting that. I'll leave it blank."

Ifan let it go quicker than she thought he might. "As you wish. Here, let me hold Tom while you sign it." Ifan looked too old and fragile to be entrusted with her baby son, but she passed him over anyway. "Put the kettle on, Arwel, that's a boy," Ifan asked absent-mindedly. Mona signed and Arwel witnessed.

"We're out of fresh milk." Arwel had sniffed the carton and found it wanting.

"Any chance you can fetch some, lad? I'm gasping," Ifan asked. The young man was obviously used to his dogsbody role, and left without a murmur.

Ifan waited a minute or so, but as soon as the Welsh started to leave his mouth, she was powerless. "Mona, little Tom's cold, he's *freezing* cold. Do you know what would warm him up? Some water. How about some of that boiling water in the kettle?" Mona stared at the kettle. The Welsh words were so compelling that even that abhorrent thought sounded reasonable. Of course the boiling water would warm him up. Tom couldn't get cold, after all. "Yes, that's right; bring it here, right over here. Look, I'll undo his blanket, and let's take off his little vest; the water will warm him up much quicker that way." Tom was peering up at Ifan; his tiny arms and hands colouring with purple and white blotches as his body heat leaked away into the icy room. "Look, he's starting to cry, Mo. Quick! Just pour it over him, he'll warm up in no time."

Mona obeyed the seductive words directly, tipping the kettle of water forwards. Steam billowed out of the spout as the scalding water splashed to the floor at Ifan's feet.

The old man had stopped talking and was now holding Tom up – high and out of harm's way. He stared, incredulous, at Mona, whose knuckles had whitened over the kettle's handle. She put it down very carefully and advanced on the old man.

Snatching Tom from Ifan's grasp, Mona settled the baby into the crook of her left arm, then snaked out with her right. Pinching Ifan around his neck, she drove him back against the wall to his rear. "It was an experiment," he choked. "I had to see how badly you were affected."

Mona squeezed harder at the memory of what she had almost done. "Never again. You will die if you ever even consider it again," she growled at him murderously through gritted teeth. Mona released her grip and the old man fell to the ground, coughing and rubbing his neck.

≈

Later Rob held her, held them both, as she wept out her remorse. Siân blamed the 'baby blues', which was for the best: the truth could never be told.

33

Falmouth

By the time Tom was six weeks old, Rob and Mona had become two cogs in one relentless parental machine. They shared everything but the feeding, and Rob would try to make sure he was around for that, even if it meant getting up at some horrible hour of the morning.

They were gritty-eyed and hollow-cheeked. The only thing that got Rob through it was Bryn, but Mona found her comfort in the patterns. She had restarted her training as soon as she was able to walk again, and was rediscovering the joys of her old, dependable love every day.

Mona pushed her body to the limit, stretching herself a little more at each additional session. After a couple of weeks, she began sparring with anyone who had the time and energy. Bryn was a solid opponent, Dai was quick and subtle, Sioned had improved beyond all recognition – but it was Cai that Mona craved, even after all this time.

She had a feeling that as the anniversary of their departure approached, something official would be said. And at that point Mona would be free to leave. Something awful had happened to the man she might have loved. Everyone knew that it couldn't take a year to circumnavigate Britain, no matter what the weather.

≈

The engine was fitted, the boat slipped back into the water and the journey back began again. The crew had stopped making predictions about when they'd finally reach home, fearing that this would only invite further disaster. An air of superstitious doom pervaded the fleet, and it seemed to Cai that they were all just waiting for the next catastrophe to befall them.

The shipping forecast remained his constant companion, and there were still weather setbacks around North Foreland and Beachy Head, halting their progress south and west for days at a time. The White Cliffs of Dover seemed to last all the way to Dorset, and the further west they ventured, the busier and more expensive the amenities became. The sea around the Isle of Wight was filled with the most idiotic, indecisive people that the crew had ever encountered, and the four boats motored out of the mayhem as briskly as they could.

The weather was consistently glorious this far south, and Cai was on board Dafydd's boat, enjoying the feel of the sun on his body. "I'm going to try to recruit some reinforcements," Dafydd told him. "We've no idea what to expect back home." His voice tightened with feeling. "There's a spy at the *Conway* and we may have a battle on our hands."

Cai squinted over at his uncle; the same thought had occurred to him. "Yes, we should motor straight to Kernow; it's the only sizeable community of us left in England."

Dafydd opened his eyes with a lazy smirk. "What do you think I've been doing while you've been chasing around after secretaries?" Cai waited for the surprise. "I've contacted all the chiefs in Cornwall. We're going straight to Falmouth, where we'll meet Cadan. He'll coordinate everything from there."

Past The Needles, the idiocy and the traffic eased, and there was a united moment of calm as the Druids gazed westwards. It was the summer solstice by the time they passed into Cornish waters; the sun was high and hot, beating down on a rugged coast of turquoise coves and white sands. Falmouth Bay opened up before them.

Cai reluctantly handed over the mooring fees to the harbour master. At twelve pounds a boat per night, he didn't plan to stay here long, but they wanted to meet up with Cadan at the earliest opportunity. Leaving Glyn and Dewi to organise the crews, they set off on the short walk to the Lifeboat Station.

≈

Rob was on leave with Bryn, enjoying a little well-deserved free time. Mona knew straightaway that it was Arwel at the door; there was an unmistakeable mix of deference and firmness to his knock that made her smile. Tom would be waking up any minute, demanding to be fed, but Arwel was typically unfazed by breastfeeding.

"Come in, Blondie."

Arwel drew somebody else into the room with him – someone dark, petite and rounded – along in his wake. The girl whose hand he clutched had a pretty face, polished with youth and now crimson with embarrassment. Mona knew her well; it was Rhona, Nesta's granddaughter, a colleague of Rob's in the nursery and one of her very first pupils.

"Come in you two, I'll put the kettle on," Mona sang out in an overly breezy manner. Tom started to stir in his wicker basket, causing Rhona's glance to dart in his direction. "Would you mind holding him while I make the tea, Rhona?" Mona asked, and the girl was over at Tom's side like a shot, picking him up with the expertise of a professional.

"You said he looked like Cai," she whispered to Arwel, who seemed unable to leave her side. "But he's just so sparkly."

Mona glanced up at the girl's strange adjective. "Sparkly?"

Rhona stared at Arwel, who then stared at Mona and shrugged. "He's hungry," the girl informed them, hastily changing the subject.

"You'll have to take over tea duties, Al," Mona sighed, a hint of weariness creeping into her voice.

Once Tom was settled, Arwel cut to the chase. "I'm sixteen on

Saturday, and I've asked Rhona to be my partner." The girl didn't turn quite as pink-faced as earlier. "I'd like you to give me permission; you're entitled now, as a person of rank."

"Of course I'll give my permission, but wouldn't your grandfather be the best person to ask?" Mona still found it difficult to utter Ifan's name after his horrific experiment. They hadn't spoken since.

Arwel was ready with his answer. "I love my taid, but he can be foolish. I trust your judgement."

Mona knew that he was speaking the truth, but she also knew how his devious little mind worked. Arwel was an Archdruid in waiting, and Rhona was the granddaughter of the laundry maid. Ifan would never give his permission, so Arwel was using her to sidestep any confrontation.

Mona grinned at him, acknowledging the tactic, and he reciprocated his thanks with a smile of his own. "Do I have to sign something?" She did, and Arwel had it in his hand. "Are you having a party?" Mona asked as she signed her name. Both youngsters recoiled in unison, but Rhona gave him an encouraging smile.

"We haven't got anywhere to go, anywhere private. And Taid still doesn't want anyone else in Dad's rooms."

Mona looked around. She couldn't offer them this place: it was baby central. "We wondered if you thought Cai would mind us borrowing his room, seeing as he's…"

Mona was renowned for her inability to talk about the continued absence of the fleet. "I can't speak for him," she didn't let Arwel finish, "but I'm pretty sure he wouldn't mind – you are his baby brother after all."

"That's what I said," Rhona added, smiling at him.

≈

The beach was an image of paradise. Cai had never felt the sun's heat so intensely. In the dazzling light he was unable to distinguish separate colours: sky, sea and sand merged into a wall of whiteness that caused his eyes to squint and water mercilessly. Surrendering to the bright light, he closed them, content for now just to listen. He could hear children laughing, the tinny sound of a portable speaker, and the soporific crash of surf on sand. The sun seemed to penetrate his bones, and he drifted off to sleep.

When Cai woke, it was with a start. The wind had changed direction, it was now blowing offshore. Surely he couldn't have slept for that long? Even the music had stopped.

Cerys had made sure that everyone had used sun-cream this morning, but Cai suspected he'd been a little too sparing on his legs. He couldn't remember the last time he'd exposed them to the elements. The other Welshmen were the same; the contrast between their magnesium-white legs and nut-brown torsos had caused great amusement among the locals when they'd arrived on the beach this morning.

His thighs were pink now and smarted. Cai needed to get out of the sun, but hesitated at the sight of the tanned, lithe women frolicking on the beach. Now that his eyes had finally adjusted to the light, it would be such a waste not to savour the way their hips moved and their breasts wobbled as they larked about in the surf. The drowsy heat had opened the floodgates to a rising wave of sexual desire, and he couldn't help but gawk openly.

There was something familiar about the group of women nearest him. All three were attractive, but one in particular claimed his attention: she was tanned and petite, with a tumble of curling dark hair and flashing Mediterranean eyes. Her name was Carmen or something like that; they'd met last night at the RNLI boathouse, and she was from a tiny clan in Galicia. The woman was exquisitely exotic.

Looking up, she noticed his interest, and picked her way towards him across the burning sand. The woman was tying some sort of sash at her waist, though it didn't hide enough of her body to disappoint him. Cai could see that she had just come out of the water; it still lay in sparking droplets on her arms and cleavage, making the material of her bikini top translucent and causing it to cling to her perfect breasts.

He wasn't at all intimidated by her bold approach – there was no shaking or trembling, no doubts about how to respond. He breathed in her smell as she came to a halt in front of him. Cai didn't move from the deckchair as she held up a bottle of after-sun. "I thought you could use a little of this." She spoke in a sexy, broken English laced with exotic Spanish.

Carmen's cooler leg touched his burning thigh, and Cai knew he didn't need to say anything: his smile would tell her all she needed to know. "Let me help." She squeezed some of the cooling balm on to each thigh, and began to massage gently.

Cai didn't think he had any of the magic that was supposedly hidden in his bloodline, but if he had any talent at all, it was this: women responded to him, were drawn to him, with very little conscious effort on his part.

Cai knew that this woman wanted to touch him, that she enjoyed rubbing the cream into his chest and straying tantalizingly close to his waistband. He understood that if he placed his hands on her hips, right now, they would be having sex within ten minutes.

The woman had remained standing, but had straddled one of his thighs to massage his chest. Waves of female pheromones, laced with sun-cream and perfume, radiated from her deliciously warmed skin, heightening Cai's already overwhelming sense of desire. Still damp from the sea, her breasts brushed against his shoulder. This was the trigger, and Cai moved his hands to her hips. Knowing he was ready, the woman leaned in further to kiss him.

The spell was broken by a loud shout from nearby. There was an urgency to the voice that could not be ignored, and Cai levered the woman from his body so that he could get to his feet.

Dafydd was running towards him, waving his arms and shouting. Once he was sure of Cai's attention, he began to move away, gesturing at Cai to follow.

Running through the loose, hot sand required a monumental

effort and when Cai eventually caught up with Dafydd, he was panting. "What, what's happened?"

"Come with me to the boat." Cai followed quickly, trawling his mind for a possible explanation. He desperately hoped that the news wasn't too horrific.

Back at the boat, he waited patiently – and in vain – for Dafydd to explain. "And?" he finally asked.

Dafydd hadn't said a word and was now fussing with the kettle. "Tea?"

"Dafydd," Cai warned, his temper was fraying and his head was thumping.

"Cerys thought you should come in out of the sun."

Cai was stunned. "What?"

"She thought you might get sunstroke," Dafydd hedged.

Cai grunted and turned to leave; Carmen might still be there.

"Sit down, Cai, cool off." Dafydd was brusque, and Cai finally got it.

"It's *just* sex."

"Yeah, you're right. Gods, couldn't we all do with some lovely uncomplicated shagging right now." His uncle's words may have been conciliatory, but his tone wasn't, and it irritated Cai.

"Are you seriously going to lecture me?"

"Shagging Carmen will not be uncomplicated. Some of the Cornish lot have decided to come back and be trained. They're ready to fight if they have to, and I'm pretty sure this travelling Galician group will want to tag along for the ride." Dafydd crossed his arms, hard over his chest. "I'm not even sure I like Mona all that much. But don't you think it's a little harsh? Bringing a new girlfriend back home with you from your travels – seeing as you asked her to stick around till you got back?"

Shame, not the sun, burned Cai's face, and he lay back on the bunk, folding his arms over his head. All thoughts of Mona had evaporated on the beach. How had that happened?

"I just…"

Dafydd's tone had already softened. "It's been a long time, Cai; we're all feeling the strain." He poured the tea and Cai sat up. "I've been married to Nansi for ten years. I've got three kids with her, but I suspect that if I could get away with some sneaky shagging without her ever knowing…"

Dafydd's tone was lightening further, and Cai responded in kind. "I know how handy she is with a knife."

They both chuckled shakily. "There is that, but I know how I'd feel if she did the same to me. And it doesn't really bear thinking about."

Cai had no idea how Mona would react to infidelity, but even the thought of her in someone else's arms made his stomach turn.

≈

Mona had given Arwel an attractive hardback journal in which to write up his notes, together with five packs of condoms. Everything had been gratefully received, and it was only later that she learned that condoms had been part of almost every present he'd been given. Rob teased him constantly, but he bore it manfully and, to her delight, started to return the banter. Arwel really was her young *padawan*.

Mona was almost back to her pre-pregnancy fighting form, and was enjoying life more than she ever believed possible. Whatever happened now, Mona knew she would endure, and the thought made her smile as she peered down into her son's clear-eyed gaze.

Tom stopped feeding and let her breast fall from his mouth. Milk dribbled out either side of his wide, smiling lips, and his eyes, normally so dour, came alive with joy. Until that moment, Mona hadn't imagined that she could love the little person in her arms any more than she already did.

Tom generally smiled for her at least once a feed from then on, and she became addicted to his beatific expression. Mona told Sioned about the smile, and the young woman made it her mission to cajole one out of Tom for herself.

She was currently holding him in her arms, giving it another good try. "I don't believe you, Mo; he's still looking at me as if I've done something wrong. It's unnerving how much like Cai he is."

The deceit always stabbed Mona's conscience, but it was the mention of Cai's name that changed the mood. In two weeks' time, the fleet would have been absent for a year. Mona didn't speak, but she knew Sioned would. "If that many had been lost, we would have heard about it."

This was always Sioned's stock answer, but Mona had never been convinced by it. The whole Druid community had lived under the radar for millennia, of course they could keep quiet the death of twenty-four people who didn't officially exist.

Sioned went back to coaxing a smile out of Tom, and Mona looked on, hoping for another glimpse of Cai in the fierce concentration on his sister's face. "Please don't take Tom away." Sioned's quiet plea blindsided Mona. "If Cai's dead, then Tom is nearly all the family I have left."

It was a calm request, not a hysterical whine. The symmetry of their plights was horribly acute; this little boy was all they had left between them in the world.

≈

Cai was shivering when Dafydd woke him; perhaps he had spent too long in the sun. "Come on, mate, we're meeting the Cornish lads down the pub. We need to find out how many are willing to come back with us."

Cai knew he should leave his bunk and join Dafydd, but he was reticent for a number of reasons – among them fear of meeting the Galician woman again. "Don't worry. I'll protect you." Dafydd had read his mind, but he doubted his uncle's resilience against an opponent like Carmen.

The pub was an incongruous mixture of Druids and tourists. Dafydd had been told that the outsiders thought the Welsh was some sort of ancient Cornish, and in a way they were right. A band was playing in the corner, but their musicianship wasn't up to much.

Cai squeezed in between Cerys and Gwen for protection. "Coward," Cerys smirked over her pint. Cai didn't bother arguing; everyone knew about the incident on the beach, and he now realised it must have been a spectator sport. "You're not among friends here, Cai; we really thought you'd changed." His silence pleased them and he sipped his beer, legs and chest burning.

Dafydd approached, gesturing him forward into a meeting room at the back of the pub, and after a while, he mellowed into the atmosphere. They were a friendly bunch; the Welsh and Cornish Druids rubbed along fairly well, speaking with a strange mixture of their shared Celtic languages and a large dollop of English.

Only a few of the Cornish seemed happy to be part of an offensive against the Irish, and only for a while at that. Though they were extremely keen to learn some new fighting techniques, and could at least provide a couple of extra boats to bolster the fleet. It was arranged that a small combined Cornish force from several different clans would join them – as well as the three women from Galicia.

As Dafydd stood to shake hands with Cadan, their leader, there was a bustle of activity behind him. Cai looked up to see an enormous fair-haired man stride into the room, filling it with an imposing presence. He spoke in fluent Cornish at first but reverted to English when he noticed the newcomers. "Excuse me, sorry to interrupt." He glanced at Dafydd and Cai before tackling Cadan. "Jago's in bits out there." He pointed towards the seashore. "If you don't sort this out, I'm going to have to."

Cadan began to speak to the newcomer, trying and failing to placate him. As Cai studied him, he realised that the man's hair was not as fair as he'd first imagined, but more of a reddish-blonde colour. Finishing up his conversation with Cadan, the man's eyes flicked upwards to meet Cai's. The Welshman gasped with shock: he knew those grey eyes, he'd been trapped under their gaze before. All he could rasp out was one word: "Idwal." The man's glare intensified. "Idwal Jones?" It was a question, but it didn't need to be.

"I don't know you." His tone had turned threatening and he took up a defensive stance. "Military police?" he snarled in Cai's direction.

His initial shock over, Cai reasserted control over his vocal cords. "I know your sister, Mona."

Colour and composure drained from him and Idwal grasped the back of a chair for support, profound pain filling his eyes. This wasn't possible, they had all died together, five years ago now – Brendan himself had written the letter. "She's dead." Idwal somehow made these two words threatening.

"We left her safe on Ynys Môn, in July last year." It was Dafydd who now spoke, as Cai was struggling with words.

They could see the incomprehension on Idwal's face turn to scepticism. "I got a letter; he said she'd been killed, along with my parents. They died in a car crash." There was a raw pain in the big man's voice.

"Mona got one about you, too."

Idwal slumped into a chair, his hands covering his face in an attempt to hide his emotions. "How is she?"

Cai couldn't truthfully think of an adequate answer. "She's… glorious," he improvised.

Idwal exploded in booming laugher, stopping only when a young and distraught Cornishman rushed into the room. "It's Jago." Idwal rushed out after him immediately, with Dafydd and Cai following.

The cliffs weren't far from the pub, and it became immediately apparent that the Jago in question was contemplating throwing himself from them. There was a fair amount of shouting and swearing as Idwal briskly bounced up the cliff face to the youngster. "Get her," he barked sideways.

A man reappeared momentarily, pulling Carmen behind him. Cai started to feel increasingly uneasy as he began to guess the cause of Jago's despair. "I'm not going up there," she screeched at the man who'd dragged her unceremoniously across the sandy car park.

Cai approached foot of the cliff. "What's going on?" he asked them both.

"The young lad's gone crazy with love for this one." The man roughly shook her arm.

"He's a prat. Of course I was moving on." Carmen gave Cai an openly lingering smile, confirming that this had something to do with their little show on the beach.

The drop wasn't horrific; if the boy jumped he probably wouldn't die, but the chances of ending up in a wheelchair were pretty good. Cai saw a way up the cliffs on the other side; perhaps he could help prevent the tragedy.

He arrived slightly lower and nearer to Jago than Idwal, who didn't look at him but began to include Cai in the soothing conversation he was having with the young lad. "Tell him: there was nothing in it today with Carmen. Jago's under the impression you two were getting friendly on the beach."

"It wasn't like that, mate," Cai agreed, knowing it was what Idwal wanted to hear.

"Liar." The boy had been crying. His eyes were red and swollen, and his anguished expression reminded Cai of the pain he'd seen in Emlyn's eyes so many years ago.

"Why don't you come down so we can have a chat? Come on," Idwal coaxed. He pitched his voice perfectly, avoiding any patronising trace that might offend the young lad. Less certain now, Jago moved away from the cliff edge slightly. Idwal offered him a hand. "Come on. It'll be all right, I promise."

They touched fingertips, then fingers. As soon as Idwal was sure of his grip, he yanked the boy forward and into his arms. Idwal held the young lad tight against his chest, mumbling low reassurances, and even managed to coax a sad smile from the youngster as they eased down from the cliffs.

The drama was over – until Jago caught sight of Carmen. She was leaning casually against the pub wall in a light summer dress. The pose stretched the material enticingly around her tight little curves and the paleness of the fabric enriched the caramel of her skin. Jago squirmed free of Idwal and lurched towards her. For one awful moment, Cai thought that the lad was going to fall to his knees in front of her. "You lied to me." The abject tone in his voice was appalling to hear.

Cai expected Carmen to apologise in some way, but she simply laughed, regarding the boy with cruel contempt. "Your heart will mend." Her voice was entrancing, even as it tore the boy's heart apart, and Cai felt sickened.

Idwal recaptured Jago and led him away by his shoulders. The excitement over, everyone else began to gravitate back to the pub. "Nice," Cerys whispered in Cai's ear.

Idwal didn't reappear in the pub that night, though, to his shame, Cai waited and watched obsessively for him until closing time. It was more than his grey eyes that reminded him of Mona; they shared a physical confidence that he'd overlooked until tonight.

Cai also wasn't too sure how much he should reveal to Idwal about his relationship with Mona. The episode with Carmen made broaching the subject extremely awkward, and he was dubious of Idwal's possible reaction – the man was a giant and clearly not someone to be messed with.

≈

Cai and his uncle both stood up in anticipation as Idwal strode towards their berth just after dawn. "I'm finding it hard to take your word for it." It was clear he meant Mona. "How can I be sure?"

There was a moment's silence, both men hoping the other would take the lead. Dafydd spoke first. "Well, she's big, five feet ten – powerfully built, short hair, grey eyes." There was no encouragement from Idwal, who remained impassive. Dafydd ploughed on manfully. "Bit of a temper, bossy, belligerent, a good fighter."

Cai was glad now that he hadn't spoken up because, though

accurate, these would not have been the adjectives he'd have used to describe Mona. Idwal remained sceptical, though less so than previously.

"Music!" Cai exclaimed abruptly as the inspiration hit him, and Idwal suddenly became interested. "She's always listening to the mp3 player you got her for her sixteenth birthday; I think it might have been pink once."

"One song, one of her favourites," Idwal demanded, and Cai knew that he had started to believe them.

"The Prodigy, '*Breathe*.'" He could have named any of a hundred tracks, but that pleased Idwal enough to crush the air out of Cai's lungs.

"You know a lot about my sister."

It wasn't an accusation as such, but Cai felt he needed to explain. "I'm… we…"

Idwal put up a hand. "I get it."

"About Carmen." Cai had to say something about their encounter on the beach, but Idwal repeated the hand gesture.

"Someone should have warned you about our Carmen," he laughed ruefully. "She's got some strange Druid sex magic, they say. I don't know if that's true or not, but she got me the very first day I arrived." He coughed, a little embarrassed. "It took a whole week for me to realise what a nasty little cow she is. Don't worry, I won't tell Mo." Idwal now turned again to Dafydd. "When do we leave?"

Hope rose in Cai's chest. He had been afraid that Cadan was stalling, but if Idwal said they were going, he had a feeling it might happen soon indeed.

In the event, they had a few days more to wait. Knowing they might be gone for a while, the Cornish crew needed time to tie up a few loose threads. The delay was still excruciating for Cai, who knew that Ynys Môn was only a two-day motor away in such calm conditions. In the meantime, he spent the long, sunny days getting to know Idwal.

Initially, Cai wanted to warn Idwal about the ambiguous reaction to Mona and her *mark*, but the big man was exceptionally impervious to the idea of magic, so Cai didn't pursue it, and instead listened to Idwal chat about their childhood. Despite his description of Mona as an annoying little tomboy, Cai could hear the affection in Idwal's voice as he reminisced about his family. Their parents sounded like good people – in fact, it all sounded pretty rose-tinted. But when all you have are memories, that's the colour they tend to be.

Like Cai, Idwal had a reputation as a ladies' man; unlike Cai, he was still very much in the game. His romances were short-lived and didn't seem to mean a lot to him, and Cai couldn't help but cringe at the similarity between them.

≈

By mid-July, Tom was almost too heavy to carry around in the sling. Mona had started to consider some sort of backpack arrangement, but Sioned had demanded a buggy – as soon as one became available in the network of charity shops they used in Bangor.

Tom accompanied his mum every day to her favourite shaded spot. Mona performed her patterns and Tom kicked around in wild naked abandon, mirroring the movement of the branches in the wind high above his head. He had started to make excited cooing and hooting noises to accompany his dance, and he always returned her smile at the end of their exercise routine.

Mona had just finished dressing him when Sioned shattered their calm. Powering towards them at pace, Mona couldn't make out what she was shouting until Sioned stood breathless and panting in front of her. "They've been spotted... off Caernarfon... the fleet, Mo. They're back."

Mona had clenched with paranoia at Sioned's hurricane arrival and the tension heated her blood as she watched the girl's lips move. '*Death, War, Sorrow!*' it shrieked – the harsh singing of a whistling kettle. '*Love, Betrayal!*' The boiling words sang in her ears, ratcheting up to a ragged high pitched whine. *Childbirth!* it screeched. Sioned touched her arm; the screaming pressure was released and she sagged.

"You're sure?" Mona asked, now strangely detached.

"Checked and double-checked. I was on duty when the coastguard called."

"Have they made radio contact?"

"No, not yet." Sioned's face creased with burgeoning excitement.

"OK," Mona replied, squeezing Tom against her tightly. "Go to Arwel and Ifan. I'll be along as soon as I can."

Mona sat on the grass and took courage from Tom as she fed him. He was asleep by the time they walked into the meeting.

≈

Each one of the committee members was trying and failing to keep their emotions under wraps. However, Mona had allowed herself time to think during the measured walk over here. Despite the desire to celebrate, they had to be rational. Every one of the returning warriors must be considered suspect.

Both Ifan and Arwel looked up at her – they had each come to the same conclusion. "We should hold them, until we know it's safe." Arwel stated quietly.

"*Arrest them*?" Sioned blurted out in shock, and Ifan nodded.

"I'm afraid Arwel's right, my dear." He shook his head slowly. "Though I hate to say it."

"But how long can we hold them? How can we test them?" Sioned was agitated and shrill.

Mona nodded at Arwel; they were on the same page at least. If she could get near enough each one of them to smell for the tell-tale sulphur, that might constitute a test – of sorts.

"Mona will test them," Arwel stated, more bluntly now.

"How?" Sioned asked, increasingly aggrieved by his attitude.

"She bears the *mark*," Arwel replied simply and without a pause.

The finality of the statement seemed to satisfy Sioned, but she glanced over at Mona.

"Are you alright with that, Mo? I mean if Cai's…"

"Yes," she agreed hastily before having to think about her imminent reunion with Cai. "Who's to say that there's not a traitor within the ranks of the fleet? We have been betrayed. It's been over a year, and we still have no idea why, when or who is to blame."

≈

All the crews were combat ready as they passed through the Swellies, just before high water. Someone within the *Conway* had betrayed the fleet, and Cai felt sick with anticipation and dread at the thought of discovering the culprit – though his heart told him that it couldn't be Mona.

The tiny navy had been absent from Ynys Môn for a year and a day, and Cai cringed inwardly at the mythological timescale, hoping that he wasn't sailing into a Celtic tragedy. He scanned the jetty and wharf as the complex came into view, and was not alone in being staggered by their reception.

There were warriors lining the shore: women and children he'd known his entire life, stood shoulder to shoulder, armed with the swords and staffs. Ifan was implacable in their midst, and Cai realised very quickly that it wasn't a welcome party. His heart sank to his boots at the realisation that something here was terribly wrong.

The story continues in

Hiraeth
a burden – *baich*

Visit www.hiraeth.me

Notes

The Mabinogion
The collective name given to eleven medieval Welsh tales, found mainly in two manuscripts, the *White Book of Rhydderch* (c. 1350) and the *Red Book of Hergest* (c. 1382–1410)

The Táin Bó Cúailnge
An epic tale from the Irish Ulster Cycle

Cantiaci
A Celtic people living in Britain before the Roman conquest. They lived in the area now called Kent, in south-eastern England. Their capital was Durovernum Cantiacorum, now Canterbury.

Demetae
A Celtic people of Iron Age Britain. They inhabited modern Pembrokeshire and Carmarthenshire.

Silures
A powerful and warlike tribe of ancient Britain, occupying approximately the former counties of Monmouthshire, Breconshire and Glamorganshire in present-day South Wales.

Gangani
Celtic people of Iron Age Britain. They lived on the Llŷn Peninsula.

Ordovices

One of the Celtic tribes living in Britain before the Roman invasion. Their tribal lands were located in present-day Wales and England between the Silures to the south and the Deceangli to the north-east.

Brú na Bóinne (Brew na boynya)

A complex of megalithic remains dating back to the Neolithic period. The complex is sited in the Boyne Valley in County Meath, Ireland, and is best known for the impressive passage graves of Newgrange, Knowth and Dowth

Acknowledgements

Anon., *The Mabinogion*, tr. Sioned Davies (2007)

Anon., *The Táin*, tr. Ciaran Carson (2008)

Ellis, Peter Berresford, *Celtic Women* (1996)

Ellis, Peter Berresford, *The Druids* (2006)

Ellis, Peter Berresford, *The Celts* (2003)

Hutton, Ronald, *Blood and Mistletoe* (2011)

Moffat, Alistair, *The Sea Kingdoms* (2001)

Sykes, Bryan, *Blood of the Isles* (2006)